The Collected
Supernatural and Weird
Fiction of
Edward Lucas White

The Collected Supernatural and Weird Fiction of Edward Lucas White

Four Novelettes 'The Snout,' 'The Message on the Slate,' 'The Song of the Sirens,' & 'The Fasces,' Nineteen Short Stories & Two Poems of the Strange and Unusual

Edward Lucas White

LEONAUR

The Collected
Supernatural and Weird
Fiction of
Edward Lucas White
Four Novelettes 'The Snout,' 'The Message on the Slate,' 'The Song of the Sirens,' &
'The Fasces,' Nineteen Short Stories & Two Poems of the Strange and Unusual

by Edward Lucas White

FIRST EDITION

Leonaur is an imprint of Oakpast Ltd

ISBN: 978-1-78282-602-6 (hardcover)
ISBN: 978-1-78282-603-3 (softcover)

http://www.leonaur.com

Publisher's Notes

The views expressed in this book are not necessarily
those of the publisher.

Contents

Lukundoo

(A Tale from *Lukundoo and Other Stories*)

"It stands to reason," said Twombly, "that a man must accept the evidence of his own eyes, and when eyes and ears agree, there can be no doubt. He has to believe what he has both seen and heard."

"Not always," put in Singleton, softly.

Every man turned toward Singleton. Twombly was standing on the hearth-rug, his back to the grate, his legs spread out, with his habitual air of dominating the room. Singleton, as usual, was as much as possible effaced in a corner. But when Singleton spoke he said something. We faced him in that flattering spontaneity of expectant silence which invites utterance. "I was thinking," he said, after an interval, "of something I both saw and heard in Africa." Now, if there was one thing we had found impossible it had been to elicit from Singleton anything definite about his African experiences.

As with the Alpinist in the story, who could tell only that he went up and came down, the sum of Singleton's revelations had been that he went there and came away. His words now riveted our attention at once. Twombly faded from the hearth-rug, but not one of us could ever recall having seen him go. The room readjusted itself, focused on Singleton, and there was some hasty and furtive lighting of fresh cigars. Singleton lit one also, but it went out immediately, and he never relit it.

1

We were in the Great Forest, exploring for pigmies. Van Rieten had a theory that the dwarfs found by Stanley and others were a mere cross-breed between ordinary negroes and the real pigmies. He hoped to discover a race of men three feet tall at most, or shorter. We had found no trace of any such beings.

Natives were few; game scarce; food, except game, there was none; and the deepest, dankest, drippingest forest all about. We were the only novelty in the country, no native we met had even seen a white man before, most had never heard of white men. All of a sudden, late one afternoon, there came into our camp an Englishman, and pretty well used up he was, too. We had heard no rumour of him; he had not only heard of us but had made an amazing five-day march to reach us. His guide and two bearers were nearly as done up as he. Even though he was in tatters and had five days' beard on, you could see he was naturally dapper and neat and the sort of man to shave daily. He was small, but wiry.

His face was the sort of British face from which emotion has been so carefully banished that a foreigner is apt to think the wearer of the face incapable of any sort of feeling; the kind of face which, if it has any expression at all, expresses principally the resolution to go through the world decorously, without intruding upon or annoying anyone. His name was Etcham. He introduced himself modestly, and ate with us so deliberately that we should never have suspected, if our bearers had not had it from his bearers, that he had had but three meals in the five days, and those small. After we had lit up he told us why he had come.

"My chief is ve'y seedy," he said between puffs. "He is bound to go out if he keeps this way. I thought perhaps. . . ."

He spoke quietly in a soft, even tone, but I could see little beads of sweat oozing out on his upper lip under his stubby moustache, and there was a tingle of repressed emotion in his tone, a veiled eagerness in his eye, a palpitating inward solicitude in his demeanour that moved me at once. Van Rieten had no sentiment in him; if he was moved he did not show it. But he listened. I was surprised at that. He was just the man to refuse at once. But he listened to Etcham's halting, diffident hints. He even asked questions.

"Who is your chief?"

"Stone," Etcham lisped.

That electrified both of us. "Ralph Stone?" we ejaculated together. Etcham nodded.

For some minutes Van Rieten and I were silent. Van Rieten had never seen him, but I had been a classmate of Stone's, and Van Rieten and I had discussed him over many a camp-fire. We had heard of him two years before, south of Luebo in the Balunda country, which had been ringing with his theatrical strife against a Balunda witchdoctor, ending in the sorcerer's complete discomfiture and the abasement of

8

his tribe before Stone. They had even broken the fetish-man's whistle and given Stone the pieces. It had been like the triumph of Elijah over the prophets of Baal, only more real to the Balunda.

We had thought of Stone as far off, if still in Africa at all, and here he turned up ahead of us and probably forestalling our quest.

2

Etcham's naming of Stone brought back to us all his tantalizing story, his fascinating parents, their tragic death; the brilliance of his college days; the dazzle of his millions; the promise of his young manhood; his wide notoriety, so nearly real fame; his romantic elopement with the meteoric authoress whose sudden cascade of fiction had made her so great a name so young, whose beauty and charm were so much heralded; the frightful scandal of the breach-of-promise suit that followed; his bride's devotion through it all; their sudden quarrel after it was all over; their divorce; the too much advertised announcement of his approaching marriage to the plaintiff in the breach-of-promise suit; his precipitate remarriage to his divorced bride; their second quarrel and second divorce; his departure from his native land; his advent in the dark continent. The sense of all this rushed over me and I believe Van Rieten felt it, too, as he sat silent.

Then he asked: "Where is Werner?"

"Dead," said Etcham. "He died before I joined Stone."

"You were not with Stone above Luebo?"

"No," said Etcham, "I joined him at Stanley Falls."

"Who is with him?" Van Rieten asked.

"Only his Zanzibar servants and the bearers," Etcham replied.

"What sort of bearers?" Van Rieten demanded. "Mang-Battu men," Etcham responded simply. Now that impressed both Van Rieten and myself greatly. It bore out Stone's reputation as a notable leader of men. For up to that time no one had been able to use Mang-Battu as bearers outside of their own country, or to hold them for long or difficult expeditions.

"Were you long among the Mang-Battu?" was Van Rieten's next question.

"Some weeks," said Etcham. "Stone was interested in them and made up a fair-sized vocabulary of their words and phrases. He had a theory that they are an offshoot of the Balunda and he found much confirmation in their customs."

"What do you live on?" Van Rieten inquired.

"Game, mostly," Etcham lisped.

9

"How long has Stone been laid up?" Van Rieten next asked.

"More than a month," Etcham answered.

"And you have been hunting for the camp!" Van Rieten exclaimed. Etcham's face, burnt and flayed as it was, showed a flush.

"I missed some easy shots," he admitted ruefully. "I've not felt ve'y fit myself."

"What's the matter with your chief?" Van Rieten inquired.

"Something like carbuncles," Etcham replied.

"He ought to get over a carbuncle or two," Van Rieten declared.

"They are not carbuncles," Etcham explained. "Nor one or two. He has had dozens, sometimes five at once. If they had been carbuncles he would have been dead long ago. But in some ways they are not so bad, though in others they are worse."

"How do you mean?" Van Rieten queried.

"Well," Etcham hesitated, "they do not seem to inflame so deep nor so wide as carbuncles, nor to be so painful, nor to cause so much fever. But then they seem to be part of a disease that affects his mind. He let me help him dress the first, but the others he has hidden most carefully, from me and from the men. He keeps his tent when they puff up, and will not let me change the dressings or be with him at all."

"Have you plenty of dressings?" Van Rieten asked.

"We have some," said Etcham doubtfully. "But he won't use them; he washes out the dressings and uses them over and over."

"How is he treating the swellings?" Van Rieten inquired.

"He slices them off clear down to flesh level, with his razor."

"What?" Van Rieten shouted.

Etcham made no answer but looked him steadily in the eyes.

"I beg pardon," Van Rieten hastened to say. "You startled me. They can't be carbuncles. He'd have been dead long ago."

"I thought I had said they are not carbuncles," Etcham lisped.

"But the man must be crazy!" Van Rieten exclaimed.

"Just so," said Etcham. "He is beyond my advice or control."

"How many has he treated that way?" Van Rieten demanded.

"Two, to my knowledge," Etcham said.

"Two?" Van Rieten queried.

Etcham flushed again.

"I saw him," he confessed, "through a crack in the hut. I felt impelled to keep a watch on him, as if he was not responsible."

"I should think not," Van Rieten agreed. "And you saw him do that twice?"

"I conjecture," said Etcham, "that he did the like with all the rest."

"How many has he had?" Van Rieten asked.

"Dozens," Etcham lisped.

"Does he eat?" Van Rieten inquired.

"Like a wolf," said Etcham. "More than any two bearers."

"Can he walk?" Van Rieten asked.

"He crawls a bit, groaning," said Etcham simply.

"Little fever, you say," Van Rieten ruminated. "Enough and too much," Etcham declared.

"Has he been delirious?" Van Rieten asked.

"Only twice," Etcham replied; "once when the first swelling broke, and once later. He would not let anyone come near him then. But we could hear him talking, talking steadily, and it scared the natives."

"Was he talking their patter in delirium?" Van Rieten demanded.

"No," said Etcham, "but he was talking some similar lingo. Hamed Burghash said he was talking Balunda. I know too little Balunda. I do not learn languages readily. Stone learned more Mang-Battu in a week than I could have learned in a year. But I seemed to hear words like Mang-Battu words. Anyhow the Mang-Battu bearers were scared."

"Scared?" Van Rieten repeated, questioningly.

"So were the Zanzibar men, even Hamed Burghash, and so was I," said Etcham, "only for a different reason. He talked in two voices."

"In two voices," Van Rieten reflected.

"Yes," said Etcham, more excitedly than he had yet spoken. "In two voices, like a conversation. One was his own, one a small, thin, bleaty voice like nothing I ever heard. I seemed to make out, among the sounds the deep voice made, something like Mang-Battu words I knew, as *nedru, metebaba,* and *nedo,* their terms for 'head,' 'shoulder,' 'thigh,' and perhaps *kudra* and *nekere* ('speak' and 'whistle'); and among the noises of the shrill voice *matomipa, angunzi,* and *kamomami* ('kill,' 'death,' and 'hate'). Hamed Burghash said he also heard those words. He knew Mang-Battu far better than I."

"What did the bearers say?" Van Rieten asked.

"They said, '*Lukundoo, Lukundoo!*'" Etcham replied. "I did not know that word; Hamed Burghash said it was Mang-Battu for 'leopard.'"

"It's Mang-Battu for 'witchcraft,'" said Van Rieten.

"I don't wonder they thought so," said Etcham. "It was enough to make one believe in sorcery to listen to those two voices."

"One voice answering the other?" Van Rieten asked perfunctorily.

11

Etcham's face went gray under his tan. "Sometimes both at once," he answered huskily.

"Both at once!" Van Rieten ejaculated.

"It sounded that way to the men, too," said Etcham. "And that was not all." He stopped and looked helplessly at us for a moment. "Could a man talk and whistle at the same time?" he asked.

"How do you mean?" Van Rieten queried.

"We could hear Stone talking away, his big, deep-chested baritone rumbling along, and through it all we could hear a high, shrill whistle, the oddest, wheezy sound. You know, no matter how shrilly a grown man may whistle, the note has a different quality from the whistle of a boy or a woman or little girl. They sound more treble, somehow. Well, if you can imagine the smallest girl who could whistle keeping it up tunelessly right along, that whistle was like that, only even more piercing, and it sounded right through Stone's bass tones."

"And you didn't go to him?" Van Rieten cried.

"He is not given to threats," Etcham disclaimed. "But he had threatened, not volubly, nor like a sick man, but quietly and firmly, that if any man of us (he lumped me in with the men), came near him while he was in his trouble, that man should die. And it was not so much his words as his manner. It was like a monarch commanding respected privacy for a deathbed. One simply could not transgress."

"I see," said Van Rieten shortly. "He's ve'y seedy,"

Etcham repeated helplessly. "I thought perhaps. . . ."

His absorbing affection for Stone, his real love for him, shone out through his envelope of conventional training. Worship of Stone was plainly his master passion.

Like many competent men, Van Rieten had a streak of hard selfishness in him. It came to the surface then. He said we carried our lives in our hands from day to day just as genuinely as Stone; that he did not forget the ties of blood and calling between any two explorers, but that there was no sense in imperilling one party for a very problematical benefit to a man probably beyond any help; that it was enough of a task to hunt for one party; that if two were united, providing food would be more than doubly difficult; that the risk of starvation was too great. Deflecting our march seven full days' journey (he complimented Etcham on his marching powers) might ruin our expedition entirely.

3

Van Rieten had logic on his side and he had a way with him. Etcham sat there apologetic and deferential, like a fourth-form school-boy before a head master. Van Rieten wound up.

"I am after pigmies, at the risk of my life. After pigmies I go."

"Perhaps, then, these will interest you," said Etcham, very quietly. He took two objects out of the sidepocket of his blouse, and handed them to Van Rieten. They were round, bigger than big plums, and smaller than small peaches, about the right size to enclose in an average hand. They were black, and at first I did not see what they were.

"Pigmies!" Van Rieten exclaimed. "Pigmies, indeed! Why, they wouldn't be two feet high! Do you mean to claim that these are adult heads?"

"I claim nothing," Etcham answered evenly. "You can see for yourself." Van Rieten passed one of the heads to me. The sun was just setting and I examined it closely. A dried head it was, perfectly preserved, and the flesh as hard as Argentine jerked beef. A bit of a vertebra stuck out where the muscles of the vanished neck had shrivelled into folds. The puny chin was sharp on a projecting jaw, the minute teeth white and even between the retracted lips, the tiny nose was flat, the little forehead retreating, there were inconsiderable clumps of stunted wool on the Lilliputian cranium. There was nothing babyish, childish or youthful about the head, rather it was mature to senility.

"Where did these come from?" Van Rieten inquired.

"I do not know," Etcham replied precisely. "I found them among Stone's effects while rummaging for medicines or drugs or anything that could help me to help him. I do not know where he got them. But I'll swear he did not have them when we entered this district."

"Are you sure?" Van Rieten queried, his eyes big and fixed on Etcham's.

"Ve'y sure," lisped Etcham.

"But how could he have come by them without your knowledge?" Van Rieten demurred.

"Sometimes we were apart ten days at a time hunting," said Etcham. "Stone is not a talking man. He gave me no account of his doings and Hamed Burghash keeps a still tongue and a tight hold on the men."

"You have examined these heads?" Van Rieten asked.

"Minutely," said Etcham.

Van Rieten took out his notebook. He was a methodical chap. He tore out a leaf, folded it and divided it equally into three pieces. He gave one to me and one to Etcham.

13

"Just for a test of my impressions," he said, "I want each of us to write separately just what he is most reminded of by these heads. Then I want to compare the writings."

I handed Etcham a pencil and he wrote. Then he handed the pencil back to me and I wrote.

"Read the three," said Van Rieten, handing me his piece.

Van Rieten had written:

"An old Balunda witchdoctor."

Etcham had written:

"An old Mang-Battu fetish-man."

I had written:

"An old Katongo magician."

"There!" Van Rieten exclaimed. "Look at that! There is nothing Wagabi or Batwa or Wambuttu or Wabotu about these heads. Nor anything pigmy either."

"I thought as much," said Etcham. "And you say he did not have them before?"

"To a certainty he did not," Etcham asserted.

"It is worth following up," said Van Rieten. "I'll go with you. And first of all, I'll do my best to save Stone."

He put out his hand and Etcham clasped it silently. He was grateful all over.

4

Nothing but Etcham's fever of solicitude could have taken him in five days over the track. It took him eight days to retrace with full knowledge of it and our party to help. We could not have done it in seven, and Etcham urged us on, in a repressed fury of anxiety, no mere fever of duty to his chief, but a real ardour of devotion, a glow of personal adoration for Stone which blazed under his dry conventional exterior and showed in spite of him.

We found Stone well cared for. Etcham had seen to a good, high thorn *zareeba* round the camp, the huts were well built and thatched and Stone's was as good as their resources would permit. Hamed Burghash was not named after two Seyyids for nothing. He had in him the making of a *sultan*. He had kept the Mang-Battu together, not a man had slipped off, and he had kept them in order. Also he was a deft nurse and a faithful servant.

The two other Zanzabaris had done some creditable hunting. Though all were hungry, the camp was far from starvation.

Stone was on a canvas cot and there was a sort of collapsible camp-stool-table, like a Turkish *tabouret*, by the cot. It had a water-bottle and some vials on it and Stone's watch, also his razor in its case.

Stone was clean and not emaciated, but he was far gone; not unconscious, but in a daze; past commanding or resisting anyone. He did not seem to see us enter or to know we were there. I should have recognized him anywhere. His boyish dash and grace had vanished utterly, of course. But his head was even more leonine; his hair was still abundant, yellow and wavy; the close, crisped blond beard he had grown during his illness did not alter him. He was big and big-chested yet. His eyes were dull and he mumbled and babbled mere meaningless syllables, not words.

Etcham helped Van Rieten to uncover him and look him over. He was in good muscle for a man so long bedridden. There were no scars on him except about his knees, shoulders and chest. On each knee and above it he had a full score of roundish cicatrices, and a dozen or more on each shoulder, all in front.

Two or three were open wounds and four or five barely healed. He had no fresh swellings except two, one on each side, on his pectoral muscles, the one on the left being higher up and farther out than the other. They did not look like boils or carbuncles, but as if something blunt and hard were being pushed up through the fairly healthy flesh and skin, not much inflamed.

"I should not lance those," said Van Rieten, and Etcham assented. They made Stone as comfortable as they could, and just before sunset we looked in at him again. He was lying on his back, and his chest showed big and massive yet, but he lay as if in a stupor. We left Etcham with him and went into the next hut, which Etcham had resigned to us. The jungle noises were no different there than anywhere else for months past, and I was soon fast asleep.

5

Sometime in the pitch dark I found myself awake listening. I could hear two voices, one Stone's, other sibilant and wheezy. I knew Stone's voice after all the years that had passed since I heard it last. The other was like nothing I remembered. It had less volume than the wail of a new-born baby, yet there was an insistent carrying power to it, like the shrilling of an insect. As I listened I heard Van Rieten breathing near me in the dark, then he heard me and realized that I was listening, too. Like Etcham I knew little Balunda, but I could make out a word or two. The voices alternated with intervals of silence between.

Then suddenly both sounded at once and fast, Stone's *baritone* basso, full as if he were in perfect health, and that incredibly stridulous *falsetto*, both jabbering at once like the voices of two people quarrelling and trying to talk each other down.

"I can't stand this," said Van Rieten. "Let's have a look at him." He had one of those cylindrical electric night-candles. He fumbled about for it, touched the button and beckoned me to come with him. Outside of the hut he motioned me to stand still, and instinctively turned off the light, as if seeing made listening difficult.

Except for a faint glow from the embers of the bearer's fire we were in complete darkness, little star-light struggled through the trees, the river made but a faint murmur. We could hear the two voices together and then suddenly the creaking voice changed into a razor-edged, slicing whistle, indescribably cutting, continuing right through Stone's grumbling torrent of croaking words.

"Good God!" exclaimed Van Rieten.

Abruptly he turned on the light.

We found Etcham utterly asleep, exhausted by his long anxiety and the exertions of his phenomenal march and relaxed completely now that the load was in a sense shifted from his shoulders to Van Rieten's. Even the light on his face did not wake him.

The whistle had ceased and the two voices now sounded together. Both came from Stone's cot, where the concentrated white ray showed him lying just as we had left him, except that he had tossed his arms above his head and had torn the coverings and bandages from his chest.

The swelling on his right breast had broken. Van Rieten aimed the centre line of the light at it and we saw it plainly. From his flesh, grown out of it, there protruded a head, such a head as the dried specimens Etcham had shown us, as if it were a miniature of the head of a Balunda fetishman.

It was black, shining black as the blackest African skin; it rolled the whites of its wicked, wee eyes and showed its microscopic teeth between lips repulsively negroid in their red fullness, even in so diminutive a face. It had crisp, fuzzy wool on its minikin skull, it turned malignantly from side to side and chittered incessantly in that inconceivable *falsetto*. Stone babbled brokenly against its patter.

Van Rieten turned from Stone and waked Etcham, with some difficulty. When he was awake and saw it all, Etcham stared and said not one word.

"You saw him slice off two swellings?" Van Rieten asked. Etcham

16

nodded, chokingly.

"Did he bleed much?" Van Rieten demanded.

"Ve'y little," Etcham replied.

"You hold his arms," said Ven Rieten to Etcham.

He took up Stone's razor and handed me the light. Stone showed no sign of seeing the light or of knowing we were there. But the little head mewled and screeched at us.

Van Rieten's hand was steady, and the sweep of the razor even and true. Stone bled amazingly little and Van Rieten dressed the wound as if it had been a bruise or scrape.

Stone had stopped talking the instant the excrescent head was severed. Van Rieten did all that could be done for Stone and then fairly grabbed the light from me. Snatching up a gun he scanned the ground by the cot and brought the butt down once and twice, viciously.

We went back to our hut, but I doubt if I slept.

6

Next day, near noon, in broad daylight, we heard the two voices from Stone's hut. We found Etcham dropped asleep by his charge. The swelling on the left had broken, and just such another head was there miauling and spluttering. Etcham woke up and the three of us stood there and glared. Stone interjected hoarse vocables into the tinkling gurgle of the portent's utterance.

Van Rieten stepped forward, took up Stone's razor and knelt down by the cot. The atomy of a head squealed a wheezy snarl at him.

Then suddenly Stone spoke English. "Who are you with my razor?"

Van Rieten started back and stood up. Stone's eyes were clear now and bright, they roved about the hut.

"The end," he said; "I recognize the end. I seem to see Etcham, as if in life. But Singleton! Ah, Singleton! Ghosts of my boyhood come to watch me pass! And you, strange spectre with the black beard, and my razor! Aroint ye all!"

"I'm no ghost, Stone," I managed to say. "I'm alive. So are Etcham and Van Rieten. We are here to help you."

"Van Rieten!" he exclaimed. "My work passes on to a better man. Luck go with you, Van Rieten."

Van Rieten went nearer to him.

"Just hold still a moment, old man," he said soothingly. "It will be only one twinge."

"I've held still for many such twinges," Stone answered quite distinctly. "Let me be. Let me die my own way. The hydra was nothing to this. You can cut off ten, a hundred, a thousand heads, but the curse you cannot cut off, or take off. What's soaked into the bone won't come out of the flesh, any more than what's bred there. Don't hack me anymore. Promise!"

His voice had all the old commanding tone of his boyhood and it swayed Van Rieten as it always had swayed everybody.

"I promise," said Van Rieten.

Almost as he said the word Stone's eyes filmed again. Then we three sat about Stone and watched that hideous, gibbering prodigy grow up out of Stone s flesh, till two horrid, spindling little black arms disengaged themselves. The infinitesimal nails were perfect to the barely perceptible moon at the quick, the pink spot on the palm was horridly natural. These arms gesticulated and the right plucked toward Stone's blond beard.

"I can't stand this," Van Rieten exclaimed and took up the razor again. Instantly Stone's eyes opened, hard and glittering.

"Van Rieten break his word?" he enunciated slowly. "Never!"

"But we must help you," Van Rieten gasped.

"I am past all help and all hurting," said Stone. "This is my hour. This curse is not put on me; it grew out of me, like this horror here. Even now I go."

His eyes closed and we stood helpless, the adherent figure spouting shrill sentences. In a moment Stone spoke again.

"You speak all tongues?" he asked thickly.

And the emergent minikin replied in sudden English:

"Yea, verily, all that you speak," putting out its microscopic tongue, writhing its lips and wagging its head from side to side. We could see the thready ribs on its exiguous flanks heave as if the thing breathed.

"Has she forgiven me?" Stone asked in a muffled strangle.

"Not while the moss hangs from the cypresses," the head squeaked. "Not while the stars shine on Lake Pontchartrain will she forgive."

And then Stone, all with one motion, wrenched himself over on his side. The next instant he was dead.

When Singleton's voice ceased the room was hushed for a space. We could hear each other breathing. Twombly, the tactless, broke the silence.

"I presume," he said, "you cut off the little minikin and brought it home in alcohol." Singleton turned on him a stern countenance.

"We buried Stone," he said, "unmutilated as he died."

"But," said the unconscionable Twombly, "the whole thing is incredible." Singleton stiffened.

"I did not expect you to believe it," he said; "I began by saying that although I heard and saw it, when I look back on it I cannot credit it myself."

The Picture Puzzle
(A Tale from *Lukundoo and Other Stories*)

1

Of course the instinct of the police and detectives was to run down their game. That was natural. They seemed astonished and contemptuous when I urged that all I wanted was my baby; whether the kidnappers were ever caught or not made no difference to me. They kept arguing that unless precautions were taken the criminals would escape and I kept arguing that if they became suspicious of a trap they would keep away and my only chance to recover our little girl would be gone forever. They finally agreed and I believe they kept their promise to me. Helen always felt the other way and maintained that their watchers frightened off whoever was to meet me. Anyhow I waited in vain, waited for hours, waited again the next day and the next and the next. We put advertisements in countless papers, offering rewards and immunity, but never heard anything more.

I pulled myself together in a sort of a way and tried to do my work. My partner and clerks were very kind. I don't believe I ever did anything properly in those days, but no one ever brought any blunder to my attention. If they came across any they set it right for me. And at the office it was not so bad. Trying to work was good for me. It was worse at home and worse at night. I slept hardly at all.

Helen, if possible, slept less than I. And she had terrible spasms of sobs that shook the bed. She would try to choke them down, thinking I was asleep and she might wake me. But she never went through a night without at least one frightful paroxysm of tears.

In the daylight she controlled herself better, made a heart-breaking and yet heart-warming effort at her normal cheeriness over the breakfast things, and greeted me beautifully when I came home. But the moment we were alone for the evening she would break down.

I don't know how many days that sort of thing kept up. I sympathized in silence. It was Helen herself who suggested that we must force ourselves to be diverted, somehow. The theatre was out of the question. Not merely the sight of a four-year-old girl with yellow locks threw Helen into a passion of uncontrollable sobbing, but all sorts of unexpected trifles reminded her of Amy and affected her almost as much. Confined to our home we tried cards, chess and everything else we could think of. They helped her as little as they helped me.

Then one afternoon Helen did not come to greet me. Instead as I came in I heard her call, quite in her natural voice.

"Oh, I'm so glad that is you. Come and help me." I found her seated at the library table, her back to the door. She had on a pink wrapper and her shoulders had no despondent droop, but a girlish alertness. She barely turned her head as I entered, but her profile showed no signs of recent weeping. Her face was its natural colour.

"Come and help me," she repeated. "I can't find the other piece of the boat." She was absorbed, positively absorbed in a picture puzzle.

In forty seconds I was absorbed too. It must have been six minutes before we identified the last piece of the boat. And then we went on with the sky and were still at it when the butler announced dinner.

"Where did you get it?" I asked, over the soup, which Helen really ate.

"Mrs. Allstone brought it," Helen replied, "just before lunch." I blessed Mrs. Allstone.

Really it seems absurd, but those idiotic jigsaw puzzles were our salvation. They actually took our minds off everything else. At first I dreaded finishing one. No sooner was the last piece in place than I felt a sudden revulsion, a booming of blood in my ears, and the sense of loss and misery rushed over me like a wave of scalding water. And I knew it was worse for Helen.

But after some days each seemed not merely a respite from pain, but a sedative as well. After a two hours' struggle with a fascinating tangle of shapes and colours, we seemed numb to our bereavement and the bitterness of the smart seemed blunted.

We grew fastidious as to manufacture and finish; learned to avoid crude and clumsy products as bores; developed a pronounced taste for pictures neither too soft nor too plain in colour-masses; and became Connoisseurs as to cutting, utterly above the obvious and entirely disenchanted with the painfully difficult. We evolved into adepts, quick to recoil from fragments barren of any clue of shape or markings and equally prompt to reject those whose meaning was too definite and insistent. We trod delicately the middle way among segments not one of which was without some clue of outline or tint, and not one of which imparted its message without interrogation, inference and reflection.

Helen used to time herself and try the same puzzle over and over on successive days until she could do it in less than half an hour. She declared that a really good puzzle was interesting the fourth or fifth time and that an especially fine puzzle was diverting if turned face down and put together from the shapes merely, after it had been well learned the other way. I did not enter into the craze to that extent, but sometimes tried her methods for variety.

We really slept, and Helen, though worn and thin, was not abject, not agonized. Her nights passed, if not wholly without tears, yet with only those soft and silent tears, which are more a relief than suffering. With me she was nearly her old self and very brave and patient. She greeted me naturally and we seemed able to go on living.

Then one day she was not at the door to welcome me. I had hardly shut it before I heard her sobbing. I found her again at the library table and over a puzzle. But this time she had just finished it and was bowed over it on the table, shaken all over by her grief.

She lifted her head from her crossed arms, pointed and buried her face in her hands. I understood. The picture I remembered from a magazine of the year before: a Christmas tree with a bevy of children about it and one (we had remarked it at the time) a perfect likeness of our Amy.

As she rocked back and forth, her hands over her eyes, I swept the pieces into their box and put on the lid.

Presently Helen dried her eyes and looked at the table.

"Oh! why did you touch it," she wailed. "It was such a comfort to me."

"You did not seem comforted," I retorted. "I thought the con- trast—." I stopped.

"You mean the contrast between the Christmas we expected and the Christmas we are going to have?" she queried. "You mean you thought that was too much for me?"

I nodded.

"It wasn't that at all," she averred. "I was crying for joy. That picture was a sign."

"A sign?" I repeated.

"Yes," she declared, "a sign that we shall get her back in time for Christmas. I'm going to start and get ready right away."

At first I was glad of the diversion. Helen had the nursery put in order as if she expected Amy the next day, hauled over all the child's clothes and was in a bustling state of happy expectancy. She went vigorously about her preparation for a Christmas celebration, planned a Christmas Eve dinner for our brothers and sisters and their husbands and wives, and a children's party afterwards with a big tree and a profusion of goodies and gifts.

"You see," she explained, "everyone will want their own Christmas at home. So shall we, for we'll just want to gloat over Amy all day. We won't want them on Christmas any more than they'll want us. But this way we can all be together and celebrate and rejoice over our good luck."

She was as elated and convinced as if it was a certainty. For a while her occupation with preparations was good for her, but she was so forehanded that she was ready a week ahead of time and had not a detail left to arrange. I dreaded a reaction, but her artificial exaltation continued unabated. All the more I feared the inevitable disappointment and was genuinely concerned for her reason. The fixed idea that that accidental coincidence was a prophecy and a guarantee dominated her totally. I was really afraid that the shock of the reality might kill her. I did not want to dissipate her happy delusion, but I could not but try to prepare her for the certain blow. I talked cautiously in wide circles around what I wanted and I did not want to say.

2

On December 22nd, I came home early, just after lunch, in fact. Helen met me, at the door, with such a demeanour of suppressed high spirits, happy secrecy and tingling anticipation that for one moment I was certain Amy had been found and was then in the house.

"I've something wonderful to show you," Helen declared, and led me to the library. There on the table was a picture-puzzle fitted together.

She stood and pointed to it with the air of exhibiting a marvel. I looked at it but could not conjecture the cause of her excitement. The pieces seemed too large, too clumsy and too uniform in outline. It looked a crude and clumsy puzzle, beneath her notice.

"Why did you buy it?" I asked.

"I met a peddler on the street," she answered, "and he was so wretched-looking, I was sorry for him. He was young and thin and looked haggard and consumptive. I looked at him and I suppose I showed my feelings. He said:

"Lady, buy a puzzle. It will help you to your heart's desire."

"His words were so odd I bought it, and now just look at what it is." I was groping for some foothold upon which to rally my thoughts.

"Let me see the box in which it came," I asked.

She produced it and I read on the top:

Guggenheim's Double Picture
Puzzle.
Two in One.
Most for the Money.
Ask for Guggenheim's

And on the end—

Astray.
A Breath of Air. 50 Cents.

"It's queer," Helen remarked. "But it is not a double puzzle at all, though the pieces have the same paper on both sides. One side is blank. I suppose this is Astray. Don't you think so?"

"Astray?" I queried, puzzled.

"Oh," she cried, in a disappointed, disheartened, almost querulous tone. "I thought you would be so much struck with the resemblance. You don't seem to notice it at all. Why even the dress is identical!"

"The dress?" I repeated. "How many times have you done this?"

"Only this once," she said. "I had just finished it when I heard your key in the lock."

"I should have thought," I commented, "that it would have been more interesting to do it face up first."

"Face up!" She cried. "It is face up."

Her air of scornful superiority completely shook me out of my sedulous consideration of a moment before.

"Nonsense," I said, "that's the back of the puzzle. There are no colours there. It's all pink."

"Pink!" she exclaimed pointing. "Do you call that pink!"

"Certainly it's pink," I asserted.

"Don't you see there the white of the old man's beard," she queried, pointing again. "And there the black of his boots? And there the red of the little girl's dress?"

"No," I declared. "I don't see anything of the kind. It's all pink. There isn't any picture there at all."

"No picture!" she cried. "Don't you see the old man leading the child by the hand?"

"No," I said harshly, "I don't see any picture and you know I don't. There isn't any picture there. I can't make out what you are driving at. It seems a senseless joke."

"Joke! I joke!" Helen half whispered. The tears came into her eyes. "You are cruel," she said, "and I thought you would be struck by the resemblance." I was overwhelmed by a pang of self-reproach, solicitude and terror.

"Resemblance to what?" I asked gently.

"Can't you see it?" she insisted.

"Tell me," I pleaded. "Show me just what you want me to notice most."

"The child," she said pointing, "is just exactly Amy and the dress is the very red suit she had on when—"

"Dear," I said, "try to collect yourself. Indeed you only imagine what you tell me. There is no picture on this side of the sections. The whole thing is pink. That is the back of the puzzle."

"I don't see how you can say such a thing," she raged at me. "I can't make out why you should. What sort of a test are you putting me through? What does it all mean?"

"Will you let me prove to you that this is the back of the puzzle?" I asked. "If you can," she said shortly.

I turned the pieces of the puzzle over, keeping them together as much as possible. I succeeded pretty well with the outer pieces and soon had the rectangle in place. The inner pieces were a good deal mixed up, but even before I had fitted them I exclaimed:

"There look at that!"

"Well," she asked. "What do you expect me to see "What do you see?" I asked in turn.

"I see the back of a puzzle," she answered.

"Don't you see those front steps?" I demanded, pointing. "I don't see anything," she asserted, "except green."

"Do you call that green?" I queried pointing.

"I do," she declared.

"Don't you see the brickwork front of the house?" I insisted, "and the lower part of a window and part of a door. Yes and those frontsteps in the corner?"

"I don't see anything of the kind," she asseverated. "Any more than you do. What I see is just what you see. It's the back of the puzzle, all pale green."

I had been feverishly putting together the last pieces as she spoke. I could not believe my eyes and, as the last piece fitted in, was struck with amazement.

The picture showed an old red-brick house, with brown blinds, all open. The top of the front steps was included in the lower right hand corner, most of the front door above them, all of one window on its level, and the side of another. Above appeared all of one of the second floor windows, and parts of those to right and left of it. The other windows were closed, but the sash of the middle one was raised and from it leaned a little girl, a child with frowzy hair, a dirty face and wearing a blue and white check frock. The child was a perfect likeness of our lost Amy, supposing she had been starved and neglected. I was so affected that I was afraid I should faint. I was positively husky when I asked:

"Don't you see that?"

"I see Nile green," she maintained. "The same as you see." I swept the pieces into the box.

"We are neither of us well," I said.

"I should think you must be deranged to behave so," she snapped, "and it is no wonder I am not well the way you treat me."

"How could I know what you wanted me to see?" I began.

"Wanted you to see!" she cried. "You keep it up? You pretend you didn't see it, after all? Oh! I have no patience with you."

She burst into tears, fled upstairs and I heard her slam and lock our bedroom door. I put that puzzle together again and the likeness of that hungry, filthy child in the picture to our Amy made my heart ache.

I found a stout box, cut two pieces of straw-board just the shape of the puzzle and a trifle larger, laid one on top of it and slid the other under it. Then I tied it together with string and wrapped it in paper and tied the whole.

I put the box in my overcoat pocket and went out carrying the flat parcel. I walked round to MacIntyre's.

I told him the whole story and showed him the puzzle.

"Do you want the truth?" he asked.

"Just that," I said.

"Well," he reported. "You are as overstrung as she is and the same way. There is absolutely no picture on either side of this. One side is solid green and the other solid pink."

"How about the coincidence of the names on the box?" I interjected. "One suited what I saw, one what she said she saw."

"Let's look at the box," he suggested.

He looked at it on all sides.

"There's not a letter on it," he announced. "Except 'picture puzzle' on top and '50 cents' on the end."

"I don't feel insane," I declared.

"You aren't," he reassured me. "Nor in any danger of being insane. Let me look you over." He felt my pulse, looked at my tongue, examined both eyes with his ophthalmoscope, and took a drop of my blood.

"I'll report further," he said, "in confirmation tomorrow. You're all right, or nearly so, and you'll soon be really all right. All you need is a little rest. Don't worry about this idea of your wife's, humour her. There won't be any terrible consequences. After Christmas go to Florida or somewhere for a week or so. And don't exert yourself from now till after that change."

When I reached home, I went down into the cellar, threw that puzzle and its box into the furnace and stood and watched it burn to ashes.

3

When I came upstairs from the furnace Helen met me as if nothing had happened. By one of her sudden revulsions of mood she was even more gracious than usual, and was at dinner altogether charming. She did not refer to our quarrel or to the puzzle.

The next morning over our breakfast we were both opening our mail. I had told her that I should not go to the office until after Christmas and that I wanted her to arrange for a little tour that would please her. I had phoned to the office not to expect me until after New Year's.

My mail contained nothing of moment.

Helen looked up from her's with an expression curiously mingled of disappointment, concern and a pleased smile.

"It is so fortunate you have nothing to do," she said. "I spent four whole days choosing toys and favours and found most of those I selected at Bleich's. They were to have been delivered day before yesterday but they did not come. I telephoned yesterday and they said they would try to trace them. Here is a letter saying that the whole lot was missent out to Roundwood. You noticed that Roundwood station burned Monday night. They were all burnt up. Now I'll have to go and find more like them. You can go with me."

I went.

The two days were a strange mixture of sensations and emotions. Helen had picked over Bleich's stock pretty carefully and could duplicate from it few of the burned articles, could find acceptable substitutes for fewer. There followed an exhausting pursuit of the unattainable through a bewildering series of toy-shops and department-stores. We spent most of our time at counters and much of the remainder in a taxicab.

In a way it was very trying. I did not mind the smells and bad air and other mere physical discomforts. But the mental strain continually intensified. Helen's confidence that Amy would be restored to us was steadily waning and her outward exhibition of it was becoming more and more artificial, and consciously sustained, and more and more of an effort. She was coming to foresee, in spite of herself, that our Christmas celebration would be a most terrible mockery of our bereavement. She was forcing herself not to confess it to herself and not to show it to me. The strain told on her. It told on me to watch it, to see the inevitable crash coming nearer and nearer and to try to put away from myself the pictures of her collapse, of her probable loss of reason, of her possible death, which my imagination kept thrusting before me.

On the other hand Helen was to all appearance, if one had no prevision by which to read her, her most charming self. Her manner to shop-girls and other sales-people was a delight to watch. Her little speeches to me were full of her girlish whimsicality and unexpectedness. Her good will towards all the world, her resolution that everything must come right and would come right haloed her in a sort of aureole of romance. Our lunches were ideal hours, full of the atmosphere of courtship, of lovemaking, of exquisite companionship.

In spite of my forebodings, I caught the contagion of the Christmas shopping crowds; in spite of her self-deception Helen revelled in it. The purpose to make as many people as possible as happy as might be irradiated Helen with the light of fairyland; her resolve to be happy herself in spite of everything made her a sort of fairy queen. I found myself less and less anxious and more and more almost expectant. I knew Helen was looking for Amy every instant. I found myself in the same state of mind.

Our lunch on Christmas Eve was a strange blend of artificiality and genuine exhilaration. After it we had but one purchase to make.

"We are in no hurry," Helen said. "Let's take a horse-hansom for old sake's sake." In it we were like boy and girl together until the jeweller's was reached.

There gloom, in spite of us, settled down over our hopes and feelings. Helen walked to the hansom like a gray ghost. Like the whisper of some far-off stranger I heard myself order the driver to take us home.

In the hansom we sat silent, looking straight in front of us at nothing. I stole a glance at Helen and saw a tear in the corner of her eye. I sat choking.

All at once she seized my hand. "Look!" she exclaimed, "Look!"

I looked where she pointed, but discerned nothing to account for her excitement. "What is it?" I queried.

"The old man!" she exclaimed.

"What old man?" I asked bewildered.

"The old man on the puzzle," she told me. "The old man who was leading Amy."

Then I was sure she was demented. To humour her I asked:

"The old man with the brown coat?"

"Yes," she said eagerly. "The old man with the long gray hair over his collar."

"With the walking stick?" I inquired.

"Yes," she answered. "With the crooked walking stick."

I saw him too! This was no figment of Helen's imagination. It was absurd of course, but my eagerness caught fire from hers. I credited the absurdity. In what sort of vision it mattered not she had seen an old man like this leading our lost Amy.

I spoke to the driver, pointed out to him the old man, told him to follow him without attracting his attention and offered him anything he asked to keep him in sight.

Helen became possessed with the idea that we should lose sight of the old man in the crowds. Nothing would do but we must get out and follow him on foot. I remonstrated that we were much more likely to lose sight of him that way, and still more likely to attract his notice, which would be worse than losing him. She insisted and I told the man to keep us in view.

A weary walk we had, though most of it was mere strolling after a tottering figure or loitering about shops he entered.

It was near dusk and full time for us to be at home when he began to walk fast. So fast he drew away from us in spite of us. He turned a corner a half a square ahead of us. When we turned into that street he was nowhere to be seen.

Helen was ready to faint with disappointment. With no hope of helping her, but some instinctive idea of postponing the evil moment I urged her to walk on, saying that perhaps we might see him. About the middle of the square I suddenly stood still.

"What is the matter?" Helen asked.

"The house!" I said.

"What house?" she queried.

"The house in the puzzle picture," I explained. "The house where I saw Amy at the window." Of course she had not seen any house on the puzzle, but she caught at the last straw of hope. It was a poor neighbourhood of crowded tenements, not quite a slum, yet dirty and unkempt and full of poor folks.

The house door was shut, I could find no sign of any bell. I knocked. No one answered. I tried the door. It was not fastened and we entered a dirty hallway, cold and damp and smelling repulsively. A fat woman stuck her head out of a door and jabbered at us in an unknown tongue. A man with a fez on his greasy black hair came from the back of the hallway and was equally unintelligible.

"Does nobody here speak English?" I asked.

The answer was as incomprehensible as before. I made to go up the stairs.

The man, and the woman, who was now standing before her door, both chattered at once, but neither made any attempt to stop me. They waved vaguely explanatory, deprecating hands towards the blackness of the stairway. We went up.

On the second floor landing we saw just the old man we had been following. He stared at us when I spoke to him.

"Son-in-law," he said, "son-in-law."

He called and a door opened. An oldish woman answered him in apparently the same jargon. Behind was a young woman holding a baby.

"What is it?" she asked with a great deal of accent but intelligibly. Three or four children held on by her skirts.

Behind her I saw a little girl in a blue-check dress. Helen screamed.

4

The people turned out to be refugees from the settlement about the sacked German Mission at Dehkhargan near Tabriz, Christianized Persians, such stupid villagers that they had never thought or had been

30

incapable of reporting their find to the police, so ignorant that they knew nothing of rewards or advertisements, such simple-hearted folk that they had shared their narrow quarters and scanty fare with the unknown waif their grandfather had found wandering alone, after dark, months before.

Amy, when we had leisure to ask questions and hear her experiences, declared they had treated her as they treated their own children. She could give no description of her kidnappers except that the woman had on a hat with roses in it and the man had a little yellow moustache. She could not tell how long they had kept her nor why they had left her to wander in the streets at night.

It needed no common language, far less any legal proof, to convince Amy's hosts that she belonged to us. I had a pocket full of Christmas money, new five and ten dollar gold pieces and bright silver quarters for the servants and children. I filled the old grandfather's hands and plainly overwhelmed him. They all jabbered at us, blessings, if I judged the tone right. I tried to tell the young woman we should see them again in a day or two and I gave her a card to make sure.

I told the cabman to stop the first taxicab he should see empty. In the hansom we hugged Amy alternately and hugged each other.

Once in the taxicab we were home in half an hour; more, much more than half an hour late. Helen whisked Amy in by the servants' door and flew upstairs with her by the back way. I faced a perturbed and anxious parlourful of interrogative relatives and in-laws.

"You'll know before many minutes," I said, "why we were both out and are in late. Helen will want to surprise you and I'll say nothing to spoil the effect."

Nothing I could have said would have spoiled the effect because they would not have believed me. As it was Helen came in sooner than I could have thought possible, looking her best and accurately playing the formal hostess with a feeble attempt at a surprise in store. The dinner was a great success, with much laughter and high spirits, everybody carried away by Helen's sallies and everybody amazed that she could be so gay.

"I cannot understand," Paul's wife whispered to me, "how she can ever get through the party. It would kill me in her place."

"It won't kill her," I said confidently. "You may be sure of that." The children had arrived to the number of more than thirty and only the inevitably late Amstelhuysens had not come. Helen announced that she would not wait for them.

"The tree is lighted," she said. "We'll have the doors thrown open and go in." We were all gathered in the front parlour. The twins panted in at the last instant. The grown-ups were pulling motto-crackers and the children were throwing confetti. The doors opened, the tree filled all the back of the room. The candles blazed and twinkled. And in front of it, in a simple little white dress, with a fairy's wand in her hand, tipped with a silver star, clean, healthy-looking and full of spirits was Amy, the fairy of the hour.

The Snout

(A Tale from *Lukundoo and Other Stories*)

1

I was not so much conning the specimens in the Zoological Garden as idly basking in the agreeable morning sunshine and relishing at leisure the perfect weather. So I saw him the instant he turned the corner of the building. At first, I thought I recognised him, then I hesitated.

At first he seemed to know me and to be just about to greet me; then he saw past me into the cage. His eyes bulged; his mouth opened into a long egg-shaped oval, till you might almost have said that his jaw dropped; he made an inarticulate sound, partly a grunt, partly the ghost of a howl, and collapsed in a limp heap on the gravel. I had not seen a human being since I passed the gate, some distance away. No one came when I called. So I dragged him to the grass by a bench, untied his faded, shiny cravat, took off his frayed collar and unbuttoned his soiled neckband.

Then I peeled his coat off him, rolled it up, and put it under his knees as he lay on his back. I tried to find some water, but could see none. So I sat down on the bench near him. There he lay, his legs and body on the grass, his head in the dry gutter, his arms on the pebbles of the path. I was sure I knew him, but I could not recall when or where we had encountered each other before. Presently he answered to my rough and ready treatment and opened his eyes, blinking at me heavily. He drew up his arms to his shoulders and sighed.

"Queer," he muttered, "I come here because of you and I meet you. Still I could not remember him and he had revived enough to read my face. He sat up. "Don't try to stand up!" I warned him.

He did not need the admonition, but clung to the end of the bench, his head bowed wagglingly over his arms.

"Don't you remember," he asked thickly. "You said I had a pretty good smattering of an education on everything except Natural History and Ancient History. I'm hoping for a job in a few days, and I thought I'd put in the time and keep out of mischief brushing up. So I started on Natural History first and—"

He broke off and glared up at me. I remembered him now. I should have recognized him the moment I saw him, for he was daily in my mind. But his luxuriant hair, his tanned skin and above all his changed expression, a sort of look of acquired cosmopolitanism, had baffled me.

"Natural History!" he repeated, in a hoarse whisper. His fingers digging in the slats of the bench he wrenched himself round to face the cage.

"Hell!" he screamed. "There it is yet!" He held on by the end iron-arm of the bench, shaking, almost sobbing. "What's wrong with you?" I queried. "What do think you see in that cage?"

"Do you see anything in that cage?" he demanded in reply.

"Certainly," I told him.

"Then for God's sake," he pleaded. "What do you see?"

I told him briefly.

"Good Lord," he ejaculated. "Are we both crazy?"

"Nothing crazy about either of us," I assured him. "What we see in the cage is what is in the cage."

"Is there such a critter as that, honest?" he pressed me. I gave him a pretty full account of the animal, its habits and relationships.

"Well," he said, weakly, "I suppose you're telling the truth. If there is such a critter let's get where I can't see it."

I helped him to his feet and assisted him to a bench altogether out of sight of that building. He put on his collar and knotted his cravat. While I had held it I had noticed that, through its greasy condition, it showed plainly having been a very expensive cravat. His clothes I remarked were seedy, but had been of the very best when new.

"Let's find a drinking fountain," he suggested, "I can walk now." We found one not far away and at no great distance from it a shaded bench facing an agreeable view. I offered him a cigarette and we smoked. I meant to let him do most of the talking.

"Do you know," he began presently. "Things you said to me run in my head more than anything anybody ever said to me. I suppose it's because you're a sort of philosopher and student of human nature and what you say is true. For instance, you said that criminals would get off clear three times out of four, if they just kept their mouths shut, but they have to confide in some one, even against all reason. That's just the way with me now."

"You aren't a criminal," I interrupted him. "You lost your temper and made a fool of yourself just once. If you'd been a criminal and had done what you did, you'd have likely enough got off, because you'd have calculated how to do it. As it was you put yourself in a position where everything was against you and you had no chance. We were all sorry for you."

"You most of all," he amplified. "You treated me bully."

"But we were all sorry for you," I repeated, "and all the jury too, and the judge. You're no criminal."

"How do you know," he demanded defiantly, "what I have done since I got out?"

"You've grown a pretty good head of hair," I commented.

"I've had time," he said. "I've been all over the world and blown in ten thousand dollars."

"And never seen—" I began.

He interrupted me at the third word.

"Don't say it," he shuddered. "I never had, nor heard of one. But I wasn't after caged animals while I had any money left. I didn't remember your advice and your other talk till I was broke. Now, it's just as you said, I've just got to tell you. That's the criminal in me, I suppose."

"You're no criminal," I repeated soothingly.

"Hell," he snarled, "a year in the pen makes a man a criminal, if he never was before."

"Not necessarily," I encouraged him.

"It's pretty sure to," he sighed. "They treated me mighty well and put me to bookkeeping, and I got my full good-conduct allowance. But I met professionals, and they never forget a man."

"Now it don't make any difference what I did when I got out, nor what I tried to do nor how I met Rivvin, nor how he put Thwaite after me.. No, nor how Thwaite got hold of me, nor what he said to me, nor anything, right up to the very night, till after we had started."

He looked me in the eye. His attitude became alert. I could see him warming to his narrative. In fact, when after very little rumination he began it, his early self dropped from him with his boyhood dialect and the jargon of his late associates. He was all the easy cosmopolitan telling his tale with conscious zest.

35

2

As if it had been broad day Thwaite drove the car at a terrific pace for nearly an hour. Then he stopped it while Rivvin put out every lamp. We had not met or overtaken anything, but when we started again through the moist, starless blackness it was too much for my nerves. Thwaite was as cool as if he could see. I could not so much as guess at him in front of me, but I could feel his self-confidence in every quiver of the car. It was one of those super-expensive makes which are, on any gear, at any speed, on any grade, as noiseless as a puma. Thwaite never hesitated in the gloom; he kept straight or swerved, crept or darted, whizzed or crawled for nearly an hour more.

Then he turned sharp to the left and uphill. I could feel and smell the soaked, hanging boughs close above and about me, the wet foliage on them, and the deep sodden earth mould that squelched under the tyres. We climbed steeply, came to a level and then backed and went forward a length or so a half dozen times, turning. Then we stopped dead. Thwaite moved things that clicked or thumped and presently said:

"Now I'll demonstrate how a man can fill his gasoline tank in the pitch dark if he knows the touch system."

After some more time he said: "Rivvin, go bury this."

Rivvin swore, but went. Thwaite climbed in beside me. When Rivvin returned he climbed in on the other side of me. He lit his pipe, Thwaite lit a cigar and looked at his watch. After I had lit too, Thwaite said:

"We've plenty of time to talk here and all you have to do is to listen. I'll begin at the beginning. When old Hiram Eversleigh died—"

"You don't mean—" I interrupted him.

"Shut up!" he snapped, "and keep your mouth shut. You'll have your say when I've done." I shut up.

"When old man Eversleigh died," he resumed, "the income of the fortune was divided equally among his sons. You know what the others did with their shares: palaces in New York and London and Paris, *châteaux* on the Breton Coast, deer and grouse moors in Scotland, steam yachts and all the rest of it, the same as they have kept it up ever since. At first Vortigern Eversleigh went in for all that sort of thing harder than any one of his brothers. But when his wife died, more than forty years ago, he stopped all that at once. He sold everything else, bought this place, put the wall round it and built that infinity of structures inside.

"You've seen the pinnacles and roofs of them, and that's all any-body I ever talked to has ever seen of them since they were finished about five years after his wife's death. You've seen the two gate-houses and you know each is big even for a millionaire's mansion. You can judge of the size and extent of the complication of buildings that make up the castle or mansion-house or whatever you choose to call it. There Vortigern Eversleigh lived. Not once did he ever leave it that I can learn of. There he died. Since his death, full twenty years ago, his share of the Eversleigh income has been paid to his heir. No one has ever seen that heir.

"From what I'll tell you presently you'll see as I have that the heir is probably not a woman. But nobody knows anything about him, he has never been outside these miles of wall. Yet not one of the greedy, selfish Eversleigh grandsons and grand-daughters, and sons-in-law and daughters-in-law, has ever objected to the payment to that heir of the full entire portion of Vortigern Eversleigh, and that portion has been two hundred thousand dollars a month, paid in gold on the first banking day of each month. I found that out for sure, for there have been disputes about the division of Wulfstan Eversleigh's share and of Cedric Eversleigh's share and I made certain from the papers in the suits.

"All that money, or the value of it, has been either reinvested or spent inside that park wall. Not much has been reinvested. I got on the track of the heir's purchases. He buys musical instruments any quan-tity and at any price. Those were the first things I made sure of. And artists' materials, paints, brushes, canvas, tools, woods, clay, marble, tons of clay and great blocks of superfine-grained marble. He's no magpie collecting expensive trash for a whim; he knows what he wants and why; he has taste. He buys horses and saddlery and carriages, furniture and carpets and tapestries, pictures, all landscapes, never any figure pictures, he buys photographs of pictures by the ten thousand, and he buys fine porcelains, rare vases, table silver, ornaments of Venetian glass, silver and gold filigree, jewellery, watches, chains, gems, pearls, rubies, emeralds and— diamonds; diamonds!"

Thwaite's voice shook with excitement, though he kept it soft and even.

"Oh, I did two years investigating," he went on, "I know. People blabbed. But not any of the servants or grooms or gardeners. Not a word could I get, at first or second or third hand, from them or any of their relatives or friends. They keep dumb. They know which side their bread is buttered on. But some of the discharged tradesmen's assistants told all I wanted to know and I got it straight, though not direct. No one from outside ever gets into that place beyond the big paved courtyards of the gate-houses. Every bit of supplies for all that regiment of servants goes into the brownstone gate-house. The outer gates open and the wagon or whatever it is drives under the archway. There it halts.

"The outer gates shut and the inner gates open. It drives into the courtyard. Then the *major-domo* (I suppose that wouldn't be too big a name for him) makes his selections. The inner gates of the other gateway open and the wagon drives under the archway and halts. The inner gates close fast and the outer gates open. That's the way with every wagon and only one enters at a time. Everything is carried through the gate-house to the smaller inner courtyard and loaded on the wagons of the estate to be driven up to the mansion.

"Everything like furniture, for instance, comes into the courtyard of the green-stone gate-house. There a sort of auditor verifies the inventory and receipts for the goods before two witnesses from the dealers and two for the estate. The consignment may be kept a day or a month; it may be returned intact or kept entire; any difference is settled for at once upon return of what is rejected. So with jewellery. I had luck. I found out for certain that more than a million dollars worth of diamonds alone have gone into this place in the last ten years and stayed there."

Thwaite paused dramatically. I never said a word and we sat there in the rear seat of that stationary auto, the leather creaking as we breathed, Rivyin sucking at his pipe, and the leaves dripping above us; not another sound.

"It's all in there," Thwaite began again. "The biggest stack of loot in North America. And this is going to be the biggest and most successful burglary ever perpetrated on this continent. And no one will ever be convicted for it or so much as suspected of it. Mark my words."

"I do," I broke in, "and I don't feel a bit better than when we started. You promised to explain and you said I'd be as eager and confident as you and Rivvin. I acknowledge the bait, admitting all you say is true, and it doesn't seem likely. But do you suppose any recluse millionaire eccentric is going to live unguarded? If he is careless himself his household are the reverse. By what you tell of the gate-houses there are precautions enough. Diamonds are tempting if you like, but so is the bullion in the mint. By your account all this accumulation of treasure you imagine is as safe where it is as the gold reserve in the United States Treasury. You scare me, you don't reassure me."

"Keep your head," Thwaite interrupted. "I'm no fool. I've spent years on this scheme. After I was sure of the prize I made sure of the means. There are precautions a-many, but not enough. How simple to put a watchman's cottage every hundred yards on the other side of the road across from the wall? They haven't done it. How simple to light the road and the outside of the wall? They haven't done that. Nor have they thought of any one of the twenty other simple outside precautions. The park's big enough to be lonely. And outside the wall is all dark, lonely road and unfenced, empty woods like this. They're over-confident. They think their wall and their gate-houses are enough. And they are not. They think their outside precautions are perfect.

"They are not. I know. I've been over that wall ten times, twenty times, fifty times. I've risked it and I have risked man-traps and spring guns and alarm wires. There aren't any. There isn't any night patrol, nor any regular day patrol, only casual gardeners and such. I know. I made sure of it by crawling all over the place on my belly like an Iroquois Indian in one of Cooper's novels. They are so confident of the potency of their wall that they haven't so much as a watch dog, nor any dog of any kind."

I was certainly startled. "No dog!" I exclaimed. "Are you sure?"

"Dead sure!" Thwaite returned, triumphantly, "And sure there never has been a dog on the place."

"How could you be sure of that?" I cavilled.

"I'm coming to that," Thwaite went on, "I could not get anybody that ever belonged to the place to talk, but I managed to arrange to overhear two of them talking to each other; and more than once, too. Most of what they said was no use to me, but I overheard scraps I could piece together. There's a cross-wall that divides the park. In the smaller division, into which the lodge gates lead, are the homes of all the caretakers and servants, of the overseers and manager and of the estate doctor; for there is an estate doctor. He has two assistants, young men, frequently changed. He is married like most of the retinue. There is a sort of village of them inside the outer wall, outside the inner cross-wall. Some of them have been there thirty-five years. When they get too old they are pensioned off and sent away, somewhere; far off, for I could not get a clue to any pensioner.

"The valets or keepers, whichever they are, and there are many of them, to relieve each other, are all unmarried except two or three of the most trusted. The rest are all brought over from England and shipped back usually after four or five years of service. The men I overheard were two of these, an old hand soon to finish his enlistment, as he called it, and go home, and the lad he was training to take his place. All these specials have plenty of time off to spend outside. They'd sit over their beer for two or three hours at a time, chatting on, Appleshaw giving points to Kitworth or Kitworth asking questions. I learnt from them about the cross-wall."

"Never's been a woman t' other side of it since it was built," Appleshaw said. "I shouldn't have thought it," Kitworth ruminated.

"Can you imagine a woman," Appleshaw asked, "standin' him?"

"No," Kitworth admitted, "I hardly can. But some women'll stand more'n a man."

"Anyhow," Appleshaw added, "he can't abide the sight of a woman."

"Odd," said Kitworth, "I've heard his kind are all the other way."

"They are, as we know," Appleshaw replied, "havin' watched 'em; but he ain't. He can't endure 'em."

"I suppose it's the same way about dogs," Kitworth reflected.

"No dog'd ever get used to him," Appleshaw agreed, "and he's that afraid of dogs, they're not allowed inside the place anywhere. Never's been one here since he was born, I'm told. No, nor any cat, either, not one even."

Another time I heard Appleshaw say:

"He built the museums, and the pavilion and the towers, the rest was built before he grew up." Generally I could not hear much of Kitworth's utterances, he talked so low. I once heard Appleshaw reply:

'Sometimes nights and nights he'll be quiet as anybody, lights out early and sleep sound for all we know. Again he'll be up all night, every window blazin', or up late, till after midnight.

Whoever's on duty sees the night out, nobody else's business, unless they send an alarm for help, and that ain't often; not twice a year. Mostly he's as quiet as you or me, as long as he's obeyed.

"His temper's short though. Now he'll fly into a rage if he's not answered quick; again he'll storm if the watchers come near him uncalled."

Of long inaudible whispers I caught fragments.

Once:

"Oh, then he'll have no one near. You can hear him sobbing like a child. When he's worst you'll hear him, still nights, howlin' and

40

screamin' like a lost soul."

Again:

"Clean-fleshed as a child and no more hairy than you or me."

Again:

"Fiddle? No violinist can beat him. I've listened hours. It makes you think of your sins. An' then it'll change an' you remember your first sweetheart, an' spring rains and flowers, an' when you was a child on your mother's knee. It tears your heart out."

The two phrases that seemed to mean most were: "He won't stan' any interference."

And:

"Never a lock touched till daylight after he's once locked in."

"Now what do you think?" Thwaite asked me.

"It sounds," I said, "as if the place were a one-patient asylum for a lunatic with long lucid intervals."

"Something like that," Thwaite answered, "but there seems to be more in it than that. I can't make all the things I hear fit."

Appleshaw said one thing that runs in my head:

"Seein' him in the suds give me a turn:'

And Kitworth said once:

"It was the bright colours alongside of it that made my blood run cold."

And Appleshaw said more than once, in varying words, but always with the same meaning tone:

"You'll never get over bein' afraid of him. But you'll respect him more and more, you'll almost love him. You won't fear him for his looks, but for his awful wisdom. He's that wise, no man is more so."

Once Kitworth answered: "I don't envy Sturry locked in there with him."

"Sturry nor none of us that's his most trusted man for the time bein' is not to be envied," Appleshaw agreed. "But you'll come to it, as I have, if you're the man I take you for."

"That's about all I got from listening," Thwaite went on, "the rest I got from watching and scouting. I made sure of the building they call the Pavilion, that's his usual home. But sometimes he spends his nights in one or the other of the towers, they stand all by themselves. Sometimes the lights are all out after ten o'clock or even nine; then again they're on till after midnight. Sometimes they come on late, two o'clock or three. I have heard music too, violin music, as Appleshaw described it, and organ music, too; but no howling. He is certainly a lunatic, judging by the statuary."

"Statuary?" I queried.

"Yes," Thwaite said, "statuary. Big figures and groups, all crazy men with heads like elephants or American eagles, perfectly crazy statuary. But all well-done. They stand all about the park. The little, square building between the Pavilion and the green tower is his sculpture studio."

"You seem to know the place mighty well," I said.

"I do," Thwaite assented, "I've gotten to know it well. At first I tried nights like this. Then I dared starlight. Then I dared even moonlight. I've never had a scare. I've sat on the front steps of the Pavilion at one o'clock of starlight night and never been challenged. I even tried staying in all day, hiding in some bushes, hoping to see him."

"Ever see him?" I inquired.

"Never," Thwaite answered, "I've heard him though. He rides horseback after dark. I've watched the horse being led up and down in front of the Pavilion, till it got too dark to see it from where I was hid. I've heard it pass me in the dark. But I could never get the horse against the sky to see what was on it. Hiding and getting downhill of a road, close to it, don't go together."

"You didn't see him the day you spent there?" I insisted.

"No," Thwaite said, "I didn't. I was disappointed too. For a big auto purred up to the Pavilion entrance and stood under the *porte cochère*. But when it spun round the park there was nobody in it, only the chauffeur in front and a pet monkey on the back seat."

"A pet monkey!" I exclaimed.

"Yes," he said. "You know how a dog, a Newfoundland, or a terrier, will sit up in an auto and look grand and superior and enjoy himself? Well, that monkey sat there just like that turning his head one way and the other taking in the view."

"What was he like?" I asked.

"Sort of dog-faced ape," Thwaite told me, "more like a mastiff."

Rivvin grunted.

"This isn't business," Thwaite went on, "we've got to get down to business. The point is the wall is their only guard, there's no dog, perhaps because of the pet monkey as much as anything else. They lock Mr. Eversleigh up every night with only one valet to take care of him. They never interfere whatever noise they hear or light they see, unless the alarm is sent out and I have located the alarm wires you are to cut. That's all. Do you go?"

Rivvin was sitting close to me, half on me. I could feel his great muscles and the butt of his pistol against my hip.

"I come with you," I said. "Of your own accord?" Thwaite insisted. The butt of that pistol moved as Rivvin breathed. "I come of my own accord," I said.

3

Afoot Thwaite led as confidently as he had driven the car. It was the stillest, pitchiest night I ever experienced, without light, air, sound or smell to guide anyone: through that fog Thwaite sped like a man moving about his own bedroom, never for a second at a loss.

"Here's the place," he said at the wall, and guided my hand to feel the ring-bolt in the grass at its foot. Rivvin made a back for him and I scrambled up on the two. Tiptoe on Thwaite's shoulders I could just finger the coping.

"Stand on my head, you fool!" he whispered.

I clutched the coping. Once astraddle of it I let down one end of the silk ladder. "Fast!" breathed Thwaite from below.

I drew it taut and went down. The first sweep of my fingers in the grass found the other ring-bolt. I made the ladder fast and gave it the signal twitches. Rivvin came over first, then Thwaite. Through the park he led evenly. When he halted he caught me by the elbow and asked:

"Can you see any lights?"

"Not a light," I told him.

"Same here," he said, "there are no lights. Every window is dark. We're in luck." He led again for a while. Stopping he said only:

"Here's where you shin up. Cut every wire, but don't waste time cutting any twice. The details of his directions were exact. I found every handhold and foothold as he had schooled me. But I needed all my nerve. I realized that no heavyweight like Rivvin or Thwaite could have done it. When I came down I was limp and tottery.

"Just one swallow!" Thwaite said, putting a flask to my lips. Then we went on. The night was so black and the fog so thick that I saw no loom of the building till we were against its wall.

"Here's where you go in," Thwaite directed.

Doubly I understood why I was with them. Neither could have squeezed through that aperture in the stone. I barely managed it. Inside, instead of the sliding crash I had dreaded, I landed with a mere crunch, the coal in that bin was not anthracite. Likewise the bin under the window was for soft-coal. I blessed my luck and felt encouraged. The window I got open without too much work. Rivvin and Thwaite slid in. We crunched downhill four or five steps and stood on a firm floor. Rivvin flashed his electric candle boldly round. We were between a suite of trim coal-bins and a battery of serried furnaces.

There was no door at either end of the open space in which we stood. I had a momentary vision of the alternate windows and coal-chutes above the bins, of two big panels of shiny, coloured tiling, of clear brick-work, fresh-painted, jetty iron and dazzling-white brass-ringed asbestos, of a black vacancy between two furnaces. Toward that I half heard, half felt Rivvin turn. During the rest of our adventure he led, Thwaite followed and I mostly tagged or groped after Thwaite, often judging of their position or movement by that combination of senses which is neither hearing nor touch, though partly both.

Rivvin's torch flashed again. We were in a cement-floored, brick-walled passage, with a door at each end and on the side facing us doors in a bewildering row. In the darkness that came after the flash I followed the others to the right. Well through the doorway we stood still, breathing and listening. When Rivvin illuminated our environ-ment we saw about us thousands of bottles, all set aslant, neck down, in tiers of racks that reached to the ceiling. Edging between them we made the circuit of the cellar, but found no sign of any door save that by which we had entered. A whispered growl from Rivvin, a nudge from Thwaite and we went back the full length of the passage. Again we found ourselves in a wine vault, the duplicate of that we had left, and with the same peculiarity.

Our curiosity overcame any prudence. Rivvin, instead of flashing his torch at intervals, kept the light steady, and we scrutinized, exam-ined and whispered our astonishment. As in its fellow there was not in all this vault any spare space, the aisles were narrow, the racks reached the girders supporting the flat arches, every rack was so full that a holder empty of its bottle was scarcely findable. And there was not in all that great cellar, there was not among all those tens of thousands of bottles a magnum, or a quart or even a pint. They were all splits. We handled a number and all had the same label. I know now what the device was, from seeing it so often and so much larger afterwards, but there it seemed a picture of a skirt-dancer leading an alligator by a dog chain. There was no name of any wine or liquor on any bottle, but each label had a red number, 17, or 45 or 328, above the picture, and under it:

"Bottled for Hengist Eversleigh."

"We know his name now," Thwaite whispered.

Back in the passage Rivvin took the first door to the left. It brought us to an easy stone stair between walls, which turned twice to the left at broad landings. When we trod a softer footing we stood a long time breathing cautiously and listening. Presently Rivvin flashed his light. It showed to our left a carpeted stair, the dull red carpet bulging up over thick pads and held down by brass stair-rods; the polished quartered oak of the moulded door-jamb or end of wainscot beyond it; the floor-covering of brownish-yellow or yellowish brown linoleum or something similar, made to look like inlaid wood; and the feet, legs and thighs of a big stocky man. The light shone but the fraction of a second, yet it showed plain his knee-breeches, tight stockings on his big calves, and bright buckles at his knees and on his low shoes.

There was no loud sound, but the blurred brushy noise of a mute struggle. I backed against a window-sill and could back no further. All I could hear was the shuffling, rasping sounds of the fight, and panting that became a sort of gurgle.

Again the light flashed and stayed full bright. I saw that it was Thwaite struggling with the man, and that one of his big hands was on Thwaite's throat. Thwaite had him round the neck and his face was against Thwaite's chest. His hair was brownish. Rivvin's slung-shot crunched horribly on his skull. Instantly the light went out.

Thwaite, radiating heat like a stove, stood gasping close by me. I heard no other noise after the body thudded on the floor except that on the carpeted stair I seemed to hear light treads, as it were of a big dog or of a frightened child, padding away upward.

"Did you hear anything?" I whispered.

Rivvin punched me.

After Thwaite was breathing naturally, he turned on his torch and Rivvin did the same. The dead man was oldish, over fifty I should judge, tall, large in all his dimensions, and spare, though heavy. His clothing was a gold-laced livery of green velvet, with green velvet knee breeches, green silk stockings and green leather pumps. The four buckles were gold.

Thwaite startled me by speaking out loud.

"I take it, Rivvin," he said, "this is the trusted valet. He would have yelled if there had been anybody to call. Either we have this building to ourselves or we have no one to deal with except Mr. Hengist Eversleigh."

Rivvin grunted.

"If he is here," Thwaite went on, "he's trying to send the alarm over the cut wires, or he's frightened and hiding. Let's find him and finish him, if he's here, and then find his diamonds. Anyway let's find those diamonds."

Rivvin grunted.

Swiftly they led from room to room and floor to floor. Not a door resisted. We had been curious and astonished in the wine-vaults; above we were electrified and numb. We were in a palace of wonders, among such a profusion of valuables that even Rivvin, after the second or third opportunity, ceased any attempt to pocket or bag anything. We came upon nothing living, found no door locked and apparently made the tour of the entire building.

When they halted, I halted. We were delirious with amazement, frantic with inquisitiveness, frenzied with curiosity, incredulous, hysterical, dazed and quivering.

Thwaite spoke in the dark.

"I'm going to see this place plain, all over it, if I die for it." They flashed their torches. We were right beside the body of the murdered footman. Rivvin and Thwaite did not seem to mind the corpse. They waved their torches until one fell on an electric-light button.

"Hope those wires are underground," Thwaite remarked. He pushed the button and the electric lights came on full and strong. We were apparently at the foot of the back stairs, in a sort of lobby, an expanded passage-way out of which opened several doors.

We all three regarded the knobs of those doors. As we had half seen by flashlight on every door everywhere each door had two knobs, one like any doorknob, the other about half way between it and the floor. Rivvin opened one which proved to lead into a broom closet. He tried the knobs, Thwaite and I watching too. The lock and latch were at the upper knob, but controlled by either knob indifferently. They tried another door, but my eyes would roam to the dead body.

Rivvin and Thwaite paid no more attention to it than if it had not been there. I had never seen but one killed man before and neither wanted to be reminded of that one nor relished the sight of this one. I stared down the blackness of the stone stair up which we had come or glanced into the dimness of the padded stairway.

Then Rivvin, feeling inside the open door, found the button and turned on the lights. It was a biggish dining-room, the four corners cut off by inset glass-framed shelved closets, full of china and glassware. The furniture was oak.

"Servants dining-room," Thwaite commented.

Turning on the lights in each we went through a series of rooms; a sort of sitting-room, with card-tables and checker-boards; a library walled with bookcases and open book-shelves, its two stout oak tables littered with magazines and newspapers; a billiard room with three tables, a billiard-table, a pool-table and one for bagatelle; a sort of lounging room, all leather-covered sofas and deep armchairs; an entry with hat-hooks and umbrella-stands, the outer door dark oak with a great deal of stained glass set in and around it.

"All servants' rooms," Thwaite commented. "Every bit of the furniture is natural man-size. Let's go on."

Back we went along a passage and into a big kitchen beyond the dining-room. "Never mind the pantries till we come down again," Thwaite commanded. "Let's go upstairs. We'll do the banqueting-hall after those bedrooms, and the writing rooms and study last. I want a real sight of those pictures."

They passed the dead flunkey as if he had not been there at all. On the floor above Thwaite touched Rivvins' elbow.

"I forgot these," he said.

We inspected a medium-sized sitting-room with a round centre-table, an armchair drawn up by it, and in the armchair a magazine and a sort of wadded smoking-jacket. Next this room was a bedroom and a bathroom.

"Mr. Footman's quarters," Thwaite remarked, staring unconcernedly at a photograph of a dumpy young woman and two small children, set on the bureau. "All man-size furniture here, too."

Rivvin nodded.

Up the second flight of that back-stair we went again. It ended in a squarish hallway or lobby or room with nothing in it but two settees. It had two doors.

Rivvin pushed one open, felt up and down for the electric button and found it. We all three gasped; we almost shouted. We had had glimpses of this gallery before, but the flood of light from a thousand bulbs under inverted trough-reflectors dazzled us; the pictures fairly petrified us.

The glare terrified me.

"Surely we are crazy," I objected, "to make all this illumination. It's certain to give the alarm."

"Alarm nothing," Thwaite snapped. "Haven't I watched these buildings night after night. I told you he is never disturbed at any hour, lights or no lights."

My feeble protest thus brushed away I became absorbed, like the others, in those incredible paintings. Rivvin was merely stupidly dazed in uncomprehending wonder, Thwaite keenly speculative, questing for a clue to the origin of their peculiarities, I totally bewildered at the perfection of their execution, shivering at their uncanniness.

The gallery was all of ninety feet long, nearly thirty wide and high. Apparently it had a glass roof above the rectangle of reflectors. The pictures covered all four walls, except the little door at either end. None was very small and several were very large. A few were land-scapes, but all had figures in them, most were crowded with figures.

Those figures.

They were human figures, but not one had a human head. The heads were invariably those of birds, animals or fishes, generally of animals, some of common animals, many of creatures I had seen pic-tures of or had heard of, some of imaginary creatures like dragons or griffons, more than half of the heads either of animals I knew nothing of or which had been invented by the painter.

Close to me when the lights blazed out was a sea picture, blurred grayish foggy weather and a heavy ground-swell; a strange other-world open boat with fish heaped in the bottom of it and standing among them four human figures in shining boots like rubber boots and wet, shiny, loose coats like oilskins, only the boots and skins were red as claret, and the four figures had hyenas' heads. One was steering and the others were hauling at a net. Caught in the net was a sort of merman, but different from the pictures of mermaids. His shape was all human except the head and hands and feet; every bit of him was covered with fish-scales all rainbowy. He had flat broad fins in place of hands and feet and his head was the head of a fat hog. He was thrash-ing about in the net in an agony of impotent effort. Queer as the pic-ture was it had a compelling impression of reality, as if the scene were actually happening before our eyes.

Next it was a picnic in a little meadow by a pond between woods with mountains behind it higher up. Every one of the picnickers about the white tablecloth spread on the grass had the head of a dif-ferent animal, one of a sheep, one of a camel, and the rest of animals like deer, not one of them known to me.

Then next to that was a fight of two compound creatures shaped like centaurs, only they had bulls' bodies, with human torsos growing out of them, where the necks ought to be, the arms scaly snakes with

48

open-mouthed, biting heads in place of hands; and instead of human heads roosters' heads, bills open and pecking. Under the creatures in place of bulls' hoofs were yellow roosters' legs, stouter than chickens' legs and with short thick toes, and long sharp spurs like game roosters'. Yet these fantastic chimeras appeared altogether alive and their movements looked natural, yes that's the word, natural.

Every picture was as complete a staggerer as these first three. Everyone was signed in the lower left hand corner in neat smallish letters of bright gold paint:

"Hengist Eversleigh"

and a date.

"Mr. Hengist Eversleigh is a lunatic that's certain," Thwaite commented, "but he unquestionably knows how to paint."

There must have been more than fifty pictures in that gallery, maybe as many as seventy-five, and every one a nightmare.

Beyond was a shorter gallery of the same width, end on to the side of the first, and beyond that the duplicate of the first; the three taking up three sides of the building. The fourth side was a studio, the size of the second gallery; it had a great skylight of glass tilted sideways all along over one whole wall. It was white-washed, very plain and empty-looking, with two easels, a big one and a little one.

On the little one was a picture of some vegetables and five or six little fairies, as it were, with children's bodies and mice's heads, nibbling at a carrot.

On the big one was a canvas mostly blank. One side of it had a palm-tree in splashy, thick slaps of paint and under it three big crabs with cocoanuts in their claws. A man's feet and legs showed beside them and the rest was unfinished.

The three galleries had fully three hundred paintings, for the smaller gallery contained only small canvases. Besides being impressed with the grotesqueness of the subjects and the perfection of the drawing and coloring, two things struck me as to the pictures collectively.

First, there was not represented in any one of all those paintings any figure of a woman or any female shape of any kind. The beast-headed figures were all, whether clothed or nude, figures of men. The animals, as far as I could see, were all males.

Secondly, nearly half of the pictures were modifications, or parallels or emulations (I could hardly say travesties or imitations), of well-known pictures by great artists, paintings I had seen in public galleries or knew from engravings or photographs or reproductions in books or magazines.

There was a picture like Washington crossing the Delaware and another like Washington saying farewell to his generals. There was a batch of Napoleon pictures; after the paintings of Napoleon at Austerlitz, at Friedland, giving the eagles to his regiments, on the morning of Waterloo, coming down the steps at Fontainebleau, and on the deck of the ship going to St. Helena. There were dozens of other pictures of generals or kings or emperors reviewing victorious armies; two or three of Lincoln. One that hit me hardest, obviously after some picture I had never seen or heard of, of the ghost of Lincoln, far larger than a life-size man, towering above the surviving notabilities of his time on the grandstand reviewing the homecoming Federal army marching through Washington.

In every one of these pictures, the dominant figure, whether it stood for Lincoln, Napoleon, Washington, or some other general or ruler; whatever uniform or regalia clothed its human shape, had the same head. The heads of the fighting men in all these pictures were those of dogs, all alike in any one picture, but differing from one to another; terriers or wolf-hounds or mastiffs or what not. The heads of any men not soldiers were those of oxen or sheep or horses or some other mild sort of animal. The head of the dominant figure I then took to be invented, legendary, fabulous—oh, that's not the word I want."

"Mythological?" I suggested, the only interruption I interjected into his entire narrative. Yes, mythological, he returned. I thought it was a mythological creature. The long-jawed head, like a hound's; the little pointed yellow beard under the chin; the black, naked ears, like a hairless dog's ears and yet not doggy, either; the ridge of hair on top of the skull; the triangular shape of the whole head; the close-set, small, beady, terribly knowing eyes; the brilliant patches of colour on either side of the muzzle; all these made a piercing impression of individuality and yet seemed not so much actual as mythological.

It takes a great deal longer to tell what we saw on that third floor than it took to see it. All round the galleries under the pictures were cases of drawers, solidly built in one length like a counter and about as high. Thwaite went down one side of the gallery and Rivvin down the other, pulling them out and slamming them shut again. All I saw held photographs of pictures. But Rivvin and Thwaite were taking no chances and looked into every drawer. I had plenty of time to gaze about me and circulated at a sort of cantering trot around the green-velvet miniature sofas and settees placed back to back down the middle of the floor-space. It seemed to me that Mr. Hengist Eversleigh was a great master of figure and landscape drawing, colour, light and perspective.

As we went down the duplicate staircase at the other corner from where we came up Thwaite said:

"Now for those bedrooms."

By the stair we found another valet's or footman's apartment, sitting-room, bedroom and bathroom, just like the one by the other stair. And there were four more between them, under the studio and over the lounging-rooms.

On the east and west sides of the building were "the" bedrooms, twelve apartments, six on each side; each of the twelve made up of a bedroom, a dressing-room and a bathroom.

The beds were about three feet long, and proportionately narrow and low. The furniture, bureaus, tables, chairs, chests-of-drawers and the rest, harmonized with the dimensions of the beds, except the cheval-glasses and wall-mirrors which reached the ceilings. The bathtubs were almost pools, about nine feet by six and all of three feet deep, each a single block of porcelain.

The shapes and sizes and styles of the furniture were duplicated all through, but the colours varied, so that the twelve suites were in twelve colours; black, white, gray and brown, and light and dark yellow, red, green and blue; wall coverings, hangings, carpets and rugs all to match in each suite. The panels of the walls had the same picture, however, repeated over and over, two, four or six times to a room and in every suite alike.

This picture was the design I had failed to make out on the labels of the bottles. It was set as a medallion in each panel of the blue or red walls, or whatever other colour they were. The background of the picture was a vague sort of palish sky and blurred, hazy clouds above tropical-looking foliage. The chief figure was an angel, in flowing white robes, floating on silvery-plumed wings widespread. The angel's face was a human face, the only human face in any picture in that palace, the face of a grave, gentle, rather girlish young man.

The creature the angel was leading was a huge, bulky crocodile, with a gold collar about its neck, and a gold chain from that, not to the angel's hand, but to a gold fetter about his wrist.

Under each picture was a verse of four lines, always the same.

Let not your baser nature drag you down.
Utter no whimper, not one sigh or moan,
Hopeless of respite, solace, palm or crown
Live out your life unflinching and alone.

I saw it so often I shall never forget it.

The bathrooms were luxurious in the extreme, a needle-bath, a shower-bath, two basins of different sizes in each, besides the sunk pool-tub. The dressing-rooms has each a variety of wardrobes. One or two we opened, finding in each several suits of little clothes, as if for a boy under six years old. One closet had shelf above shelf of small shoes, not much over four inches long.

"Evidently," Thwaite remarked, "Hengist Eversleigh is a dwarf, whatever else he is." Rivvin left the wardrobes and closets alone after the first few.

Each bedroom had in it nothing but the bed and on each side of it a sort of wine-cooler, like a pail with a lid, but bigger, set on three short legs so that its top was level with the bed. We opened most of them; every one we opened was filled with ice, bedded in which were several half-pint bottles. Every one of the twelve beds had the covers carefully turned down. Not one showed any sign of having been occupied. The wine-coolers were solid silver but we left them where they were. As Thwaite remarked, it would have taken two full-sized freight cars to contain the silver we had seen.

In the dressing-rooms the articles like brushes and combs on the bureaus were all of gold, and most set with jewels. Rivvin began to fill a bag with those entirely of metal, but even he made no attempt to tear the backs off the brushes or to waste energy on any other breakage. By the time we had scanned the twelve suites Rivvin could barely carry his bag.

The front room on the south side of the building was a library full of small, showily-bound books in glass-fronted cases all the way to the ceiling, covering every wall except where the two doors and six windows opened. There were small, narrow tables, the height of those in the dressing-rooms. There were magazines on them and papers. Thwaite opened a bookcase and I another and we looked at three or four books. Each had in it a book-plate with the device of the angel and the crocodile.

Rivvin did not find the electric button in the main hallway and we went down the great broad, curving stair by our electric candles.

Rivvin turned to the left and we found ourselves in the banquet hall as Thwaite had called it, a room all of forty by thirty and gorgeous beyond any description.

The diminutive table, not three feet square, was a slab of crystal-white glass set on silver-covered legs. The tiny armchair, the only chair in the big room, was solid silver, with a crimson cushion loose in it.

The sideboards and glass-fronted closets paralyzed us. One had fine china and cut glass; wonderful china and glass. But four held a table service of gold, all of pure gold; forks, knives, spoons, plates, bowls, platters, cups, everything; all miniature, but a profusion of everything. We hefted the pieces. They were gold. All the pieces were normal in shape except that instead of wine-glasses, goblets and tumblers were things like broad gravy-boats on stems or short feet, all lopsided, with one projecting edge like the mouth of a pitcher, only broader and flatter. There were dozens of these. Rivvin filled two bags with what two bags would hold. The three bags were all we three could carry, must have been over a hundred and fifty pounds apiece.

"We'll have to make two trips to the wall," Thwaite said. "You brought six bags, didn't you, Rivvin?"

Rivvin grunted.

At the foot of the grand staircase Rivvin found the electric button and flooded the magnificent stairway with light.

The stair itself was all white marble, the rails yellow marble, and the panelling of the dado malachite. But the main feature was the painting above the landing. This was the most amazing of all the paintings we had come upon.

I remembered something like it, an advertisement of a root-beer or talcum powder, or some other proprietary article, representing all the nations of the earth and their rulers in the foreground congratulating the orator.

This picture was about twenty feet wide and higher than its width. There was a throne, a carved and jewelled throne, set on an eminence. There was a wide view on either side of the throne, and all filled with human figures with animal heads, an infinite throng, all facing the throne. Nearest it were figures that seemed meant for all the presidents and kings and queens and emperors of the world. I recognized the robes or uniforms of some of them. Some had heads taken from their national coat of arms, like the heads of the Austrian and Russian eagles. All these figures were paying homage to the figure that stood before the throne; the same monster we had seen in place of Lincoln or Washington or Napoleon in the paintings upstairs.

He stood proudly with one foot on a massive crocodile. He was dressed in a sort of revolutionary uniform, low shoes, with gold buckles, white stockings and knee-breeches, a red waistcoat, and a bright blue coat. His head was the same beast-head of the other pictures, triangular and strange, which I then though mythological.

Above and behind the throne floated on outspread silver wings the white-robed angel with the Sir Galahad face.

Rivvin shut off the lights almost instantly, but even in the few breaths while I looked I saw it all.

The three sacks of swag we put down by the front door. The room opposite the banquet-hall was a music room, with an organ and a piano, both with keys and keyboards far smaller than usual; great cases of music books; an array of brass instruments and cellos and more than a hundred violin cases. Thwaite opened one or two.

"These'd be enough to make our fortune," he said. "If we could get away with them." Beyond the music-room was the study. It had in it four desks, miniature in size and the old-fashioned model with drawers below, a lid to turn down and form a writing surface, and a sort of bookcase above with a peaked top. All were carved and on the lids in the carving we read:

Journal Music Criticism
Business

Thwaite opened the desk marked *business* and pulled open the drawers. In pigeon-holes of the desk were bundles of new, clean greenbacks and treasury notes of higher denominations; five each of fives, tens, twenties, fifties and hundreds. Thwaite tossed one bundle of each to me and Rivvin and pocketed the rest.

He bulged.

One drawer had a division down the middle. One half was full of ten-dollar gold pieces, the other half of twenties.

"I've heard of misers," said Thwaite, "but this beats hell. Think of that crazy dwarf, a prisoner in this palace, running his hands through this and gloating over the cash he can never use.

Rivvin loaded a bag with the coin and when he had them all he could barely lift the bag. Leaving it where it lay before the desk he strode the length of the room and tried the door at the end.

It was fast.

Instantly Rivvin and Thwaite were like two terriers after a rat.

"This is where the diamonds are," Thwaite declared, "and Mr. Hengist Eversleigh is in there with them."

He and Rivvin conferred a while together.

"You kneel low," Thwaite whispered. "Duck when you open it. He'll fire over you. Then you've got him. See?"

Rivvin tip-toed to the door, knelt and tried key after key in the lock. There were at least twenty bulbs in the chandelier of that room and the light beat down on him. His red neck dew-lapped over the low collar of his lavenderish shirt, his great broad back showed vast and powerful.

On the other side of the doorway Thwaite stood, his finger at the electric button. Each had his slung-shot in his left hand. They had spun the cylinders of their revolvers and stuck them in their belts in front before Rivvin began work on the lock.

I heard a click.

Rivvin put up his hand.

The lights went out.

In the black dark we stood, stood until I could almost see the outlines of the windows; less black against the intenser blackness.

Soon I heard another click, and the grate of an opened door. Then a kind of snarl, a thump like a blow, a sort of strangling gasp, and the cushiony sounds of a struggle.

Thwaite turned on the lights.

Rivvin was in the act of staggering up from his knees. I saw a pair of small, pink hands, the fingers intertwined, locked behind Rivvin's neck. They slipped apart as I caught sight of them.

I had a vision of small feet in little patent leather silver-buckled low-shoes, of green socks, of diminutive legs in white trousers flashing right and left in front of Rivvin, as if he held by the throat a struggling child.

Next I saw that his arms were thrown up, wide apart.

He collapsed and fell back his full length with a dull crash. Then I saw the snout!

Saw the wolf-jaws vised on his throat!

Saw the blood welling round the dazzling white fangs, and recognized the reality of the sinister head I had seen over and over in his pictures.

Rivvin made the fish-out-of-water contortions of a man being killed. Thwaite brought his slung-shot down on the beast-head skull.

The blow was enough to crush in a steel cylinder. The beast wrinkled its snout and shook its head from side to side, worrying like a bull-dog at Rivvin's throat.

Again Thwaite struck and again and again. At each blow the portentous head oscillated viciously. The awful thing about it to me was the two blue bosses on each side of the muzzle, like enamel, shiny and hard looking; and the hideous welt of red, like fresh sealing-wax, down between them and along the snout.

Rivvin's struggles grew weaker as the great teeth tore at his throat. He was dead before Thwaite's repeated blows drove in the splintered skull and the clenched jaws relaxed, the snout crinkling and contracting as the dog-teeth slid from their hold.

Thwaite gave the monster two or three more blows, touched Rivvin and fairly dashed out of the room, shouting.

"You stay here!"

I heard the sound of prying and sawing. There alone I looked but once at the dead cracksman. The thing that had killed him was the size of a four to six year old child, but more stockily built, looked entirely human up to the neck, and was dressed in a coat of bright dark blue, a vest of crimson velvet, and white duck trousers. As I looked the muzzle wriggled for the last time, the jaws fell apart and the carcass rolled sideways. It was the very duplicate in miniature of the figure in the big picture on the staircase landing.

Thwaite came dashing back. Without any sign of any qualm he searched Rivvin and tossed me two or three bundles of greenbacks.

He stood up.

He laughed.

"Curiosity," he said, "will be the death of me." Then he stripped the clothing from the dead monster, kneeling by it.

The beast-hair stopped at the shirt collar. Below that the skin was human, as was the shape, the shape of a forty-year-old man, strong and vigorous and well-made, only dwarfed to the smallness of a child.

Across the hairy breast was tattooed in blue,

Hengist Eversleigh.

"Hell," said Thwaite.

He stood up and went to the fatal door. Inside he found the electric button. The room was small and lined with cases of little drawers, tier on tier, rows of brass knobs on mahogany.

Thwaite opened one.

It was velvet lined and grooved like a jeweller's tray and contained rings, the settings apparently emeralds.

Thwaite dumped them into one of the empty bags he had taken from Rivvin's corpse. The next case was of similar drawers of rings set with rubies. The first of these Thwaite dumped in with the emeralds.

But then he flew round the room pulling out drawers and slamming them shut, until he came upon trays of unset diamonds. These he emptied into his sack to the last of them, then diamond rings on them, other jewellery set with diamonds, then rubies and emeralds till the sack was full.

He tied its neck, had me open a second sack and was dumping drawer after drawer into that when suddenly he stopped.

His nose worked, worked horridly like that of the dead monster.

I thought he was going crazy and was beginning to laugh nervously, was on the verge of hysterics when he said:

"Smell! Say what you smell."

I sniffed. "I smell smoke," I said.

"So do I," he agreed. "This place is afire."

"And we locked in!" I exclaimed.

"Locked in?" he sneered. "Bosh. I broke open the front door the instant I was sure they were dead. Come! Drop that empty bag. This is no time for haggling."

We had to step between the two corpses. Rivvin was horridly dead. The colours had all faded from the snout. The muzzle was all mouse-colour.

When we had hold of the bag of coin, Thwaite turned off the electric lights and we struggled out with that and the bag of jewels, and went out into the hallway full of smoke.

"We can carry only these," Thwaite warned me. "We'll have to leave the rest." I shouldered the bag of coin, and followed him down the steps, across a gravel road, and, oh the relief of treading turf and feeling the fog all about me.

At the wall Thwaite turned and looked back. "No chance to try for those other bags," he said. In fact the red glow was visible at that distance and was fast becoming a glare. I heard shouts.

We got the bags over the wall and reached the car. Thwaite cranked up at once and we were off.

How we went I could not guess, nor in what directions, nor even how long. Ours was the only vehicle on the roads we darted along.

When the dawn light was near enough for me to see Thwaite stopped the car. He turned to me.

57

"Get out!" he said.

"What?" I asked.

He shoved his pistol muzzle in my face. "You've fifty thousand dollars in bank bills in your pockets," he said. "It's a half a mile down that road to a railway station. Do you understand English? Get out!"

I got out.

The car shot forward into the morning fog and was gone.

4

He was silent a long time.

"What did you do then?" I asked. "Headed for New York," he said, "and got on a drunk. When I came round I had barely eleven thousand dollars. I headed for Cook's office and bargained for a ten thousand dollar tour of the world, the most places and the longest time they'd give for the money; the whole cost on them. I not to need a cent after I started."

"What date was that?" I asked.

He meditated and gave me some approximate indications rather rambling and roundabout. "What did you do after you left Cook's?" I asked.

"I put a hundred dollars in a savings bank," he said. "Bought a lot of clothes and things and started.

"I kept pretty sober all round the world because the only way to get full was by being treated and I had no cash to treat back with.

"When I landed in New York I thought I was all right for life. But no sooner did I have my hundred and odd dollars in my pockets than I got full again. I don't seem able to keep sober."

"Are you sober now?" I asked.

"Sure," he asserted.

He seemed to shed his cosmopolitan vocabulary the moment he came back to everyday matters.

"Let's see you write what I tell you on this," I suggested, handing him a fountain-pen and a torn envelope, turned inside out.

Word by word after my dictation he wrote.

Until you hear from me again

Yours truly,

No Name.

I took the paper from him and studied the handwriting. "How long were you on that spree?" I asked.

"Which?" he twinkled.

"Before you came to and had but eleven thousand dollars left," I explained.

"I don't know," he said, "I didn't know anything I had been doing."

"I can tell you one thing you did," I said.

"What?" he queried.

"You put four packets, each of one hundred hundred-dollar bills, in a thin manila clasp-envelope, directed it to a New York lawyer and mailed the envelope to him with no letter in it, only a half sheet of dirty paper with nothing on it except: 'Keep this for me until I ask for it,' and the signature you have just written."

"Honest?" he enunciated incredulously.

"Fact!" I said.

"Then you believe what I've told you," he exclaimed joyfully.

"Not a bit I don't," I asseverated.

"How's that?" he asked.

"If you were drunk enough," I explained, "to risk forty thousand dollars in that crazy way, you were drunk enough to dream all the complicated nightmare you have spun out to me.

"If I did," he argued, "how did I get the fifty thousand odd dollars?"

"I'm willing to suppose you got it with no more dishonesty on your part," I told him, "than if you had come by it as you described."

"It makes me mad you won't believe me," he said.

"I don't," I finished.

He gloomed in silence. Presently he said: "I can stand looking at him now," and led the way to the cage where the big blue-nosed mandril chattered his inarticulate bestialities and scratched himself intermittently.

He stared at the brute. "And you don't believe me?" he regretted.

"No, I don't," I repeated, "and I'm not going to. The thing's incredible."

"Couldn't there be a mongrel, a hybrid?" he suggested.

"Put that out of your head," I told him, "the whole thing's incredible."

"Suppose she'd seen a critter like this," he persisted, "just at the wrong time?"

"Bosh!" I said. "Old wives' tales! Superstition! Impossibility!"

"His head," he declared, "was just like that." He shuddered.

"Somebody put drops in some of your drink," I suggested. "Anyhow, let's talk about something else. Come and have lunch with me."

Over the lunch I asked him:

"What city did you like best of all you saw?"

"Paris for mine," he grinned, "Paris forever."

"I tell you what I advise you to do," I said.

"What's that?" he asked, his eyes bright on mine. "Let me buy you an annuity with your forty thousand," I explained, "an annuity payable in Paris. There's enough interest already to pay your way to Paris and leave you some cash till the first quarterly payment comes due."

"You wouldn't feel yourself defrauding the Eversleighs?" he questioned.

"If I'm defrauding any people," I said, "I don't know who they are."

"How about the fire?" he insisted. "I'll bet you heard of it. Don't the dates agree?"

"The dates agree," I admitted. "And the servants were all dismissed, the remaining buildings and walls torn down and the place cut up and sold in portions just about as it would have been if your story were true."

"There now!" he ejaculated. "You do believe me!"

"I do not!" I insisted. "And the proof is that I'm ready to carry out my annuity plan for you."

"I agree," he said, and stood up from the lunch table.

"Where are we going now?" he inquired as we left the restaurant.

"Just you come with me," I told him, "and ask no questions."

I piloted him to the Museum of Archæology and led him circuitously to what I meant for an experiment on him. I dwelt on other subjects nearby and waited for him to see it himself.

He saw.

He grabbed me by the arm. "That's him!" he whispered. "Not the size, but his very expression, in all his pictures." He pointed to that magnificent, enigmatical black-diorite twelfth-dynasty statue which represents neither Anubis nor Seth, but some nameless cynocephalus god.

"That's him," he repeated. "Look at the awful wisdom of him." I said nothing.

"And you brought me here!" he cried. "You meant me to see this! You do believe!"

"No," I maintained. "I do not believe."

After I waved a farewell to him from the pier I never saw him again. We had an extensive correspondence six months later when he wanted his annuity exchanged for a joint-life annu-

ity for himself and his bride. I arranged it for him with less difficulty than I had anticipated. His letter of thanks, explaining that a
French wife was so great an economy that the shrinkage in his income was more than made up for, was the last I heard from him.
As he died more than a year ago and his widow is already married, this
story can do him no harm. If the Eversleighs were defrauded they will
never feel it and my conscience, at least, gives me no twinges.

Alfandega 49 A

(A Tale from *Lukundoo and Other Stories*)

1

The Alders was the last place on earth where anyone would have expected to encounter an atmosphere of tragedy and gloom. The very air of the farm seemed charged with the essence of cheerfulness and friendliness. There appeared to be diffused about the homestead some subtle influence promoting sociability and cordiality.

Perhaps it was merely that the Hibbards had miraculous luck in attracting only the right kind of boarders; possibly, they possessed an almost superhuman intuition which enabled them to avoid accepting any applicant likely to be uncongenial to the others, to themselves or to the place; maybe it was merely the personal effect of the Hibbards and of their welcome which seemed, in some magical fashion, to make all newcomers as much at home as if they had lived at the Alders from childhood. Certainly all their boarders were mutually congenial.

Never was summer-boarding-house so free from cliques, coteries, jealousies, enmities, bickerings and squabbles. The children played all day long apparently, but never seemed noisy or quarrelsome. The old ladies knitted or crocheted, teetering everlastingly in their rocking-chairs on the veranda, beaming at each other and at the landscape. The almost daily games of cards gave rise to scarcely any disputes. The folks at the Alders were very unlike an accidental gathering of summer boarders and much more resembled an unusually large and harmonious family.

This, I suppose, was due to the Hibbards' positive genius for managing a boarding-house and to their genial disposition. Naturally, from their temperament, they enjoyed it, they showed that they enjoyed it and they made everybody feel that they enjoyed it, so that each boarder felt like an invited guest.

The girls never seemed to have anything to do except to make everybody have a good time. Yet they had a great deal to do. In the heyday of the Alders the four girls divided their duties systematically.

Susie, the eldest, and the head of the house, rose early, oversaw the getting of the breakfast, and superintended everything. After dinner she always took a long rest and nap. Then, after supper, she stayed up until the last boarder had come indoors and said goodnight, chiefly occupying herself with seeing to it that all together were enjoying themselves, and each separately. She did it very well too. It was a sight to see her, the moment she was free from presiding at the supper table, appear out on the lawn or on the piazza, or in the parlour, according to the weather. She was tall, plump and handsome, held herself erect and had the art of making herself look well in very inexpensive dresses, mostly of her own devising.

She was always smiling, her light brown hair haloing her face, her blue eyes shining. As she came she swept one comprehensive glance over her guests, unerringly picked out that one, man or woman, lad or girl, child or baby, which seemed enjoying life least, made for that particular individual and wholeheartedly devoted herself to affording enjoyment. She could afford it, too. She was jolly and had an infectious gaiety that was irresistible. She talked well. She was a fair pianist and a really splendid singer. She played, if need be, and sang, too, indefatigably. Never did a party of boarders have a more conscientious, more solicitous or more tactful hostess.

Mattie, who was taller and stouter than Susie, with brown eyes looking out of a face generally expressionless, but sometimes lit by a sympathetic smile, habitually slept late and was abed early. But she bore valiantly the brunt of the long middle of the summer days, took upon herself all that pertained to personal dealings with the servants, engaged them, dismissed them if unsatisfactory, controlled them when restive or cajoled them if dissatisfied, oversaw the getting of the dinner and supper, and made the desserts and ices.

Among the boarders her chief activity was the foreseeing of incipient coolnesses and the tactful dissipation of any small cloud on the social atmosphere. It was chiefly due to her that no germ of antipathy ever developed, at the Alders, into dislike, that no seed of aversion, ever, in that atmosphere, ripened into enmity. She did her part so cleverly that few of the boarders realized that she ever did anything at all, or suspected that she had any social influence.

The two younger sisters superintended the sweeping, dusting, bed-making, lamp-cleaning and all the other details contributing to the comfort of the boarders outside of the dining-room. Also Anna made the always abundant and miraculously appetizing cakes in great variety.

The Alders was always full to its capacity, which meant thirty in the house and any number of boys up to nine in one of the out-buildings, a one-story stone cottage which had once been part of the slave quarters. In it were two double-beds, three canvas cots and at least seven boys; increased to eleven, sometimes, by casual transient guests of the boy-boarders.

The three boys of the family lived out there in summer with the boarders and visitors and kept them in a perpetual good humour.

The Hibbards had learnt this not by precept, but by example. They had grown up to it with their growth. For Susie had been a small girl, Buck a small boy and the rest little children when their widowed mother had begun to take boarders. They had learned much of her art, unconsciously and without knowing that they were learning it.

She was dead and gone before I first knew the Alders. But her spirit still informed the life of the place. She must have been a real lady, every fibre and breath of her, and she must have been a level-headed, practical woman. They quoted some of her aphorisms.

"You cannot make money on twenty-one really good meals a week when you only charge six dollars board," she was reputed to have said. "See that everything is eatable and every meal abundant and give them fried chicken and ice-cream, all they can eat, on Sundays and Thursdays, and they'll always be enthusiastic about the table."

"People can have a good time only in their own way. Find out what they like to do and encourage them to do it, if it is not wrong. That is the only way to please anybody."

"Either don't take boarders at all or make them feel as welcome as cousins.

"Leave out what you can't afford altogether. People never miss what no one has and no one can see. But never skimp anything you have. It is economy to offer everyone a third helping of everything."

"Season the food with good nature."

"Be easy-going about everything." They were easy-going about everything. I've seen Susie tired to death, but gaily hiding it under an exterior of spontaneous vivacity, come back into the big parlour at eleven o'clock Saturday night with two handfuls of cornmeal to scatter on the floor to make it more slippery for dancing. And she did it graciously. They all did such things, and did them instinctively.

They had the faculty of foreseeing when any amusement was palling on the participants and of starting something else before the boarders had time to find out that they were getting tired of what they were doing. They could always lead their guests into anything they began. On Sunday nights Susie sat at the piano and the rest stood around her and they all sang hymns in which all the singers on the farm invariably joined. Two or three nights a week they gathered similarly and sang college songs or popular tunes. Nearly every weekday evening they danced and of course the guests danced too.

Then there was Jack Palton, who foraged among Uncle Hibbard's guitars, found one with four strings left, tuned it like a banjo, and accompanied himself and a bevy of girls in singing glees. Mostly the boarders were too lazy to play tennis and most of the Hibbards were too easy-going to see that the court was kept in order, but nobody missed it. If they played tennis they suited themselves to the court as it was.

The Alders was an easy-going place, full of merriment, of gaiety, of diversion, of singing and dancing, of lovemaking and flirtations.

Especially of flirtations.

That was where the three boys came in strong. Inevitably the boarders at the Alders were mostly women and young women. Before they were half grown the three boys learned to act as beaux for little girls, misses, hoydens, old-maids and grass-widows. They had learned how without knowing it, without knowing it they made an art of it. They did their best, quite spontaneously, to see to it that every unmated feminine creature at the Alders had a good time.

Incidentally they had a good time, for attractive girls were always present in abundance. The result was as good as a comedy to watch.

Whenever a pretty girl, without a gallant in attendance, came to the Alders, she was promptly annexed by the second brother, who had been christened Ernest Paca Hibbard and was always known, spoken of and addressed as "Pake."

Pake was neither tall nor short. He was broad and thick. Also he was fat, not too fat, but pleasantly fat. He had a bullet head, a short neck and a round ruddy face. Withal he was good looking. He affected bright hat-bands on his new stylish straw hats; bright effective neck-ties, tan shoes, white duck trousers and blue coats. He looked attractive, felt attractive and was attractive. Nearly every newcomer liked Pake and, if he liked her, she was within three days spoken of as "Pake's girl."

He was a born flirt, could have flirted if he had been walking in his sleep, and he flirted well. Few girls could resist the charm of his frank and ingenuous overtures or the sparkle of his brown eyes.

Then after Pake had annexed the girl, Buck would look her over. He was in no hurry. He was tall, heavily built though spare, had a good-natured countenance, in which blue eyes looked out of a tanned face, and wore clothes which neither he nor anyone else ever noticed. If Buck liked a girl well enough he took her away from Pake. Nobody could ever describe or specify how he did it; but he did it. Buck's advances threw Pake completely into the shade.

Buck was the head of the family, ran the farm, gave orders to the tenant-farmer, directed the selection of the calf that was to be slaughtered every two weeks and of the two lambs killed each week, talked fascinatingly of pigs and crops, had to ask no one but himself when he wanted a horse hitched up to take a girl out driving, and was generally jovial and delightful. The girls he liked always liked him better than Pake. He had more conversation and never bored anybody.

Then after Pake had transferred his attentions to some newcomer and Buck and his girl were together during all Buck's leisure as naturally as cup and saucer, Rex would look her over deliberately. He was even less in a hurry than Buck.

Rex was slight and silent, with a melancholy air and melting yellow-brown eyes. He was, to the few girls he fancied, altogether irresistible. Therein lay his fault. Rex took flirtation too seriously. It was likely to slip into love making, which is not sound boarding-house ethics.

But Rex never caused any trouble or got into any trouble. If things looked serious to the gossips or the family, they never felt serious to Rex or the girl.

Such was the Alders in its prime, which lasted some few years, during which I was a resident there, first in the "Club," as the boys called their whitewashed stone cottage, later in the house itself. I was happy those four summers, and became almost an honorary member of the family. The honorary members of the Hibbard family were numerous. The Alders had entertained nearly two hundred individual boarders a year for fifteen years. At least one in ten of them felt like an honorary member of the family. Many of those who came there for a second summer were treated as honorary members of the family, and I had spent four summers at the Alders.

So I was treated quite as an honorary member of the family and enjoyed it. The family, in fact, was the best feature of life at the Alders. Seldom could one encounter seven brothers and sisters so loving to each other, so devoted. They had no motto, but they behaved as if their motto were "all for one, one for all." A pleasant feature of each day was the sight of their habitual morning gathering, all to themselves, on the small side porch. There they would sit for half an hour or more, holding a sort of family council on the problems of that day. They were a most united family, solicitous about each other, perpetually interested in each other's welfare.

2

The Alders changed like everything else. Susie married and lived in Baltimore, Anna married and lived in Washington. Pake went to Pittsburgh. Rex married a widow with two children and settled in Chicago. Buck was away from home a good deal. Mattie married a man who did not make the family feel enthusiastic. The Alders continued full of boarders, all in the care of Leslie, the youngest sister, whom I had last seen as a shy girl.

For I had not visited the Alders for a dozen years, and in that time had scarcely seen any of the family except Pake, jolly old Pake, a prosperous bachelor, as much of a flirt as ever, even more of a flirt than in his youth; a short, florid, jovial man, young-looking and handsome, who made love to every new girl he met as naturally as he breathed.

Then, one afternoon early in July, I encountered Rex on the platform of a railroad station, just as we were about to take trains leaving in opposite directions. He glowed over conditions at the Alders, averred that Leslie ran the place as well as ever all four sisters together had, that it was always full, that it was as delightful as ever.

Within a week I encountered Susie and her two tall girls in the waiting room of Union Station. They were off to the Alders for the summer and Susie invited me up over any Sunday I chose.

As with Rex, so also the time I had with Susie was too short for me to ask a tenth of the questions I wanted to ask or for her to tell me a tenth of what she had to tell.

The first Saturday I could get off early I ran up to the Alders. Buck met me at Jonesville station, a little more bronzed than I had last seen him, otherwise the same youthful-looking giant.

The house, of course, was the same tile-roofed brick house, big and plain, neat under a new coat of bright lemon-yellow paint. The barns were the same weathered gray, unpainted, ramshackle barns I remembered, not a bit more decayed nor less dilapidated than a dozen years before. The grove behind the barn was unaltered, not a tree gone as far as I could judge, and all its big oaks, tulip-poplars and hickories rustling delightfully.

The outbuildings near the house were as of old and the brook, just as of yore, not fifty feet from the front porch, rippled across the lawn between its rows of alders. The ailanthus trees west of the house and the locust tree by the well seemed exactly as formerly. They were so big they did not show their growth. But the catalpa by the bridge over the brook had taken on a new lease of life and was flourishing, whereas the Lombardy poplars across the brook were gone. The chief change was in the maples. In my time they had been young trees, with trunks too slender to support a hammock rope without bending when anyone sat in the hammock. Now they were large trees, shading the entire front yard from the brook to the porch with an almost continuous canopy of green.

The place was full of boarders and their children, though the family themselves took up a larger part of the house than of old. Susie was there with her two girls, Anna with her two manly boys and Rex and his wife and his two step-children. Leslie had grown into an entirely adequate housekeeper and hostess and presided admirably. As of yore, the homestead tinkled with banjo music and rang with laughter.

Mattie, of course, was not at the house, as she and her husband lived a quarter of a mile down the road on the farm that had been Aunt Cynthia's. Everything and everybody was as I expected except that I missed Pake.

"Where's Pake?" I queried.

"Pake!" Susie exclaimed. "Didn't you know Pake was in Rio de Janeiro?"

"No!" I answered; "why, I saw Pake on Washington's birthday and he said nothing about going abroad."

"He went in March," Susie rejoined; "late in March, I think. He likes it down there." Somebody interrupted and we did not mention Pake again until after supper. Then we were all out on the long front porch, grouped about Susie. Buck and Tom Brundige and I, scattered among the ladies, had our cigars drawing well. Rex, as always, was smoking one cigarette after another.

A V.M.I. cadet, a crony of one of Anna's boys, was seated on one rail of the rustic bridge over the brook, twanging a banjo at three girls who sat on the other rail facing him. In the lulls of our talk and of the banjo, the chuckle of the brook over its pebbles emphasized the silence, into which broke the undertones of a pair of lovers, swinging in a hammock off to the right. The stars twinkled through the tree-tops, the cigar ends glowed red in the darkness, which was cloven by shafts of lamplight from the windows and mitigated afar to the left where, over the long black outline of the Blue Ridge a paling sky prophesied moonrise.

Somebody had been expecting a letter and had been disappointed and was mourning over it.

"I don't understand about letters from Pake," Susie remarked. "Sometimes we don't get any letters for weeks, and then we get two or three, all at once. When we compare dates and postmarks we find that he writes every Wednesday and Saturday and mails the letters the very day they are written. How do you explain that, Billy?"

"I suppose," I said, "that the letters come different ways, perhaps some by Lisbon, some by London, others perhaps other ways. That might explain it. What do you think, Tom?"

"I fancy," said Brundige, "that you are probably right."

"I had a letter from Pake today," Susie went on. "I had not heard from him for a month. He says he don't like his business quarters. He has an expensive office and he says it is dark and hot and stuffy and he is going to change just as soon as he can find something to suit him. He says he is looking round. But he says he is most comfortably located otherwise. He is boarding, as he expresses it, 'up on Santa Teresa'; what does that mean, Billy?"

"Big, long hill," I replied. "Four hundred feet high. Splendid view over the city and harbour. Fine air all night. Lots of places to board up there, and all good. How's that now, Tom?"

"All correct," Brundige corroborated me.

"I should think," Rex put in, "that Pake would get into trouble down there."

"What sort of trouble?" Anna demanded. "Pake never gets into trouble anywhere. What sort of trouble do you mean?"

Rex lit another cigarette.

"Oh," he said, "I meant that down there those Dago Portuguese won't stand any nonsense. They're a revengeful lot, by what I hear. Pake might cut somebody out with a girl and get a knife stuck in him."

"You're teasing!" cried Anna, indignantly. "You're always up to some teasing! You ought to be ashamed of yourself." And Susie rebuked him:

"You oughtn't to suggest such awful things, Rex."

"But I wasn't suggesting anything awful," Rex persisted, "and I wasn't teasing. I only meant Pake would be likely to cause some heart-burnings down there. Pake's bound to be the same old Pake. He can't change all of a sudden. He's certain to have half a dozen girls thinking they have him on a string before he was there a week. Before he was there a month he had more than one girl on a string. Somebody's bound to be jealous. Those Dagoes are a hot-blooded lot."

"Pooh!" Buck cut in, "Pake don't know enough Portuguese to flirt with any natives and all the Americans and English down there will understand flirting."

"What's the matter with some Dago being in love with an English girl or an American girl?" Rex persevered; "Pake might cut one out with a girl that speaks English."

I saw that both Susie, who was naturally nervous, and Anna, who had been inseparable from Pake all through their childhood, were wrought up. I tried to intervene.

"Nonsense," I said, "Pake might cut out any number of gallants and never get into any trouble. Rio is as peaceable as Baltimore. To begin with, he can't flirt with any Brazilian girls, for no Brazilian girl is ever permitted to talk to a young man. Anybody going along the streets can see the fashionable Brazilians making love according to their custom. Toward sunset, when the heat is less fierce, the girls, all dressed up, lean out of the windows of the second floor drawing rooms. Their lovers stand on the other side of the street and look at them. A young man will stand that way two hours or more every afternoon for a year before he asks her father for a girl. That's the fashion. How is it now, Tom?"

"Same way now." Brundige corroborated me. "Lots of flirtation among the foreign set, though. But no danger of daggers or revenge. Rio is as peaceable as Washington. I never heard of any case of revenge or of jealousy leading to bloodshed. Never heard of a supposed case, except once."

His tone told us all there was a story coming. He was sitting next to Susie and we all hitched our chairs nearer.

"What was that, Tom?" Buck asked.

The women all looked towards Brundige. Rex lit another cigarette. The rest of us lit fresh cigars.

"It was a fellow named Orodoff Guimaraes," Brundige began.

"Guimaraes, in Portuguese, is like Smith in English, only more so. It seems as if half the Fluminenses, as they call the people of Rio, are named Guimaraes. This Orodoff Guimaraes was a cousin and name-sake of a wealthy and respected wine-merchant and rather traded on the relationship and identity of the name. He was one of those dandies who swarm in all South American cities, young men with little or no income, a great sense of their own importance, a taste for expensive pleasures, a love of ease and comfort, ungovernable passions, and an insane devotion to the latest fashion in clothes.

"Most of such idlers have no income and are too proud to have any business. This Orodoff Guimaraes was better off in both respects. He inherited a small property in real estate, and he made some money in life insurance. He had a desk in a third floor office in a building he owned, 49A Rua de Alfandega, one of the principal business streets of the old down-town part of Rio. He rented the first and second floors of the building at good rentals, and he rented desk-room on the third floor; all the back office and all the front office except his own small desk.

"He used to spend the most of his mornings at that desk, idling. He sometimes had business that took him out, sometimes he pretend-ed he had. But mostly he just sat at his desk, reading papers, smoking cigarettes or doing nothing at all. It was a pleasant place to do nothing in, a big room, nearly thirty feet wide, more than thirty feet long, with a high ceiling and three tall French windows down to the floor, all three always open. They faced south, so that they needed no awnings and they let in no glare and plenty of breeze. The office was light, but not too light, cool and airy, an ideal loafing place.

"When he was not loafing in his office Guimaraes was always making love to some girl or going through the motions of making love. No girl would have him, for no girl's father would let her marry him; he was not well enough off to marry, though he managed to dress well as a bachelor. So girl after girl whom he made love to married someone else, or got engaged to someone else. Three of them got engaged, but never got married. Their bridegrooms died before the wedding day.

"In each case Guimaraes made friends with his rival, got quite chummy with him, and induced him to rent a desk in his office. In each case the rival was killed by falling out of one of the French windows of the office, forty odd feet to the pavement of the Rue de Alfandega. In each case it was an accident. In each case Orodoff Guimaraes was out of his office when the accident happened. But while no one could say a word against Guimaraes, after the third accident no Fluminense who had been exposed in any way to Orodoff Guimaraes' real or apparent rivalry for any girl could be induced to rent desk room in his office.

"The deaths could not be imputed to him, but the coincidence of the rivalry, the friendship, the renting of a desk and the fall from the window, in three different cases, was more than even the slow-thinking fashionable Fluminenses could stand. It got on their nerves. If he hadn't committed three murders out of revenge, it seemed as if he had. Of course, he couldn't have hypnotized the victims when he was half a mile away and made them throw themselves out of the window or caused them to walk out of the window, but somehow everybody felt as if that was just about what he had done.

"And each case was spooky, too. In each case the victim's desk was close to one of the windows; in each case Orodoff Guimaraes was out, but there were two other men, renters of desk-room, at desks further back in the office; in each case the other men, seated at their desks twenty feet and more away, had been talking across the room to the victim; in each case the other men, different men each time, had turned round to look at something on their desks, had heard no sound, no movement, no cry, but when they looked round again found themselves alone in the room, and, going to the window, saw the victim crushed on the pavement below."

He stopped.

"Why don't they have a railing or a balustrade across the open window?" Rex inquired.

"Custom," Brundige rejoined. "Custom rules everything down there; custom rules everything all over South America. In Rio all upstairs offices have French windows down to the floor. It's a hot climate and no window has a rail or even a bar across it. To have unobstructed windows is the custom.

"Fool custom!" said Buck.

Just then Leslie came out and joined us. She had been attending to her household duties, or giving orders about breakfast, or entertaining a boarder or something like that.

After she was settled next Rex she said: "I had a letter from Pake this morning. He says there are some fine girls down there in Rio. Says he has had no end of fun with them. He must have been in a good humor when he wrote that letter. It's a long letter and very funny. He tells how he pretended to make love to a girl, just to annoy a fool of a dude who was always making eyes at her, how at first the dude was mad, how he saw the joke and behaved real sensibly. Pake says they got to be real good friends. He tells it all very well. I'll read it to you tomorrow."

Leslie was bubbling with merriment, as unconscious as possible and very girlish. But about the rest of us the atmosphere seemed to tingle. I could feel, as it were, the spiritual tension. Buck asked, thickly:

"Did he tell you the fellow's name?"

"No," said Leslie cheerfully. "He never mentioned his name. But he says they are real good friends."

Just then the banjo party on the little bridge stood up. We heard cheerful greetings and recognized Mattie's voice. She had strolled over on foot, her home being a very short distance down the road.

She came up on the porch, a big, solid matronly young woman. I caught a glimpse of her plump face as the lamplight through the open doorway struck on her, her brown eyes smiling merrily.

Buck sat down on the porch floor, his feet on the steps, his back against a pillar. Mattie took his chair. She also took charge and control of the conversation.

"Alf drove to Hagerstown right after supper," she said. "He ought to be back soon. I told him I was coming over here and he'll come right here when he comes out."

This was in answer to my query.

"I had a letter from Pake this morning," she went on. "He says he's got a new office that suits him perfectly. He says he didn't need as much room as he had, so he's taken desk room only in the office of a friend of his, some kind of Brazilian name, I couldn't spell and can't pronounce it. He says it's a dandy place on the third floor, big, high room, plenty of floor space to move about in and nice fellows at the other desks. It's bright and cool and airy, three big French windows open down to the floor."

Then, quite suddenly, as she paused, I felt the Alders enveloped in an atmosphere of tragedy and gloom. The Hibbards excelled in self-control; not one of them uttered a sound. There was a long silence. I could hear the ripple of the brook. The first rays of the late moon, just clearing the top of the Blue Ridge, struck through the maples.

Anna spoke first: "Have you that letter with you, Mattie?"

"Yes," Mattie replied cheerfully. "I brought it along."

"Give it to me," Anna said; "Billy and I will try to make out that name."

"Billy can do it, I'll bet," spoke Mattie brightly.

Anna, the letter in her hand, stood up. "Come on, Billy," she said. I went.

I was surprised at her asking me instead of Brundige. I had never been intimate with Anna. Susie I had known well and Mattie better, but Leslie, in the old days, had merely smiled and seldom spoken, so that I could not tell whether she liked me or not, while Anna had seemed to avoid me.

I should have expected her to call Brundige, for Tom had been in Rio longer than I, and much more recently.

She stood by the refrigerator in the back hall by the side door and leaned against it, her brown hair almost golden against the lamp that stood on the refrigerator.

"I daren't look at the letter," she said. "You read it, Billy." I found the name and it was Orodoff Guimaraes. Also, at the end of the letter he told Mattie to write to him at his office address, Rua de Alfandega, 49A.

"Come!" said Anna, in a fierce whisper.

I followed her through the side door and out into the tepid windless moonlight. She made for the barn.

The atmosphere of gloom and tragedy deepened about us. The moonlight seemed weird and ghastly, the shadows of the trees grim and menacing, the silence like that of a graveyard.

Anna leaned against the barnyard gate. "Could I send a cablegram to Rio de Janeiro for thirty dollars?" she queried. "A long one for less," I said. "When I was down there the rates were sixty-five cents a word. That's many years ago. The rates can't be over half that now. You could cable a letter for thirty dollars."

"I have three ten-dollar bills," she said. "Barton gave them to me for emergencies just before I left Washington."

"I have more than that in my pocket," I said. "Between us we are sure to have more than enough."

"Do you suppose," she asked, "that I could send a cable from Jonesville this late Saturday night?"

"We might try," I said.

"If we can't," she pressed me, "will you drive into Hagerstown with me "Yes," I promised.

"Oh," she said, "I can't bear it. I can see him lying dead on those cruel paving stones. I can't bear it."

I remembered that, just as Rex and Leslie had been inseparable all through their childhood, so Anna and Pake had been comrades from the cradle on. I said nothing.

"Can you hitch up without the lantern?" she demanded. "Has the stable been altered?" I asked.

"Not a bit," she said.

In fact my hand in the dark found in the same places what might have been the same hickory harness-pegs and on them what seemed like the same old sets of harness.

"Which stall?" I asked.

"Laddie's old stall," she directed me; "call her Nell." I harnessed the mare and led her out to the carriage shed. Anna climbed into the buggy. I opened the gate into the grove and closed it after she had driven through. At the far end of the grove I got out of the buggy again and let down the bars. After I had put them up and was at last in the buggy she handed the reins to me.

"Nell can trot," she said.

Nell trotted, the snaky black shadows lay inky dark across the road. We tore past Grotto station. We neared Jonesville. I had no sense of ineptitude or futility in what we were trying to do. I did not feel I was on a wild goose chase. I did not feel absurd. I took our errand most seriously. We were on our way to warn Pake against the devilish machinations of a fiend who had contrived and compassed three ingenious murders. We were racing against time to warn him before it was too late. I was wrought up to the highest pitch of excitement over the gravity and urgency of our mission.

We found the telegraph operator still awake. We persuaded him to do as we asked. Anna wrote and I amended till we agreed on:

Change your office immediately. Do not enter it again on any account. Get another office at once. Act instantly; this is a matter of life and death. Explanations by letter.

                                                                    Anna.

When the cablegram was sent off we drove homeward, at Nell's natural pace, which was not slow.

We felt only partly relieved.

A dozen times Anna sighed: "I hope we were in time; oh, I hope we were in time!" The atmosphere of gloom and tragedy pursued us as we returned, enveloped the Alders when again we were seated on the porch.

Hardly were we seated when Mattie's husband came. I had heard he had been consumptive, but had recovered completely. He looked to me like a dying man; haggard, gray-checked, sunken-eyed, trembling. He greeted people like a sleep-walker.

As soon as greetings were over he said: "Buck, I want to talk business to you a moment." Buck stood up. He had the Hibbard faculty of intuition and unexpectedness. I was used to both, of old. But I was very much astonished when he pinched me as he passed and indicated that I was to come, too.

In the back hall by the refrigerator Alf looked up at Buck like a hunted animal at bay.

"My God, Buck," he said. "How'll we ever break it to the girls?"

"Break what?" Buck queried, his voice dry and thin.

"There was a cablegram for you at Hagerstown," Alf replied. "Beesore had sense enough not to telephone it out here. He saw me and gave it to me. Pake's dead."

"Let's look at the cablegram," Buck said thickly.

He looked, holding it closely to the kerosene lamp on the refrigerator. Then he handed it to me.

I read:

E. P. Hibbard instantly killed by a fall from a window.

G. Swanwick.

The Message on the Slate

(A Tale from *Lukundoo and Other Stories*)

1

Mrs. Llewellyn had always held—in so far as she ever thought about the subject at all—that to consult a clairvoyant was not merely an imbecile folly, but a degrading action, nearly akin to crime. Now that she felt herself overmasteringly driven to such an unconscionable unworthiness she could not bring herself to do it openly. Anything underhand or secretive was utterly alien to her nature. She was a tall woman, notably well shaped, with unusual dignity of demeanour. The poise of her head would have appeared haughty but for the winning kindliness of her frequent smile. Her dark hair, dark eyes and very white skin accorded well with that abiding calm of her bearing which never seemed mere placidity in a face habitually lighted with interested comprehension.

Like a cloudless springtime sunrise over limitless expanses of dewy prairies, she was enveloped in an atmosphere of spacious serenity of soul, and her appearance was entirely in consonance with her character. She was still a very beautiful woman, high-souled as she was beautiful and exceedingly straight-forward. Yet to drive in open day to a house bearing the displayed sign of a spirit-medium was more than she could do. Bidding her footman call for her later, much later, at her hairdresser's, she dismissed her carriage at the main entrance of a department store.

Leaving it by another entrance, she took a street car for the neighbourhood she sought. The neighbourhood was altogether different from what she had anticipated; the houses, by no means small, were even handsome; not least handsome that of the clairvoyant. And it was very well kept, the pavement and the steps clean, the plate glass window panes bright, the shades and curtains new and tasteful, the silver doorknobs and door-bell fresh polished. There was a sign, indeed, but not the flaming horror her imagination had constructed from memories of signs seen in passing. This was a bit of glass set inside the big, bright pane of one of the parlour windows. It bore in small gold letters only the name, *Salathiel Vargas,* and the word, *Clairvoyant.*

A neat maid opened the door. Yes, Mr. Vargas was in; would she walk into the waiting room? The untenanted waiting room was a dignified parlour, furnished in the costliest way, but with a restraint as far as possible from ostentation. The rug was Persian, each piece of furniture different in design from any other, yet all harmonizing, while the ten pictures were paintings by well-known artists. Before Mrs. Llewellyn had time for more than one comprehensive and surprised glance about, when she had barely seated herself, the retreating maid struck two sharp notes on a silvery gong.

Almost immediately the door leading to the rear room was opened. In it appeared a man under five feet tall, not dwarfish, but deformed. His patent-leather shoes were boyish, his trousers hung limp about legs shrivelled to mere skeletal stems, and his left knee was bent and fixed at an unchanging angle, so that his step was a painful hobble. Above the waist he was well made; a deep chest; broad, square shoulders; a huge head with a vast shock of black, curly hair. He had the look of a musician or artist; with a wide forehead; delicately curved eyebrows; nose hooked, sharp and assertive; eyes, wide apart, large, dark brown with sparkles of red and green; and a mouth whose curled upper lip was almost too short.

The mouth and eyes held Mrs. Llewellyn at first glance, and the instant change in them startled her. He had appeared with a suave mechanical smile, with a look of easy expectancy. As his gaze met hers his lips set and their redness dulled; his eyes were full of so poignant a dismay that she would not have been surprised had he abruptly retreated and slammed the door between them. Without a word he clung to the knob, staring at her. Then he drew the door to after him and leaned against it, still holding to the knob with one hand behind his back. When he spoke it was in a dry whisper.

"You here, of all women!"

"You know me!" she exclaimed; "I have never seen you."

"You are seen of many thousands you never note," he replied. "Everyone knows Mrs. David Llewellyn. Everyone knew Constance Palgrave."

"You flatter me," she said coldly, with the air of one resenting an unwelcome familiarity.

"Flattery is part of my trade," he replied. "But I do not flatter you. So little that I have forgotten my manners. I should have asked you to step into my consulting room. Pray, enter it."

She passed him as he held the door open for her. The inner room was not less seemly than the outer. Except for three doors and one broad window looking out on an area, it was walled with bookcases some eight feet high, broken only where there were set into them two small cabinets with drawers below. The glass doors of the bookcases were of small panes, and the books within were in exquisite bindings. Topping the cases were several splendid bronze busts. The furniture was completed by a round mahogany centre-table, several small chairs and three tapestried armchairs.

When Mrs. Llewellyn had seated herself in one the clairvoyant took another. His agitation was so extreme that had she been capable of fear it would almost have frightened her; her curiosity it greatly piqued. He was as pale as a swarthy man can be, his lips bloodless and twitching, dry and moistening themselves one against the other as he mechanically swallowed in his nervousness. She herself was perturbed in soul, but an eye less practised than his would have discerned no signs of emotion beneath her easy exterior. They faced each other in silence for some breaths; then he spoke:

"For what purpose have you come here?"

"To consult you," she answered. "Is it astonishing? Do not all sorts of persons come to consult you?"

"All sorts," he replied. "But none such as you. Never any such as you."

"I have come, it seems," she said simply, "and to consult you."

"In what way do you mean to consult me?" he queried. "People consult me in various ways."

"I had in mind," she said, "the answers you give by writing on the inside of a shut slate."

"You have come to the wrong man," he said harshly, with an obvious effort that made his voice unnatural. "Go elsewhere," and he rose.

She gazed at him in astonishment without moving. "Why do you say that?" she demanded.

He opened each of the three doors, looked outside and then made sure that each was latched. He looked out of the window, glancing at each of the other windows visible from it. He hobbled once or twice up and down the room, mopping his forehead and face with his handkerchief; then he seated himself again.

"Mrs. Llewellyn," he said, "I must request your promise of entire and permanent secrecy for what I am about to tell you."

"Anyone would suppose," she said, "that you were the client and I the clairvoyant."

"Acknowledging that," he replied. "Let it pass, I beg of you. I have told you that you have come to the wrong man. I bade you go elsewhere. You ask for an explanation. I have fortified myself to give it to you. But I must have your pledge of silence if you desire an explanation."

"I do desire it and you have my promise."

He looked around the room with the movement of a rat in a cage. His eyes met hers, but shifted uneasily, and his shamefaced gaze fell to the floor. His hands clutched each other upon his lame knee.

"*Madame*," he said, "I tell you to go elsewhere because I am a charlatan, an impostor. My trances are mere pretence, the method of my replies a farcical mummery, the answers transparent concoctions from the hints I extract from my dupes."

"You say this to try me," she cried; "you are subjecting me to some sort of test."

"*Madame*," he said, "look at me. Am I like a man playing a part? Do I not look in earnest?" She regarded him, convinced.

"But," she wondered. "Why do you thrust this confession upon me?"

"I fear," he hesitated, "that a truthful answer to that question would displease you."

"Your behaviour," she said, "and your utterances are so unexpected and amazing to me, coming here as I have, that I must request an explanation."

Vargas straightened himself in his chair and looked her in the eyes, not aggressively, but timidly. He spoke in a low voice.

"*Madame*," he said solemnly, "I have told you the truth about myself because you are the one human being whom I am unwilling to harm, wrong or cheat."

"You mean,"—she broke off, bridling.

"Ah, *Madame*," he cried, "I mean nothing that has in it any tinge of anything that might offend you. What does the north star know or care how many frail, storm-tossed barks struggle to steer by it? Is it any the less radiant, pure, high because so many to whom it is and shall remain forever unattainable strive to win from its rays guidance towards havens of safety? A woman such as you cannot guess, much less know, to how many she is the one abiding heavenly beacon. How could you, who need no such help from without, realize what the mere sight of you afar off must mean to natures not blest with such a heritage of goodness? How many have been strengthened at sight of your face, wherein they could not but see the visible outward expression of that inward peace and serenity that comes from right instincts unswervingly adhering to noble ideals? You have been to me the incarnate token of the existence of that righteousness to which I might not attain."

Mrs. Llewellyn had borne his torrent of verbiage with a look of intolerant toleration, of haughty displeasure curbed by astonishment. When he paused for breath she said, in a voice half angry, half repressed:

"I quite understand you, I have heard enough, I have heard altogether too much of this; we will change the subject, if you please."

"I spoke at your command," Vargas apologized, abashed, "and only to convince you of my sincerity in telling you that I am not worthy of being consulted by you."

"But," she protested, carried away by her surprise, "you are called the greatest clairvoyant on earth."

"And I have schemed, advertised lavishly, spent money like water, bribed reporters, bought editors, cajoled managers, hoodwinked owners and won over their wives and daughters through laborious years to produce that impression. It is no growth of accident, no spontaneous recognition of self-evident merit.

"But," she argued, "are you a fiend doing all this for the delight of deceiving for deception's sake? Are you a man wealthy by inheritance and choosing this form of activity for the pleasure it gives you?"

"By no means *Madame*," he denied, "I live by my wits."

"Your surroundings tell me that you live well," she suggested. "Better than my surroundings reveal," he rejoined.

"Then your wits are good wits," she ventured.

"None better of their kind on earth," he naïvely admitted, wholly off his guard. "And they are not overtaxed?" she asked.

"Deception is not hard," he told her, "the world is full of fools and even the sensible are easy to deceive."

"From what I have read," she continued, "you do not deceive. Your advice is good. Your precepts guide your clients right. Your suggestions lead to success. Your predictions come to pass, your conjectures are verified."

"All that is true enough," he allowed. "Then how can you call your clients dupes, your methods mummeries, your answers lies?" She wound up triumphantly.

"I did not call my answers lies," he disclaimed. "Mummeries I deal in and to dupes. Dupes they are all. They pour gold into my lap to tell them what they already knew if they but reasoned it out calmly with themselves. They babble to me all they need to know and pay me insensately for it when I fling back to them a patchwork of the fragments I have extracted from their stories of expectations, apprehensions and memories."

"But if you do all that you must be a real judge of human nature, a genuine reader of hearts, a keen-brained counsellor."

"I am all that and more," he bragged. He had lost every trace of agitation and bore himself with a dashing self-confidence of manner, extremely engaging. "I cannot minister to a mind diseased; but I am called on to prescribe for all sorts of delusions, follies, blunders, miseries and griefs. I could count by thousands the men and women I have saved, the lives I have made happy, the difficulties I have annihilated, the aspirations I have guided aright."

"Then you must have an immense experience of human frailties and human needs."

"Vast, enormous, incalculable," he declared.

"Your advice then should be valuable."

"It is valuable," he boasted.

"Then advise me, I am in extreme distress. I have felt that no one could help me. The belief that you might has given me a ray of hope. You have expressed a regard for me altogether extraordinary. Will it not lead you to help me?"

"Any advice and help, any service in my power you may be sure shall be yours," he said earnestly. "But let me ask you first, how was it that you did not seek the advice of some business-man, lawyer or clergyman? You are not at all of the light-headed type of those frivolous women who flock to me and to others like me. You have common sense, unalterable principles, rational instincts and personal fastidiousness, why did you not go to one of the recognized, established, honoured advisers of humanity? Tell me that if you please?"

"It was because of the dream," she faltered.

"The dream!" he exclaimed. "A dream sent you to me? What sort of a dream?"

"I had come to feel that there could be no hope for me," she said. "But about a month ago I had a dream in which I was told 'The seventh advertisement in the seventh column of the seventh newspaper in the seventh drawer of the linen room will point for you the way to escape from your miseries and win what you desire.' There should have been no papers in my linen-room and it made me feel foolish to want to go and look. Also the servants knew I never went there, so I had to watch until the housekeeper was out and no maids were on that floor. Sure enough I found seven old newspapers in the seventh drawer, and on the seventh page of the lowermost paper, on the seventh column, the seventh advertisement was yours."

"And you came to me because of that dream?"

"Yes:—and;—" she hesitated.

"Well," he interrupted, "the reasons why you came are not so important. What I want to be sure of is this. Even if you were led to come by a mere coincidence acting on your feelings, are you now, from cool, deliberate reflection, determined to consult me? Would it not be better to take my advice at this point and go to one of the world's regular, accredited dispensers of wisdom?"

"I have made up my mind to consult you," she said. "It is not a passing whim, but a settled resolve."

"Then *Madame*," he said, his manner wholly changing, "you must tell me all your troubles without any reservation of any kind. If I am to help you I must know your case as completely as a physician would have to know your symptoms in an illness. Tell me plainly what your trouble is."

She began to pluck at her veil with her gloved hands.

"Oh," she gasped, "let me moisten my lips. Just a swallow of water." For all his lameness he was surprisingly agile, as he wrenched himself up, tore open the rear door and almost instantly hobbled back with a glass and silver pitcher on a small silver tray.

She took off her veil and one glove. Several swallows were required to compose her. When she was calm again he sat looking at her with a face full of inquiry, but without uttering any questions.

"You do not know," she said, "how hard it is to begin."

"For the third time, *Madame*," he said, "I advise you not to consult me, to go elsewhere."

"Are you not willing to help me?" she asked, softly.

"Utterly willing," he said, "but timid, timid as a doctor would be about prescribing for his own child. Yours is the first case ever brought to me in which I feared the effect of personal bias dimming my insight or deflecting my judgment. I have a second confession to make to you. Before you married, a man desperately in love with you came to me for help. Among other things he gave me the day, hour and minute of your birth and of his and asked me to cast both horoscopes and infer his chances of success. I had and have no faith in astrology, yet I had cast my own horoscope long before from mere curiosity. When I cast yours I was amazed at the clear indications of a connection between your fate and mine. I did not believe anything of the Babylonian absurdities, yet the coincidence struck me. Perhaps I am influenced by it yet. Under such an influence, even more than under that of my feeling for yourself, my acumen is likely to be impaired. I again advise you to go elsewhere."

"I am all the more determined to consult you and you only."

He bowed without any word and waited in silence for her to go on. She stared at him with big melting eyes, her face very pale.

"My husband does not love me," she said.

"Not love you?" Vargas exclaimed, startled. "Do you mean seriously to tell me that, you who have been loved by hundreds, been adored, worshipped, courted by so many, for despair of gaining whom men have gone mad, who have had your choice of so many lovers, are not prized by the man who succeeded in winning you?"

"Yes," she barely breathed. "He does not prize me, nor love me at all."

"Does he love anyone else?"

Out of her total paleness she flushed rose pink from throat to hair. "Yes," she admitted.

"Who is she?" Vargas demanded.

"His first wife."

Vargas staggered to his feet. "I did not so much as know that your husband had been married before," he gasped, "let alone that he was divorced."

"He was not divorced," she stated. "Not divorced," he quavered.

"No, he was a widower when I married him." Vargas collapsed back into his chair.

"I do not understand," he told her. "Does he love a dead woman?"

"Just that," she asseverated.

"This will not do," the clairvoyant told her, "I cannot come nearer to helping you at this rate. Try to give me the information you think necessary, not by splinters and fragments, but as a whole. Make a connected exposition of the circumstances. Begin at the beginning.

"That is harder," she mused, "I always want to begin anything at the last chapter."

"Woman fashion," he commented. "You are above that in most things, I know. Try a straight story from the beginning."

She reflected:

"The beginning," she said, "was before I began to remember. David and I were playmates before we could talk. Boy and girl, lad and lass, we always belonged to each other, there was no love-making between us, I think, for it was all love-living. I do not believe he ever asked me to marry him or promised to marry me, or so much as talked marriage. But we had a clear understanding that we were to marry as soon as we could, at the earliest possible day. He did not merely seem wrapped up in me, he was. God knows he was all my life. Then he had no more than seen Marian Conway when he fell in love with her. There is no use in dwelling on what I suffered. He married almost at once and I gave myself up to that empty life of frivolity which made me a reigning beauty and brought me scores of suitors for none of whom I cared anything and which gave me not a particle of satisfaction.

"Then after they had lost both their children Marian died. David was frightfully overcome by his loss. He had loved her inconceivably and he showed his grief in the most heart-rending ways. He had the coffin opened over and over after it had been closed. He had it even lifted out of the grave and opened yet once more for one more look at her face. He spent every moment from her death to her burial in a sort of adoration of her corpse, and he did stranger things. I do not know whether it was Mr. Llewellyn's valet who told, but at any rate the story got out among the servants.

"The night before she was buried he had her laid out in her coffin and a second coffin exactly like it set beside her's. He stayed locked in the room all night. They believed he lay in the other coffin. At any rate in the morning it was closed, and he did not allow it to be opened. What he had placed in it no one knew. They said it was as heavy as the other. Two hearses, one behind the other, carried the coffins to the graveyard. Her grave is not under the monument—you have seen the monument?"

"No," he said, "only a picture of it."

"Well, she is not buried under it, and the second coffin was placed on hers." She stopped.

"Go on," he said.

"Oh," she cried, "it is so hard to go on. But it is true. As soon as David was free I felt I had an object in life. I—I followed him, I might almost say pursued him all over the world, and when we met I courted him, and it seems strange, but I asked him to marry me. And—" she hesitated—"he refused twice."

"He did not want to marry you?" Vargas asked incredulously.

"He refused. It was at Cairo, that first time. He said he could not love anyone any more, all his love, his very self, was buried in Marian's grave. The second time was at Hong Kong. Then he said he always had cared for me and still cared for me, but that affection was as nothing compared to his passion for Marian, that he would never marry, and especially he would not marry me because of his regard for me, that I would not be contented or happy with him, that I was thinking of the lad he had been and that boy was buried in his wife's grave, that he was nothing more than a walking ghost, a wraith of what he had been, a spirit condemned to wander its allotted time on earth until his hour should come and he be called to join Marian.

"The third time was in Paris. He said he was indifferent to everything, to anything, to love or hate or death or life; that he cared nothing whether he married me or not. If I cared as much as I seemed to he would marry me to please me. I told him that what I had always wanted was to be with him, that what I most wanted was to spend with him as much as possible of my time until death parted us. He said if that was what I wanted I could have it, but he was nothing more than a shadow of his old self and I was sure to be unhappy.

"And I am unhappy. He is generosity, gentleness, kindness and consideration itself, but he does not care. I hoped, of course, that his grief for Marian would soften, fade away and vanish, that he would cease to mourn for her, that his interest in life would reawaken, that I could win his love and that we would both be happy. But I am not. His utter indifference to me, to anything, to everything is preying on my feelings, I must do something. I shall lose my mind."

"Is that all?" Vargas asked.

"It is enough," she asserted, "and more than enough. Do you think it a small matter?"

"Not in the least," he declared, "I comprehend your disappointment in respect to your hopes, your chagrin at your baffled efforts to win him back to be his old self, your pain at his inertness. But by your own showing you have no grievance against your husband."

"That I have not," she maintained. "Not a shadow of a griev-ance against him. My grievance is for him as much as for myself and against—against the way the world is made."

Vargas looked at her for some little time.

"You do not say what you are thinking," she interrupted.

"I am considering how to express it," he said. "However I express it I am sure to offend you."

"Not a bit," she replied. "Say it at once."

"You must realize that if I am to advise you truly I must speak plainly," he hesitated.

"I do realize it," she told him.

"You will then pardon what I have to say?" he ventured.

"I will pardon anything except beating about the bush," she rapped out.

"Well," he said slowly, "it seems to me that your coming to me, your state of mind, your trouble, as you have related it all turns upon a piece of femininity to which you should be altogether superior, to which I should have imagined you were altogether superior. You look, and I have always imagined you, free from any trace of the eter-nal feminine. Here it crops out. Men in general find that women in general have no feeling for the mutuality of a contract. Some women may be exceptions, but women habitually ignore the other side of a contract and see only their own side. Here you display the same defect. Mr. Llewellyn practically proposed a contract to you: on his side he to marry you, on your side, you to put up with his complete indifference to you, to everything, and be content with his actual companionship such as he is. He has fulfilled and is fulfilling his part of the contract, you seek escape from yours."

"I think," she snapped. "You are insufferably brutal."

"The eternal feminine again," he retorted.

"Worse and more of it. I told you I should offend you."

"You do offend me. I have confidence in you, but I did not come here to be scolded or to be preached at. I do not want criticism, I want advice. Don't tell me my shortcomings, real or imaginary, think over my troubles and my needs and tell me what to do."

"That is plain enough," he asserted. "Do your obvious duty. Keep your part of your contract with your husband. Give no sign that you suffer from the absence of feeling of which he warned you. Make the most of your life with him. Hope for a change in him but do not try to force it, do not rebel if it does not come."

"I know I ought to endure," she wailed. "But I cannot, I must do something. I must act. I must."

"You have asked for my advice," he said, "and you have it."

"And what good is it to me?" she objected, "I ask for help and you string out platitudinous precepts like a snuffy, detestable old-fashioned evangelical dominie. Is this all the help you can give me?"

"All," said Vargas humbly. "If I knew of any other it should be at your service."

"You could consult your slate for me, as I proposed," she suggested.

"Great heavens above!" he cried, "I have told you that all that is imposture."

"It might turn out genuine for once," she persisted. "Don't people have real trances? Don't many people believe in the answers from slates and *planchettes* and Ouija boards?"

"Perhaps they do," Vargas admitted. "But I never had a real trance, never saw one, never knew of one. And to my knowledge no slate or other such device ever gave any answer or wrote anything unless I or some other shuffler made it write or answer."

"But could you not try just once for my sake," she implored.

"Why on earth," he demanded, "are you, so sane and sensible in appearance, so set on this mummery?"

"Because of the other dream," she faltered.

"The other dream!" he exclaimed. "You had another dream?"

"Yes," she said, "I was going to tell you but you interrupted me. The dream about the advertisement did not convince me. I felt it might be coincidence after all. That was more than a month ago and I disregarded it. But night before last I dreamed I was told, 'The message on the slate will be true.' I fought against it all day yesterday, all last night. Today I gave up and came. I want you to consult your slate for me."

"*Madame*," he said, "this is dreadful. Can nothing make you see the truth. There is not anything supernatural about this trade of mine. It is as simple as a Punch and Judy show. There the puppets do nothing save as the showman controls them; so of my slate and of my trances."

"But it might surprise you," she persisted. "It might come true once. Won't you try for me?"

"I know," he mused, "that there is such a thing as auto-hypnotism. To humour you I might try to put myself into a genuine trance. But there would be nothing about it to help you, just a mere natural sleep, artificially induced. If I babbled in it the words would have no significance, and no writing would appear on the slate unless I put it there."

"Just try," she pleaded, "for my sake, to quiet me. If there is nothing, then I shall believe you."

"There will be nothing on the slate," he maintained. "But suppose I should mumble some fragments of words. You might take those accidental vocables for a revelation, they might become an obsession upon you, they might warp your judgment and do you great harm. I feel we should be running a foolish risk. Give up this idea of the trance and the slate, I beg of you."

"And I beg of you to try it. You said you would do anything for me. That is what I want and nothing else."

He shook his head, his expression crestfallen, baffled, puzzled, even alarmed.

"If you insist—" he faltered.

"I do insist," she said.

"You wish," he inquired, "to proceed exactly as I usually do with my simulated trance and pretended spirit replies?"

"Precisely," she affirmed.

He opened a drawer below one of the cabinets and took out a hinged double slate. It was made like a child's school-slate, but the rims instead of being wood, were of silver, the edges beaded and the flat of each rim chased in a pattern of pentacles, swastikas and pentagrams; a pentacle, a right-hand swastika, a pentagram, a left-hand swastika and so on all round. In the drawer was a box of fresh slate-pencils. This he held out to her and told her to choose one. At his bidding she broke off a short fragment and put it between the two Leaves of the slate, the four faces of which were entirely blank.

"Settle yourself in your chair," he instructed her, "hold the slate in your lap. Hold it fast with both hands. First take off your other glove."

As she did this he settled himself into the armchair opposite her, took a silver paper-knife from the table and held it upright, gazing at its point.

"You are not to move or speak until I tell you," he directed her.

So they sat, she holding in her lap the slate shut fast upon the pencil within, her fingers enforcing its closure; he gazing intently at the point of the scimitar-shaped paper-knife. She became aware of the slow, pompous tick of a tall clock in the hallway; of faint noises, as of activity in a pantry, proceeding from somewhere in the rear of the house and barely audible through the closed window. She had expected to see him stiffen, his eyes roll up or some such manifestation appear.

Nothing of the kind happened. For a long time, a very long time, she watched him staring fixedly at the sharp end of the paper-cutter. Then she saw it waver, saw his eyes close and his head, propped against the back of the armchair, move ever so little sideways, as the neck-muscles relaxed. His hands opened, the knife dropped on his knee and he was to all appearances peacefully asleep. Presently his even, regular breathing was a sound more apparent than the tick of the clock outside.

All of a sudden Mrs. Llewellyn felt herself ridiculous. Here she was, holding a childish toy, facing a strange man with whom she was entirely alone and who was apparently enjoying a needed snooze. She had an impulse to laugh and was on the point of rising, disembarrassing herself of her burden and leaving the house.

At that instant she felt a movement between the fast-shut slates. They lay level upon her lap, firmly set. She had not jarred or tilted them, yet she felt the pencil move. Felt it move and heard it too. Her mood of impatient self-contempt and irritated derision was instantly obliterated under a wave of terrified awe. She controlled a spasm of panic, an impulse to let go her hold upon her frightful charge, to scream, to run away. Rigid, trembling, breathing quick, her heart hammering her ribs, she sat, her fingers gripping the slates, listening for another movement.

It came. Faintly at first, she felt and heard it, then more distinctly. Slowly, very slowly, with intervals of silence, the bit of pencil crawled, tapped and scratched about. While listening to it, and still more while listening for it, she was under so terrific a tension that she felt if nothing happened to relieve her, she must faint or shriek. When she continued listening for a long, an interminable, an unbearable time and heard nothing but the clock in the hall and Vargas' breathing in the room, she felt she was about to do both.

Then the clairvoyant uttered a choked sound, the incipience of that feeble wailing groan or groaning wail of a sleeper in a nightmare. His feet moved, his undeformed leg stiffened, his hands clenched, his head rolled from side to side, he writhed, the effort expended at each successive groan was more and more excessive, each sound feebler and more pitiful.

Then Mrs. Llewellyn did scream.

Instantly Vargas struggled into a sitting posture, his face contorted, his eyes bulging, staring at her.

"Did I speak, did I speak?" he gasped.

Mrs. Llewellyn was past articulation, but she shook her head. "I passed into a real trance, a real trance," he babbled.

She could only cling to the slate and gaze.

"I had a frightful dream," Vargas panted, "I dreamed there was a message on the plate. It frightened me, but what it was has escaped me."

"There is a message on the slate," she managed to utter, "I heard the pencil writing." Vargas, holding to the back of his chair, assisted himself to his feet. From her fingers, mechanically clenched on it, he gently disengaged the slate and put it on the table. Opening one of the cabinets he took out a decanter and two glasses, half filling one he placed it in her numb grasp.

"Drink that," he dictated, draining the other full glass as he spoke.

Half dazed she obeyed him. Her face flushed angrily and the glass broke as she set it down. "You have given me brandy!" she cried in indignation.

"You needed it," he asserted. "It will steady you, but you will not feel it. Compose yourself and we will look at the slate."

She stood up beside him and he laid the slate open. There was writing on each leaf of it, on one side legible, on the other reversed.

"Oh," she said and sat down heavily. He brought a small chair, set it beside hers and seated himself upon it, the slates open in his hands, before them both. Fine-lined, legible, plainly made by the point of the pencil, was the writing, on one leaf of the slates; on the other reversed writing with coarse strokes, plainly made by the splintered end, which was worn slightly at one place. All the writing was in the same individual script.

"This is not my handwriting," said Vargas. "It is my husband's," she gasped. The words on the slate were: "That which is buried in that coffin is alive. If disinterred it will die." Vargas opened the other cabinet. The inside of its door was a mirror. Before this he held the slates. On the other leaf the broad-stroked script showed the same words.

"What does it mean?" she pleaded, "oh! what does it mean?"

"It doesn't mean anything," said Vargas, roughly.

"How can that be," she moaned. "It must mean something. It does mean something. I feel it does."

"That is just the point," he said, "that is what I feared before, and warned you of. Here are some chance words. They mean nothing, except that you or I or both of us have been intensely strung up with emotion. But if you cannot see that or be made to see that, you are lost. If you feel that they mean something, then they do mean that something to you, that that is your danger. Do not yield to it."

"Do you mean to tell me, to try to convince me that those words, twice written, in the same handwriting, in my husband's hand of all hands, formed upon those slates while I held them myself, came there by accident?"

"Not by accident," he argued. "By some operation of unguessed forces set in motion by your excitement or mine or both; but blind forces, meaningless as the voices in dreams."

"Am I to believe meaningless," she demanded, "the voices in my dreams that sent me to that advertisement and to you and told me expect an answer from the slates, a true answer?"

"*Madame*," he reasoned, "the series of coincidences is startling, but it is nothing but a series of coincidences. Try to rise superior to it."

"And you won't help me," she wailed. "You won't tell me what this message means—"

"I have told you my belief as to how it originated," he said, "I have told you that I do not attach any other significance to it."

"Oh," she groaned, "I must go home."

"Your carriage is at the door," he said.

"My carriage!" she exclaimed. "How did it get there?"

"Not your own carriage," he explained, "but one for you. I telephoned for it."

"You have not left me an instant," she asserted incredulously.

"When I brought you a glass of water I told the maid to telephone for a carriage and tell it to wait. It will be there."

"I thank you," she said, "and now, what do I owe you? What is your fee?" Vargas flushed all over his face and neck, a deep brownish-red.

"Mrs. Llewellyn," he said with great dignity, "I take pay from my dupes for my fripperies of deception. But no money, not all the money on earth could pay me to do what I have done for you today, no sum could induce me to go through it again for anyone else. For you I would do anything. But what I have done was not done for payment, nor will anything I may do be done except for you, for whom I would do any service in my power."

"I ask your pardon," she said. "Where is the carriage? I shall faint if I stay here."

Some weeks later, in the same room, the clairvoyant and the lady again faced each other.

"I had hoped never to see you again," he said.

"Did you imagine that I could escape from the compulsion of all that series of manifestations?" she asked.

"I tried to believe that you might," he answered.

"Have you been able to shake off its hold on you?" she demanded.

"Not entirely," he confessed. "But dazing as the coincidences were, the effect on my emotions will wear off, like the smart of a burn; and, as one forgets the fury of past sufferings, I shall forget the turmoil of my feelings. There was no clear intelligibility, no definite significance in it at all."

"Not in that message!" she exclaimed.

"Certainly not," he asseverated.

"Yes there was," she contradicted.

"*Madame*," he said earnestly, "if you fancy you perceive any genuine coherence in those fortuitous words you have put the meaning there yourself, your imagination is riveting upon your soul fetters of your own forging."

"My imagination and my soul have nothing to do with my insight into the spirit of that message," she said calmly. "My heart cries out for help and my intellect has pondered at leisure upon what you call a fortuitous series of coincidences, a chance string of meaningless words. I see no incoherence, rather convincing coherence, in the sequence of your reading of horoscopes, my dreaming of dreams, leading up to the imperative behest given me from your slate."

"*Madame*," he cried, "this is heart-rending. I told you I dreaded the effect upon you of any sort of mummery. You forced me to it. I should have had strength to refuse you. I yielded. Now my cowardice will ruin you."

"Was not your trance genuine?" she queried. "Entirely genuine, entirely too genuine."

"Did not the writing appear upon the slate independent of your will or of mine?" she demanded.

"It did," he admitted.

"Can you explain how it came there?" she wound up.

"Alas, no," he confessed, shaking his head.

"You can scarcely reproach me for accepting it as a message," she concluded triumphantly.

"I do not reproach you," he said, "I reproach myself as culpable."

"I rather thank you for what you have done for me," she almost smiled at him. "It gives me hope. I have meditated carefully upon the message and I am convinced that I comprehend its meaning."

"That is the worst possible state of mind you could get into," he groaned. "Can I not make you realize the truth? It is not as you think you see it."

"I do not think," she said. "I know. I am convinced, and I mean to act on my convictions."

"This is terrible," he muttered. Then he controlled himself, shifted his position in his chair and asked: "And what are your convictions? What do you mean to do?"

"My conviction," she said, "is that David's love for Marian is in some way bound up with whatever he had buried in that coffin. I mean to have the coffin disinterred."

"*Madame*," he said, "this thing gets worse the more you tell me of it. You are in danger of coming under the domination of a fixed idea, even if you are not already under its sway. Fight against it. Shake it off."

"There is no use in your talking that way to me," she said. "I mean to do it. I shall do it."

"Has your husband consented?" Vargas asked.

"He has," she replied.

"Do you mean to tell me that he has agreed to your opening his wife's grave?"

"He has agreed," she asserted.

"But did he make no demur?" the clairvoyant inquired.

"He said he did not care what I did, I could do anything I pleased."

"Was that all he said?" Vargas persisted.

"Not all," she admitted. "He asked me if I had not told him that what I wanted in this life was to spend as much as possible of my time on earth with him, for us two to be together as much as circumstances would allow, and as long as death would permit. I told him of course I had said it, not once but over and over. He asked me if I still felt that way. I told him I did. He said it made no difference to him he was past any feelings, but if that was what I really wanted he advised me to let that grave alone."

"Take his advice, by all means," Vargas exclaimed. "It is good advice. You let that grave alone."

"I am determined," she told him.

"*Madame*," he said, "will you listen to me?"

"Certainly," she replied. "If you have anything to say to the purpose. But not to fault-findings or to scoldings."

"Mrs. Llewellyn," Vargas began, "what happened during your former visit to me has demolished the entire structure of my spiritual existence. I had the sincerest disbelief in astrology, in prophecy, in ghosts, in apparitions, in superstitions, each and all, in supernaturalism in general, in religions, individually and collectively, in the idea of future life. Upon the most materialistic convictions my intellectual life was placid and unruffled, and my soul-life, if I had any, undisturbed by anything save occasional and very evanescent twinges of conscience over the contemptible duplicity of my way of livelihood. Intermittently only I despised myself.

"Mostly I only despised my dupes and generally not even that. Rather I merely smiled tolerantly at the childishness of their profitable credulity. Never did I have the remotest approach to any shadow of belief that there could be anything occult beneath or behind any such jugglery as I continually made use of. The matter of your horoscope and mine I took as mere coincidence. It might affect my feelings, never my reason; my heart, never my head. My head is involved now, my reason at fault. In the writing on that slate I am face to face with something, if not supernatural, at least preternatural.

"The thing is beyond our ordinary experience of the ordinary operation of those forces which make the world go. It depends upon something not yet understood, not necessarily inexplicable, but unexplained. It is uncanny. I don't like it. Yet I do not yield to its influence. I am not swept away. If I dwell upon it, I know it will unsettle my reason. I do not mean to dwell upon it, I mean to get away from it, to ignore it, to forget it, and I counsel you to do likewise."

"Your counsel," she said, "has a long-winded preamble, but is entirely unacceptable."

"I have more to say," he went on. "Mere bewilderment of mind is not an adequate ground for action. There is a fine old proverb that says, '*When in doubt, do nothing.*' Take its advice and your husband's; do nothing."

"But I am not in doubt," she protested. "I am convinced that I was meant to come to you, that the message was meant for me, and that I know what it means. I am determined to act upon it."

He shook his head with a gesture of despair, but continued:

"I have more yet to say and on another point. I advise you to go away from all this. You should and you can. You have your own wealth and your husband's opulence at your disposal. You have one of the finest steam-yachts on the seas awaiting your pleasure. Much as you have travelled, the globe has many fascinating regions still new to you. Your husband and you have practically not travelled at all since your marriage. You should still hope for your husband's recovery of his spirits by natural means. Travel is the most obvious prescription.

"Try that. Because your husband had not emerged from his brooding upon his loss and grief during two years of wandering alone with a valet; because he has not recovered his spirits after two years of matrimony spent in the neighbourhood of his first wife's grave, in mansions full of memories of her, is no reason for not hoping that his elasticity will revive during months or years spent with you among delightful scenes of novelty, far from anything to recall his mind to old associations."

"I have no hope in any such attempt," she said wearily. "When I cannot bear my life here with a mate who is no more than a likeness of the man I loved, why drag this soulless semblance about the oceans of the earth in the hope of seeing it awake to love me? Shall I expect a miracle from salt air or the rays of the Southern cross?"

"Mrs. Llewellyn," Vargas said, "I have taken the liberty of making inquiries, quite unobtrusively, concerning your husband's treatment of you. I find that it is the general impression that he is a very uxorious, a very lovely husband. Except the barest minimum required for his affairs, he spends his entire time with you. His best friends, his boyhood's chums, his life-long cronies he never converses with, never chats with, hardly talks to, and for all his genial cordiality and courtesy, barely more than greets in passing. He is seldom seen at his clubs and very briefly. To all appearances he devotes himself to you wholly. You have all the external trappings of happiness: health, beauty, a devoted husband, the most desirable intimates, countless friends, luxurious surroundings, and unlimited affluence. It is for you to put life into all this, it is your duty to recall to it what you miss. You should leave no natural means untried turning to what you propose."

"My determination is irrevocably taken," she said.

"But what do you expect to find in the coffin?" he queried.

"I have no expectations, not even any anticipations," she said. "We may find keepsakes of some kind; there cannot be love-letters, for they scarcely separated a day after they met, or an hour after they married. There may be nothing in the coffin. But I am convinced that whatever it does or does not contain, David's love for Marian is bound up with the closure of that coffin. I believe that if it is opened he will be released from his passion of grief and be free to love me.

"You mean practically to resort to an incantation, a sort of witchcraft. The notion is altogether unworthy of you, especially while so natural a device as travel remains untried."

"You do not understand," she said, "that I feel compelled to do something."

"Is not going for a cruise doing something?" he asked.

"Practically doing nothing," she replied. "Just being with David and watching for the change that never comes. You don't know how that makes me feel forced to take some action."

"I do not know," he said, "because you have not told me."

"I cannot tell you," she said, "because I cannot find any words to express what I feel. I could not convey it to you, the loneliness that overwhelms me when I am alone with David. It is worse than being alone; I cannot imagine feeling so lonely lost in a wilderness, solitary in the desert, adrift on a raft in mid-ocean. Being with David, as he is, makes me feel—"(her voice sank to a whisper and her face grew pale, her lips gray)"oh, it makes me feel as if I were worse than with nobody. It makes me feel as if I were with nothing, with nothing at all."

"I sympathize with you deeply," said Vargas. "But all you say only deepens my conviction that your one road to safety lies in striving to overcome these feelings; your best hope is change of scene and travel. Above all let that grave alone."

"My determination is irrevocably taken," she repeated.

"Mrs. Llewellyn," Vargas asked, "how, in your belief, did the writing you saw upon the slate come there?"

"I have no conception at all as to how it came there," she replied. "None at all?" he probed.

"None definitely," she said. "Vaguely I suppose I conceive it came there by the power of some consciousness and will beyond our ken."

"Do you mean," he queried, "by the intervention of a ghost, or spirit or some such disembodied entity?"

"Perhaps," she admitted, "but I have not thought it out at all."

"Granted a spirit," he suggested, "might it not be a malignant sprite, an imp bent on doing you harm, upon entrapping you to your destruction?"

"I don't credit such an idea for a moment," she said. "The message has given me hope. Your innuendoes seek to rob me of my hope."

"I seek to save you," Vargas said, "to dislodge you from your fortalice of resolve."

"For the third time," she said, "I tell you that my determination is irrevocably taken." Vargas awkwardly stood up. He clung to the back of a chair and gazed at her steadily. His face, from a far-off solemn look of resigned desperation gradually took on an expression of prophetic resolve.

"Pardon me," he said, "if I must shock you. I wish to put to you a question."

"Put it," she said coldly.

"Mrs. Llewellyn," the clairvoyant asked in a deep, slow voice. "Have you kept your marriage vows?"

"Sir," she said angrily, rising. "You are insulting me."

"Not a particle," he persisted. "You have not answered my question."

"To answer it is superfluous," she said, facing him in trembling wrath. "Of course I have kept them. You know how utterly I love my husband."

"You regard your vows as sacred?" he asked relentlessly. "Of course," she said wearily.

"Why then," he demanded, "do you attach less sanctity to your verbal compact with your husband? Your duty as a wife is to keep one compact as well as the other. Keep both. Do not be recalcitrant against the terms of your agreement. Endure his indifference and strive patiently to win his love. It is your duty, as much as it is your duty to keep your marriage vows."

"You assume a role," she said, "very unsuitable for you. Preaching misfits you, and it has no effect on me. I know and feel all this. But there is the plain meaning of that message. I shall open that grave."

"I have done all I can," he said dispiritedly. "I cannot dissuade you."

"You cannot," she said.

"How then can I serve you?" he asked. "I have not yet discovered to what I owe the honour of this second visit. Why are you here?"

"I wish you to be present at the opening of the coffin," she said.

"Are you sure," he demanded, "that that would not be most unseemly? The first Mrs. Llewellyn, I believe, left no near relatives. But would not even her cousins resent such an intrusion as my presence there? Would not your husband still more resent it? Would it not be in very bad taste?"

"I do not make requests," she said, "that are in bad taste. As for my husband, he resents and will resent nothing, as he approves and will approve of nothing. My brother will be there and he will not find anything unseemly in your presence."

"Nevertheless I hesitate to agree," said Vargas.

"You have expressed," said she, "a very deep regard for me, will you not do this since I ask it?"

"I will," he said with an effort.

"Then whenever I write you and send a carriage for you, you will be there at the time named?"

"I promise," he said.

Sometime before the appointed hour, at that spot where a driveway approached nearest to the Llewellyn monument, Vargas painfully emerged from a closed carriage, the blue shades of which were drawn down. He spoke to someone inside and shut the door. He had taken but two or three hobbling steps, when another carriage closely followed his stopped where his had stopped. Its shades were also drawn down. When its door opened a well dressed man got out. As Vargas had done he spoke to someone inside and closed the door.

When he turned Vargas saw a man of usual, very conventional appearance, the sort of man visible by scores in fashionable clubs. His build and carriage were those of a man naturally jaunty in his movements. His well-fleshed, healthy face, smooth shaven except for a thick brown moustache, was such a face as lends itself naturally to expressions of good fellowship and joviality. His brown eyes were prone to merriment. But there was no sparkle in them, no geniality in his air, no springiness in his movements. He wore his brown derby a trifle, the merest trifle, to one side, but his expression was careworn, he looked haggard. He had the air of a man used to having his own way, but he held himself now without any elasticity. He looked the deformed clairvoyant up and down with one quick glance, fixed him with a direct gaze as he approached and greeted him with an engaging air of easy politeness, neither stiff nor familiar.

"My name is Palgrave," he said, "I presume you are Mr. Vargas."

"The same," said the clairvoyant, with not a little constraint.

"Pleased to meet you," said the other holding out his hand and diminishing Vargas' embarrassment by the heartiness of his handshake. "Glad to have a chance for a talk with you. My sister has told me of her visits to you."

Vargas controlled his expression, but shot one lightning glance at the other's face, reading there instantly how much Mrs. Llewellyn had told her brother and how much she had not told him.

There was something very taking about Mr. Palgrave's manner, which put Vargas completely at his ease. It was more than conciliatory, it was almost friendly, almost sympathetic. It not so much expressed readiness to admit to a confidential understanding, as gave the impression of continuing a well-established natural attitude of entire trust and complete comprehension. It had an unmistakable tinge, as unexpected as gratifying, of level esteem and unspoken gratitude.

There was a rustic seat by the path and by a common impulse both moved toward it. At the club-man's courteous gesture, the cripple, with his unavoidable wrenching jolt, lowered himself painfully to the level of the bench. Mr. Palgrave seated himself beside him, crossed his knees and half turned toward him. He rested his left elbow on the back of the bench. His other hand held his cane, which he tapped against the side of his foot. The waiting carriages, one behind the other, were under a big elm some distance off; their drivers lay on the grass beside them. No one else was in sight except where, rather farther off in another direction, six labourers, their coats off, sat with a superintendent near them, in the shade of a Norway maple, near the Llewellyn monument; which dominated the neighbourhood from its low, broad knoll.

The brief silence Mr. Palgrave broke.

"If you will pardon my saying it, you don't look at all like my idea of a clairvoyant." Vargas smiled a wan smile. The tone of the words was totally disarming.

"I don't feel like my idea of a clairvoyant," he said, "I am usually clear-sighted in any matter I take up; usually so clear-sighted in respect to any personality that my advice, as it often is, seems to my clients a mere echo of their own thoughts, a mere confirmation of their own judgments, a mere additional reason for what they would have done anyhow. I am used to touching unerringly the strongest springs of action. So far I have utterly failed to gain that clue to Mrs. Llewellyn's character necessary to make my advice acceptable."

"In every other respect you seem to have been as clear-sighted as possible," Mr. Palgrave told him. "No advice could have been better nor more judiciously urged, nor more entirely disinterested."

"Rather utterly interested," said Vargas.

"In an altogether different sense," said the other. "She told me. Until I saw you I was astonished that she had not resented it."

"She did resent it, and of course," said the cripple.

"Not as she would from any other man," said Mr. Palgrave. "There are some things—" Vargas began. His voice thinned out and he broke off.

"Yes, I understand," said her brother, "and I want to say that I feel under much obligation to you for the way you behaved and for the manliness and the straightforwardness of your whole attitude."

"I am greatly complimented," Vargas replied.

"You deserve complimenting," said Mr. Palgrave. "You acted admirably. Your consideration, I might say your gentleness shows that you really have her best interests at heart."

"I truly have," said Vargas fervently, "and I am more disturbed in mind than I can express."

"That must be a great deal," said the clubman, a momentary gleam of his usual self, fading instantly from his eyes. "I certainly cannot express how much I am upset. I hate worry or anxiety and always put such troubles away and forget them. I can't forget this. I have idolized my sister since we were babies. I have hardly slept since she talked to me. She won't hear of a doctor. She don't admit that there could be any pretext for her consulting a doctor, and I can't talk to anyone about her. I can talk to you. You seem a very sensible man. I should like to hear your opinion of her condition. Do you think her mind is unsettled?"

"Not as bad as that," Vargas told him.

"This grave-opening idea seems to me out and out lunacy," said the other.

"Not as bad as that," Vargas repeated. "It shows a trend of thought which may develop into something worse; but in itself it is only a foolish whim. The worst of it is that it produces a situation of great delicacy, and high tension which may have almost any sort of bad result."

"I can't imagine," said Palgrave, "any rational or half rational basis for her whim. I can't conceive what she thinks she will accomplish by opening that coffin or why she wants it opened. I was at Marian's funeral and the two coffins made a precious lot of talk, I can tell you. I assumed that Llewellyn had some wild, sentimental notion of the second coffin waiting there for him. Constance declares it was not empty, but she won't say what she expects to find in it and I believe she don't say because she has no idea at all."

"You are right," said the clairvoyant, "she hasn't."

"Well," said the other, "what do *you* think she will find in it?"

"I have no opinions whatever," said Vargas, "as to whether it is empty or not or as to what may be in it. I have no basis of conjecture. But whether empty or not or whatever may be in it, I dread the effect on her. She is sure to be baffled in her hopes. Her present state of mind is a sort of reawakening in a civilized, educated, cultured woman of the primitive, childish, savage faith in sorcery, almost in rudimentary fetishism. She would not acknowledge it, but her attitude is very like that of a fetish-worshipper. Her mind does not reason. She is possessed of a blind, vague feeling that her welfare is implicated with whatever is in that coffin, and a compelling hope in the efficiency of the mere act of opening it, as a sort of magic rite. She is buoyed up with uncertainty. Whether she finds something or nothing she will be brought face to face with final unmistakable disappointment. I dread the moment of that realization."

"I felt something like that," said her brother. "Anyhow I brought a doctor with me, but she must not suspect that as long as we don't need him."

"That is why your carriage has the shades down,"Vargas hazarded.

"Is that the reason yours has its shades down?" the other inquired.

"That is it,"Vargas confessed. "I brought a doctor too."

"Two doctors," commented Palgrave. "Like a French duel. Hope it will end as harmlessly as the average French duel."

"That is almost too much to hope for," said Vargas. "She may pass the critical instant safely. But even if she does she will be thrown back into brooding over her troubles."

"Her troubles seem to me largely imaginary," said the clubman.

"All the more danger in that," said Vargas. "If merely subjective."

"In this case they ought to evaporate," said her brother, "if she acted sensibly, and yet they are not wholly imaginary. I don't wonder that she is troubled. David Llewellyn is not himself at all. His dead-and-alive demeanour is enough to prey on anybody's mind. Moping about here with him makes it worse. But going for a cruise might cure both of them and would be likely to wake him up and certain to clear her head. She ought to take your advice."

"She will not," said Vargas dejectedly, "and I scarcely wonder at her determination. Her dreams were enough to affect anybody. And the message on that slate was enough to influence anyone. Believing it addressed directly to her she is irresistibly urged to act upon it. I myself, merely a spectator, have been thrown by it into a terrible confusion of my whole mentality. I have believed in no real mystery in the universe. I am confronted by an unblinkable, an insoluble puzzle. My reliance upon the laws of space and time, as we think we know them, is, for the time being, wrenched from its foundations. My faith in the indestructibility of matter, in the continuity of force, in the fundamental laws of motion, is shaken and tottering.

"My belief in the necessary sequence of cause and effect, in causation and causality in general, is totally shattered. I could credit any marvel, could accept any monstrous portent as altogether to be expected. The universe no longer seems to me a scene, at least in front of the great, blank curtain of the unknowable, filled by an orderly progress of more or less cognizable and predictable occurrences, depending upon interrelated causes; it seems the playground of the irresponsible, prankish, malevolent somethings, productive of incalculabilities. I am in a delirium of dread, in a daze of panic."

"I hardly follow your meaning," said the other, "but I feel we can do nothing."

"No," said Vargas, "we can only hope for the best and fear the worst."

"And what will be the worst?" her brother demanded.

"I conceive," said Vargas, "that upon the opening of the coffin she will suffer some sort of shock, whether it be from disappointment, surprise, or whatever else. At the worst she might scream and drop dead before our eyes or shriek and hopelessly lose her reason.

"Yes," said Mr. Palgrave, "that would be the worst, I suppose."

"And yet," said Vargas, "I cannot escape from the feeling that the worst, in some incalculable, unpredictable, inconceivable way, will be something a great deal worse than that; something unimaginably, unutterably, ineffably worse than anything I can definitely put into words or even vaguely think."

"I cannot express myself as fluently as you can," her brother responded, "but I have had much the same sort of feeling. I have it now. I feel as if I were not now in a cemetery for the purpose of being present at the opening of a grave; but far away, or long ago, about to participate in some uncanny occurrence fit to make Saul's experience at Endor or Macbeth's with the witches seem humdrum and commonplace."

"I feel all that," said Vargas, "and more; as if we were not ourselves at all, but the actors in some vast drama of wretchedness, apocalyptically ignorant of an enormous shadow of unescapable doom steadily darkening over our impotence. We cannot modify, we cannot alter, we cannot change, we cannot ward off, we cannot even postpone what is about to happen."

"What is about to happen," said his companion, "is going to happen now. Here they come. The two men rose and watched the Llewellyn carriage draw up where theirs had stopped. Its door opened and a large man stepped down.

Vargas had previously seen David Llewellyn only momentarily at a distance, and now scrutinized him with much attention. He was a tall man, taller than his brother-in-law and was solidly and very compactly made. His manner, as he turned to the carriage, was solicitous, and deferential as he helped his wife out. As they approached, walking side by side, Vargas eyed the man. He was powerfully built and showed an immense girth of chest. His close-cut beard did not disguise the type of his countenance, the face belonged to an athletic college-bred man, firm chin, set lips, straight nose and clear gray eyes. He was very handsome and reminders of what had been downright beauty in his boyhood were manifest not only in the face but in the general effect of his presence.

Without any word, barely nodding to the two men, he halted some steps away, leaving his wife to advance alone. She greeted Vargas and, slipping her hand through the bend of her brother's arm, passed on along the path with him. Vargas remained where he was, waiting for Mr. Llewellyn to go first. He seemed, by a subtle and intangible something in his look and attitude, to signify that he disclaimed any participation in what was to take place. By an almost imperceptible nod of negation and a barely discernible gesture of affirmation he indicated that the clairvoyant was to precede him. Vargas complied and hobbled after the brother and sister. The superintendent came forward to meet them, and walked beside Mrs. Llewellyn, listening to her instructions, and then going toward his assistants.

The space around their monument which was occupied by the Llewellyn graves was encircled by a low hedge, not more than knee-high. It had an opening facing the monument and through this Mrs. Llewellyn and her brother passed, Vargas some steps behind them. They stopped a pace or two from the foot of the grave, and turned about. Vargas, keeping his distance, stopped likewise and likewise turned. Mr. Llewellyn, treading noiselessly, had stepped aside from the path and took his stand just inside the hedge. The workmen straggled past him, the superintendent convoying them. When they had begun to dig, Vargas, like the rest, watched them.

Presently he began to look about him and survey the cemetery, of which the knoll afforded an extensive view. The weather gave the prospect an unusual quality, the late spring or early summer warmth was unrelieved by any positive breeze, the light air stirred aimlessly, the cloudiness which completely overcast the sky was too thin to cut off the heat of the sun-rays, the foliage was dusty and the landscape a sickly yellowish green in the weak tepid sunshine. This eery quality of the scene Vargas felt rather than saw. While the time taken up with digging postponed the all-important moment, his attention was divided between the monument and Mr. Llewellyn. He stood with his weight nearly all on one foot, leaning on the cane his left hand held, the other gloved hand, holding his hat, hanging at his side.

Gazing straight in front of him toward the monument, rather than at it, there was about him the look of something inanimate, of something made, not grown, of an object immovably planted in carven, expressionless impassivity. The monument, which Vargas saw for the first time, gave from the perfectly coordinated harmonies of its architectural design, its delicate reliefs, and its exquisite statuary, an impression of individuality striking enough to any one at any time and all the more now by contrast. Any one of its figures seemed instinct with more life than the man facing it. That member of the little gathering who should have been most moved, showed no emotion and Vargas himself felt much.

As the digging proceeded, he mostly gazed into the deepening pit, or watched Mrs. Llewellyn's back as she stood clinging to her brother's arm, leaning against him. When the workmen began to raise the coffin, he found the emotions of his strained forebodings overmastering him. His breath quickened and came hard, his heart thumped at his ribs, his eyes were unexpectedly, inexplicably moist. Glancing back at the immobile man behind him, through the iridescent film upon his lashes, he saw but a blurred, vague shape. He strove to regain his composure, conning the outline of his own barely discernible shadow.

The outer box containing the raised coffin was now supported upon two pieces of wood thrust under it across the grave. The men unscrewed the lid and laid it aside. The coffin was of ebony and as fresh as if just made.

The men, at the superintendent's bidding, shambled away round the monument and through the opening in the hedge behind it to the tree they had left.

The superintendent began to take out the silver screws which held down the lid over the glass front of the coffin-head. As they were removed one by one, Vargas again glanced behind him. He saw worse than ever. The outline of the big figure was almost indefinite, its bulk almost hazy.

As he turned his gaze again to the coffin his sight seemed to clear entirely. He saw even the silver rims round the screw-holes and the head of the last screw. As the superintendent lifted the lid, Mrs. Llewellyn, now at the foot of the coffin, leaned forward, and her brother and Vargas, now just behind her, leaned even more. Through the glass they saw a face, David Llewellyn's face. Mrs. Llewellyn screamed. All three turned round. Save themselves and the superintendent and the distant workmen there was no human shape in sight anywhere. The big, solid presence had vanished.

Again screaming Mrs. Llewellyn threw herself on the coffin, the two men, scarcely less frantic than she, close by her. Through the glass they could see the face working, the eyelids fluttering. The superintendent toiled furiously at the catches of the glass front. When he lifted it away the eyes opened, gazing straight into Mrs. Llewellyn's. Almost at once they glazed, and a moment later the jaw dropped.

Amina

(A Tale from *Lukundoo and Other Stories*)

Waldo, brought face to face with the actuality of the unbelievable—as he himself would have worded it—was completely dazed. In silence he suffered the consul to lead him from the tepid gloom of the interior, through the ruinous doorway, out into the hot, stunning brilliance of the desert landscape. Hassan followed, with never a look behind him. Without any word he had taken Waldo's gun from his nerveless hand and carried it, with his own and the consul's.

The consul strode across the gravelly sand, some fifty paces from the southwest corner of the tomb, to a bit of not wholly ruined wall from which there was a clear view of the doorway side of the tomb and of the side with the larger crevice.

"Hassan," he commanded, "watch here."

Hassan said something in Persian.

"How many cubs were there?" the consul asked Waldo. Waldo stared mute. "How many young ones did you see?" the consul asked again.

"Twenty or more," Waldo made answer.

"That's impossible," snapped the consul.

"There seemed to be sixteen or eighteen," Waldo asserted. Hassan smiled and grunted. The consul took from him two guns, handed Waldo his, and they walked around the tomb to a point about equally distant from the opposite corner. There was another bit of ruin, and in front of it, on the side toward the tomb, was a block of stone mostly in the shadow of the wall.

"Convenient," said the consul. "Sit on that stone and lean against the wall, make yourself comfortable. You are a bit shaken, but you will be all right in a moment. You should have something to eat, but we have nothing. Anyhow, take a good swallow of this."

107

He stood by him as Waldo gasped over the raw brandy. "Hassan will bring you his water-bottle before he goes," the consul went on; "drink plenty, for you must stay here for some time. And now, pay attention to me. We must extirpate these vermin. The male, I judge, is absent. If he had been anywhere about, you would not now be alive. The young cannot be as many as you say, but, I take it, we have to deal with ten, a full litter. We must smoke them out. Hassan will go back to camp after fuel and the guard. Meanwhile, you and I must see that none escape."

He took Waldo's gun, opened the breech, shut it, examined the magazine and handed it back to him.

"Now watch me closely," he said. He paced off, looking to his left past the tomb. Presently he stopped and gathered several stones together.

"You see these?" he called.

Waldo shouted an affirmation.

The consul came back, passed on in the same line, looking to his right past the tomb, and presently, at a similar distance, put up another tiny cairn, shouted again and was again answered. Again he returned.

"Now you are sure you cannot mistake those two marks I have made?"

"Very sure indeed," said Waldo.

"It is important, warned the consul. "I am going back to where I left Hassan, to watch there while he is gone. You will watch here. You may pace as often as you like to either of those stone heaps. From either you can see me on my beat. Do not diverge from the line from one to the other. For as soon as Hassan is out of sight I shall shoot any moving thing I see nearer. Sit here till you see me set up similar limits for my sentry—go on the farther side, then shoot any moving thing not on my line of patrol. Keep a lookout all around you. There is one chance in a million that the male might return in daylight—mostly, they are nocturnal, but this lair is evidently exceptional. Keep a bright lookout.

"And now listen to me. You must not feel any foolish sentimentalism about any fancied resemblance of these vermin to human beings. Shoot, and shoot to kill. Not only is it our duty, in general, to abolish them, but it will be very dangerous for us if we do not. There is little or no solidarity in Mohammedan communities, but on the comparatively few points upon which public opinion exists it acts with amazing promptitude and vigour. One matter as to which there is no disagreement is that it is incumbent upon every man to assist in eradicating these creatures. The good old Biblical custom of stoning to death is the mode of lynching indigenous hereabouts. These modern Asiatics are quite capable of applying it to anyone believed derelict against any of these inimical monsters. If we let one escape and the rumour of it gets about, we may precipitate an outburst of racial prejudice difficult to cope with. Shoot, I say, without hesitation or mercy."

"I understand," said Waldo.

"I don't care whether you understand or not," said the consul, "I want you to act. Shoot if needful, and shoot straight." And he tramped off.

Hassan presently appeared, and Waldo drank from his water-bottle as nearly all of its contents as Hassan would permit. After his departure Waldo's first alertness soon gave place to mere endurance of the monotony of watching and the intensity of the heat. His discomfort became suffering, and what with the fury of the dry glare, the pangs of thirst and his bewilderment of mind, Waldo was moving in a waking dream by the time Hassan returned with two donkeys and a mule laden with brushwood. Behind the beasts straggled the guard.

Waldo's trance became a nightmare when the smoke took effect and the battle began. He was, however, not only not required to join in the killing, but was enjoined to keep back. He did keep very much in the background, seeing only so much of the slaughter as his curiosity would not let him refrain from viewing. Yet he felt all a murderer as he gazed at the ten small carcasses laid out arow, and the memory of his vigil and its end, indeed of the whole day, though it was the day of his most marvellous adventure, remains to him as the broken recollections of a phantasmagoria.

On the morning of his memorable peril Waldo had waked early. The experiences of his sea-voyage, the sights at Gibraltar, at Port Said, in the canal, at Suez, at Aden, at Muscat, and at Basrah had formed an altogether inadequate transition from the decorous regularity of house and school life in New England to the breathless wonder of the desert immensities. Everything seemed unreal, and yet the reality of its strangeness so besieged him that he could not feel at home in it, he could not sleep heavily in a tent. After composing himself to sleep, he lay long conscious and awakened early, as on this morning, just at the beginning of the false dawn.

The consul was fast asleep, snoring loudly. Waldo dressed quietly and went out; mechanically, without any purpose or forethought, taking his gun. Outside he found Hassan, seated, his gun across his knees, his head sunk forward, as fast asleep as the consul. Ali and Ibrahim had left the camp the day before for supplies. Waldo was the only waking creature about; for the guards, camped some little distance off, were but logs about the ashes of their fire. Meaning merely to enjoy, under the white glow of the false dawn, the magical reappearance of the constellations and the short last glory of the star-laden firmament, that brief coolness which compensated a trifle for the hot morning, the fiery day and the warmish night, he seated himself on a rock, some paces from the tent and twice as far from the guards. Turning his gun in his hands he felt an irresistible temptation to wander off by himself, to stroll alone through the fascinating emptiness of the arid landscape.

When he had begun camp life he had expected to find the consul, that combination of sportsman, explorer and archaeologist, a particularly easygoing guardian. He had looked forward to absolutely untrammelled liberty in the spacious expanse of the limitless wastes. The reality he had found exactly the reverse of his preconceptions. The consul's first injunction was:

"Never let yourself get out of sight of me or of Hassan unless he or I send you off with Au or Ibrahim. Let nothing tempt you to roam about alone. Even a ramble is dangerous. You might lose sight of the camp before you knew it."

At first Waldo acquiesced, later he protested. "I have a good pocket compass. I know how to use it. I never lost my way in the Maine woods."

"No Kourds in the Maine woods," said the consul.

Yet before long Waldo noticed that the few Kourds they encountered seemed simple-hearted, peaceful folk. No semblance of danger or even of adventure had appeared. Their armed guard of a dozen greasy tatterdemalions had passed their time in uneasy loafing. Likewise Waldo noticed that the consul seemed indifferent to the ruins they passed by or encamped among, that his feeling for sites and topography was cooler than lukewarm, that he showed no ardour in the pursuit of the scanty and uninteresting game. He had picked up enough of several dialects to hear repeated conversations about "them."

"Have you heard of any about here?"

"Has one been killed?"

"Any traces of them in this district?" And such queries he could make out in the various talks with the natives they met, as to what "they" were he received no enlightenment.

110

Then he had questioned Hassan as to why he was so restricted in his movements. Hassan spoke some English and regaled him with tales of Afrits, ghouls, spectres and other uncanny legendary presences; of the *jinn* of the waste, appearing in human shape, talking all languages, ever on the alert to ensnare *infidels*; of the woman whose feet turned the wrong way at the ankles, luring the unwary to a pool and there drowning her victims; of the malignant ghosts of dead brigands, more terrible than their living fellows; of the spirit in the shape of a wild ass, or of a gazelle, enticing its pursuers to the brink of a precipice and itself seeming to run ahead upon an expanse of sand, a mere mirage, dissolving as the victim passed the brink and fell to death; of the sprite in the semblance of a hare feigning a limp, or of a ground bird feigning a broken wing, drawing its pursuer after it till he met death in an unseen pit or well shaft.

Ali and Ibrahim spoke no English. As far as Waldo could understand their long harangues, they told similar stories or hinted at dangers equally vague and imaginary. These childish bogy- tales merely whetted Waldo's craving for independence.

Now, as he sat on a rock, longing to enjoy the perfect sky, the clear, early air, the wide, lonely landscape, along with the sense of having it to himself, it seemed to him that the consul was merely innately cautious, overcautious. There was no danger. He would have a fine leisurely stroll, kill something perhaps, and certainly be back in camp before the sun grew hot. He stood up.

Some hours later he was seated on a fallen coping stone in the shadow of a ruined tomb. All the country they had been traversing is full of tombs and remains of tombs, prehistoric, Bactrian, old Persian, Parthian, Sassanian, or Mohammedan, scattered everywhere in groups or solitary.

Vanished utterly are the faintest traces of the cities, towns, and villages, ephemeral houses or temporary huts, in which had lived the countless generations of mourners who had reared these tombs.

The tombs, built more durably than mere dwellings of the living, remained. Complete or ruinous, or reduced to mere fragments, they were everywhere. In that district they were all of one type. Each was domed and below was square, its one door facing eastward and opening into a large empty room, behind which were the mortuary chambers.

In the shadow of such a tomb Waldo sat. He had shot nothing, had lost his way, had no idea of the direction of the camp, was tired, warm, and thirsty. He had forgotten his water-bottle.

He swept his gaze over the vast, desolate prospect, the unvaried turquoise of the sky arched above the rolling desert. Far reddish hills along the skyline hooped in the less distant brown hillocks which, without diversifying it, hummocked the yellow landscape. Sand and rocks with a lean, starved bush or two made up the nearer view, broken here and there by dazzling white or streaked, grayish, crumbling ruins. The sun had not been long above the horizon, yet the whole surface of the desert was quivering with heat.

As Waldo sat viewing the outlook a woman came round the corner of the tomb. All the village women Waldo had seen had worn *yashmaks* or some other form of face covering or veil. This woman was bareheaded and unveiled. She wore some sort of yellowish-brown garment which enveloped her from neck to ankles, showing no waist line. Her feet, in defiance of the blistering sands, were bare.

At sight of Waldo she stopped and stared at him as he at her. He remarked the un-European posture of her feet, not at all turned out, but with the inner lines parallel. She wore no anklets, he observed, no bracelets, no necklace or earrings. Her bare arms he thought the most muscular he had ever seen on a human being. Her nails were pointed and long, both on her hands and feet. Her hair was black, short, and tousled, yet she did not look wild or uncomely. Her eyes smiled and her lips had the effect of smiling, though they did not part ever so little, not showing at all the teeth behind them.

"What a pity," said Waldo aloud, "that she does not speak English."

"I do speak English," said the woman, and Waldo noticed that as she spoke, her lips did not perceptibly open. "What does the gentleman want?"

"You speak English!" Waldo exclaimed, jumping to his feet. "What luck! Where did you learn it?"

"At the mission school," she replied, an amused smile playing about the corners of her rather wide, unopening mouth. "What can be done for you?" She spoke with scarcely any foreign accent, but very slowly and with a sort of growl running along from syllable to syllable.

"I am thirsty," said Waldo, "and I have lost my way."

"Is the gentleman living in a brown tent, shaped like half a melon?" she inquired, the queer, rumbling note drawling from one word to the next, her lips barely separated.

"Yes, that is our camp," said Waldo.

"I could guide the gentleman that way," she droned; "but it is far, and there is no water on that side."

"I want water first," said Waldo, "or milk."

"If you mean cow's milk, we have none. But we have goat's milk. There is to drink where I dwell," she said, sing-songing the words. "It is not far. It is the other way."

"Show me," said he.

She began to walk, Waldo, his gun under his arm, beside her. She trod noiselessly and fast. Waldo could scarcely keep up with her. As they walked he often fell behind and noted how her swathing garments clung to a lithe, shapely back, neat waist, and firm hips. Each time he hurried and caught up with her, he scanned her with intermittent glances, puzzled that her waist, so well-marked at the spine, showed no particular definition in front; that the outline of her from neck to knees, perfectly shapeless under her wrappings, was without any waistline or suggestion of firmness or undulation. Likewise he remarked the amused flicker in her eyes and the compressed line of her red, her too-red lips.

"How long were you in the mission school?" he inquired. "Four years," she replied.

"Are you a Christian?" he asked.

"The Free-folk do not submit to baptism," she stated simply, but with rather more of the droning growl between her words.

He felt a queer shiver as he watched the scarcely moved lips through which the syllables edged their way.

"But you are not veiled," he could not resist saying.

"The Free-folk," she rejoined, "are never veiled."

"Then you are not a Mohammedan?" he ventured.

"The Free-folk are not Moslems."

"Who are the Free-folk?" he blurted out incautiously. She shot one baleful glance at him. Waldo remembered that he had to do with an Asiatic. He recalled the three permitted questions.

"What is your name?" he inquired.

"Amina," she told him.

"That is a name from the 'Arabian Nights'," he hazarded.

"From the foolish tales of the believers," she sneered. "The Free-folk know nothing of such follies." The unvarying shutness of her speaking lips, the drawly burr between the syllables, struck him all the more as her lips curled but did not open.

"You utter your words in a strange way," he said. "Your language is not mine," she replied.

"How is it that you learned my language at the mission school and are not a Christian?"

"They teach all at the mission school," she said, "and the maidens of the Free-folk are like the other maidens they teach, though the Free-folk when grown are not as town-dwellers are. Therefore they taught me as any town-bred girl, not knowing me for what I am."

"They taught you well," he commented.

"I have the gift of tongues," she uttered enigmatically, with an odd note of triumph burring the words through her unmoving lips.

Waldo felt a horrid shudder all over him, not only at her uncanny words, but also from mere faintness.

"Is it far to your home?" he breathed.

"It is there," she said, pointing to the doorway of a large tomb just before them. The wholly open arch admitted them into a fairly spacious interior, cool with the abiding temperature of thick masonry. There was no rubbish on the floor. Waldo, relieved to escape the blistering glare outside, seated himself on a block of stone midway between the door and the inner partition wall, resting his gun butt on the floor. For the moment he was blinded by the change from the insistent brilliance of the desert morning to the blurred gray light of the interior

When his sight cleared he looked about and remarked, opposite the door, the ragged hole which laid open the desecrated mausoleum. As his eyes grew accustomed to the dimness he was so startled that he stood up. It seemed to him that from its four corners the room swarmed with naked children. To his inexperienced conjecture they seemed about two years old, but they moved with the assurance of boys of eight or ten.

"Whose are these children?" he exclaimed. "Mine," she said.

"All yours?" he protested.

"All mine," she replied, a curious suppressed boisterousness in her demeanour.

"But there are twenty of them," he cried.

"You count badly in the dark," she told him. "There are fewer."

"There certainly are a dozen," he maintained, spinning round as they danced and scampered about.

"The Free-people have large families," she said.

"But they are all of one age," Waldo exclaimed, his tongue dry against the roof of his mouth. She laughed, an unpleasant, mocking laugh, clapping her hands. She was between him and the doorway, and as most of the light came from it he could not see her lips.

"Is not that like a man! No woman would have made that mistake." Waldo was confused and sat down again. The children circulated around him, chattering, laughing, giggling, snickering, making noises indicative of glee.

"Please get me something cool to drink," said Waldo, and his tongue was not only dry but big in his mouth.

"We shall have to drink shortly," she said, "but it will be warm." Waldo began to feel uneasy. The children pranced around him, jabbering strange, guttural noises, licking their lips, pointing at him, their eyes fixed on him, with now and then a glance at their mother.

"Where is the water?"

The woman stood silent, her arms hanging at her sides, and it seemed to Waldo she was shorter than she had been.

"Where is the water?" he repeated.

"Patience, patience," she growled, and came a step near to him. The sunlight struck upon her back and made a sort of halo about her hips. She seemed still shorter than before. There was a something furtive in her bearing, and the little ones sniggered evilly.

At that instant two rifle shots rang out almost as one. The woman fell face downward on the floor. The babies shrieked in a shrill chorus. Then she leapt up from all fours with an explosive suddenness, staggered in a hurled, lurching rush toward the hole in the wall, and, with a frightful yell, threw up her arms and whirled backward to the ground, doubled and contorted like a dying fish, stiffened, shuddered and was still. Waldo, his horrified eyes fixed on her face, even in his amazement noted that her lips did not open.

The children, squealing faint cries of dismay, scrambled through the hole in the inner wall, vanishing into the inky void beyond. The last had hardly gone when the consul appeared in the doorway, his smoking gun in his hand.

"Not a second too soon, my boy," he ejaculated. "She was just going to spring." He cocked his gun and prodded the body with the muzzle.

"Good and dead," he commented. "What luck! Generally it takes three or four bullets to finish one. I've known one with two bullets through her lungs to kill a man.

"Did you murder this woman?" Waldo demanded fiercely.

"Murder?" the consul snorted. "Murder! Look at that." He knelt down and pulled open the full, close lips, disclosing not human teeth, but small incisors, cusped grinders, wide-spaced; and long, keen, overlapping canines, like those of a greyhound: a fierce, deadly, carnivorous dentition, menacing and combative.

Waldo felt a qualm, yet the face and form still swayed his horrified sympathy for their humanness.

"Do you shoot women because they have long teeth?" Waldo insisted, revolted at the horrid death he had watched.

"You are hard to convince," said the consul sternly. "Do you call that a woman?" He stripped the clothing from the carcass.

Waldo sickened all over. What he saw was not the front of a woman, but more like the underside of an old fox-terrier with puppies, or of a white sow, with her second litter; from collarbone to groin ten lolloping udders, two rows, mauled, stringy, and flaccid.

"What kind of a creature is it?" he asked faintly.

"A Ghoul, my boy," the consul answered solemnly, almost in a whisper.

"I thought they did not exist," Waldo babbled. "I thought they were mythical; I thought there were none.

"I can very well believe that there are none in Rhode Island," the consul said gravely. "This is in Persia, and Persia is in Asia."

The Pig-Skin Belt

(A Tale from *Lukundoo and Other Stories*)

1

Be it noted that I, John Radford, always of sound mind and matter-of-fact disposition, being entirely in my senses, here set down what I saw, heard and knew. As to my inferences from what occurred I say nothing, my theory might be regarded as more improbable than the facts themselves. From the facts anyone can draw conclusions as well as I.

The first letter read:

> San Antonio, Texas,
> January 1st, 1892.
>
> My dear Radford:
>
> You have forgotten me, likely enough, but I have not forgotten you nor anyone (nor anything) in Brexington. I saw your advertisement in the New York *Herald* and am glad to learn from it that you are alive and to infer that you are well and prosperous.
>
> I need a lawyer's help. I want to buy real estate and I mean to return home, so you are exactly the man I am looking for. I am writing this to ask that you take charge of any and all of my affairs falling within your province, and to learn whether you are willing to do so.
>
> I am a rich man now, and without any near ties of kin or kind. I want to come home to Brexington, to live there if I can, to die there if I must. Along with other matters which I will explain if you accept I want to buy a house in the town and a farm nearby, if not the Shelby house and estate then some others like them.
>
> If willing to act for me please reply at once care of the Hotel

117

Menger. Remember me to any cousins of mine you may see.

Faithfully yours,

Cassius M. Case.

The name I knew well enough, of course, but my efforts to recall the individual resulted only in a somewhat hazy recollection of a tall, thin, red-cheeked lad of seventeen or so. It was almost exactly twenty-eight years since Colonel Shelby Case had left Brexington taking with him his son. Colonel Shelby had died some six years later. I remembered hearing of his death, in Egypt, I thought. Since his departure from Brexington I had never heard of or from Cassius.

My reply I wrote at once, professing my readiness to do anything in my power to serve him. As soon as the mails made it possible, I had a second letter from him.

My dear Radford:

Your kind letter has taken a load off my mind. I am particular about any sort of arrangements I make, exacting as to the accurate carrying out of small details and I feared I might have difficulty in finding a painstaking man in a community so easy-going as Brexington. I remember your precise ways as a boy and am basking in a sense of total relief and complete reliance on you.

I should buy the Shelby house and estate on your representations, but I must see for myself first. If they are the best I can get I shall take them anyhow. But please be ready to show me over every estate of five hundred acres or more, lying within ten miles of the Court House. I wish to examine every one which is now for sale or which you can induce the owners to consider selling. I want the best which is to be had. Also I want a small place of fifty acres or so, two miles or more from the larger place I buy. Money is no object to me and the condition of the buildings on the places will not weigh with me at all.

So with the town house: I may tear it down entirely and rebuild from the cellar up. What I want in the town is a place of half an acre to two acres carrying fine, tall trees, with well-developed trunks. I want shade and plenty of it, but no limbs or branches growing or hanging within eight feet of the ground. I do not desire shrubbery, but if there is any I can have it removed, while I cannot create stout trees. Those I must have on the place when I buy it, for I will have the shade and I will have a clear sweep for air and an unobstructed view all round.

I am not at the Menger as you naturally suppose. I merely have my mail sent there. I am living in a tent half a mile or more from the town. At Los Angeles I had the luck to fall in with a Brexington nigger, Jeff Twibill. He knew of another, Cato Johnson, who was in Frisco. I have the two of them with me now, Jeff takes care of the horses and Cato of me and I am very comfortable.

That brings me to the arrangements I want you to make for me. Buy or lease or rent or borrow a piece of a field, say four acres, free of trees or bushes and sloping enough to shed the rain. Be sure there is good water handy. Have four tents; one for me, one for the two niggers (and make it big enough for three or four); one to cook in and one for my four horses, they are luxurious beasts and live as well as I do. Have the tents pitched in the middle of the field so I shall have a clear view all around. The field must be clear of bushes or trees, must be at least four acres and may he any size larger than that: forty would be none too big for me. I want no houses too close to me.

You see I am at present averse to houses, hotels and public conveyances. I mean to ride across the continent camping as I go. And in Brexington I mean to tent it until I have my own house ready to live in. I am resolute to be no man's guest nor any man's lodger, nor any company's passenger.

I am coming home, Radford, coming home to be a colonel with the rest of them. And I shall be no mere colonel-by-courtesy: I have won my right to the title, I won it twice over, years ago in Egypt and later in Asia.

Thank you for all the news of the many cousins, I did not realize they were so very numerous. I am sorry that Mary Mattingly is dead, of all the many dear people in Brexington I loved her best.

I shall keep you advised of my progress across the continent. And as questions come up about the details of the tent-equipment you can confer with me by letter.

Gratefully yours,

Cassius M. Case.

I showed the letters to one and another of my elder acquaintances, who remembered Cassius. Dr. Boone said:

"I presume it is a case of advanced tuberculosis. He should have remained in that climate. Of course, he may live a long time here, tenting in the open or living with the completest fresh air treatment. His punctiliousness in respect to self isolation does him credit, though he carries it further than is necessary. We must do all we can for him."

Beverly said: "Poor devil. 'Live if he can, die if he must.' He'll die all right. They'd call him a 'lunger' out there and he had better stay there."

The minister said:

"The lode-star of old sweet memories draws him homeward. 'Mary Mattingly,' yes we all remember how wildly he loved Mary Mattingly. While full of youth he could find forgetfulness fighting in strange lands. Now he must be near her although she lies in her grave. The proximity even of her tomb will be a solace to his last days."

We were prepared to do all that sympathy could suggest. Mr. Hall and Dr. Boone gravely discussed together the prolongation of Case's life and the affording of spiritual support. Beverly I found helpful on my line of finances and creature comforts. As Case's leisurely progress brought him nearer and nearer our interest deepened. When the day came on which he was to arrive Beverly and I rode put to meet him.

2

Language has no words to picture our dumbfounded amazement. And we were astonished in more ways than one. Chiefly, instead of the lank invalid we expected to see, we beheld a burly giant every characteristic of whom, save one, bespoke rugged health. He was all of six foot three, big boned, overlaid with a surplus of brawn, a Samsonian musculature that showed plain through his negligent, loose clothing; and withal he was plump and would have been sleek but for the roughness of his weather-beaten skin.

He wore gray; a broad-brimmed felt hat, almost a *sombrero*; a flannel shirt, a sort of jacket, and corduroy trousers tucked into his boots. It was before the days of khaki.

His head was large and round, but not at all a bullet head, rather handsome and well set. His face was round too, and good-natured, but not a particle as is the usual round face, vacuous and like a full-moon. His was agreeable, but lit with character and determination. His neck was fat but showed great cords through its rotundity. He had a big barrel of a chest and his voice rumbled out of it. He dominated the landscape the moment he entered it.

Even in our astonishment three things about him struck me, and, as I afterwards found out, the same three similarly struck Beverly.

One was his complexion. He had that build which leads one to expect floridity of face, a rubicund countenance or, at least, ruddy cheeks. But he was dead pale, with a peculiar tint I never had seen before. His face showed an abundance of solid muscle and over it a skin roughened by exposure, toughened, even hardened by wind and sun. Yet its colour was not in agreement with its texture. It had the hue which belongs to waxy skin over suety, tallowy flesh, an opaque whiteness, a pallidity almost corpse-like.

The second was his glance: keen, glittering, hard, blue-gray eyes he had, gallant and far younger than himself. But it was not the handsome eyes so much as their way of looking that whetted our attention. They pierced us through and through, they darted incessantly here and there, they peered to right and left, they kept us generally in view, indeed, and never let us feel that his attention wandered from us, yet they incessantly swept the world about him. You should say they saw all they looked at, looked at everything seeable.

The third was his belt, a mellowed old belt of pig-skin, with two capacious holsters, from each of which protruded the butt of a large-calibre revolver.

He greeted us in the spirit of old comradeship renewed. Behind him Jeff and Cato grinned from their tired mounts. He sat his big horse with no sign of fatigue and surveyed the landscape from the cross-roads' knoll where we had met him.

"I seem to recall the landmarks here," he said, "the left hand road by which you came, would take me through to Brexington."

Beverly confirmed his recollection.

"The one straight ahead," he went on, "goes past the big new distillery you wrote me about."

"Right again," I said.

"The road to the right," he continued, "will take us by the old mill, and I can swing round to my camp without nearing town."

"You could," Beverly told. "But it is a long way round."

"Not too far for me," he announced positively. "No towns or distilleries for me. I go round. Will you ride with me, gentlemen?"

We rode with him.

On the way I told him I expected him to supper that evening. "With all my writing, Radford," he said. "You don't seem to get the idea. I flock by myself for the present and eat alone. If you insist I'll explain tomorrow."

Beverly and I left him to his camp supper.

Dr. Boone and Mr. Hall were a good deal taken aback upon learning that their imagined invalid had no existence and that the real Colonel Case needed neither medical assistance nor spiritual solace. We four sat for some time expressing our bewilderment.

Next morning I drove out to Case's Camp. I found him sitting in his tent, the flaps of which were looped up all around. He was as pale as the day before. As I approached I saw him scrutinize me with a searching gaze, a gaze I found it difficult to analyze.

He wore his belt with the holsters and the revolver-butts showed from those same holsters. I was astonished at this. When I saw it on him the day before I had thought the belt a piece of bad taste. It might have been advisable in portions of his long ride, might have been imperatively necessary in some districts; but it seemed a pose or a stupidity to wear it so far east. Pistols were by no means unknown in our part of the world, but they were carried in the seclusion of the hip-pocket or inside the breast of one's coat, not flaunted in the face of the populace in low-hung pig-skin holsters.

Case greeted me cheerily.

"I got up too early," he stated. "I've had my breakfast and done my target practice twice over. Apparently you expect me to go with you in that buggy?"

I told him that I did.

"Come in and sit down a moment," he said in a somewhat embarrassed way. 'This suggestion of our driving together is in line with your kind invitation for last night. I see I must explain somehow."

He offered me a cigar and though I seldom smoke in the morning, I took it, for, I thought smoking would fill up the silences I anticipated.

He puffed a while, in fact.

"Have you ever been among feudists in the mountains?" he queried. "More than a little," I told him.

"Likely enough then," he went on, "you know more about their ways than I do. But I saw something of them myself, before I left America. Did you ever notice how a man at either focus of a feud, the king-pin of his end of it so to speak, manifests the greatest care to avoid permitting others to expose themselves to any degree of the danger always menacing him; how such men, in the black shadow of doom, as it were, are solicitous to prevent outsiders from straying into the penumbra of the eclipse which threatens themselves?"

"I have observed that," I replied. "Have you noticed on the other hand," he continued, "that they never show any concern for acquaintances who comprehend the situation, but pay them the compliment of assuming that they have sense enough to know what they are doing and to take care of themselves?"

"I have observed that same too," I affirmed.

He puffed again for a while.

"My father," he returned presently, "used to say that there are two ends to a quarrel, the right end and the wrong end, but that either end of a feud is the wrong end. I am one end of a feud. Wherever I am is one focus of that feud. The other focus is local, and I have removed myself as far as may be from it. But I am not safe here, should not be safe anywhere on earth; doubt if I should be safe on the moon, or Mars, on a planet of some other sun, or the least conspicuous satellite of the farthest star. I am obnoxious to the hate of a power as far-reaching" . . . he took off his broad felt hat and looked up at the canvas of the tent-roof . . . "as far-reaching as the displeasure of God."

"And as implacable," he almost whispered. "As the malice of Satan." He looked sane, healthy and self-possessed.

"I am nowhere safe," he recommenced in his natural voice, "while my chief adversary is alive. My enemies are many and malignant, enough, but their power is negligible, and their malignancy vicarious. Without fomenting their hostility would evaporate. Could I but know that my chief enemy were no more I should be free from all alarm. But while that arch-foe survives I am liable to attack at any moment, to attacks so subtle that I am at a loss to make you comprehend their possible nature, so crude that I could not make you realize the danger you are in at this instant."

I looked at him, unmoved.

"I shall say no more to you," he said. "You must do as you please. If you regard my warnings as vapours, I have at least warned you. If you are willing to share my danger, in such degree as my very neighbourhood is always full of danger, you do so at your own risk. If you consider it advisable to have no more to do with me, say so now."

"I see no reason," I told him without even a preliminary puff, "why your utterances should make any difference in my treatment of you."

"I thought you would say that," he said. "But my conscience is clear."

"Shall we proceed to business?" I asked.

"There is one point more," he replied. "Have you ever been in mining camps or amid other frontier conditions?"

"Several times," I answered, "and for some time at that."

"Have you ever noticed that when two men have been mutually threatening to shoot each other at sight, pending the final settlement, neither will expose women or children to danger by being in their neighbourhood or permitting them in his, if he can prevent their nearing them?"

"Such scrupulosity can be observed," I told him dryly, "nearer home than mining camps or frontier towns."

"So I have heard," he replied stiffly. "When I left America the personal encounter had not yet taken the place of the formal duel in these regions."

He puffed a bit.

"However," he continued, "it makes no difference from what part of the world you draw the illustration; it is equally in point. The danger of being near me is a hundred times, a thousand times greater than that of running the risk of stopping a wild or random bullet. I cannot bring myself to expose innocent beings to such danger."

"How about Jeff and Cato?" I asked.

"A nigger," declared Colonel Case (and he looked all the colonel as he spoke it) "is like a dog or a horse, he shares his master's dangers as a matter of course. I speak of women and children and unsuspecting men. I am resolute to sit at no man's table, to enter no man's house, uninvited or invited. All who come to me knowingly I shall welcome. When you bring any one with you I shall assume that he has been forewarned. But I shall intrude upon no one."

"How then are you to inspect," I queried, "the properties I expected to show you?"

"Business," said Colonel Case, "is different. When people propose to do business they assume any and all risks. Are you afraid to assume the risk of driving me about in that buggy of yours?"

"Not a particle," I disclaimed. "Are you willing to expose the people of Brexington to these dangers on which you descant so eloquently and which I fail to comprehend?"

Colonel Case fixed me with a cold stare. He looked every inch a warrior, accustomed to dominate his environment, to command and be obeyed, impatient of any opposition, ready to flare up if disbelieved in the smallest trifle.

"Radford," he said, slowly and sternly, "I am willing to take any pains to avoid wronging anyone, I am unwilling to make myself ridiculous by attempting impossibilities."

"I see," I concluded. "Let us go.

As we drove through the town he said:

"This is like coming back to earth from another world. It is like a dream too. Some streets are just as they were, only the faces are unfamiliar. I almost expect to see the ghosts of thirty years ago."

I made some vague comment and as we jogged along talked of the unchanged or new owners of the houses. Then I felt him make a sudden movement beside me, and I looked round at him. He could not turn any paler than he was, yet there had been a change in his face.

"I do see ghosts," he said slowly and softly.

I followed his glance as he gazed past me. We were approaching the Kenton homestead and nearly opposite it. It had an old-fashioned classic portico with four big white columns. At the top of the steps, between the two middle columns, stood Mary Kenton, all in pink with a rose in her jetty hair. She was looking intently at us, but not at me. Case stared at her fixedly.

"Mary Kenton is the picture of her mother," I told him.

"Her very image," he breathed, his eyes steadily on her. She continued gazing at us. Of course she knew whom I was driving. My horses were trotting slowly and when we were opposite her, she waved her hand.

"Welcome home, Cousin Cassius," she called cheerily.

Colonel Case waved his hat to her and bowed, but said nothing.

The Shelby mansion did not suit Colonel Case. What he wanted, he said, was a house at the edge of the town. When he had made his selection he bought it promptly. He had the outbuildings razed, the shrubbery torn up and the trees trimmed so that no limb hung within ten feet of the ground; above they were left untouched, tall and spreading as they were and almost interlacing with each other. The house he practically rebuilt. Its all-round veranda he had torn down and replaced by one even broader, but at the front only, facing the entrance, the only entrance he left. For he entirely closed the back-way to the kitchen and side-gate to the stable, cutting instead a loop-drive around the house from the one front entrance.

Except for this stone-posted carriage-gate with the little foot-path gate beside it, he had the whole place surrounded with a fence the like of which Brexington had never seen. The posts were T-beams, of rolled steel, eight feet tall above ground, reaching six feet below it and bedded down in rammed concrete. To these was bolted a four-foot continuous, square-mesh wire fencing, the meshes not over six inches at its top and as small as two inches at the bottom, which was sunk a hand's breadth below the surface and there held by close-set clamps upon sections of gas-pipe, extending from post to post and bolted to them.

Inside this mesh-fencing, as high as it reached, and above it to the top of the posts, were strung twenty strands of heavy barbed wire, the upper wires six inches apart, the lower strands closer. Inside the fence he had set a close hedge. As the plants composing it were large and vigorous when they arrived from the nursery-man, this was soon thick and strong. It was kept clipped to about three feet high. The flower-beds he abolished and from house to drive and drive to hedge soon had the whole place in well-kept turf.

Behind the house he had two outbuildings erected; at one corner a small carriage-house and stable, capable of holding two vehicles and three horses; at the other a structure of about the same size as the stable, half wood-shed and half hen-house.

Watching the carpenters at work on this and regarding the nine-days-wonder of a fence, several negroes stood in talk one day as I passed. They were laughing and I overheard one say:

"Mahs'r Case shuah am' gwine tuh lose no hains awf he roos'. Mus be gwine tuh be powerful fine hains he gwine raise. He sutt'nly mus' sot stoah by he hains. He sutt'nly dun tuk en' spain' cunnsdd'ble money awn he faince."

The interior of the house was finished plainly and furnished sparingly. The very day it was ready for occupancy he moved into it and ceased his camp life. Besides Cato, an old negro named Samson acted as cook, and another named Pompey as butler. These three made up all his household. Jeff was quartered in a room over the carriage-house.

Before his residence was prepared and while he was still camping he bought Shelby Manor.

"Nothing like obliging one's cousins," he said. He also bought two adjoining farms, forming a property of over a thousand acres. This he proceeded to equip as a stud farm, engaging a competent manager; re-fitting the house for him and the two smaller houses for his assistants, the overseer and farmer; abolishing the old outbuildings; putting up barns and stables in the most lavish fashion. He bought many blooded mares and created an establishment on a large scale.

About two miles out of town on the road past his house, nearly half way to Shelby Manor, he bought a worthless little farm of some forty acres. This he had fenced and put in grass, except a small garden-patch by the house, which he had made snug and where he had installed an elderly negro couple as caretakers. The old man had formerly belonged to the colonel's father, and was named Erastus Everett. All the other buildings he had removed, except a fair-sized hay barrack standing on a knoll near the middle of the largest field. This he had new roofed and repaired and given two coats of shingle stain, moss green on the roof and weather gray on the sides. In it he had ranked up some forty cords of fat pine wood. Near the house was built a small stable, which harboured the two mules Case allowed Uncle Rastus.

Besides this he had built a number of low sheds, opening on spaces enclosed with wire netting. Soon the enclosures swarmed with dogs, not blooded dogs, but mere mongrel curs. Not a small dog among them, all were big or fairly large. Uncle Rastus drove about the country in his big close-covered wagon, behind his two mules. Wherever he found an utterly worthless dog of some size he bought it, if it could be had cheap, and turned it in with the rest. Before a year had passed Uncle Rastus had more than a hundred no-account brutes to feed and care for.

Colonel Case was not a man to whom anyone, least of all a stranger, would put a direct unsolicited question. Uncle Rastus was more approachable. But the curious gained little information from him.

"Mahs'r Cash ain' tole muh wuff'r he keepin' awl dees yeah houns. He ain' spoke nuffin. He done tole muh tur buy 'um, he done tole muh to feed 'um. Ahze buyed 'um en' Ah feeds 'um."

Once he had established himself Case lived an extremely regular life. He rose early, breakfasted simply, and whatever the weather, drove out to Shelby Manor. He never rode in the forenoon. At his estate he had a pistol-range and a rifle-range. He spent nearly an hour each morning in pistol and rifle practice. He never used a shot-gun, but shot at targets, running marks, and trap-sprung clay-pigeons with both repeating rifle and revolver. He always carried his two repeating rifles with him, and brought them back with him. Several times, when I happened to accompany him, I watched him shoot.

The first time I was rather surprised. He emptied the chambers of one revolver, made some fifty shots with it, cleaned it, replaced the six cartridges which had been in it, and put it in its holster. Then he did the like with the other. Then he similarly emptied the magazines of one of his rifles, made some fifty shots with that, cleaned it and reloaded it with the original cartridges. So with the second rifle.

I asked him why he did so.

"The cartridges I go about with," he said, "are loaded with silver bullets. I can't afford to fire away two or three pounds of silver every day. Lead keeps my hand in just as well as silver, and the silver bullets are always ready for an emergency."

Against such an imaginary emergency, I conceived he wore his belt and kept his two rifles always at hand.

After his target practice he talked with his manager, looked over the place, discussed his stock or watched his jockeys exercising their mounts, for an hour or two. Once a week or so on his way back to town he stopped to inspect Uncle Rastus' charges, and investigate his doings. His early lunch was almost as simple as his breakfast. After his lunch he slept an hour or more. Later he took a long ride, seldom toward Shelby Manor. Always, both in going and in returning, he rode past Judge Kenton's mansion. At first his hour of starting on his ride varied. Before many days he so timed his setting forth as to pass the Kenton house when Mary was likely to be at her window, and his riding homeward when she was likely to be on the portico.

After a time she was sure to be at her window when he passed and on the portico when he repassed, and his departure and return occurred with clock-work regularity. When she was at her window, they never gave any sign of mutual recognition, but when she was on the portico she waved her hand to him and he his hat to her.

Towards dusk in summer, after lamp-light in winter, he ate a deliberate dinner. It never seemed to make a particle of difference to him how early he went to bed or how late, or whether he went to bed at all. He was quite capable of sitting all night at cards if the game was especially interesting. Yet he never made a habit of late hours. He was an inveterate card-player, but play at his house generally ceased before midnight and often much earlier. He could drink all night long, four fingers deep and often, and never seem the worse for it. Yet it was very seldom he did so. Habitually he drank freely after dinner, but no effects of liquor were ever visible on him. His liquors were the best and always set out in abundance. His cigars were as good as his liquors and spread out in similar profusion. His wines at dinner were unsurpassable and numerous.

The dinners themselves could not have been beaten. Uncle Samson was an adept at marketing and a superlative cook. Pompey was an ideal butler. They seemed always ready to serve dinner for their master alone without waste or for a dozen more also without any sign of effort or dismay. As Case made welcome to his dinner table as to his card table anyone who happened to drop in, he had no lack of guests. All the bachelors of Brexington flocked to him as a matter of course. The heads of families were puzzled. One after another they invited him to their houses. His refusals were courteous but firm: for explanations he referred them to me.

Most of them accepted my dilution of his utterances and acquiesced in his lop-sided hospitality. One or two demurred and laid special siege to him. Particularly Judge Kenton would not be denied. When he was finally convinced that Colonel Case would not respond to any invitation, he declared his resolution not to cross Case's threshold until his several visits there were properly acknowledged by a return call at his house. Intercourse between him and Case thereupon ceased. Judge Kenton, however, was alone in his punctilious attitude. Everybody else frequented Case's house and table. His house indeed became a sort of informal club for all the most agreeable men of the town and neighbourhood.

It was not mere creature comforts or material attractions which drew them there, but the very real charm of the host. Even while he was tenting, before the house was ready for occupancy, he had made friends, according to their degree, with every man in and about Brexington, white or black. Everybody knew him, everybody liked him, everybody wondered at him.

4

Case was in fact the most discussed man in our region of the world. Some called him a lunatic, dwelling especially on his dog-ranch, as he called it, and his everlasting pig-skin belt with the holstered revolvers, without which he was never seen at any hour of the day, by anyone. It was difficult for his most enthusiastic partisans to assign any colourable reason why he should maintain a farm for the support of some two hundred totally worthless dogs. Their worthlessness was the main point which uncle Rastus made in buying them. Often he rejected a dog proffered for little or almost nothing.

"No seh," he would say. "Dat ar dawg ain' no 'count enuff. Mah'sr Cash he dun awdah muh dat Ah ain' buy no dawg wut am' pintedly no 'count. Dey gotter be no 'count. Ah ain' buyin' um lessen dey's wuffless en' onery."

Scarcely less easy was it to defend his wearing his twin revolvers even with dinner-dress, for he put on evening-dress for dinner, with the punctiliousness of an Englishman in the wilderness, put it on as often as he dined and yet wore it so naturally and unobtrusively, that no more than the incongruous belt did it embarrass the guests he made at home in any kind of clothes they happened to be wearing. His admirers pointed to this as a kind of exploit, as something of which only a perfectly sane and exceptionally fine man could be capable. They adduced his clear-headed business sense, his excellent judgment on matters pertaining to real estate, his knowledge of horseflesh, his horsemanship, his coolness, skill and exceptional good temper at cards, as cumulative proofs of his perfect sanity.

They admitted he was peculiar on one or two points but minimized these as negligible eccentricities. They were ready to descant to any extent on his personal charm, and this indeed all were agreed upon. To attract visitors by good dinners, good liquors, good cigars and endless card playing was easy. To keep his visitors at their ease and entertained for hours with mere conversations while seated on his veranda, was no small feat in itself and a hundred times a feat when their host obtruded upon them the ever visible butts of his big revolvers and kept a repeating rifle standing against each jamb of his front door. This tension of perpetual preparedness for an imminent attack might well have scared away everybody and left Case a hermit. It did nothing of the kind. It was acquiesced in at first, later tacitly accepted and finally ignored altogether. With it was ignored his strange complexion.

I had myself puzzled over this: after long groping about in my mind I had realized what it reminded me of, and I found others who agreed with me in respect to it. It was like the paleness one sees for the half of a breath on the face of a strong, healthy man when in sudden alarm, astonishment or horror his blood flows momently back to his heart. Under such stress of unforeseen agitation a normal countenance might exhibit that hue for a fraction of a second, on Case's visage it was abiding, like the war paint on an armour-clad, drab-gray and dreary. Yet it produced no effect of gloom in his associates. He not only did not put a damper upon high spirits but diffused an atmosphere of gaiety and good fellowship.

And he did so not only in spite of his ever-visible weapons and of his uncanny, sombre complexion, but also in spite of the strange and daunting habit of his eyes. I had seen something like it once and again in a frontiersman who knew that his one chance of surviving his enemy was to shoot first and who expected the crucial instant at any moment. I had watched in more than one town the eyes of such an individual scan each man who approached with one swift glance of inquiry, of keen uncertainty dying instantly into temporary relief.

Such was the look with which Case invariably met me. It had in it hesitation, doubt, and, as it were, an element of half-conscious approach to alarm. It was as if he said to himself:

"Is that Radford? It looks like him. If it is Radford, all right. But is it really Radford after all?" I grew used in time to this lightning scrutiny of me every time he caught sight of me. His other friends grew used to it. But it was the subject of endless talk among us. His eyes had an inexplicable effect on everyone. And not the least factor in their mystery was that he bestowed this glance not only upon all men, but upon women, children, animals, birds, even insects. He regarded a robin or a butterfly with the same flash of transient interest which he bestowed upon a horse or a man. And his eyes seemed to keep him cognizant of every moving thing before, behind and above him. Nothing living which entered his horizon seemed to escape his notice.

Beverly remarked:

"Case is afraid of something, is always looking for something. But what the devil is it he is looking for? He acts as if he did not know what to expect and suspected everything."

Dr. Boone said:

"Case behaves somewhat as if he were suffering from a delusion of persecution. But most of the symptoms are conspicuously absent. I am puzzled like the rest of you."

The effect upon strangers of this eerie quality of Case's vision was by no means pleasant. Yet his merest acquaintances soon became used to it and his intimates ceased to notice it at all. His personal charm made it seem a trifle. Night after night his card room was the scene of jollity. His table gathered the most desirable comrades the countryside afforded. Evening after evening his cronies sat in the comfortable wicker chairs on his broad veranda, little Turkish tables bearing decanters and cigars set among them, Colonel Case the centre and life of the group.

He talked easily and he talked well. To start him talking of the countries he had seen was not easy, but, once he began, his stories of Egypt and Abyssinia, of Persia and Burmah, of Siam and China were always entertaining. Very seldom, almost never did he tell of his own experiences. Generally he told of having heard from others the tales he repeated, even when he spoke so that we suspected him of telling events in which he had taken part.

It was impossible to pin him down to a date, almost as hard to elicit the definite name of a locality. He gave minute particulars of incidents and customs, but dealt in generalities as to place and time. Especially he was strong in local superstitions and beliefs.

He told countless tales, all good, of crocodiles and *ichneumons* in Egypt, gazelles and ghouls in Persia, elephants and tigers in Burmah, deer and monkeys in Siam, badgers and foxes in China and sorcerers and enchanters anywhere. He spoke of the last two in as matter-of-fact a tone as of any of the others.

He told legends of the contests of various Chinese sages and saints, with magicians and wizards; of the malice and wiles of these wicked practitioners of sombre arts; of the sort of super-sense developed by the adepts, their foes, enabling them to tell of the approach or presence of a sorcerer whatever disguise he assumed, even if he had the power of making himself invisible.

Several legendary anecdotes turned on this point of the invisibility of the wicked enemy and the prescience of his intended victim.

One was of a holy man said to have lived in Singan Fu about the time of the crusades. Knowing that he was threatened with the vengeance of a wizard, he provided himself with a sword entirely of silver, since the flesh of a wizard was considered proof against all baser metals. He likewise had at hand a quantity of the ashes of a sacred tree.

While seated in his study he felt an inimical presence. He snatched up his silver blade, stood upon the defensive and shouted a signal previously agreed upon. Hearing it his servants locked the doors of the house and rushed in with boxes of the sacred ashes. Scattering it on the floor, they could see on the fresh ashes the footsteps of the wizard. One of the servants, according to his master's instructions, had brought a live fowl. Slicing off its head he waved the spouting neck towards the air over the footprints.

According to Chinese belief fowls' blood has the magical property of disclosing anyone invisible through incantation. In fact where the blood drops fell upon the wizard, they remained visible, there appeared a gory eye and cheek. Slashing at his revealed enemy the sage slew him with the silver sword, after which his body was with all speed burned to ashes. This was the invariable ending of all his similar tales.

Stories like this Case delighted in, but beyond this penchant for the weird and occult, for even childish tales of distant lands, his conversation in general showed no sign of peculiarity or eccentricity. Only once or twice did he startle us. Some visitors to town were among the gathering on his veranda and fell into a discussion of the contrasting qualities of Northerners and Southerners. Inevitably the discussion degenerated into a rather acrimonious and petty citation of all the weak points of each section and a rehash of all the stale sneers at either. The wordy Alabamian who led one side of the altercation descanted on the necessary and inherited vileness of the descendants of the men who burnt the Salem witches. Case had been listening silently. Then he cut in with an emphatic, trenchant directness unusual to him. "Witches," he announced, "ought to be burnt always and everywhere."

We sat a moment startled and mute.

The Alabamian spoke first.

"Do you believe in witches, Sir?" he asked.

"I do," Case affirmed.

"Ever been bewitched?" the Alabamian queried. He was rather young and dogmatically assertive.

"Do you believe in Asiatic cholera?" Case queried in his turn."

"Certainly, Sir," the Alabamian asserted.

"Ever had it?" Case inquired meaningly.

"No," the Alabamian admitted. "No, Sir, never."

"Ever had yellow fever?" Case questioned him.

"Never, Sir, thank God," the Alabamian replied fervently.

"Yet I'll bet," Case hammered at him, "that you would be among the first to join a shotgun quarantine if an epidemic broke out within a hundred miles of you. You have never had it, but you believe in it with every fibre of your being.

"That's just the way with me. I've never been bewitched, but I believe in witchcraft. Belief in witchcraft is like faith in any one of a dozen fashionable religions, not a subject for argument or proof, but a habit of mind. That's my habit of mind. I won't discuss it, but I've no hesitation about asserting it.

"Witchcraft is like leprosy, both spread among nations indifferent to them, both disappear before unflinching severity. The horror of both among our ancestors abolished both in Europe and kept them from gaining a foothold in this country. Both exist and flourish in other corners of the world, along with other things undreamed of in some complacent philosophies. Leprosy can be repressed only by isolation, the only thing that will abolish witchcraft is fire, fire Sir."

That finished that discussion. No one said another word on the subject. But it started a round of debates on Case's mental condition, which ran on for days, everywhere except at Case's house, and which brought up all that could be said about personal aloofness, pensioned dogs, exposed revolvers and pig-skin belts.

5

The mellow fall merged into Indian Summer. The days were short and the afternoons chill. The weather did not permit the evening gatherings on Case's veranda. No more did it allow Mary Kenton to sit in her rocker between the two left-hand columns of the big white portico. Yet it was both noticeable and noticed that she never failed to step out upon that portico, no matter what the weather, each afternoon; that in the twilight or in the late dusk the wave of her hand and the sweep of the horseman's big, broad-brimmed felt hat answered each other unfailingly.

The coterie of Case's chums, friends and hangers-on gathered then mostly around the generous log-fire in his ample drawing-room, when they were not in the card-room, the billiard-room or at table. I made one of that coterie frequently and enjoyed my hours there with undiminished zest. When I dined there I habitually occupied the foot of the long table, facing Case at the head. The hall door of the dining-room was just at my right hand.

One evening in early December I was so seated at the foot of the table. The weather had been barely coolish for some days, the skies had been clear and everything was dry. That night was particularly mild. We had sat down rather early and it was not yet seven o'clock when Pompey began to pass the cigars. No one had yet lit up. Someone had asked Case a question and the table was still listening for his answer. I, like the rest, was looking at him. Then it all happened in a tenth, in a hundredth of the time necessary to tell it; so quickly that, except Case, no one had time to move a muscle.

Case's eyes were on his questioner. I did not see the door open, but I saw his gaze shift to the door, saw his habitual glance of startled uncertainty. But instead of the lightning query of his eyes softening into relief and indifference, it hardened instantaneously into decision. I saw his hand go to his holster, saw the revolver leap out, saw the aim, saw his face change, heard his explosive exclamation:

"Good God, it is!" saw the muzzle kick up as the report crushed our ear drums and through the smoke saw him push back his chair and spring up.

The rest of us were all too dazed to try to stand. Like me they all looked toward the door. There stood Mary Kenton, all in pink, a pink silk opera cloak half off her white shoulders, a single strand of pale coral round her slender throat, a pink pompom in her glossy hair. She was standing as calmly as if nothing had happened, her arms hidden in the cloak, her right hand holding it together in front. Her rings sparkled on her fingers as her breast-pin sparkled on her low corsage.

"Cousin Cassius," she said, "you have a theatrical way of receiving unexpected visitors."

"Good God, Mary," he said. "It is really you. I saw it was really you just in time.

"Of course it is really I," she retorted. "Whom or what did you think it really was?"

"Not you," he answered thickly. "Not you."

His voice died away.

"Now you know it is really I," she said crisply, "you might at least offer me a chair." At that the spell of our amazement left us and we all sprang to our feet.

She seated herself placidly to the right of the fireplace.

"I hear your port is excellent," she said laughingly. Before Case could hand her the glass she wavered a little in the chair, but a mere swallow revived her.

"I had not anticipated," she said, "so startling a reception."

We stood about in awkward silence.

"Pray ask your guests to be seated, Cousin Cassius," she begged. "I did not mean to disturb your gaiety."

We took our chairs, but those on her side of the table were turned outward toward the fireplace, where Case stood facing her.

"I owe you an explanation," she said easily. "Milly Wilberforce is staying with me and she bet me a box of Maillard's that I would not pay you a call. As I never take a dare, as the weather is fine, and as we have all your guests for chaperons, I thought a brief call between cousins could do no harm."

"It has not," said Case fervently; "but it very nearly did. And now will you let me escort you home? The Judge will be anxious about you."

"Papa doesn't know I am here, of course," she said. "When he finds out, I'll quiet him. If you won't come to see me, at least I have once come to see you."

Case held the door wide for her, shut it behind him, and left us staring at the bullet hole in the door frame.

One morning of the following spring Case was driving me townward from Shelby Manor, when, not a hundred feet in front of us, Mary Kenton's buggy entered the pike from a cross-road. As it turned, mare, vehicle and all went over sideways with a terrific crash. Mary must have fallen clear for the next instant she was at the mare's head.

Case did succeed in holding his fiery colts and in pulling them to a standstill alongside the wreck, but it was all even he could do. I jumped out, meaning to take the colts' bits and let Case help Mary. But she greeted me imperiously.

"Cousin Jack, please come sit on Bonnie's head." I took charge of Bonnie in my own fashion and she stood up entirely unhurt.

"How on earth did you come to do it, Mary?"

Colonel Case wondered, for she was a perfect horsewoman.

"Accidents will happen," she answered lightly, "and I am glad of this one. You have really spoken to me, and that is worth a hundred smashes."

"But I wrote to you," he protested. "I wrote to you and explained."

"One letter," she sniffed contemptuously. "You should have kept on, you silly man, I might have answered the fifth or sixth or even the second."

He stared at her and no wonder for she was fascinatingly *coquettish*.

"I don't mind Jack a bit, you know," she went on. "Jack is my loyal knight and unfailing partisan. He keeps my secrets and does everything I ask of him. For instance, he will not demur an atom now when I ask him to throw Bonnie's harness into the buggy and ride her to town for me.

"You see," she smiled at him dazzlingly, "another advantage of my upset is that the buggy is so smashed that you cannot decently refuse to drive me home."

"But Mary," he protested, "I explained fully to you."

"You didn't really expect me to believe all that fol-de-rol?" she cried. "Suppose I did, I don't see any dwergs around, and if all Malebolge were in plain sight I'd make you take me anyhow."

Inevitably he did, but that afternoon their daily ceremony of hand-wave from the portico and hat-wave from horseback was resumed and was continued as their sole intercourse.

6

It was full midsummer when a circus came to Brexington. Case and I started for a ride together on the afternoon of its arrival, passed the tents already raised and met the procession on its way through town from the freight yard of the railroad. We pulled our horses to one side of the street and sat watching the show.

There were Cossacks and cowboys, Mexican *vaqueros* and Indians on mustangs. There were two elephants, a giraffe, and then some camels which set our mounts snorting and swerving about. Then came the cages, one of monkeys, another of parrots, cockatoos and macaws, others with wolves, bears, hyenas, a lion, a lioness, a tiger, and a beautiful leopard.

Case made a movement and I heard a click. I looked round and beheld him with his revolver cocked and pointed at the leopard's cage. He did not fire but kept the pistol aimed at the cage until it was out of range. Then he thrust it back into its holster and watched the fag-end of the procession go by. All he said was:

"You will have to excuse me, Radford, I have urgent business at home."

Towards dusk Cato came to me in great agitation.

"Mahs'r Cash done gone off'n he haid," he declared. "He shuah done loss he sainsus." I told him to return home and I would stroll up there casually.

I found Case in the woodshed, uncle Rastus with him. Hung by the hind legs like new-slaughtered hogs were a dozen of the biggest dogs of which Rastus had had charge. Their throats were cut and each dripped into a tin pail. Rastus, his ebony face paled to a sort of mud-gray, held a large tin pail and a new white-washer's brush.

Case greeted me as usual, as if my presence there were a matter of course and he were engaged upon nothing out of the common.

"Uncle," he said, "I judge those are about dripped out. Pour it all into the big pail." He took the brush from Rastus, who followed him to the gate.

There Case dipped the brush into the blood and painted a broad band across the gravel of the drive and the flagstones of the footpath. He proceeded as if he were using lime white-wash to mark off a lawn-tennis court in the early days of the game, when wet markers were not yet invented and dry markers were still undreamed of. He continued the stripe of blood all round his place, just inside the hedge. He made it about three inches wide and took great pains to make it plain and heavy.

When he had come round to the entrance again he went over the stripe on the path and drive a second time. Then he straightened up and handed the brush to Rastus.

"Just enough," he remarked. "I calculated nicely."

I had so far held my tongue. But his air of self-approval, as if in some feat of logic led me to blurt out:

"What is it for?"

"The Chinese," said Case, "esteem dogs' blood a defence against sorcery. I doubt its efficacy, but I know of no better fortification."

No reply seemed expected and I made none.

That evening I was at Case's, with some six or seven others. We sat indoors, for the cloudy day had led up to a rainy evening. Nothing unusual occurred.

Next day the town was plastered with posters of the circus company offering five hundred dollars reward for the capture of an escaped leopard.

Cato came to my office just as I was going out to lunch.

"Mahs'r Cash done gone cunjuhin' agin," he announced. I found out that a second batch of dogs had been brought in by uncle Rastus in his covered wagon behind his unfailing mules, had been butchered like the former convoy and the band of blood gone over a second time. Case had not gone outside that line since he first made it, no drive to Shelby Manor that morning.

The day was perfect after the rain of the day before, and the bright sunlight dried everything. The evening was clear and windless with a nearly full moon intensely bright and very high. Practically the whole population went to the circus.

Beverly and I dined at Case's. He had no other guests, but such was his skill as a host that our dinner was delightfully genial. After dinner the three of us sat on the veranda.

The brilliance of the moonlight on and through the unstirred trees made a glorious spectacle and the mild, cool atmosphere put us in just the humour to enjoy it and each other. Case talked quietly, mostly of art galleries in Europe, and his talk was quite as charming and entertaining as usual. He seemed a man entirely sane and altogether at his ease.

We had been on the veranda about half an hour and in that time neither team nor pedestrian had passed. Then we saw the figure of a woman approaching down the middle of the roadway from the direction of the country. Beverly and I caught sight of her at about the same instant and I saw him watching her as I did, for she had the carriage and bearing of a lady and it seemed strange that she should be walking, stranger that she should be alone, and strangest that she should choose the road instead of the footpath which was broad and good for half a mile.

Case, who had been describing a carved set of ivory chessmen he had seen in Egypt, stopped speaking and stared as we did. I began to feel as if I ought to recognize the advancing figure, it seemed unfamiliar and yet familiar too in outline and carriage, when Beverly exclaimed:

"By Jove, that is Mary Kenton."

"No," said Colonel Case in a combative, resonant tone like the slow boom of a big bell. "No, it is not Mary Kenton."

I was astonished at the animus of his contradiction and we intensified our scrutiny. The nearing girl really suggested Mary Kenton and yet, I felt sure, was not she. Her bearing made me certain that she was young, and she had that indefinable something about her which leads a man to expect that a woman will turn out to be good looking. She walked with a sort of insolent, high-stepping swing.

When she was nearly opposite us Case exclaimed in a sort of chopped-off, guttural bark:

"Nay, not even in that shape, foul fiend, not even in that."

The tall, shapely young woman turned just in front of the gateway and walked towards us. "I think," said Beverly, "the lady is coming in."

"No," said Colonel Case, again with that deep, baying reverberation behind his voice. "No, not coming in."

The young woman laid her hand on the pathway gate and pushed it open. She stepped inside and then stopped, stopped suddenly, abruptly, with an awkward half-stride, as if she had run into an obstacle in the path, a low obstruction like a wheelbarrow. She stood an instant; looked irresolutely right and left, and then stepped back and shut the gate. She turned and started across the street, fairly striding in a sort of incensed, wrathful haste.

My eyes, like Beverly's, were on the figure in the road. It was only with a sort of sidelong vision that I felt rather than saw Case whip a rifle from the door jamb to his shoulder and fire. Almost before the explosion rent my ear drums I saw the figure in the roadway crumple and collapse vertically. Petrified with amazement I was frozen with my stare upon the huddle on the macadam. Beverly had not moved and was as dazed as I. My gaze still fixed as Case threw up a second cartridge from the magazine and fired again, I saw the wretched heap on the piking leap under the impact of the bullet with the yielding quiver of totally dead flesh and bone. A third time he fired and we saw the like. Then the spell of our horror broke and we leapt up, roaring at the murderer.

With a single incredibly rapid movement the madman disembarrassed himself of his rifle and held us off, a revolver at each of our heads.

"Do you know what you have done?" we yelled together.

"I am quite sure of what I have done," Case replied in a big calm voice, the barrels of his pistols steady as the pillars of the veranda. "But I am not quite so clear whether I have earned five hundred dollars reward. Will you gentlemen be kind enough to step out into the street and examine that carcass?"

Woodenly, at the muzzles of those unwavering revolvers, we went down the flagged walk side by side, moving in a nightmare dream.

I had never seen a woman killed before and this woman was presumably a lady, young and handsome. I felt the piking of the roadway under my feet, and looked everywhere, except downward in front of me.

I heard Beverly give a coughing exclamation:

"The leopard!"

Then I looked, and I too shouted: "The leopard!"

She lay tangible, unquestionable, in plain sight under the silver moonrays with the clear black shadows of the maple leaves sharp on her sleek hide.

Gabbling our excited astonishment we pulled at her and turned her over. She had six wounds, three where the bullets entered and three where they came out, one through spine and breastbone and two through the ribs.

We dropped the carcass and stood up. "But I thought . . ." I exclaimed.

"But I saw . . ." Beverly cried.

"You gentlemen," thundered Colonel Case, "had best not say what you saw or what you thought you saw."

We stood mute, looking at him, at each other, and up and down the street. No one was in sight. Apparently the circus had so completely drained the neighbourhood that no one had heard the shots.

Case addressed me in his natural voice: "If you will be so good Radford, would you oblige me by stepping into my house and telling Jeff to fetch the wheelbarrow. I must keep watch over this carrion."

There I left him, the two crooked revolvers pointed at the dead animal. Jeff, and Cato with him, brought the wheelbarrow. Upon it the two negroes loaded the warm, inert mass of spotted hide and what it contained. Then Jeff lifted the handles and taking turns they wheeled their burden all the way to Uncle Rastus', Case walking on one side of the barrow with his cocked revolvers, we on the other, quite as a matter of course.

Jeff trundled the barrow out to the hay barrack on the knoll. He and Cato and Uncle Rastus carried out cord-wood until they had an enormous pile well out in the field. Then they dug up a barrel of kerosene from near one corner of the barrack. When the leopard had been placed on the top of the firewood they broached the barrel and poured its contents over the carcass and its pyre. When it was set on fire Case gave an order to Jeff, who went off.

We stood and watched the pyre burn down to red coals. By that time Jeff had returned from Shelby Manor with a double team.

Case let down the hammers of his revolvers, bolstered them, unbuckled his belt and threw it into the dayton.

Never had we suspected he could sing a note. Now he started "Dixie" in a fine, deep baritone and we sang that and other rousing songs all the way home. When we got out of the dayton he walked loungingly up the veranda steps, his belt hanging over his arm. He took the rifles from the door jamb.

"I have no further use for these trusty friends," he said. "If you like, you may each have one as a souvenir of the occasion. My defunct pistols and otiose belt I'll even keep myself."

Next morning as I was about to pass Judge Kenton's house I heard heavy footsteps rapidly overtaking me. Turning I saw Case, not in his habitual gray clothes and broad-brimmed semi-*sombrero*, but wearing a soft brown felt hat, a blue serge suit, set off by a red necktie and tan shoes. He was conspicuously beltless.

"You might as well come with me, Radford," he said. "You will probably be best man later anyhow."

We found Judge Kenton on his porch, and Mary, all in pink, with a pink rose in her hair, seated between her father and her pretty stepmother.

"I sent Jeff with a note," Case explained as we approached the steps, "to make sure of finding them."

After the greetings were over Case said:

"Judge, I am a man of few words. I love your daughter and I ask your permission to win her if I can."

"You have my permission, Suh," the Judge answered. Case rose.

"Mary," he said, "would you walk with me in the garden, say to the grape arbour?" When they returned Mary wore a big ruby ring set round with diamonds. Her colour was no bad match for the ruby. And, beyond a doubt, Case's cheeks showed a trace of colour too.

"Father," Mary said as she seated herself, "I am going to marry Cousin Cassius."

"You have my blessing, my dear," the Judge responded. "I am glad of it."

"Everybody will be glad, I believe," said Mary. "Cassius is glad, of course, and he is glad of two other things. One is that he feels free to dine with us tonight, he has just told me so.

"The other" (a roguish light sparkled in her eyes) "he has not confessed. But I just know that, next to marrying me, the one thing in all this world that makes him gladdest is that now at last he feels at liberty to see a horse race and go to the races every chance he gets."

In fact, when they returned from their six-months' wedding tour, they were conspicuous at every race meeting. Case's eyes had lost their restlessness and his cheeks showed as healthy a colouring as I ever saw on any human being.

It might be suggested that there should be an explanation to this tale. But I myself decline to expound my own theory. Mary never told what she knew, and her husband, in whose afterlife there has been nothing remarkable as far as I know, has never uttered a syllable.

The House of the Nightmare

(A Tale from *Lukundoo and Other Stories*)

I first caught sight of the house from the brow of the mountain as I cleared the woods and looked across the broad valley several hundred feet below me, to the low sun sinking toward the far blue hills. From that momentary viewpoint I had an exaggerated sense of looking almost vertically down. I seemed to be hanging over the checker-board of roads and fields, dotted with farm buildings, and felt the familiar deception that I could almost throw a stone upon the house. I barely glimpsed its slate roof.

What caught my eyes was the bit of road in front of it, between the mass of dark-green trees about the house and the orchard opposite. Perfectly straight it was, bordered by an even row of trees, through which I made out a cinder side path and a low stone wall.

Conspicuous on the orchard side between two of the flanking trees was a white object, which I took to be a tall stone, a vertical splinter of one of the tilted lime-stone reefs with which the fields of the region are scarred.

The road itself I saw plain as a box-wood ruler on a green baize table. It gave me a pleasurable anticipation of a chance for a burst of speed. I had been painfully traversing closely forested, semi-mountainous hills. Not a farmhouse had I passed, only wretched cabins by the road, more than twenty miles of which I had found very bad and hindering. Now, when I was not many miles from my expected stopping-place, I looked forward to better going, and to that straight, level bit in particular.

As I sped cautiously down the sharp beginning of the long descent the trees engulfed me again, and I lost sight of the valley. I dipped into a hollow, rose on the crest of the next hill, and again saw the house, nearer, and not so far below.

The tall stone caught my eye with a shock of surprise. Had I not

143

thought it was opposite the house next the orchard? Clearly it was on the left-hand side of the road toward the house. My self-questioning lasted only the moment as I passed the crest. Then the outlook was cut off again; but I found myself gazing ahead, watching for the next chance at the same view.

At the end of the second hill I only saw the bit of road obliquely and could not be sure, but, as at first, the tall stone seemed on the right of the road.

At the top of the third and last hill I looked down the stretch of road under the over-arching trees, almost as one would look through a tube. There was a line of whiteness which I took for the tall stone. It was on the right.

I dipped into the last hollow. As I mounted the farther slope I kept my eyes on the top of the road ahead of me. When my line of sight surmounted the rise I marked the tall stone on my right hand among the serried maples. I leaned over, first on one side, then on the other, to inspect my tyres, then I threw the lever.

As I flew forward, I looked ahead. There was the tall stone—on the left of the road! I was really scared and almost dazed. I meant to stop dead, take a good look at the stone, and make up my mind beyond peradventure whether it was on the right or the left—if not, indeed, in the middle of the road.

In my bewilderment I put on the highest speed. The machine leaped forward; everything I touched went wrong; I steered wildly, slewed to the left, and crashed into a big maple.

When I came to my senses, I was flat on my back in the dry ditch. The last rays of the sun sent shafts of golden-green light through the maple boughs overhead. My first thought was an odd mixture of appreciation of the beauties of nature and disapproval of my own conduct in touring without a companion—a fad I had regretted more than once. Then my mind cleared and I sat up. I felt myself from the head down. I was not bleeding; no bones were broken; and, while much shaken, I had suffered no serious bruises.

Then I saw the boy. He was standing at the edge of the cinderpath, near the ditch. He was so stocky and solidly built; barefoot, with his trousers rolled up to his knees; wore a sort of butternut shirt, open at the throat; and was coatless and hatless. He was tow-headed, with a shock of tousled hair; was much freckled, and had a hideous harelip. He shifted from one foot to the other, twiddled his toes, and said nothing whatever, though he stared at me intently.

I scrambled to my feet and proceeded to survey the wreck. It seemed distressingly complete. It had not blown up, nor even caught fire; but otherwise the ruin appeared hopelessly thorough. Everything I examined seemed worse smashed than the rest. My two hampers, alone, by one of those cynical jokes of chance, had escaped—both had pitched clear of the wreckage and were unhurt, not even a bottle broken.

During my investigations the boy's faded eyes followed me continuously, but he uttered no word. When I had convinced myself of my helplessness I straightened up and addressed him:

"How far is it to a blacksmith's shop?"

"Eight mile," he answered. He had a distressing case of cleft palate and was scarcely intelligible.

"Can you drive me there?" I inquired.

"Nary team on the place," he replied; "nary horse, nary cow."

"How far to the next house?" I continued.

"Six mile," he responded.

I glanced at the sky. The sun had set already. I looked at my watch: it was going—seven thirty-six.

"May I sleep in your house tonight?" I asked.

"You can come in if you want to," he said, "and sleep if you can. House all messy; ma's been dead three year, and dad's away. Nothin' to eat but buckwheat flour and rusty bacon."

"I've plenty to eat," I answered, picking up a hamper. "Just take that hamper, will you?"

"You can come in if you've a mind to," he said, "but you got to carry your own stuff." He did not speak gruffly or rudely, but appeared mildly stating an inoffensive fact.

"All right," I said, picking up the other hamper; "lead the way." The yard in front of the house was dark under a dozen or more immense ailanthus trees. Below them many smaller trees had grown up, and beneath these a dank underwood of tall, rank suckers Out of the deep, shaggy, matted grass. What had once been, apparently, a carriage-drive, left a narrow, curved track, disused and grass-grown, leading to the house. Even here were some shoots of the ailanthus, and the air was unpleasant with the vile smell of the roots and suckers and the insistent odour of their flowers.

The house was of grey stone, with green shutters faded almost as grey as the stone. Along its front was a veranda, not much raised from the ground, and with no balustrade or railing. On it were several hickory splint rockers. There were eight shuttered windows toward the porch, and midway of them a wide door, with small violet panes on either side of it and a fanlight above.

"Open the door," I said to the boy.

"Open it yourself," he replied, not unpleasantly nor disagreeably, but in such a tone that one could not but take the suggestion as a matter of course.

I put down the two hampers and tried the door. It was latched but not locked, and opened with a rusty grind of its hinges, on which it sagged crazily, scraping the floor as it turned. The passage smelt mouldy and damp. There were several doors on either side; the boy pointed to the first on the right.

"You can have that room," he said.

I opened the door. What with the dusk, the interlacing trees outside, the *piazza* roof, and the closed shutters, I could make out little.

"Better get a lamp," I said to the boy. "Nary lamp," he declared cheerfully. "Nary candle. Mostly I get abed before dark." I returned to the remains of my conveyance. All four of my lamps were merely scrap metal and splintered glass. My lantern was mashed flat. I always, however, carried candles in my valise. This I found split and crushed, but still holding together. I carried it to the porch, opened it, and took out three candles.

Entering the room, where I found the boy standing just where I had left him. I lit the candle. The walls were white-washed, the floor bare. There was a mildewed, chilly smell, but the bed looked freshly made up and clean, although it felt clammy.

With a few drops of its own grease I stuck the candle on the corner of a mean, rickety little bureau. There was nothing else in the room save two rush-bottomed chairs and a small table. I went out on the porch, brought in my valise, and put it on the bed. I raised the sash of each window and pushed open the shutter. Then I asked the boy, who had not moved or spoken, to show me the way to the kitchen. He led me straight through the hall to the back of the house. The kitchen was large, and had no furniture save some pine chairs, a pine bench, and a pine table.

I stuck two candles on opposite corners of the table. There was no stove or range in the kitchen, only a big hearth, the ashes in which smelt and looked a month old. The wood in the woodshed was dry enough, but even it had a cellary, stale smell. The axe and hatchet were both rusty and dull, but usable, and I quickly made a big fire. To my amazement, for the mid-June evening was hot and still, the boy, a wry smile on his ugly face, almost leaned over the flame, hands and arms spread out, and fairly roasted himself.

"Are you cold?" I inquired.

"I'm allus cold," he replied, hugging the fire closer than ever, till I thought he must scorch. I left him toasting himself while I went in search of water. I discovered the pump, which was in working order and not dry on the valves; but I had a furious struggle to fill the two leaky pails I had found. When I had put water to boil I fetched my hampers from the porch.

I brushed the table and set out my meal—cold fowl, cold ham, white and brown bread, olives, jam, and cake. When the can of soup was hot and the coffee made I drew up two chairs to the table and invited the boy to join me.

"I ain't hungry," he said; "I've had supper."

He was a new sort of boy to me; all the boys I knew were hearty eaters and always ready. I had felt hungry myself, but somehow when I came to eat I had little appetite and hardly relished the food. I soon made an end of my meal, covered the fire, blew out the candles, and returned to the porch, where I dropped into one of the hickory rockers to smoke. The boy followed me silently and seated himself on the porch floor, leaning against a pillar, his feet on the grass outside.

"What do you do," I asked, "when your father is away?"

"Just loaf 'round," he said. "Just fool 'round."

"How far off are your nearest neighbours?" I asked.

"Don't no neighbours never come here," he stated. "Say they're afeared of the ghosts."

I was not at all startled; the place had all those aspects which lead to a house being called haunted. I was struck by his odd matter-of-fact way of speaking—it was as if he had said they were afraid of a cross dog.

"Do you ever see any ghosts around here?" I continued.

"Never see 'em," he answered, as if I had mentioned tramps or partridges. "Never hear 'em. Sort o' feel 'em 'round sometimes."

"Are you afraid of them?" I asked.

"Nope," he declared. "I ain't skeered o' ghosts; I'm skeered o' nightmares. Ever have nightmares?"

"Very seldom," I replied.

"I do," he returned. "Allus have the same nightmare—big sow, big as a steer, trying to eat me up. Wake up so skeered I could run to never.

Nowheres to run to. Go to sleep, and have it again. Wake up worse skeered than ever. Dad says it's buckwheat cakes in summer."

"You must have teased a sow some time," I said.

"Yep," he answered. "Teased a big sow wunst, holding up one of her pigs by the hind leg. Teased her too long. Fell in the pen and got bit up some. Wisht I hadn't a' teased her. Have that nightmare three times a week sometimes. Worse'n being burnt out. Worse'n ghosts. Say, I sorter feel ghosts around now."

He was not trying to frighten me. He was as simply stating an opinion as if he had spoken of bats or mosquitoes. I made no reply, and found myself listening involuntarily. My pipe went out. I did not really want another, but felt disinclined for bed as yet, and was comfortable where I was, while the smell of the ailanthus blossoms was very disagreeable. I filled my pipe again, lit it, and then, as I puffed, somehow dozed off for a moment.

I awoke with a sensation of some light fabric trailed across my face. The boy's position was unchanged.

"Did you do that?" I asked sharply.

"Ain't done nary thing," he rejoined. "What was it?"

"It was like a piece of mosquito-netting brushed over my face."

"That ain't netting," he asserted; "that's a veil. That's one of the ghosts. Some blow on you; some touch you with their long, cold fingers. That one with the veil she drags acrosst your face—well, mostly I think it's ma."

He spoke with the unassailable conviction of the child in *We Are Seven*. I found no words to reply, and rose to go to bed.

"Goodnight," I said.

"Goodnight," he echoed. "I'll sit out here a spell yet." I lit a match, found the candle I had stuck on the corner of the shabby little bureau, and undressed. The bed had a comfortable husk mattress, and I was soon asleep.

I had the sensation of having slept some time when I had a nightmare—the very nightmare the boy had described. A huge sow, big as a dray horse, was reared up with her forelegs over the foot-board of the bed, trying to scramble over to me. She grunted and puffed, and I felt I was the food she craved. I knew in the dream that it was only a dream, and strove to wake up.

Then the gigantic dream-beast floundered over the foot-board, fell across my shins, and I awoke.

I was in darkness as absolute as if I were sealed in a jet vault, yet the shudder of the nightmare instantly subsided, my nerves quieted; I realised where I was, and felt not the least panic. I turned over and was asleep again almost at once. Then I had a real nightmare, not recognisable as a dream, but appallingly real—an unutterable agony of reasonless horror.

There was a Thing in the room; not a sow, nor any other nameable creature, but a Thing. It was as big as an elephant, filled the room to the ceiling, was shaped like a wild boar, seated on its haunches, with its forelegs braced stiffly in front of it. It had a hot, slobbering, red mouth, full of big tusks, and its jaws worked hungrily. It shuffled and hunched itself forward, inch by inch, till its vast forelegs straddled the bed.

The bed crushed up like wet blotting-paper, and I felt the weight of the Thing on my feet, on my legs, on my body, on my chest. It was hungry, and I was what it was hungry for, and it meant to begin on my face. Its dripping mouth was nearer and nearer.

Then the dream-helplessness that made me unable to call or move suddenly gave way, and I yelled and awoke. This time my terror was positive and not to be shaken off.

It was near dawn: I could descry dimly the cracked, dirty window-panes. I got up, lit the stump of my candle and two fresh ones, dressed hastily, strapped my ruined valise, and put it on the porch against the wall near the door. Then I called the boy. I realised quite suddenly that I had not told him my name or asked his.

I shouted. "Hello!" a few times, but won no answer. I had had enough of that house. I was still permeated with the panic of the nightmare. I desisted from shouting, made no search, but with two candles went out to the kitchen. I took a swallow of cold coffee and munched a biscuit as I hustled my belongings into my hampers. Then, leaving a silver dollar on the table, I carried the hampers out on the porch and dumped them by my valise.

It was now light enough to see the walk, and I went out to the road. Already the night-dew had rusted much of the wreck, making it look more hopeless than before. It was, however, entirely undisturbed. There was not so much as a wheel-track or a hoof-print on the road. The tall, white stone, uncertainty about which had caused my disaster, stood like a sentinel opposite where I had upset.

I set out to find that blacksmith shop. Before I had gone far the sun rose clear from the horizon, and was almost at once scorching. As I footed it along I grew very much heated, and it seemed more like ten miles than six before I reached the first house. It was a new frame house, neatly painted and close to the road, with a whitewashed fence along its garden front.

I was about to open the gate when a big black dog with a curly tail bounded out of the bushes. He did not bark but stood inside the gate wagging his tail and regarding me with a friendly eye; yet I hesitated with my hand on the latch and considered. The dog might not be as friendly as he looked, and the sight of him made me realise that except for the boy I had seen no creature about the house where I had spent the night; no dog or cat; not even a toad or bird. While I was ruminating upon this a man came from behind the house.

"Will your dog bite?" I asked.

"Naw," he answered; "he don't bite. Come in."

I told him I had had an accident to my automobile, and asked if he could drive me to the blacksmith shop and back to my wreckage.

"Cert," he said. "Happy to help you. I'll hitch up foreshortly. Wher'd you smash?"

"In front of the grey house about six miles back," I answered.

"That big stone-built house?" he queried.

"The same," I assented.

"Did you go a-past here?" he inquired astonished. "I didn't hear ye."

"No," I said; "I came from the other direction."

"Why," he meditated, "you must'a' smashed about sun-up. Did you come over them mountains in the dark?"

"No," I replied; "I came over them yesterday evening. I smashed up about sunset."

"Sundown!" he exclaimed. "Where in thunder've ye been all night?"

"I slept in the house where I broke down."

"In that big stone-built house in the trees?" he demanded.

"Yes," I agreed.

"Why," he answered excitedly, "that there house is haunted! They say if you have to drive past it after dark, you can't tell which side of the road the big white stone is on."

"I couldn't tell even before sunset," I said.

"There!" he exclaimed. "Look at that, now! And you slep' in that house! Did you sleep, honest?"

"I slept pretty well," I said. "Except for a nightmare, I slept all night."

"Well," he commented, "I wouldn't go in that there house for a

150

farm, nor sleep in it for my salvation. And you slep'! How in thunder did you get in?"

"The boy took me in," I said.

"What sort of boy?" he queried, his eyes fixed on me with a queer, countrified look of absorbed interest.

"A thick-set, freckle-faced boy with a harelip," I said.

"Talk like his mouth was full of mush?" he demanded. "Yes," I said; "bad case of cleft palate."

"Well!" he exclaimed. "I never did believe in ghosts, and I never did half believe that house was haunted, but I know it now. And you slep'!"

"I didn't see any ghosts," I retorted irritably. "You seen a ghost for sure," he rejoined solemnly. "That there harelip boy's been dead six months."

Sorcery Island

(A Tale from *Lukundoo and Other Stories*)

When I regained consciousness I was on my feet, standing erect, near enough to my burning aeroplane to feel the warmth radiated by the crackling flames with which every part of it was ablaze; far enough from it to be, despite the strong breeze, much more aware of the fierce heat of the late forenoon sunrays beating down on me from almost overhead out of the cloudless sky. My shadow, much shorter than I, was sharply outlined before me on the intensely white sand of the beach; which dazzling expanse, but a few paces to my right, ended abruptly in an almost straight line, at a little bank of about eight inches of exposed blackish loam, beyond which was dense tropical vegetation gleaming in the brilliant sunshine.

Not much farther away on my left were great patches, almost heaps, fathoms long, yards wide and one or even two or three feet high, of unwholesome looking grayish white slimy foam, like persistent dirty soap-bubbles, strung along the margin of the sparkling dry sand, between it and the swishes of hissing froth that lashed lazily up from the sluggish breakers in which ended the long, broad-backed, sleepy swells of the endlessly recurrent ocean surges. As there was no cloud in the dark blue firmament, so there was no sail, no funnel-smoke in sight on the deep blue sea. Overhead, against the intense blue sky, whirled uncountable flocks of garishly pink flamingos, some higher, some lower, crossing and recrossing each other, grotesque, flashing, and amazing in their myriads.

To my scrutinizing gaze, as to my first glance, it was manifest that there was no indication of wreckage, breakage or injury to any part of my aeroplane visible through the flames now fast consuming it. No bone of me was broken, no ligament strained. I had not a bruise on me, not a scratch. I did not feel shaken or jarred, my garments were untorn and not even rumpled or mussed. I conjectured at once, what is my settled opinion after long reflection, that I, in my stupor or trance or daze or whatever it was, had made some sort of a landing, had unstrapped myself, had clambered out of the fuselage, had staggered away from it, and had fainted; and that, while I was unconscious, someone had set fire to my aeroplane.

As I stood there on the beach I was flogging my memory to make it bridge over my interval of unconsciousness and I recollected vividly what had preceded my lapse and every detail of my sensations. I had been flying my aeroplane between the wide blue sky, unvaried by any cloud, and the wide blue sea, unbroken by any sign of sail, steamer or island. Then I descried a difference of appearance at one point of the horizon forward and on my right and steered towards it. Soon I made sure of a low island ahead of me.

Up to that instant I had never, in all my life, had anything resembling a delusion or even any thoughts that could be called queer. But, just as I made certain that I was approaching an island, there popped into my head, for no assignable reason, the recollection of the flock of white geese on my grandmother's farm and of how I, when seven years old or so, or maybe only six or perhaps even younger, used to make a pet of an unusually large and most uncommonly docile and friendly white gander, used to fondle him, and, in particular, used to straddle him and fairly ride about on him, he flapping his wings and squawking.

While I was wondering what in the world had made me think of that gander, all of a sudden, as I neared the island and would soon be over it, I had an indubitable delusion. Instead of seeing before me and about me the familiar parts of my aeroplane, I seemed to see nothing but sky and sea and myself astraddle of an enormous white gander, longer than a canoe, and bigger than a dray-horse; I seemed to see his immense, dazzlingly white wings, ten yards or more in spread, rhythmically beating the air on either side of me; I seemed to see, straight out in front of me, his long white neck, the flattened, rounded top of his big head, and the tip of his great yellow bill against the sky; what was more, instead of seeing my knees clad in khaki, my calves swathed in *puttees* and my feet in brown boots.

I seemed to see my knees in blue corduroy knickerbockers, my legs in blue ribbed woollen stockings, against the white feathers of that gigantic dream-gander's back, and my feet sticking out on either side of him encased in low, square-toed shoes of black leather, of the cut one sees in pictures of Continental soldiers or of Benjamin Franklin as a lad, their big silver buckles plain to me against the blueness of the ocean far below me.

After being swallowed up in this astounding hallucination, which I vividly recalled, I remembered nothing until I came to myself, standing on the beach by what was left of my blazing aeroplane.

While struggling to recollect what I could remember and trying to surmise what had happened during my unconsciousness, I had been surveying my surroundings. On one hand I saw only the limitless and unvaried ocean from which came the cool sea-breeze that fanned my left cheek and stirred my hair under the visor of my cap; on the other opened a wide, flat-floored valley, bounded by low hills, the highest, at the head of the valley, not over ninety feet above sea-level, crowned by a huge palatial building of pinkish stone, its two lofty stories topped by an ornate carved balustrade above which no roof showed, so that I inferred that the roof was flat. The hills shutting in my view on either side, lower and lower towards the sea, were rounded and covered with a dense growth of scrubby trees, not quite tall enough to be called forest.

Close to the beach and hills, on each side of the valley, was what looked like a sort of model garden village. That on my right, as I faced inland, was of closely-set one-story cottages, bowered in flowering vines, under a grove of handsome, exotic-looking trees. The other, which I saw beyond the slackening flames above the embers of my aeroplane, was of roomy, broad-verandahed, two-story villas, generously spaced, beneath magnificent young shade-trees, mostly loaded with brilliant flowers.

As I was looking at the valley, the villages, the palace on the hilltop and from one to the other, with now and then a glance overhead at the hosts of wheeling flamingos, I thought I had a second hallucination. I seemed to see, along a path through the riotous greenery, a human figure approaching me, but, when it drew near and I seemed to see it more clearly, I felt that it must be a figment of my imagination.

It was that of a tall, perfectly formed and gracefully moving young man. But, under the scorching rays of that caustic sunshine he was bare-headed and his shock of abundant, wavy and brilliantly yellow golden hair was bobbed off short below his ears like the hair of Italian pageboys in early Florentine and Venetian paintings. His eyes were very bright and a very light blue, his cheeks rosy, his bare neck pinkish. He was clad only in a tight-fitting stockinet garment of green silk, something like the patent underwear shown in advertising pictures. It looked very new, very silky and very green, and as unsuitable as possible for the climate, for its long, clinging sleeves reached to his wrists and the tight legs of it sheathed him to his ankles. His feet were encased in high laced shoes of a very bright, and apparently very soft, yellow leather, with (I was sure he was an hallucination) *every one of the five toes of each foot formed separately.*

Just as I was about to rub my eyes to banish this disconcerting apparition, I recognized him and saw him recognize me.

It was Pembroke!

His face, as he recognised me, did not express pleasure; what mine expressed, besides amazement, I could not conjecture. All in a flash my mind ran over what I knew of him and had heard. We had first met as freshmen and had seen little of each other during our life as classmates. Pembroke, at college, had been noted as the handsomest student of his day; as the youngest student of his class; as surrounding himself with the most luxurious furnishings, the most beautiful and costly pictures, bronzes, porcelains and art objects ever known in the quarters of any student at our college; as very self-indulgent, yet so brilliantly gifted that he stood fifth or sixth in a large class with an unusual proportion of bright students; as daft about languages, music and birds, and, frequently descanting on the wickedness and folly of allowing wild bird-life to be all-but exterminated; as so capricious and erratic that most of his acquaintances thought him odd and his enemies said he was cracked.

I had not seen him since our class dispersed after its graduation and the attendant ceremonies and festivities. I had heard that, besides having a very rich father, he had inherited, on his twenty-first birthday, an income of over four hundred thousand dollars a year and a huge accumulation of ready cash; that he had at once interested himself in the creation of refuges for migratory, rare and picturesque birds; that his fantastic whimsicalities and eccentricities had intensified so as to cause a series of quarrels and a complete estrangement between himself and his father; that he had bought an island somewhere and had absorbed himself in the fostering of wild bird-life and in the companionship of very questionable associates.

He held out his hand and we shook hands.

"You don't seem injured or hurt at all, Denbigh," he said. "How did you manage to get out of that blazing thing alive, let alone without any sign of scratch or scorch?"

"I must have gotten out of it before it caught fire," I replied. "I must have gone daffy or lost my wits as I drew over your island. I have no idea how I landed or why. The whole thing is a blank to me."

"You are lucky," he said, matter-of-factly, "to have landed at all. If your mind wandered, it is a miracle you did not smash on the coral rocks on the other side of the island or on one of the outlying keys, or fall into the ocean and drown.

"However, all's well that ends well. Nothing can be salvaged from the wreckage of your conveyance, that is clear. What you need is a bracer, food, rest, a bath, sleep, fresh clothes and whatever else will soothe you. Come along. I'll do all I can for you."

I followed him past the remnants of my aeroplane, along the beach, to the group of villas. Close to them and to the beach was a sort of park or open garden, with fountains playing and carved marble seats set here and there along concrete walks between beds of flowers, shrubberies, and trim lawns, all canopied by astonishingly vigorous and well-grown ornamental trees.

As we approached the nearest villa I saw a family group on its veranda, obviously parents and children; also I heard someone whistling "Annie Laurie" so exquisitely as to evidence superlative artistry. As we passed the entrance to the villa I was amazed to recognize Radnor, another classmate. But, as he ran down the steps to greet me, I reflected that there was nothing really astonishing in a man as opulent as Pembroke having as dependable a physician as he could engage resident on his island nor anything unnatural in his choosing an acquaintance.

"Denbigh," said Pembroke, "has dropped on us out of the wide blue sky. His aeroplane has been demolished, so he'll sojourn with us a while."

"You don't seem to need me," Radnor commented, conning me. "I see no blood and no indications of any broken bones. Can I patch you up, anywhere?"

"Not a bruise on me, as far as I know," I replied.

"Then," he laughed, "my prescription is two hours abed. Get undressed and horizontal and stay so till you really feel like getting up. And not more than one nip of Pembroke's guest-brandy, either. Get flat with no unnecessary delay and sleep if you can."

As we went on I noted that neither Radnor close by nor Mrs. Radnor on the veranda seemed aware of anything remarkable in Pembroke's attire; they must be habituated by him to it or to similar or even more fantastic raiment.

We appeared to walk the length or width of the village, to the villa farthest from the beach. As we entered I had a glimpse on one hand of a parlour with an ample round centre-table, inviting armchairs and walls lined with bookcases, through whose doors I espied some handsome bindings; on the other hand of a cosy dining-room with a polished table and beyond it a sideboard loaded with silverware and decorated porcelain.

By the newel-post of the broad, easy stair stood a paragon of a Chinese butler.

"Wu," said Pembroke, "Mr. Denbigh is to occupy this house. Show him to his bedroom and call Fong. Mr. Denbigh needs him at once. And tell Fong that Mr. Denbigh has lost all his baggage and needs a change of clothes promptly."

Without any sudden movement or appearance of haste, without a word, he turned and was out of the villa and away before I could speak.

I found myself domiciled in an abode delightfully situated, each outlook a charming picture, and inside admirably designed and lavishly provided with every imaginable comfort and luxury. The servants were all Chinese. One took care of the lawn, flowers and shrubberies, another swept the rooms; there was an unsurpassable Chinese cook, whom I never saw, and something I heard made me infer that he had a helper. I had at my beck a Chinese valet, a Chinese errand-boy and the deferential butler, who managed the house and anticipated my every want.

Except for frequent baths I think I slept most of the ensuing forty-eight hours. What I swallowed I took in bed. My second breakfast on the island I ate in the dainty, exquisitely appointed dining-room. After that I had energy enough to loll in one of the rattan lounging-chairs on the veranda, comfortably clad in neat, cool, well-cut, well-fitting garments chosen from the amazing abundance which Fong had ready for me, how so exactly suitable for me I could not conjecture. I had not been long on the veranda when Radnor strolled by, whistling "The Carnival of Venice." He came up and joined me. Early in our chat he said:

"Probably you will be unable to refrain from asking questions; but I fancy that I shall feel at liberty to answer very few of your queries. Nearly everything I know about this island and about happenings on it I have learned not as a mere man or as a mere dweller here, but as Pembroke's resident physician; it is all confidential. Most of what you learn here you'll have to absorb by observation and inference. And I don't mind telling you that the less you learn the better will Pembroke be pleased, and I likewise."

He did tell me that the villas were tenanted chiefly by the members of Pembroke's private orchestra and band, mostly Hungarians, Bohemians, Poles and Italians, with such other satellites as a sculptor, an architect, an engineer, a machinist, a head carpenter, a tailor and an accountant. The other village was populated entirely by Asiatics, Chinese, Japanese, Hindoos, and others; who performed all the labour of the island.

The next morning, about the same time, as I was similarly lounging on my veranda, Pembroke appeared, in the same bizarre attire, or lack of attire, in which I had previously seen him. He sat with me a half hour or so, asked courteously after my health and comfort and remarked:

"I am glad you feel contented: you'll probably abide here some time."

I said nothing. He glanced away from me, up under the edge of the veranda roof through the overarching boughs. My eyes followed his. I caught glints of pink from far-off flamingos.

"Glorious birds!" Pembroke exclaimed, rapturously. "They nest on several of the low outlying keys, which, with the coral-reefs scattered between them, make it impossible for any craft bigger than a cat-boat to approach this side of the island. They have multiplied amazingly since I began shepherding them. I love them! I glory in them!"

At the word he left me, as abruptly and swiftly as after our first encounter. Thereafter, for some weeks of what I can describe only as luxuriously comfortable and very pleasant captivity, I diverted myself by reading the very well-chosen and varied books of the villa's fairly large library, by getting acquainted with the inhabitants of the other villas, and by roaming about the lower part of the valley. The very evening of our chat Radnor had invited me to dinner, for which Fong fitted me out irreproachably, and at which I found Mrs. Radnor charming and the other guests, Conway the architect, and his wife and sister, very agreeable companions. After that I was a guest at dinner at one or another of the villas each evening, so that I lunched and breakfasted alone at my abode, but never dined there.

Once only I inspected the other village and found its neatness and the apparent contentment of its inhabitants, especially the women and children, very charming. But I seemed to divine that they felt the presence of a European or American as an intrusion: I avoided the village thereafter.

Some of the men of that village tended the trees, shrubberies, vines and gardens of the valley, and kept it a paradise, luxuriant with every sort of fruit and vegetable which could be grown in that soil and climate.

I saw nothing more of Pembroke and found that I could not approach his palace on the hill-top, for there was an extremely adequate steel fence of tall L-irons, sharp at the top, across the valley and down to the beach beyond either village, which barrier was patrolled by heavily-built, muscular guards, seemingly Scotch and not visibly armed, who respectfully intimated that no one passed any of its gates, or along either beach, without Mr. Pembroke's express permit. Very seldom did I so much as catch a glimpse of Pembroke on the terraces of his palace, but I did see on them knots, even bevies, of women whose outlines, even at that distance, suggested that they were young and personable, certainly that they were gayly clad in bright-coloured silks. Near or with them I saw no man, excepting Asiatic servitors, and Pembroke himself, who powerfully suggested an oriental despot among his *sultanas*.

By the inadvertent utterance of someone, I forget whom, I learned that the guards had a cantonment or barrack on the other side of the island.

I enjoyed rambling about the valley, as far as I was permitted, for both the variety and the beauty of its products were amazing.

Still more amazing to me was the number of ever-flowing ornamental fountains. The Bahamas are proverbially hampered by scanty water supply. But here I found, apparently, a superabundance of clear, pure, drinkable water. There was a fountain near the village, where a seated bronze figure, seemingly of some Asiatic god or saint unknown to me, held in each hand a great serpent grasped by its throat, and from the open mouth of each snake poured a spout of water into the basin before the statue.

There were other fountains, each with a figure or group of figures of bronze, in the formal garden by the village of villas. And beyond it, set against the scooped-out flank of one of the range of enclosing hills, was a huge concrete edifice of basins and outstanding groups of statuary and statues and groups in niches, more or less reminiscent of the Fountain of Trevi. I was dumbfounded at the flow of water from this extravagantly ornate and overloaded structure. There were many jets squirting so as to cross each other in the air, even to interlace, as it were. But midway of the whole construction, behind the middle basin, was a sort of grotto with, centrally, an open entrance like a low doorway or manhole, on either side of which were two larger apertures like low latticed windows, filled in with elaborately patterned bronze gratings, through the lower part of which flowed two streams of water as copious as brooks, which cascaded into the main basin.

Beyond this *rococo* fountain was a plot of ground enclosed by a hedge, serving as garden for a tiny cottage of one low story. In it lived an old Welsh woman, spoken of by the inhabitants of the village as "Mother Bevan." She always wore the hideous Welsh national costume and hobbled about leaning on a stout Malacca walking-stick with an ivory cross-head tipped with gold bosses. She cared for and delighted in a numerous flock of snow-white geese which somehow seemed thriving in this, one would suppose, for them far too tropical climate. Among them was a large and very handsome gander, which reminded me of my childhood's pet. The flock spent much of its time swimming and splashing in the basins of the enormous grotto-fountain.

When I asked Radnor about the abundance of water and its apparent waste, he said:

"No mystery there nor any secrets. Pembroke could spend anything he pleased on wildcat artesian drilling and had the perverse luck to strike a generous flow just as his drillers were about to tell him that no humanly constructed implements could drill any deeper. It's no spouting well, though, and a less opulent proprietor than Pembroke could not afford to pump it as he does. The power-station is on the other side of the island, near the harbour. It uses oil fuel of some kind. There is never any stint of water for any use and the surplus is made to do ornamental duty, as you see."

I was interested in the old Welsh woman and in her tiny cottage, so oddly discordant with the Italianate concrete fountain near it and the spacious villas not far off. Except the Asiatics of the village and the barrier-guards I had found affable every dweller on the island; most of them sociable. I accosted the grotesque old crone, as she leaned over her gate and discovered in her the unexpected peculiarity that all her answers were in rhyming lines, rather cleverly versified, which she uttered, indeed, slowly, in a measured voice, but without the slightest symptom of hesitation. Her demeanour was distinctly forbidding and her words by no means conciliatory. I recall only one of her doggerels, which ended our first interview:

160

"Man fallen out of the sky." "God never intended us to fly." "It's impious to ascend so high." "'Twas wicked of you ever to try." "No lover of reprobates am I."

Except for this queer old creature I encountered no unfriendly word or look from any of my neighbours. I enjoyed the dinners to which I was invited and liked my fellow-guests at them; indeed I disliked no one with whom I talked; but, on the other hand, I was attracted to no one, and, while I felt entirely welcome wherever I was invited and altogether at my ease, and pleased to be invited again later, at no household did I feel free to drop in at odd times for casual chat. I found many congenial fellow-diners, but no one increasingly congenial, no one who impressed me as likely to be glad to have me call uninvited.

Therefore, as I always loved the open air, as I somehow felt lonely on my own veranda and nowhere intimate enough to lounge on any other, I took to spending many hours of the mornings, before the heat of the midday grew intense, out in the shade of the little park, to which I was attracted by many of its charming features, especially by the pink masses of flowering bougainvillea here and there through it. I always carried a book, sometimes I read, oftener I merely gazed about at the enchanting *vistas*, overhead at the uncountable flamingos, or between the trees out to seaward at the dazzling white heaps of billowy cumulus clouds, like titanic snow-clad mountains, bulging and growing on the towering thunder-heads forming against the vivid blue sky out over the ocean.

I think it was on my second morning in the park that I caught a glimpse of Mother Bevan crossing a path at some distance. Later I caught other glimpses of her crossing other paths. Each morning I caught similar glimpses of her. On the fifth or sixth morning I suddenly became conscious of an inward impression that she was, again and again, making the circuit of the park, circling about me as it were, like a witch weaving a spell about an intended victim.

Next morning I affected an absorption in my book and kept an alert, and I was certain, an imperceptible watch in all directions. I made sure that Mother Bevan was indeed perambulating the outer portions of the park, stumping along, leaning heavily on her cross-headed cane, and I made sure also that after she had completed one circuit about me she kept on her way and completed another and another.

I was curious, puzzled, incensed; derisive of myself for so much as entertaining the idea of any one, in 1921, attempting witchcraft;

concerned for fear that my wits were addled; and, while unable to rid myself of the notion, yet completely sceptical of any effect on me and unconscious of any.

But, the very next day, seated on the same marble bench, by the same fountain, among the same pink masses of bougainvillea in flower, I was aware not only of Mother Bevan circumambulating the outskirts of the park, but also of her numerous flock of noisy, self-important, white geese waddling about, not far from me, and indubitably walking round and round me in ever lessening circles, the big gander always nearest me.

At first I felt incredulous, then silly, then resentful. And, as the gander, now and then honking, circled about me for the fifth or sixth time, I became conscious of an inner impulse, of an all but overmastering inner impulse, to seek out Pembroke and to tell him that I was willing to do anything he wanted me to do; to pledge myself to do anything he wanted me to do.

I took alarm. I felt, shamefacedly, but vividly, that I was being made the subject of some sort of attempted necromancy. All of a sudden I found myself aflame with resentment, with hatred of that gander. I leapt to my feet, I hurled my book at him, I ran after him, I threw at him my bamboo walking stick, barely missing him. I retrieved the walking-stick and pursued the retreating bird, and threw the cane at him a second time, almost hitting him.

The geese half waddled, half flew towards the beetling atrocities of the ornate rococo hill-side fountain; I followed, still infuriated. There was, along the walk before the fountain, an edging of lumps of coral rock defining the border of the flower-beds. I picked up an armful of the smaller pieces of angular coral rock, chased the geese into the big main basin of the fountain and pelted that gander with jagged chunks of coral. He fled through the central manhole into the grotto and hissed at me through one of the gratings, behind which he was safe from my missiles.

Suddenly overwhelmed by a revulsion of shame and a tendency to laugh at myself, I beat a retreat to my veranda. There I sat, pondering my situation and my experiences.

I recalled that, at every dinner to which I had been invited, there had been, practically, but two subjects of conversation: the boredom of life on tropical islands in general and on Pembroke island in particular; and the worth, the fine qualities, the charm, the perfection of Pembroke himself.

I watched a chance to find Radnor at leisure, to waylay him, to entice him to my veranda. When the atmosphere of our talk seemed auspicious, I said:

"See here, Radnor! I know you said you meant to elude any queries I might put to you, but there is one question you'll have to answer, somehow. Why are all these people here?"

"That is easy," Radnor laughed. "I have no objection to answering that question. They are here because Pembroke wants them here."

"I didn't phrase my question well," I said, "but you know what I mean. No one I have met really likes being here. Why do they stay?"

"That's easy, too," Radnor smiled. "Almost anyone will stay almost anywhere if lodged comfortably and paid enough. Pembroke provides his hirelings with an overplus of luxuries and is more than liberal in payment."

"That does not explain what intrigues me," I pursued. "I haven't yet hit on the right words to express my idea. But you really understand me, I think, though you pretend you don't. All the inhabitants of these villas are not merely uneasy, they are consciously homesick, acutely homesick, homesick to a degree which no luxurious surroundings, no prospective savings could alleviate. They are pining for home. What keeps them here?"

"Put it down," said Radnor, weightily, "to the unescapable charm of the island. That keeps them here."

"Did you say witchery or enchantment?" I queried, meaningly.

Radnor was emphatic.

"I said charm!" he uttered. "Let it go at that."

"I am not in the least inclined," I retorted, "to let it go at that. I take it that this is no joke, certainly not anything to be dismissed by a clever play on words. I insist on knowing what makes all these people stay here. They all declare, at every opportunity, that they are dying of *ennui*, that the climate is uncongenial, that they long for temperate skies, for northern vegetation, for frosty nights. What keeps them here?"

"I tell you," said Radnor, "that, like me, most human beings will do anything, anything lawful and reasonable, if paid high enough."

"The rest aren't like you," I asserted. "You and Mrs. Radnor impress me as free agents, doing, for a consideration, what you have been asked to do, and what you both, after weighing the pros and cons, have agreed to do. All the others, Europeans, Americans and Asiatics, except Mother Bevan, appear like beings hypnotized and moving in a trance, mere living automatons, without any will of their own, actuated solely by Pembroke's will; as much so as if they were mechanical dolls. They impress me as being mesmerized or bewitched. I seriously vow that I believe they have been subjected to some supernatural or magical influence. They are as totally dominated by Pembroke as if they were the ends of his fingers."

Radnor looked startled. "It will do no good," I cried, "to contradict me or to deny it."

"I believe you," Radnor said, as if thinking out loud. He went on: "You are right. Except Mother Bevan and me and Lucille every human being on this island is completely under Pembroke's influence, gained largely through the help of Mother Bevan."

"Why not you and your wife?" I queried.

"Lucille, because of me," he replied. "Pembroke found out, by trying Melville here and Kennard, that, after being put under his influence, while retaining surgical skill, a physician loses all ability to diagnose and prescribe. He had to ship Kennard and Melville back home, and pension them till their faculties recovered their tone."

I looked him straight in the eyes. He forestalled my impending outburst by saying: "As far as I can discern, Pembroke's influence over his retainers does them no harm, physical or mental. Kennard and Melville have as large incomes and as many patients and are as successful and prosperous, as popular and prominent among their fellow-physicians as if they had never sojourned here. Except in their enthusiasm for and admiration of Pembroke every human being on this island appears to me as healthy as if not under any influence of any kind."

"Even so," I blurted out, "you ought not to abet any such deviltries."

"I don't admit," said Radnor, hotly, "that any deviltries exist on this island or that there is any approach to deviltry in what you have partly divined. Also I abet nothing, as I ought, but, as I also ought, I conceive that I am under obligations not to thwart Pembroke in any way. I am the island's resident physician and his personal physician; I am here to treat injuries, cure maladies, relieve pain, and do all I can to keep healthy every dweller on this island. I live up to my conception of my duty. Don't attempt to preach at me.

"I am impatient," I said, "at my enforced stay here, and revolted at the idea of succumbing to Pembroke's influence."

Radnor laughed.

"You are," he said, "the only human being who has reached the island, since Pembroke bought it, uninvited. You'll get away by and by. And you are most unlikely to be affected by anything he or Mother Bevan may have in their power to do. Neither Kennard nor Melville ever suspected anything, or grew suspicious. You alone have half seen through the situation here. You are Mother Bevan's most refractory subject, so far. Have no fear."

He went off, whistling Strauss' Blue Danube Waltz.

I had frequent and recurrent fears, but I dissembled them. I think, among all the terrors which haunted me during the remainder of my sojourn on the island, that I came nearest to panic and horror within an hour after Radnor had left me. Hardly was he gone when Pembroke, arrayed precisely as before and reminding me of a stage-frog in a goblin pantomime, sauntered up and seated himself by me.

I sweated with tremors of dismay, I was ready to despair, when I found myself, however I tried, unable to utter a word to him concerning the gander, Mother Bevan, or my suspicions; unable even to allude to the subject in any way, although he asked me bluntly:

"Have you anything to complain of?"

"Only that I am here," I replied.

"I had nothing to do with your coming here," he retorted. 'You came uninvited, of your own accord, or by accident. I trust I have been a courteous host, but I have not tried to pretend that you are welcome. I am endeavoring to arrange that your departure shall not entail upon me any inconvenience or any danger of disadvantageous consequences. Believe me, I am doing all I can to expedite your return to your normal haunts. Meantime you'll have to be patient."

I was most impatient and very nearly frantic at finding myself, no matter how I struggled inwardly, totally unable so much as to refer or allude to what lay heaviest on my mind.

We exchanged vaguely generalized sentences for awhile and he left as abruptly as before, left me quivering with consternation, dreading that my inability to broach the subject on which I was eager to beard him was a premonition of my total enthrallment to Pembroke's influence.

As the days passed I became habituated to stoning that uncanny gander, chasing him into the basin of the fountain and having him hiss at me from behind one of the gratings; I became indifferent to the glimpses I caught of Mother Bevan hovering in the middle distance. I had a good appetite for my meals: in fact, the food set before me at my abode would have awakened the most finicky dyspeptic to zest and relish, even to voracity; while the dinners to which I was invited were delectable.

But from night to night I slept less and less, until I was near insomnia. And, from day to day, I found it more and more difficult to absorb myself in reading, to keep my mind on what I read; even to read at all.

Again I waylaid Radnor. I described to him my progressively worsening discomfort and distress.

"I am now," I said, "or soon shall be, not merely in need of your help, but beyond any help from you or anybody. If you don't do something for me I'll go crazy, I'll do something desperate, I'll commit suicide."

"I have been pondering," he said, "how to help you, and I have almost bit upon a method. Your condition does not yet justify my giving you anything to make you sleep. As yet I do not want to give you any sort of drug, not even the simplest sedative. Honestly try to get to sleep tonight. Before tomorrow I think I'll hit upon an entirely suitable prescription salutary for you and yet avoiding any appearance any hint, of my antagonising Pembroke."

I did try to sleep that night, but I was still wide awake long after midnight. So tossing and turning on my comfortable bed, I heard outside in the moonless darkness someone whistling a tune. As the sound came nearer I made sure it was Radnor. Also I recognized the tune.

It was that of "The Ballad of Nell Flaherty's Drake."

The tune brought to my mind the words of the song's refrain:

The dear little fellow,
His legs were so yellow,
He could fly like a swallow and swim like a hake!
Bad luck to the tober,
The haythen cashlober,
The monsther thot murthered Nell Flaherty's drake"

All of a sudden I conceived that this was Radnor's method of intimating to me by indirection what he did not dare to utter to me in plain words. thought I knew what he meant as well as if it had been put into the plainest words. I rolled over, was asleep in three breaths, and slept till Fong ventured to waken me.

After breakfast I went upstairs again and rummaged about in the closet where Fong had deposited what I had worn when I came under his care. I found there everything I remembered to have had about me. My automatic was well oiled and in good working order and its clip of cartridges was full. My belt, with the extra clips of cartridges, was as it had been when I last put it on. I put it on, over my feather-weight hot-weather habiliments; I strapped on my automatic; I strolled out, intent on somehow coming within speaking distance of Pembroke.

Chance, or some unconscious whim, guided my footsteps to the beach and, in spite of the rapidly intensifying heat of the sun rays, along it to the remaining fragments of my wreck, barely visible under a great accumulation of beach foam, left by the breakers, hurled shorewards during the thunder storm which had raged while I slept.

Not far beyond those vestiges of what had been an aeroplane, approaching me along the beach, I encountered Pembroke.

I found I had now no difficulty in speaking out my mind.

"Pembroke," I said, "I'm outdone with confinement on this island of yours. I'm irritated past endurance. If you don't promptly speed me on my way elsewhere the tension inside me is going to get too much for me. Something inside me is going to snap and I'll do something desperate, something you'll regret."

He looked me straight in the eyes, handsome in his fantastic toggery; calm and cool, to all appearance.

"Are you, by any chance," he drawled, "threatening to shoot me?"

"I haven't made any threats," I retorted, hotly, "and I have no intentions of shooting you or anybody. I realize that this island of yours is part of the British Empire and that in no part of it are homicides or murderous assaults condoned or left unpunished. But, since you use the word 'threat,' I am ready to make a threat. If you don't soon set me free of my present captivity, if you don't soon put me in the way of getting home, I'll not shoot you or any human being, but I will shoot that devilish gander; and, I promise you, if I shoot at him I'll hit him and if I hit him I'll kill him. I fancy those are plain words and I conjecture that you understand me fully, with all the implications of what I say."

Pembroke's expression of face appeared to me to indicate not only amazement and surprise, but the emotions of a man at a loss and momentarily helpless in the face of wholly unexpected circumstances.

"You come with me!" he snapped.

I followed him along the beach to the village, and, as we went, wondered to see him apparently comfortable in his tight-fitting suit and bare headed beneath the fierce radiance of the merciless sun rays, while I rejoiced in my flimsy garments and at being sheltered under the very adequate Panama I had chosen from the headgear Fong had offered me.

We passed the end of the steel picket fence, the two beach guards saluting Pembroke, and, I thought, suppressing a tendency to grin at me. Just around the point was a wide aviation field with a long row of hangars opposite the beach. I marvelled, for I had caught no glimpse of any avion in the air over or about the island.

A half dozen Asiatics, apparently Annamites, rose as we approached and stood respectfully, eyes on Pembroke. He uttered some sort of order in a tongue unknown to me and two of them set wide open the doors of one of the hangars. In it, to my amazement, I saw a Visconti biplane, one of the fastest and most powerful single-seaters ever built.

"What do you think of that?" Pembroke queried.

"I am astonished," I answered. "I was certain that no specimen of this type of machine had ever been on this side of the Atlantic."

"This is the first and only Visconti to be set up on this side of the ocean," he replied. "The point is; could you fly it?"

"I think I could," I said, "and I am sure I could try."

"Try then," Pembroke snapped. "I make you a present of it. The sooner you're off and away the better I'll be pleased."

He spoke at some length, apparently in the same unknown tongue, and strode off towards his palace.

I spent that day and most of the next going over that Visconti biplane, with the deft, quick assistance of the docile Annamites. If there was anything about it defective, untrustworthy or out of order I could not find it. On the third morning (I had dined at Radnor's both evenings), equipped admirably by Fong, who instantly provided me with whatever I asked for, I rose in that Visconti biplane, and, contrary to my fears, reached Miami in safety. But I was so overstrained by anxiety that it required six weeks in a sanatorium to make me myself again. During those, apparently, endless hours in the air I had been expecting every moment that something cunningly arranged beforehand and undiscoverable to my scrutiny in my inspections and reinspections, was going to go wrong with my conveyance and instantaneously annihilate me. The strain all but finished me. However, all's well that ends well.

The Whirlpool Gorge

(*Sunset Magazine* August 1910)

Fowcha Nipsilath had been a thief, pilfering from families of his own tribe and incorrigibly thievish among them. Slow of wrath are they against their own, indulgent and easy-going. His roguery had been beyond forgiveness. The marks of trial and conviction he bore for life upon both hands, where the hatchet of justice had lopped off three digits of each and left him only to itch for others' belongings.

He had a habit of twiddling his little fingers against his thumbs and watching them as he sat silent, his narrow eyes staring down his thin nose, his gaze meditative but not regretful, rather sly and cheerful.

So he sat just now, a slender, brown figure, naked save for waist-cloth and turban, his sallow face expressionless and secretive.

"Why do you tell me this?" Uttarity asked.

"Solitary," he said, "I possess not the force to extricate the effigy."

Fowcha Nipsilath had learned English at the mission school long before he lost his fingers. He not only spoke English but read it, had read everything he could lay his hands on in English, even the school dictionary, which had been one of his prizes for scholarship at the mission. Not once nor twice, but scores of times he had read it through. Mentally translating from his vernacular—for however much he read and talked English he had never come to think in it—he chose the mouth-filling words by preference.

"Dalkeith is stronger than I am," Uttarity demurred.

"Mister Dalkeith," Fowcha Nipsilath spoke slowly, "abides ineffably autocratical. Co-partner of my secret, he would impropriate the entirety, relegate me to the subordinancy of cat's-pawship and arrogate himself proprietor of the total bonanza. Upon your even-handedness I can repose."

Uttarity said nothing.

His thought was:

"Yes, you designing scoundrel, you know Dalkeith too keen and wary to be fooled at any step of the proceedings. You think you can use me and pit me out of the way at your convenience."

There was just enough decency in Uttarity for him to feel for a moment that the only safe, as the only honest, course was to wait for Dalkeith and tell him the whole story. His avarice and self-conceit got the better of him as the Oriental had calculated. He felt cocksure of being able to outwit Fowcha Nipsilath. His dominant idea was to land the prize and get away before Dalkeith returned. He did not even formulate a plan of evasion, but trusted to the vague possibilities he saw in his mind's eye and to his cleverness at a pinch.

He questioned Fowcha Nipsilath as to distances and directions.

"But that will take us over the border," he protested.

Fowcha Nipsilath nodded.

Uttarity became serious, even gloomy. The temptation was severe, but the risk was daunting. He did not hesitate long over Dalkeith's wrath at his breaking their parole or over troubles with the authorities on the way down. He staked everything on being off before Dalkeith returned and on reaching the coast ahead of any rumour of his perjury that might trickle down country. But the actual danger was enough to scare a bolder man than he. His greed triumphed. Prudence he ignored as well as decency.

Thereupon he catechised Fowcha Nipsilath rigorously. Presently a light broke on his intelligence.

"Why," he exclaimed, "that will take us mighty close to the Miang-Miangs."

"Their confines," Fowcha Nipsilath stated placidly, "border upon the verge of the precipices eastwardly."

"We might as well cut our own throats now," said Uttarity, "as venture that near to them."

"I have returned alive," Fowcha Nipsilath reminded him.

"But," Uttarity demurred, "we may have to wait more than one day for our chance. They are certain to see us."

"Into the chasm," Fowcha Nipsilath explained, "no Miang-Miang ever ventures for fear of the *nats* and *phees* with which their tribal superstitions people its abysses."

Uttarity conceived that this might be true. His innate recklessness reinforced his cupidity. The fascination of excitement lured him on where greed of gain beckoned. To match his wits against those of the treacherous native seemed a prospect, an exhilarating game. The narrow margin by which he might win added to its enticement. He made sure of one fact only that they would return in a single march without sleeping. True, he must take Fowcha Nipsilath's word for this, but he flattered himself that he had put the questions too indirectly for their purpose to be conjectured. He might sleep fearlessly until the loot was in their possession.

Methodically he prepared for the expedition. He must omit nothing available which they might need, must carry not one ounce of superfluous weight.

Fowcha Nipsilath was wiry and enduring. Burdened to the utmost, he accepted the load without a murmur. Uttarity himself carried little besides his rifle and cartridge-belt, with his revolver in its holster.

His Celtic blood tempted him to venture unarmed. But they might encounter a tiger, and were likely to meet more than one leopard, while his fighting gorge rose at the thought of being captured without resistance. Also, the arms would strengthen his superiority on the march home. He would have been more comfortable and freer for threading the jungle with Fowcha Nipsilath as gun-bearer. But it would intensify the difficulties of his diplomacy to assume all the weapons only after the treasure as in hand.

Fowcha Nipsilath in the lead, they set out. The last sight Uttarity had of the camp was when he glanced back through the big trees and closing undergrowth and saw the Chinese cook still staring after them.

In one respect Fowcha Nipsilath was entirely to be trusted. Between Tawang and Lung-Chau, from Tasso southward, there was no better woodsman. His sense of direction was perfect, his deviations and doublings genuine savings of effort and ultimate economies in both time and distance. Uttarity followed without question or comment, but every sense he could spare from immediate obstacles was bent on his compass or on landmarks and bearings.

They rested in the hottest part of the day and pushed on until dusk. The last two hours were a heart-breaking climb through dense underwood up broken, rocky gullies. Fowcha Nipsilath did not halt till it was too dark to see to travel. They fed hastily, and Uttarity, at least, slept at once. His last sensation as he drowsed was hearing the short, shrill yelp of a barking muntjac deer, some distance off in the scrub.

The next morning, they reached the crest in a short half-hour and came out into a vast rock-amphitheatre full of the roar of water. At first Uttarity caught mere glimpses of sunlit cliff-tops against the intense, clear sky, but after much sliding and zigzagging they emerged upon a treeless shelf from which the entire enormous bowl was visible. Behind and above them the great, red cliff down which they had scrambled towered a full two thousand feet to ragged pinnacles, whose rampart extended east and west and curved round to the northward more than three-quarters of a full circle. Facing them from due north a huge wedge of grim, black rock jutted out, like the prow of an ocean liner. Uttarity felt the resemblance and mentally calculated that an ocean liner, with a prow like that, would be more than eleven miles long. To the left of it, through a widening forested valley, opening from the tree-clad gorge, the river wound snakily away north-westward.

Far as he could see, Uttarity could not conjecture the curve where it must turn south again. Its shining surface was visible in diminishing streak beyond streak on the broadening *vista*. To the right of the prodigious black chisel-edge, between it and the beetling pink precipice, was the menacing and forbidding throat of the narrow chasm down which the river snarled and fought its way. Below them, a thousand feet below them, the whirlpool churned and growled. The moan of baffled and groping currents found a guttural undertone to the boom of the falls and rapids and the bellowing of ten thousand impounded echoes.

From the warm sunlight they dived into wet woods, at first streaming and suffocating, later dank and almost chill. Finally, Fowcha Nipsilath led Uttarity out upon a ten-foot apology for a beach barely above the water level, half sandbank, half mud-flat. Gnarled and crooked teak trees, misbegotten in that soggy soil, hung over it; flecks of brown foam and blistery patches of viscous, muddy bubbles streaked it near the water's edge; little waves lapped lazily along it and their silty lips sucked at it as the sleepy current sulked past. That current, the outermost movement of the mighty vortex, crawled deceptively slow. Yet its unhurried motion heaved and throbbed with sudden uneven swirls too strong for any swimmer.

Out of the mud-bank points of rock projected, and a sort of ring of them, sharp as dogs' fangs, stuck out of the water at its right-hand end forming a sheltered pool. Some thirty to forty feet beyond them a rock stood clear of the water. It was jagged with worn cusps, like the shark-tooth projections around the pool and through the sand-bar. Beyond it the surface of the whirlpool eddied and hurtled, leaping up in spray, boiling in circles that spread and broke, contracted and vanished.

The torrent issuing from the chasm was tilted sideways as it rushed into the pool spurting out highest at the foot of the titanic, black wedge of jutting cliff. The effect was as Fowcha Nipsilath had described—all floating things were shot into the vortex and there whirled round and round forever. The gush of the current hurled them back again and again. Nothing on the surface of the whirlpool ever went down river.

There were many things on the surface: entire trees with splintered, stripped branches; logs bare of bark and frayed against the rocks; bits of wood of all sizes from mere chips to bulky, squared balks; even a raft of mountain pine, still holding together.

"I do not see it," Uttarity said.

"Contemplate unremittingly," Fowcha Nipsilath responded. "Espial will eventually ensue."

Uttarity's gaze swept the surface of the whirlpool and conned every salient object, every difference of colour, every glint of light.

Far to their left it seemed he could descry two long, cleanish stretches of shingle.

"Why did we not go there?" he inquired.

"No flotsam trends thither its destination," said Fowcha Nipsilath, pointing to the bits of wood stranded at their feet, split sticks, like firewood, three logs about a foot thick and some ten feet long, and a peeled sapling trunk slender and thin, not four inches thick at the butt, and all of thirty feet in length.

Uttarity took this and sounded the little pool between the tusky rocks. The butt of the sapling, totally waterlogged, went straight down as if it had been an iron pole. It knocked against smooth sides of stone slabs, but touched no bottom. He tried beyond the rocks where he could reach the outer water. The pole sank as easily as before, then suddenly its buoyancy asserted itself, it pushed gently upward against Uttarity's thrust. The resistance grew stronger, grew rapidly stronger, and though he clung to it with both hands it tore itself from his grasp, leapt lance-like into the air for more than half its length and toppled over on the mud-flat.

Doggedly Uttarity tried it again. Again it touched no bottom. But this time, as he probed with it, it pulled against him, almost dragged him down, was wrenched from his clutch and vanished into the depths. Uttarity watched for its reappearance and watched long in vain.

So watching he became fascinated. He climbed between the teak trees, found a point of view on a rock and sat and watched. After a while he came down to the mud-flat and watched from there. Between the two he alternated as his whim took him. No art was long the same. Tumultuous upbursts of white spray and boiling foam abated to tossing waves, to jostling wavelets, to slapping ripples and quieted in oily rings that swirled slowly, then in accelerating whirls. Gathering speed, the new vortex would hasten its rotation till the shreds of bark and bits of wood began to be sucked under. Faster and faster the gyration spun until it dragged down into its maw beams, logs, even perhaps one of the great trees entire.

Then the smooth funnel of foamless water would deepen and spin awhile, sometimes a long while, sometimes only a moment, until its centre slowly or suddenly lifted, the rotation slowed and stopped, the surface smoothed to an oily flat, heaved, creased into ropy curves, pulsed, leapt, and shot up into a spout of hissing foam and silvery spray.

From watching the alterations of the surface Uttarity passed to following the fates of its playthings. The big trees now sailed languidly, now levered sideways, now rolled over lumberingly, their branches sweeping in slow arcs like stiff arms of uneasy sleepers. He saw one drawn bodily down, its rigid boughs like palsied fingers beckoning vainly for help. Many a log and beam he saw disappear. Most spun dizzily, upended and plunged almost vertically down, but the smaller sometimes went under suddenly flatwise into the wider and stronger indrafts. The larger logs occasionally rode out a vortex and sailed on; the big trees generally, the raft, though twice it seemed about to yield, never wholly was submerged.

It remained mostly near the centre of the pool. The trees circled about it, it and the dozen of them changing places and weaving in and out among each other. When one or another of them came round to the mouth of the chasm it accelerated its speed, was caught in the down-rush, whirled over and over against the cross-current and hurled back into the pool. Beams and logs so drawn always went under, but always reappeared, though sometimes after a long interval.

From noting their vanishings Uttarity passed to watching for their reappearances. Some he watched for in vain. They might be held under for hours. The sapling pole with which he had sounded he did not see again for half the day.

So intent, he became aware that many captive derelicts never came wholly into view. He grew absorbed in watching for half-guessed tantalising hints of what milled about below the surface. Out of the space where a vortex had dissipated or in the calmer intervals a half-seen momentary difference of colour told of some sudden shape that failed to reach the air. Roundish things shouldered cumbrously into the sunlight, wallowed like a porpoise on the flank of an ocean billow, and sank again. Watching for these and greedily eyeing them, Uttarity, after more than an hour in a cramped position of intenseness, caught a glint of blue, as it were of *lapia lazuli*, awash in the greenish blackness of a foamless quake and reel of currents.

As he thought he saw it Fowcha Nipsilath yelled shrilly.

Uttarity saw him pointing where the glimpse of blue had vanished. "You beheld?" Fowcha Nipsilath cried. "You credit my veracity?"

Uttarity turned again to the pool.

The sun was visibly lowering and the shadow of the black cliff lay broad on the slope behind them, when, out of an oily swell, emerged what he had hoped to see. The hair of the head was gilded, the face a ruddy, brownish pink. The eyes, as Fowcha Nipsilath had narrated, white crystals of great size, flashing with rainbow tints. The teeth, two rows of them, were manifestly pearls, and the three-strand necklace around the neck was all of great rubies, flat-cut but very large.

Evidently it was an escape from some flood-ravaged temple of some nameless cult in the vast mysterious region known to Uttarity, and indeed to all Europeans, merely as "upriver".

The painted robe was blue, a brilliant enamel-surfaced blue, and in the two hands was clasped to its wooden bosom the figure of a horse, painted blood-red.

The face of the idol was not that of a *Buddha*, nor yet of any Hindu god. Its nose was high and aquiline, its cheekbones broad.

The force of the up current shot it out into the air, nearly to its robed knees. Its blue length toppled with a sort of reluctant dignity and it lay awash. So, barely visible, they kept it in view as it swam slowly round to below the chasm, was caught in the down-rush and swept under in the twirl of the crosscurrents.

Fowcha Nipsilath slept heavily all the night, or certainly as much of it as Uttarity was wakeful, which was nearly all.

The dawn showed the idol in full view, not ten feet beyond the rock opposite their beach. It floated slowly round and round the pool. On its third journey it came between them and the rock. Uttarity had no time nor any materials for making harpoons. The sheaf of native spears which Fowcha Nipsilath had selected from Dalkeith's collection served as substitutes. The most of that day they spent in watching for chances, hurling spears at the image and trying to haul it ashore. One spear they lost because Fowcha Nipsilath's knots were insecure, two the sudden malice of a down-current dragged under and wrenched away. Three times they struck the idol, once a glancing blow that did not hold. Another strike was a disappointment because the spear pulled out. The other, made about noon, was a clean throw from a good aim, Fowcha Nipsilath being in perfect form.

A hundred times that day Uttarity had marvelled at the strength of his mere thumb grasp and at his accurate balance. This time the spear bit deeply, the rope tightened, the prize voyaged easily toward them, almost into reach of the pole-hook Fowcha Nipsilath had made from Uttarity's sounding-sapling when it returned to their foothold. At that crisis the suck of the water checked its course, pulled the rope through their hands and out of sight, the only submergence the statue offered all that day. When it came again to the surface the spear and rope had vanished.

The next day at dawn, waking suddenly from the long, deep slumber of exhaustion, Uttarity saw the god not ten feet from the bank. The pole-hook failed to catch it. Fowcha Nipsilath staggered to his feet, drunk with drowsiness and his throw missed entirely; his second throw, for he had time to throw again, just nudged the idol on its way.

The next time it came near, after pirouetting about all over the midst of the pool, was afternoon and it floated right to their hands, feet first. Uttarity caught the splintered toes and guided it between the two nearest rock-points into the little pool.

With a shout of triumph, he straightened up, his face to the sun, his arms flung wide and high, his fingers spread, yelling his exultation to the sapphire sky.

That instant Fowcha Nipsilath had him round the waist with the momentum of a calculated rush.

Uttarity was a born wrestler. Totally at a disadvantage as he was, he did not instantly lose his footing and he did instantly clutch his assailant.

Along the oozy flay they struggled, neither ever down, each often almost in the air. At its lower end they pitched off into the water, Fowcha Nipsilath further from the shore. As they fell an upward seethe swept them out.

Uttarity was a strong swimmer. He reached the rock with his last strength, after a battle that lasted some minutes and seemed to him to have lasted hours.

When he looked about for Fowcha Nipsilath he saw him on the raft, far away across the commotion of waters. The raft sailed round, farther from the centre of the whirlpool than Uttarity had yet seen it, and passed within a few yards of the rock. The baffled, cunning and impotent hate on Fowcha Nipsilath's face, Uttarity hardly noticed; Fowcha Nipsilath seemed as distant as Lake Titicaca, as far off as Achilles.

The idol was still in the little pool, teetering slowly on the tiny ripples. Somehow it did not seem as remote as Fowcha Nipsilath. He watched it intently as if he might ever hope to touch it again. It bobbed up and down less slowly. Eyeing it and the tusks of rock about it, he saw that the water was rising. Conning the marge of the mud-flat, he made sure of it. Within an hour he had made the mortification of seeing the idol, after much bumping against the rocks, edge its way on the slow current out between the two widest-set rock-points, and drift away to the outer confusion. He followed it with his eyes and it went under.

Then he fell to watching Fowcha Nipsilath, where the raft now staggered and tossed in the centre of the turmoil.

So watching he began to feel as if his eyes were fixed scrutinizingly on himself from behind.

He turned.

Some twenty sallow-skinned, nearly naked men stood or squatted on the mud-flat, silently regarding him. For an instant he thought them Miang-Miangs. Then a difference, many differences, the peculiar make of their clubs, spears, and bows, a greater breadth of shoulder, a stockier build, a more striking show of brawn, an intenser ferocity of expression revealed to him the probable reason why the Miang-Miangs kept out of the gorge. All wore necklaces of teeth, some of several strands. One, the tallest and heaviest, wore the horse-jaw head-ornament of a hill *Tsobwa* and carried a gun, a muzzle-loading smooth-bore of an antique pattern recognisable even at that distance.

Presently one of the youngest rose and poised his spear. Uttarity did not pray; he was not a praying man. His one thought was not to disgrace his fellow Europeans in the eyes of the savages. He found it took all his self-control to conserve an appropriately defiant expression and attitude.

The lance would have undoubtedly have finished Uttarity had not the spearman's aim been spoiled by the clubbed gun-butt of the *Tsobwa*, which thudded on his skull the fraction of a second before he loosed his weapon.

There followed a great deal of jabbering. Uttarity needed no interpreter to convey to him that, in the *Tsobwa's* opinion, a quick death was too good for him. The chief apparently explained to his men that the thought of the intruder dying by inches on his hopeless perch would be a relishable pleasure for days to come.

This, or whatever else was their subject, satisfactorily settled and the rash youth properly subordinated to the *Tsobwa's* authority, the Singphoos or whatever they might be, examined his revolver, belt, cartridges, and rifle, ate everything eatable, made various derisive gestures towards Fowcha Nipsilath and Uttarity and departed in single file, the Tsobwa in the lead. Of the adventurer's outfit they left not a vestige.

A hazy murkiness crept over the sun, the sky clouded over, the twilight was unusually long.

Night came with but one or two stars, then the impenetrable blackness of windless, lowering darkness settled over Uttarity.

His Celtic optimism was no worthless asset. He fitted himself into the depressions of the rock, composed himself and slept off and on; the thunderous roar aft about him soothed him and he was not yet weak and his hunger was bearable.

Sometime in the night it began to rain, a chilling and depressing drizzle. Through the greyness of this dawn light filtered. The drizzle increased and became a downpour. Uttarity, even in his discomfort, remarked its astonishing effect in beating down the spasm of the eddies. Fowcha Nipsilath on his raft circulated evenly, passing Uttarity's rock within fifty feet at each round. Not far from the raft, slower in its wider orbit, was a sixty-foot squared beam of newly hewn timber. The idol was nowhere in view.

When the light became full day the rain stopped suddenly and within a few moments blue sky showed overhead. Uttarity turned his face to the mud-bank and ignored what went on beyond him. Within a half an hour after he had adopted this posture of contempt, the statue, as little battered as when he first saw it, slid out of the depths a mere arm's-length from his rock. He grasped it easily. For a time, the water about the crag was as still as a horse pond. Between him and the shore no current showed. For a breath Uttarity was tempted to swim for it. Then he towed the idol to the left extremity of his rock, aimed it toward the widest opening between the protecting rocks about the little pool, took a firm hold of its feet and pushed. Released from his grasp, with the impetus of his thrust, it forged majestically across the interval and its head jolted on the rock-points; passed between them and there the statue rested, caught firmly by the neck.

Uttarity regretted that he had not ventured to swim. But scarcely was the idol fast in the fork of the two rocks when a vicious uprush of water bodied fiercely past. He was glad of his foothold.

Then he sat down and wondered and wondered why he had sent that idol ashore. He perceived that he had some crazy idea of afterwards reaching the shore himself. He might have hauled it up on his rock and dug the gems out of it. Might? He had no knife or tool of any kind and the rocks had scant room for himself. He comforted his chagrin by reflecting that he might not have been able to pull the statue clear of the water: he had no idea how heavy it might be.

He felt his arms and legs. He was not weak yet, nor did he feel faint. The night had not stiffened his muscles, chilly as he had been in his coatless condition. He was still hopeful. He sat and thought.

So sitting, he saw the big new-hewn balk pass between him and the mud-bank. After a long interval it came round again, farther from him. Its end butted into the innermost rock-point about the little pool. It did not bound back, but nosed joltily against the rocks. Its other end swung out from shore.

Uttarity became tense with expectancy.

Slowly the beam swung outward, rolling a trifle in the gentle current. Slowly it neared his rock. It was, yes, it was, longer than the interval of water.

It jammed solidly against his crag. Uttarity slid down, clinging cautiously to the cusps of the rock, reaching eagerly for a grasp on the balk. His feet were in the water, his legs.

A clutch, a vice-like grip of a talon of a thumb and a claw of a finger, gripped his right ankle.

Instinctively and with his best possible judgement, Uttarity threw all his strength into gripping the rock. He kicked, too, kicked with all his strength. Kicking under water the force of his strength was muffled.

He realised, too, that Fowcha Nipsilath, with Asiatic malignity, had put by all hope of the jewels, of escape, even of life. The concentrated venom of his malevolence was focused on killing Uttarity, he was not merely ready to sacrifice his life for that end, but had already resigned any expectation of survival; he meant to die with him and was not trying for anything beyond.

He dared not lessen either hand-hold, dared not try to look round, could only struggle blindly. Once he did catch a glimpse of Fowcha Nipsilath's black shock head, barely out of the water. The splendid barbarian was throwing himself low, risking the swish of the next eddy, to drag Uttarity down.

Face down on the crag Uttarity clung weakening.

A rifle shot rang out.

The clutch on his ankle loosened.

He collapsed on the rock.

When he opened his eyes a crimson commotion in the water by the crag was the first sight he beheld.

Then he saw that the beam was still bridging the gulf.

Dalkeith's reassuring voice sounded full and strong above the thunder of the waters

"Stop where you are till you are rested."

The balk chafed and champed against the crag and Uttarity made as if to start across it.

"Take your time," Dalkeith yelled, and then, "can you catch it?"

Uttarity signalled an affirmation.

It was a half-pint flask that he caught, full of brandy.

Next Dalkeith deftly threw him a small size tin of their precious Berlin meat-biscuits and last a cake of Swiss chocolate.

While he ate, Uttarity watched Dalkeith and Vudjva Laiwaporn drag the statue up on the bank.

Unhurriedly Dalkeith gouged out the inlaid gems.

Uttarity saw him pile them in two heaps on the flat of his spread coat, an eye in each pile, wrap each heap up separately and put both packages inside his shirt.

Only after that did Dalkeith call to him to catch a rope.

Vudjva Laiwaporn threw it accurately. With this tied about his body he essayed the crossing, the horizontal climb along the bobbing balk. Once the undertow sucked greedily at his legs. Otherwise he might have been in a vat.

Dalkeith and Vudjva Laiwaporn, grinning sociably, leaned over and drew him to shore. While he rested they stood and watched him. When he stood up and stretched himself, Dalkeith put his hand inside his shirt, drew out one of the packets and handed it to him. Uttarity pocketed it without a word.

"And now," Dalkeith said, "we'd best be off."

"How did you find me?" Uttarity asked.

"Lung Chung is no fool," Dalkeith answered, "and Vudjva Laiwaporn can follow any trail. Getting here was easy. The point is, getting back. If we can steal a march on the gentry who left these tracks we have half a chance of dodging the Miang-Miangs."

The Ghoula

(*Narrative Lyrics*)

Because my mate did not return,
And since my little ones must eat,
I sallied forth alone to learn,
Myself, to win my children meat.

Whatever man upon my way,
Hunter or villager robust,
I met alone and marked for prey,
My smile would lull his first distrust;

My beauty touched his heart at length,
And in my form he could not guess
A hint of that titanic strength
Which even female ghouls possess.

At dusk, at sundawn, or at noon
I lured him from ravine or road
To where the ruins are. And soon
We feasted in our dim abode.

Men s flesh is best. If none came near,
I caught some bullock, sheep, or goat,
Or, waiting at a pool the deer,
Leapt like a panther at its throat.

Three days, and to my younglings cries
I brought but pilfered scraps of food.
I saw the famine in their eyes
And hunted in no gentle mood.

Next day above the desert plain

Our Persian sky arched blue and clear.
From the lookout where I had lain
I saw a figure drawing near;

An Englishman who strayed alone,
Careless of nomads, ghouls, or spells,
To beat the waste of sand and stone
For hares or bustards or gazelles.

He spoke our homely Persian tongue;
I found him nowise hard to fool;
And yet, he was so tall and young,
I wished that he had been a ghoul.

My hunting had engrossed my mind,
Since of my mate I was bereft.
Now, staring through the months behind,
I felt how lonely I was left.

My starved mouth watered at the view
Of pink cheeks, tender, plump, and nigh,
And yet it seemed a pity too;
He looked too comely far to die.

As by my side he idly paced,
Before the ruins we had neared,
Between two boulders on the waste,
Some distance off, a doe appeared.

He raised his rifle and took aim.
Then, as I watched to see her spring,
He stopped and said: "It seems a shame
"To kill the pretty, dainty thing."

It startled me to find this youth,
So heedless, hale, and lithe of limb,
Felt for his game the self-same ruth
Which I had felt at sight of him.

She stood and stared before she ran.
"What good to us that she should roam,"
I said: "Best shoot her while you can,
We have no meat at all at home."

His bullet missed. The creature fled.

He flushed, surprised, chagrined, and vexed.
Then, smiling cheerily, he said:
"I may do better with the next.

"That lean doe was not worth regret,
You may get meat some other way."
I answered, with my purpose set,
"Indeed, I rather think I may."

How cool the shadowed archway smelt,
Pleasant and softly lit inside!
His arm went round my waist. I felt
My young would not have long to bide.

They cowered huddling in our lair.
Their pangs I knew they would endure
In silence, rather than to scare
Quarry of which I was not sure.

Inebriated with my charms,
He held me closely, unaware
That he was helpless in my arms
As is a rabbit in a snare.

Time after time our lips had met;
His curly head to mine I drew,
A kiss upon his throat I set
And bit the windpipe through and through.

Firm flesh to eat, clean blood to drink,
Fitted to make my dear ones thrive,
And yet, since then, I often think
He was so handsome when alive.

Who knows, but for my darlings need
I might have softened, let him go?
I find it in my heart indeed
To wish that he had shot the doe.

The Song of the Sirens

(A.k.a. *The Man Who Had Seen Them*)
(A Tale from *The Song of the Sirens and Other Stories*)

I first caught sight of him as he sat on the wharf. He was seated on a rather large seaman's chest, painted green and very much battered. He wore gray, his shirt was navy-blue flannel, his necktie a flaring red bandana handkerchief knotted loosely under the ill-fitting lop-sided collar, his hat was soft, gray felt and he held it in his hands on his knees. His hair was fine, straight and lightish, his eyes china-blue, his nose straight, his skin tanned. His features were those of an intelligent face, but there was in it no expression of intelligence, in fact no expression at all. It was this absence of expression that caught my eye. His face was blank, not with the blankness of vacuity, but with the insensibility of abstraction. He sat there amid the voluble negro loafers, the hurrying stevedores, the shouting wharf-hands, the clattering tackles, the creaking shears and all the hurry and bustle of unloading or loading four vessels, as imperturbable as a bronze statue of Buddha in meditation.

His gaze was fixed unvaryingly straight before him and he seemed to notice and observe more distant objects; the larger panorama of moving craft in the harbour, the fussy haste of the scuttling tugboats tugging nothing, the sullen reluctance of the urged scows, the outgoing and incoming *pungies* and schooners, the interwoven pattern they all formed together, the break in it now and again from the dignified passage of a towed bark or ship or from the stately progress of a big steamer.

Of all this he seemed aware, but of what went on about him he seemed not only unaware but unconscious, with an impassivity not as if intentionally aloof nor absorbingly preoccupied but as if utterly unconscious or totally insensible to it all. During my long, fidgety wait that first morning I watched him at intervals a good part of the time.

Once a pimply, bloated boarding-master, patrolling the wharf, stopped full in front of him, caught his eye and exchanged a few words with him, otherwise no one seemed to notice him, and he scarcely moved, bare-headed all the while in the June sunlight. When I was at last notified that the *Medorus* would not sail that day, went over her side, and left the pier, I saw him sitting as when I first caught sight of him.

Next morning I found him in almost the same spot, in precisely the same attitude, and with the same demeanour. He might have been there all night.

Soon after I reached the *Medorus* the second morning the bloated boarding-master came on board with that rarity, a native American seaman. I was sitting on the cabin-deck by the saloon-skylight, Griswold on one side of me and Mr. Collins on the other. Captain Benson, puffy, pasty-faced and shifty-eyed, was sitting on the booby-hatch, whistling in an exasperatingly monotonous, tuneless and meaningless fashion. As soon as the Yankee came up the companion-ladder he halted, turned to the boarding master who was following him and blurted out.

"What! Beast Benson! Me ship with Beast Benson!" And back he went down the ladder and off up the pier.

Benson said never a word, but recommenced his whistling. It was part of his undignified shiftlessness that he aired his shame on deck. Almost any captain, fool or knave or both, would have kept his cabin or sat by his saloon table. Benson advertised his helplessness to crew, loafers and passersby alike.

The boarding master walked up to Mr. Collins and said:

"You see. Sir. I can't do anything. You've lucky enough to be only two hands short for a crew and luckier to have gotten a second mate to sign. Wilson's the best I can do for first mate. He's willing and he's the only man I can get. Not another boarding-master will so much as try for you."

Mr. Collins kept his irritating set smile, his mean little eyes peering out of his narrow face, his stubby scrubbing-brush pepper-and-salt moustache bristling against his nose. He made no reply to the boarding-master but turned to Griswold.

You're a doctor, aren't you?" he queried.

'Not yet,' Griswold replied. Well," said Mr. Collins impatiently, "you know pretty much what doctors know?"

"Pretty much, I trust," Griswold answered cheerfully.

"Can you tell whether a man is deaf or not?" Mr, Collins pursued.

I fancy I could," Griswold declared, gaily. 'Would you mind testing that man over there for me?" Mr. Collins jerked his thumb toward the impassive figure on the seaman's chest.

Griswold stared.

"He looks deaf enough from here," he asserted.

"Try him nearer," Mr. Collins insisted.

Griswold swung off the cabin deck, lounged over to the companion ladder, went down it leisurely and sauntered toward the seated mariner. Griswold had a taking way with him, a jaunty manner, an agreeable smile, a charming demeanour and plenty of self-confidence. He usually got on immediately with strangers. So now you could see him win at once the confidence of the man. He looked up at him with a sentient and interested personal glance. They talked some little time and then Griswold sauntered back. He did not speak but seated himself by me as before, lit a fresh cigarette and smoked reflectively.

Is he deaf?" Mr. Collins inquired.

"Deaf is no word for it," Griswold declared, an adder is nothing to him. I'll bet he has neither tympanum, *malleus*, *incus* nor stapes in either ear, and that both *cochleas* are totally ossified; that the middle ear is annihilated and the inner ear obliterated on both sides of his head. His hearing is not defective, it is abolished, non-existent. I never saw or heard of a man who impressed me as being so totally deaf."

"What did I tell you?" broke in Captain Benson from the booby-hatch.

"Benson, shut up," said Mr. Collins. Benson took it without any change of expression or attitude.

"You seemed to talk to him," Mr. Collins said to Griswold.

"He can read lips cleverly," Griswold replied. "Only once did I have to repeat anything."

"Did you ask him if he was deaf?" Mr. Collins inquired,

"I did," said Griswold, "and he told the truth instanter."

"Impressed you as truthful, did he?" Mr. Collins queried.

"Notably," Griswold said. "There is a gentlemanly something about him. He is the kind of man you respect from the first, and truthful as possible."

"You hear that, Benson?" Mr. Collins asked.

"What's truthfulness of a pitch-dark night in a gale of wind!" Benson snorted, "The man's stone deaf."

Mr. Collins flared up.

"You may take your choice of three ways," he said, "the *Medorus*

186

tows out at noon. If you can find a first-mate to suit you by then, or if you take Wilson as first-mate, you take her out. If not, I'll find another master for her and you can find another ship."

Benson lumbered off the booby-hatch and disappeared down the cabin companion-way. The cabin-boy came up whistling, went briskly over the side, and scampered some little distance up the pier to where three boarding-masters stood chatting. One of them came back with him, three or four half sober sailors tagging after him. These he left by the deaf man's sea-chest. Its owner came aboard with him and together they went down into the cabin.

"Look here, Mr. Collins," I said, "I've half a mind to back out of this and stay ashore?"

"Why?" he queried, his little gray eyes like slits in his face.

"I hear this captain called Beast Benson, I see he has difficulty in getting a crew and before me you force him to take a deaf mate. An unwilling crew, a defective officer and an unpopular captain seem to me to make a risky combination."

"All combinations are risky at sea, as far as that goes," said Mr. Collins easily. "Most crews are unwilling and few captains popular. Benson is not half a bad captain. He always has bother getting a crew because he is economical of food with them. But you'll find good eating in the cabin. He has never had any trouble with a crew, once at sea. He is cautious, takes better care of his sails, rigging and tackle than any man I know, is a natural genius at seamanship, humouring his ship, coaxing the wind and all that. And he is a precious sharp hand to sell flour and buy coffee, I can tell you. You'll be safe with him. I should feel perfectly safe with him. I'm sorry I can't go, I can tell you."

"But the deaf mate," I persisted.

"He has good discharges," said Mr. Collins, "and is well spoken of. He's all right."

At that moment the boarding-master came out of the cabin and went over the side. Two of the sailors picked up the first-mate's chest and it was soon aboard. The two men went down into the cabin to sign articles. As they went down and as they came up I had a good look at them. One was a Mecklenburger, a lout of a hulking boy, with an ugly face made uglier by loathsome swellings under his chin. The other was a big, stout Irishman, his curly hair tousled, his fat face flushed, his eyes wild and rolling with the after-effects of a shore debauch. His eyes were notable, one bright enamel-blue, the other skinned-over with an opaque, white, film. He lurched against the companion-hatch, as he came up, and half-rolled, half-stumbled forward He was still three-quarters drunk.

The *Medorus* towed out at noon. Mr. Collins and Griswold stayed aboard till the tug cast loose, about dusk. After that we worked down the bay under our own sail. Even in the bay I was seasick and for some days I took little interest in anything. I had made some attempt to eat, but beyond calling the first-mate Mr. Wilson and the second mate Mr. Olsen, my brief stays at table had profited me little. I had brought a steamer-chair with me and lolled in it most of the daylight, too limp to notice much of anything.

I couldn't help noticing Captain Benson's undignified behaviour. A merchant captain, beyond taking the sun each morning and noon and being waked at midnight by the mate just off watch to hear his report, plotting his course on his chart and keeping his log, concerns himself not at all with the management of his ship, except when he takes the wheel at the critical moment of tacking, or of box-hauling, if the wind changes suddenly, or when a dangerous storm makes it incumbent upon him to take charge continually.

Otherwise he leaves all routine matters to the mate on watch. Benson transgressed sea-etiquette continually in this respect. He was forever nosing about and interfering with one or the other mate in respect to matters too small for a self-respecting captain's notice. His mates' contempt for him was plain enough, but was discreetly veiled behind silent lips, expressionless faces and far-off eyes. The men were more open and exchanged sneering glances. The captain would sit on the edge of the cabin-deck, his feet dangling over the poop-deck, and continually nag the steersman, keeping it up for hours.

"Keep her up to the wind," he would say, "keep that royal lifting."

"Aye, aye, Sir," would come from the man at the wheel.

Next moment the captain would call out:

"Let her go off, you damn fool. You'll have her aback!"

"Let her go off. Sir," the victim would reply.

Presently again Benson would snarl:

"Where are you lettin' her go to? Keep her up to the wind."

"Keep her up to the wind. Sir," would come the reply and so on in maddening reiteration.

A day or two after we cleared the capes the big one-eyed Irishman had the wheel. His name, I found afterwards, was Terence Burke and he was from Five Rivers, Canada. He had been a mariner all his life; knew most of the seas and ports of the world. He was especially proud of having been in the United States Navy and of his Civil War record. He had been one of the seamen on the *Congress* or the *Cumberland*, I forget which, and graphic were his descriptions of his sensations while the *Merrimac's* shells were tearing through the helpless ship, the men lying flat in rows on the farther side of the decks, and the six-foot live-oak splinters, deadly as the bits of shell themselves, flying murderously about as each shell burst; of how they took to their boats after dark, and reached the shore, expecting to be captured every moment; of how they saw the *Ericsson's* lights (Burke always called the *Monitor* the *Ericsson*) coming in from the sea, and took heart, Burke was justly proud that he had been one of the men detailed, as biggest and strongest, to work the *Ericsson's* guns, and that he had helped fight her big turret guns in her famous first battle.

All this about Burke I did not learn till many days later. But it was plain to be seen, even by a sea-sick land-lubber, that he was an able seaman, seasoned, competent and self-respecting. All that was manifest all over him as he stood at the wheel. Likewise it was plain that he had brought liquor aboard with him, for he was still half-drunk, and quarrelsome drunk. Even I could see that in his attitude, in his florid face, in his boiled eye. But Captain Benson did not see it when presently he came on deck and seated himself on the edge of the cabin-deck. He cocked his eye up the main-mast and presently growled.

"Let her go off."

Burke shifted the wheel a quarter of a spoke, his jaws clenched, his lips tight shut.

Benson chewed on his big quid and kept his eye aloft. Again he growled:

"Keep her up to the wind."

Burke shifted the wheel back a quarter of a spoke, again without any word.

"I'll learn ye sea-manners," Benson snarled, "I'll learn ye to repeat after me what I say. Do ye hear me?"

"Aye, aye, Sor," Burke replied, smartly enough.

Shortly Benson came at him again.

"Let her go off, you damn fool."

"Let her go off, you damn fool, Sor," Burke sang out in a rasping Celtic roar which carried to the jib boom.

It was Olsen's watch and the big Norseman was standing by the weather-rigging, his hand on one of the main shrouds. He grinned broadly, full in Captain Benson's face and then looked away to windward. Burke was clutching the spokes as if he were ready to tear them out of the wheel. He looked fighting mad all over. Captain Benson looked aft at him, looked forward, looked aloft, and then rose and went below without a word. Henceforward he worried the steersman no more, unless it were Dutch Charlie, the big loutish boy with the ulcerated chin, or Pomeranian Emil, a timid Baltic waif. Burke and the other full-grown men he let alone.

Next day Burke looked drunker and more belligerent than ever. I noted it, even in my half-daze of flabby nauseated weakness, which subdued me so totally that not even a beautiful and novel spectacle revived me. It was just before noon. The captain and the first-mate had come on deck with their sextants to determine our latitude. The day was fine with a gentle steady breeze, a clear sky and unclouded sunlight, over all the white-capped blue waters. Smoke sighted a little before turned out to be that of a British man-of-war. Just as the captain told the man at the wheel to make it eight-bells, the man-of-war crossed our bows, all white paint and gilding, her ensign spread, flags everywhere, her band playing and her crew manning the yards.

The cabin-boy said it was an English bank-holiday, and that she was bound for Bermuda. I was too flaccid to ask further or to care. I made no attempt to go below for the noon meal, I lay at length in my chair. While the captain and mates were at their dinner I could hear loud voices from the forecastle, or perhaps round the galley door. Presently the first-mate came on deck. He walked to starboard, which was to windward, and stood staring after the far off smoke of the vanished man-of-war. He was a tall, clean-built square-shouldered man, English in every detail of movement, attitude and demeanour.

He interested me, for in spite of his expressionless face he looked far too intelligent for his calling. I was watching him when I was aware of Burke puffing and snorting aft along the main deck. He puffed and snorted up the port companion-ladder to the poop-deck. His face was redder than ever and his eyes redder than his face. He carried a pan of scouse or biscuit-hash or some such mess. He approached the first-mate from behind and hailed him.

"Luke at thot, Sor," he said, "uz thot fit fude fur min?"

The mate, unaware of his presence, did not move or speak.

"Luke at thot Oi say," Burke roared, "uz thot fit to fade min on?"

The mate remained immobile.

Burke gave a sort of snarling howl, hurled at the mate the pannikin, which hit him on the back of the head, its contents going all over his neck and down his collar. As he threw it Burke leaped at the officer. He whirled round before he was seized and met the attack with a short, right-hand jab on Burke's jaw. There was not enough swing in the blow to down the sailor. He clutched both lapels of the mate's open pea-jacket and pulled him forward. The force the mate had put into the blow, and the impetus it had imparted to Burke, besides his sideways wrench, took the mate half off his feet. He got in a second jab, this time with his left hand, but again too short to be effective.

Both men lurched toward the booby-hatch and the inside breast-pockets of the mate's jolted jacket cascaded a shower of letters upon the deck, which blew hither and thither to port. My chair was on the cabin-deck just above the port companion-ladder. The booky man's instinct to save written paper shook me out of my lethargy. In an instant I was out of my chair, down the ladder and picking up the scattered envelopes. Not one, I think, went overboard. I saved three by the port rail and a half a dozen more further inboard.

As I scrambled about from one to the other I glanced again and again at the men struggling on the other side of the booby-hatch. The mate had not lost his footing. His short-arm jabs had pushed Burke back till he lost hold of the pea-jacket. The Irishman gathered himself for a rush, the mate squared off, in perfect form, met the rush with a left-hand upper cut on the seaman's chin, calculated his swing and planted a terribly accurate right-hand drive full in Burke's face. He went backward over the starboard companion-ladder down into the main deck.

Paying no more attention to him the mate turned to pick up his letters. He found several on the deck against the booby-hatch, and one by the break of the cabin. Then he looked about for more. I stepped unsteadily toward him and handed him those I had gathered up. In gathering them it had been impossible for me to help noting the address, and the stamps and the postmarks, which on several were English, on two or three French, on two Italian, on one German, on one Egyptian and on one Australian. The address the same on all, was:

Geoffrey Cecil, Esq.
C.O. Alexander Brown & Son
Baltimore, Maryland,
U. S. A.

Instinctively I turned the packet face down as I handed it to him. He took it gracefully and in his totally toneless voice said:

"Thank you very much."

As he said the words Captain Benson appeared in the cabin companion-way, his revolver in his hands. The mate in the act of stowing with his left hand the letters in his inner breast-pocket, pointed his extended index finger at the pistol.

"Put that thing away!" he commanded.

The voice was as toneless as before, but far otherwise than the blurred British evenness of his acknowledgment to me, these words rang hard and sharp. Benson took the rebuke as if he had been the mate and the other his captain, turned and shuffled fumblingly back down the companion-way. As he passed the pantry door the cabin-boy whipped out of it and popped up the companion-way to see, and the big Norse mate emerged deliberately behind him.

By this time the fat negro steward and most of the crew had come aft and gathered about the prostrate Burke.

The first-mate cleared the scouse from his neck and collar, took some tarred marline from an outside pocket of his pea-jacket, and in a leisurely way went down into the waist. He had the men turn Burke over and tie his hands behind him and his ankles together. Then he had buckets of sea-water dashed over him. Burke soon regained consciousness.

"Carry him forward and put him in his bunk," the mate commanded. "When he says he will behave cut him loose."

Captain Benson had come on deck and was standing by the booby-hatch.

"That man ought to be put in irons," he said as the mate turned.

The mate's eyes were on his face as he said it.

"He needs no irons," he retorted crisply. "*Why make a mountain out of a molehill.*"

I had been hoping that I was getting used to the sea, for I was only passively uncomfortable and mildly wretched. But sometime that night it came on to blow fresh and I waked acutely sea-sick and suffering violently from horrible surging qualms in every joint. I clambered out of my bunk, struggled into some clothes and crawled across the cabin and up the after companion-way to the wheel-deck. There I collapsed at full length into four inches of warm rain water against the lee-rail. At first the baffling breeze was comforting after the stuffy cabin, smelling of stale coffee, damp sea-biscuit, prunes, oilskins and what not. But I was soon too cold, for I was vestless and coatless, and before long my teeth were chattering and I had a general chill to add to my misery.

It was the first-mate's watch and coming aft on his eternal round he found me there. He at once went below and brought me not only vest and jacket but my mackintosh also. I was wet to the skin all over, but the mackintosh was gratefully warm. Forgetting that he could not hear I thanked him inarticulately, and relapsed into my shifting pond, where I slipped into oblivion, my head on the outer timber, the tearing dawn-wind across my face.

Sometime before noon I was again in my chair, as on the day before, and it was again the first-mate's watch. Again I saw Burke come aft. He was not puffing and snorting this time, but very silent. His florid face was a sort of gray-brown. His head was tied up and the bandage tilted sideways over his bad eye. He came up to port companion ladder half way from the waist of the poop-deck. There he stood holding on to the top of the rail, looking very humble and abashed. It was some time before the first-mate noticed him or deigned to notice him. In that interval Burke said a score of times:

"Mr. Willson, Sor."

Each time he realised that he was ignored he waited meekly for a chance to try again. Finally the mate saw him speak and asked:

"What is it, Burke?"

Burke began to pour out a torrent of speech.

"Come here," said the mate.

When Burke was close to him he said:

"Speak slow."

"Shure Sor," he said, "ye wudn't go fur to call ut mutiny whan a man's droonk an' makes a fule of himsilf?"

"Perhaps not," the mate replied, his steady eyes on Burke's face.

"Ye, wudn't, I know," Burke went on confidently. "Ye see, Sor, Oi was half droonk whan Oi cum aboord. An' Oi had licker tu, more fule Oi. Mr. Olsen, he cum forrard in the dog-watch af ther ye'd taat me me place, and he routed ut out an' hove ut overboord. Oi'm sobered now Sor, with the facer ye giv me an' the cowld wather an' the slape, Oi'm sobered, an' Oi'm sobered for the voyage, Sor. Ye'll foind me quoite and rispectful Sor. Oi was droonk Sor, an' the scouse misloiked me, an' Oi made a fule ov mesilf. Ye'll foind me quoite and rispectful, Sor, indade ye wull. Ye wudn't go for to log me for mutiny for makin' a fule ov mesilf Sor, wud ye now, Sor?"

"No, Burke," said the mate. "I shall not log you. Go forward."

Burke went.

Some days later I was forward on the forecastle deck, ensconced against the big canvas-covered anchor, leaning over the side and watching the foam about the cut-water and the up spurted coveys of sudden flying fish, darting out of the waves, at the edge of the bark's shadows and veering erratically in their unpredictable flights. Burke, barefoot and chewing a large quid, was going about with a tar-bucket, swabbing mats and other such devices. He approached me.

"Mr. Ferris, Sor," he said, "ye wudn't have a bit of washin' a man cud du for ye? Ye'll be strange loike aboord ship, an' this yer foorst voyge, an' ye the only passenger, an' this a sailin' ship, tu. Ye'll be thinkin' ov a hotel, Mr. Ferris, Sor. An' there's no wan to du washin' here fur ye, Sor. The naygur cuke is no manner ov use tu ye. Ye giv me anny bits ye want washed an Oi'll wash 'em nate fur ye. A man-o-war's man knows a dale ov washin' an' ye'll pay me wut ye loike. Thin I'll not be set ashore in Rio wudout a cint, Sor."

"You'll have your wages," I hazarded.

"Not with Beast Benson," he replied, "little duh ye know Beast Benson. Oi know um. Wut didn't go into me advances ull go into the shlop-chest. Oi may have a millrace or maybe tu at Rio, divil a cint moor."

This was the beginning of many chats with Burke. He told me of Five Rivers, of his life on men-of-war, of his participation in the battle between the *Merrimac* and the *Ericsson*, as he called the *Monitor*, of unholy adventures in a hundred ports, of countless officers he had served under.

"An' niver wan uz foine a gintlemin uz Mr. Willson," he would wind up. "Niver wan ov them all. Shure, he's no Willson. He ships as John Willson, Liverpool. Now all the seas knows John Willson ov Liverpool. There's thousands ov him. He's afloat all over the wurruld. He's always the same, short and curly-headed, black-haired and dark-faced, ivery John Willson is loike ivery other wan. Ivery Liverpool Portugee uz John Willson whin he cooms to soign articles. But Mr. Willson's no Dago, no Liverpool man at all. He's a gintlemin, British all over, an' a midlander at thot an' no seaman be naature at all.

"But he's the gintlemin. Ye saa him down me. He's the foine gin-tlemin. Not a midshipman or liftenant did iver Oi see a foiner gin-tlemin than him, and how sinsible he uz. Haff the officers Oi've served tmder wuz lunies, sinsible on this or thot, but half luny on most things and luny all over on this or thot. But Juke at Mr. Willson. Sinsible all over he uz, sinsible all thru. Luke at the discipline he huz. An' no wunder. Luke at huz oi! He cudn't du a mane thing av he wanted tu, he cudn't tell a loi av he throid, thrust me Soi, Oi know, the min knows. It's loike byes at skule wid a tacher, or min in the army wid their officers. You can't fule thim, they knows, an' wull they knows a man whin they say wan. Oi'd thrust Mr. Willson annywhere and annyhow. So wud anny other sailor man or anny man. Deef he uz, deef as an anchor fouled on a rock bottom. But he hears wid huz eyes, wid huz fingers, wid the hull skin av him. He's all sinse an' trewth an' koindness."

Not any other of the sailors besides Burke did I find sociable or communicative or capable, apparently, of intelligent intercourse. Of the captain I saw and heard enough, and more than enough, at meal times. He deserved his nickname and I avoided him with detestation.

The second mate, a big Norwegian named Olaf Olsen, was a kindly soul, but dull and uncommunicative. He had a companionable eye, but felt neither any need of converse nor any promptings toward it. Speech he never volunteered, questions he answered monosyllabically. One Sunday indeed he so far unbent as to ask if he might borrow one of my books. I told him I doubted if any would please him. He looked them over disappointedly.

"Have you any books of Doomuses?" he queried.

"Doomus?" I repeated after him reflectively.

'You're a scholar, aren't you?" he demanded.

"I aim to be," I said.

"How do you pronounce, D-u-m-a-s?" he inquired.

"I am no Frenchman," I told him, "but Dumas is pretty close to it."

"That's what I said," he shouted, "and they all laughed at me and said 'Doomus, ye damn fool.' Have you any of his books?"

"No," I confessed and he ceased to regard me as worth borrowing from.

Not so Mr. Wilson. Before we ran into the doldrums I had found my sea-legs and exhausted the diversion of learning the name of every bit of rope, metal and wood on the bark, and also the amusement of climbing the rigging, I settled down to luxurious days of reading. The first Sunday afterwards Mr. Wilson asked for a book. I took him into my cabin and showed him my stock, one-volume poets mostly, the *Iliad*, the *Odyssey*, the *Greek Anthology*, Dante, Carducci, Goethe, Heine, Shakespeare, Milton, Shelley, Keats, Tennyson, Browning, Swinburne and Rosetti, and a dozen volumes of Hugo's lyrics. I watched him as he conned them over and thought I saw his eyes light over the Greek volumes, thought I saw in them both desire and resignation. He took

Milton to begin on and afterwards borrowed my English books in series. I believe he read each entire, certainly he read much during his watches below.

At first I felt equal only to the English myself. But after we entered the glorious south-east trades, I read first *Faust*, then the *Divina Commedia*, then the *Iliad*, and, as our voyage neared its end gave myself up to the delights of the *Odyssey*.

Meanwhile I had come to feel very well acquainted with the deaf mate. Generally we had spent part of each fair Sunday in conversation. He read lips so instantly and accurately that if I faced the sun and he was close to me we talked almost as easily as if he had heard perfectly. The conversations were all of his making. He was not a man whom one would question, whereas he questioned me freely after he had made sure, but very delicately managed tentative beginnings, that I did not at all object to being questioned. He was a little stiff at first, half timid, half wary.

When he found in me no disposition to intrude upon his reserve, and felt my manner untinged by either condescension, which I did not feel, or curiosity, which I sedulously repressed, he surrendered himself somewhat to the pleasure of exchanging ideas as an equal with a man of his own kind. We came to an unspoken understanding and talked openly on a level footing as two men of education, as two aspirants after culture. He relaxed his caution sufficiently to discard any concealment of his attainments and we discussed freely not only my books which he had borrowed but also whatever I had in hand. He never let slip anything which could tell me whether his spiritual background had been Oxford or Cambridge, yet I knew that only at one or the other could he have developed the mind he revealed.

Toward the end of the voyage our day-time chats usually began with his asking what I was reading. Even in the midst of the steady routine of his unremitting seamanly diligence he often paused by my chair on a weekday and delighted me with a brief talk which I enjoyed as much as he. Our Sunday talks came to take up much of his deck-watches. But what most delighted me was to listen to his monologues at night. Monologues they were, for I could neither interrupt nor reply. He would begin his watch by a double turn round the bark, twice speaking to the steersman, twice to the lookout.

Then he would pace the poop-deck, just aft of the break; from rail to rail. As he turned by the lee rail he would throw a comprehensive glance over the whole spread of the bark's canvas, so he turned by the weather rail he would stoop down, peer out under the mainsail and sweep his eyes along the horizon on our lee bow. In the early part of our voyage I had watched him night after night keep this up for an entire watch, evenly as an automaton, breaking it only by three rounds of the vessel made precisely on the hours. After we grew to knew each other he would patrol the deck only at intervals, spending most of his watch seated on the cabin-deck at the break, on the rail or on the booby-hatch, according to the position of my chair. He mostly began.

"Have you ever read—?" Or,

"Did you ever read—?"

Sometimes I had read the book, oftener I had not. In either case I was fascinated by his sane, cod judgment, equally trenchant and subtle, and by the even flow of his well-chosen words.

Our voyage neared its end sooner than I had anticipated. The south-east trades had been almost head winds for us and we had tacked through them close-hauled, a long leg on the port tack and a short leg on the starboard. Then the proximity of the land blurred the unalterable perpetuity of the trade winds and on a Sunday morning the wind came fair. It was my first experience of running before the wind and it intoxicated me with elation. We were out of sight of land, even of its loom, yet no longer in blue water, but over that enormous sixty-fathom shelf which juts out more than a hundred miles into the Atlantic between Bahia and Rio de Janeiro, or to be more precise, between Cannavieiras and Itapemirim.

The day was bright and the sky sufficiently diversified with clouds to vary pleasingly its insistent blue, the sea a pale, golden green all torn by racing white-caps and dappled with the scurrying shadows of the clouds. The bark leapt joyously, the combers overtaking her charged in smothers of foam past each counter, the delight of merely living in such a glorious day infected even the crew.

I had my chair amidships by the break of the deck, just abaft the booby-hatch. There I was reading the *Odyssey*. The mate came and sat down by me on the booby-hatch.

"What are you reading?" he asked as usual.

"About the Sirens," I answered.

The strangest alteration came over his expression.

"Did you ever notice," he asked, "how little Homer really tells about them?"

"I was meditating on just that," I replied. "He tells only that there were two of them and that they sang. I was wondering where the popular notions' of their appearance came from,"

"What is your idea of the popular notions of their appearance?" he demanded.

I have a very vague idea," I confessed. "They are generally supposed to have had bird's feet. It seems to me I have seen figures of them as so depicted on Greek tombs and coins. And there is Boecklin's picture."

"Boecklin?" he ruminated. "The Munich man? The morbid man?"

"If you choose to call him so?" I assented. "I shouldn't call him morbid."

"His ugly idea is a mere personal conception," he said.

"I grant you that," I agreed, "as far as the age and the ugliness go. But the birds' feet of some kind are in the general conception."

"The general conception is wrong," he asserted, with something more like an approach to heat than anything I had seen in him.

"You seem to feel very sure," I replied.

"I do not feel," he answered, "I know."

"How do you know?" I inquired.

"I have seen them," he asserted.

"Seen them?" I puzzled.

"Yes, seen them," he asseverated. "Seen the twain Sirens under the golden sun, under the silver moon, under the countless stars; watched them singing as they are singing now!"

"What?" I exclaimed.

My face must have painted my amazement, my tone must have betrayed my startled bewilderment.

His face went scarlet and then pale. He sprang up and strode off to the weather rail. There he stood for a long time. Presently he wheeled, crossed the deck, the booby-hatch between us, and plunged down the cabin companion-way without looking at me.

He did not once meet my eye during the remaining days of the voyage, let alone approach me. He was again the impassive, inscrutable figure I had first seen him on the wharf at Baltimore.

We drew near Rio harbour, late of a perfect tropic September day, just too late to enter before sunset. In the brief tropic dusk we anchored under the black beetling shoulder of Itaipu inside the little islands of Mai and Pai. There we lay wobbling at anchor, there I watched the cloudless sky fill with the infinite multitudes of tropic stars, and gazed at the lights of the city, plainly visible through the harbour mouth between Morro de Sao Joao and the Sugar Loaf, twinkling brighter than the stars, not three miles away.

It must have been somewhere toward midnight when he approached me. My chair was by the rail on which he half sat, leaning down to me. So placed he began such a monologue as I had often heard from him, a monologue I could neither question nor modify, which I must listen to entire or break off completely.

"You were astonished," he said, "when I told you I had seen the Sirens, but I have. It was about six years ago, in 1879. I was in New York and I had my usual difficulty getting a ship on account of my deafness. My boarding-master tried a Captain George Andrews of the *Joyous Castle*. Andrews looked me over and said he liked me. Then he talked to me alone.

"'We are bound on an adventure,' he said, 'and I want a man who will obey orders and keep his mouth shut.'

"I told him I was his man for whatever risk. With a light mixed cargo, hardly more than half a cargo, hardly more than ballast, we cleared for Guam and a market. I was second mate. The first mate was a big Swede named Gustave Obrink. The very first meal I ever sat down to with him he made an impression on me as one of the greediest men I had ever seen. He not only ate enormously, but he seemed more than half unsatisfied after he had stuffed himself with an amazing quantity of food. He seemed to possess an unbluntable zest in the act of swallowing, an ever fresh gusto for any and every food flavour.

"I never saw a man relish his food so. He was an equally inordinate drinker, the quantity of coffee he could swill at one meal was amazing. Between meals he was always thirsty and drank incredible quantities of water. He was forever going to the butt by the galley door and drinking from it. And he would smack his lips over it and enjoy it as a connoisseur would a rare wine.

"When we came to choose watches Captain Andrews told us to choose a bo'sun for each watch. Obrink wanted to know why.

"The captain told him it was none of his business to ask questions. The Swede assented and backed down. We chose each an Irishman. Obrink, a tall, loose-jointed man named Pat Ryan and I, a compact stocky fellow named Mike Leary. Next day the captain had the boatswains shift their dunnage and bunk and mess aft. They were nearly as great gluttons as Obrink. They fed like animals and the subject of food and drink was the backbone of their conversation,

"The crew were hearty eaters as well and Captain Andrews catered to their likings. The *Joyous Castle* was amazingly well found, the cabin fare very abundant and varied, the fore-castle food plenty and good.

"Soon after Captain Andrews was sure that the crew had entirely sobered up from their shore-drinking he called them aft one noon and announced that the steward was to serve grog daily until further notice. Naturally they cheered. After that we had a good, cheap wine daily in the cabin. When Captain Andrews had made up his mind that both mates and both boatswains were sober men he had a bottle of whisky placed on the rack over the table and kept filled. It was a curiosity to watch Obrink, Ryan and Leary patronize that bottle. Not one of the three but was cautious, not one of the three but could have drunk three times as much as he did. But the way they savoured every drop they took, the affectionate satisfaction they exhibited over each nip, their eager anticipation of the next made a spectacle.

"Captain Andrews kept good discipline, we crossed the line and rounded the cape of Good Hope without any event.

"When we were off Madagascar, Obrink, going below to get his sextant, missed it from its place. The ship was searched and Captain Andrews held an inquisition. But the sextant was never found, nor any light thrown on how it had disappeared. After that the captain alone took the observations.

"Then began a series of erratic changes of our course. We kept on dodging about for six weeks, until the crew talked of nothing else and openly said the captain was trying to lose us; certainly not one of us except the captain could have designated our position. We knew we were south of the line, not ten degrees south of it, and between 50 and 110 east longitude, but within those limits we might be almost anywhere.

"We had had nothing that could be called a storm since we left New York. When a storm struck us it was a storm indeed. When it blew over it left us making water fast. After a day and a night at the pumps, we took to our boats. Captain Andrews had the cook and the cabin boy in his boat, gave each boatswain a dory and two men, and directed us to steer north by east. When Obrink and I asked for our latitude and longitude he said that was his business. He had had the boats provisioned while we pumped and they were well supplied. We left the ship under a clear sky, the wind light after the storm, the ground-swell running heavy and slow. We lowered near sunset.

"Next morning the captain's boat had vanished, and there we were, two whale boats, two dories, twenty men in all and no idea of our position.

"The third day we sighted land. It was a low atoll, not much more than a mile across, nearly circular as far as we could make out, with the usual cocoa palms all along its ring, the surf breaking on interrupted reefs off shore, and, as we drew nearer, a channel into the lagoon facing us; as we threaded it we saw about the centre of the lagoon a steep, narrow, pinkish crag, maybe fifty feet high, with a bit of flat island showing behind it. Otherwise the lagoon was unbroken. We made a landing on the atoll near the channel where we had entered, found good water, cocoanuts in abundance and hogs running wild all about, but no traces of human beings. I shot a hog and the men roasted it at once.

"As they ate they talked of nothing but the short rations they had had in the boats. They were all docile enough and good natured, but I believe every man of them said a dozen times how much he missed his grog and, Obrink, who had kept himself and his boat-load well in hand, said a score of times how much he would like to serve out grog, but must take care of his small supply. They talked a great deal of their hunger in the boats and of their relish for the pork; they ate an astonishing number of cocoanuts. It seemed to me that they were as greedy a set of men as could be met with.

"We cut down five palm-trees, and on supports made of the others set one horizontally as a ridge pole. Over this we stretched the sails of the whale-boats. So we camped on the sand- beach of the lagoon. I slept utterly. But when I waked I understood the men one and all to complain of light and broken sleep, of dreams, of dreaming they heard a queer noise like music, of seeming to continue to hear it after they woke. They breakfasted on another hog and on more cocoanuts.

"Then Obrink told me to take charge of the camp. I agreed. He had everything removed from his whale-boat and into it piled all the men, except a little Frenchman who went by no name save 'Frenchy,' a New Englander named Peddicord, a short red-headed Irishman named Mullen, Ryan, my boatswain and myself. Those of my watch who wanted to go I let go. They rowed off, across the lagoon toward the pink crag.

"After Obrink and the men were gone I meant to take stock of our stores. I sent Ryan with Frenchy around the atoll in one direction and Peddicord, who had sense for a foremast hand, with Mullen in the other direction. I then went over the stores. Fairly promising for twenty men they were, even a random boat-voyage in the Indian Ocean. With unlimited cocoanuts and abundant hogs they were a handsome provision, and need only be safeguarded from the omnipresent rats.

"Very shortly my four men returned, the two parties nearly at the same time. It was nearly noon, and no sign of Obrink or the boat. I had followed the whale-boat with my glass till it rounded the pink crag, a short half mile away, and had disappeared. Ryan asked my permission to take one dory and go join the rest on the crag. I readily agreed, for I had not yet *cached* the spirits. They rowed off as the others had.

"I made use of their welcome absence to conceal the liquor in four different places, carefully writing, in my note-book, the marks by which I was to find the *caches* again. I did the like with most of the ammunition. I had no idea of trying to get the upper hand of Obrink. I meant to tell him of my proceedings and expected him to approve.

"I expected the men bade about two hours before sunset. No sign of them appeared. No sign of them near sunset, nor at sunset. Of course I had waited inactive till it was too late for me to venture alone on the unknown lagoon at night, and there would have been no sense in one man going to look for nineteen anyhow. Moreover I must protect our stores from hogs and rats. I turned over in my mind a thousand conjectures and slept little.

"Next morning I slung what I could of our stores from our jury-ridge-pole, out of the reach of hogs and rats, made sure that the remaining whale-boat would not get adrift, prepared the remaining dory with cocoanuts, biscuits, a keg of water, liquor, some miscellaneous stores, medicine, ammunition, repeating rifle, my glass and my compass. I carried two revolvers. I knew by this time something was wrong and I rowed warily across the placid lagoon toward the pink crag.

"As I approached it I could not but remark the peacefulness and beauty of my surroundings. The sky was deep tropic blue, the sun not an hour high, the wind a mild breeze, hardly more than rippling the lagoon, my horizon was all the tops of palms on the atoll except the one glimpse of white surf on the reef beyond the channel where we had entered.

"I rowed slowly, for the dory was heavy, and kept looking over my shoulder.

"The crag rose sheer out of deep water. It might have been granite, but I could not tell what sort of stone it was. It was very pink and nothing grew on it, not anything whatever. It was just sheer naked rock. As I rounded it I could see the flattish island beyond. There was not a tree on it and I could see nothing but the even beach of it rising some six or eight feet above high water mark. Nothing was visible beyond the crest of the beach. I knew our men had meant to land on it and I stopped and considered. Then I rowed round the base of the crag. Facing the flat islet was a sort of a shelf of the pink rock, half submerged, half out of the water, sloping very gently and just the place to make a landing.

"I rowed the dory carefully till its bottom grated on the flat top of this shelf, the bow in say a foot of water, the stern over water may be sixty fathom deep, for I could see no bottom to its limpid blue, I stepped out and drew the dory well up on the shelf. Then I essayed to climb the crag. I succeeded at once, but it was none too easy and I had no leisure to look behind me till I reached the top. Once on the fairly flat top, which might have been thirty feet across, I turned and looked over the islet

"Then I sat down heavily and took out my flask. I took a big drink, shut my eyes, said a prayer, I think, and looked again. I saw just what I had seen before.

"There was about a ship's-length of water between the crag and the islet, which might have been four ships-lengths across and was nearly circular. All round it was a white beach of clean coral-sand sloping evenly and rising perhaps ten feet at most above high-water mark. The rest of the island was a meadow, nearly level but cupping ever so little from the crest of the beach. It was covered with short, soft-looking grass, of a bright pale green, a green like that of an English lawn in Spring.

"In the centre of the island and of the meadow was an oval slab of pinkish stone, the same stone, apparently, as made up the crag on which I sat. On it were two shapes of living creatures, but shapes which I rubbed my eyes to look at. Midway between the slab and the crest of the beach a long windrow heap of something white swept in a circle round the slab, maybe ten fathom from it. I did not surely make out what the windrow was composed of until I took my glasses to it.

"But it needed no glass to see our men, all nineteen of them, all sitting, some just inside the white windrow, some just outside of it, some on it or in it Their faces were turned to the slab.

"I took my glass out of my pocket, trembling so I could hardly adjust it. With it I saw clearly, the windrow as I had guessed, the shapes on the slab as I had seemed to see them with my unaided eyes.

"The windrow was all of human bones. I could see them clearly through the glass.

"The two creatures on the slab were shaped like full-bodied young women. Except their faces nothing of their flesh was visible. They were clad in something close-fitting, and pearly gray, which clung to every part of them, and revealed every curve of their forms; as it were a tight-fitting envelopment of fine mole-skin or chinchilla. But it shimmered in the sunlight more like eider-down.

"And their hair! I rubbed my eyes. I took out my handkerchief and rubbed the lenses of my glasses. I looked again. I saw as before. Their hair was abundant, and fell in curly waves to their hips. But it seemed a deep dark blue, or a dull intense shot-green or both at once or both together. I could not see it any other way.

"And their faces!

"Their faces were those of white women, of European women, of young handsome gentlewomen.

"One of them lay on the slab half on her side, her knees a little drawn up, her head on one bent arm, her face toward me, as if asleep. The other sat, supporting herself by one straight arm. Her mouth was open, her lips moved, her face was the face of a woman singing. I dared not look any more. It was so real and so incredible.

"I scanned our men through my glass. I could see their shoulders heave as they breathed, otherwise not one moved a muscle, while I looked him.

"I shut my glass and put it in my pocket. I shouted. Not a man turned. I fixed my gaze so as to observe the whole group at once. I shouted again. Not a man moved. I took my revolver from its holster and fired in the air. Not a man turned.

"Then I started to clamber down the crag. I had to turn my back on the islet, regard the far horizon, fix my gaze on the camp, discernible by the white patch, where the white sails were stretched over the palm trunk and try to realize the reality of things before I could gather myself together to climb down.

"I made it, but I nearly lost my hold a dozen times.

"I pushed off the dory, rowed to the islet, and beached the dory between the other and the whale-boat. Both were half adrift and I hauled them up as well as I could.

"Then I went up the beach. When I came to its crest and saw the backs of our men I shouted again. Not a man turned his head. I approached them, their faces were set immovably towards the rock and the two appearances on it.

"Peddicord was nearest to me, the windrow of bones in front of him was not wide nor high. He stared across it. I caught him by the shoulders and shook him, then he did turn his head and look up at me, just a glance, the glance of a peevish, protesting child disturbed at some absorbing play, an unintelligent vacuous glance, unrecognizing and uncomprehending.

"The glance startled me enough, for Peddicord had been a hard-headed, sensible Yankee. But the change in his face, since yesterday, startled me more. Of a sudden I realized that Peddicord, Ryan, Mullen and Frenchy had been without food or water since I last saw them, that they had been just where I found them since soon after they left me, had been exposed the day before to a tropical sun for some six hours, had sat all night also without moving, or sleeping. At the same instant I realized that the rest had been in the same state for some hours longer, some hours of a burning, morning tropical sun. The realization of it lost my head completely. I ran from man to man, I yelled, I pulled them, I struck them.

"Not one struck back, or answered, or looked at me twice. Each shook me off impatiently and, relapsed into his intent posture, even Obrink.

"Obrink, it is true, partially opened his mouth, as if to speak.

"I saw his tongue!

"I ran to the boat, took a handful of ship-biscuit and a pan of water, with these I returned to the men.

"Not one would notice the biscuit, not one showed any interest in the water, not one looked at it as if he saw it when I held it before his face, not one tried to drink, not one would drink when I tried to force it on him.

"I emptied my flask into the water, with that I went from man to man. Not even the smell of the whisky roused them. Each pushed the pan from before his face, each resisted me, each shoved me away.

"I went back to the boat, filled a tin cup with raw whisky and went the round with that. Not one would regard it, much less swallow it.

'Then I myself turned to the slab of stone.

"There sat the sirens. Well I recognised now what they were. Both were awake now and both singing. What I had seen through the glass was visible more clearly, more intelligibly. They were indeed shaped like young, healthy women; like well-matured Caucasian women. They were covered all over with close, soft plumage, like the breast of a dove, coloured like the breast of a dove, a pale, delicate, iridescent, pinkish gray. As a woman's long hair might trail to her hips, there trailed from their heads a mass of long, dark strands. Imagine single strands of ostrich feathers, a yard long or more, curling spirally or at random, coloured the deep, shot, blue-green of the eye of a peacock feather, or of a game-cock's shackles. That was what grew from their heads, as I seemed to see it.

"I stepped over the windrow of bones. Some were mere dust; some bleached gray by sun, wind and rain; some white. Skulls were there, five or six I saw in as many yards of the windrow near me and more beyond. In some places the windrow was ten feet wide and three feet deep in the middle. It was made up of the skeletons of hundreds of thousands of victims.

"I took out my other revolver, spun the cylinder, and strode toward the slab.

"Forty feet from it I stopped. I was determined to abolish the superhuman monsters. I was resolute. I was not afraid. But I stopped. Again and again I strove to go nearer, I braced my resolutions. I tried to go nearer. I could not.

"Then I tried to go sideways. I was able to step. I made the circuit of the slab, some forty feet from it Nearer I could not go. It was as if a glass wall were between me and the sirens.

"Standing at my distance, once I found I could go no nearer, I essayed to aim my revolver at them. My muscles, my nerves refused to obey me. I tried in various ways. I might have been paralyzed. I tried other movements, I was capable of any other movement. But aim at them I could not.

"I regarded them. Especially their faces, their wonderful faces.

"Their investiture of opalescent plumelets covered their throats. Between it and the deep, dark *chevelure* above, their faces showed ivory-smooth, delicately tinted. I could see their ears too, shell-like ears, entirely human in form, peeping from under the glossy shade of their miraculous tresses.

"They were as like each other as any twin sisters.

"Their faces were oval, their features small, clean-cut, regular and shapely, their foreheads were wide and low, their brows were separate, arched, pencilled and definite, not of hair, but of tiny feathers, of gold-shot, black, blue-green, like the colour of their ringlets, but far darker. I took out my binoculars and conned their brows. Their eyes were dark blue-gray, bright and young, their noses were small and straight, low between the eyes, neither wide nor narrow, and with moulded nostrils, rolled and fine. Their upper lips were short, both lips crimson red and curved about their small mouths, their teeth were very white, their chins round and babyish.

"They were beautiful and the act of singing did not mar their beauty. Their mouths did not strain open, but their lips parted easily into an opening. Their throats seemed to ripple like the throat of a trilling canary-bird. They sang with zest and the zest made them all the more beautiful. But it was not so much their beauty that impressed me, it was the nobility of their faces.

"Some years before I had been an officer on the private steam-yacht of a very wealthy nobleman. He was of a family fanatically devoted to the church of Rome and all its interests. Some Austrian nuns, of an order made up exclusively of noblewomen, were about to go to Rome for an audience with the Pope. My employer placed his yacht at their disposal and we took them on at Trieste. They several times sat on deck during the voyage and the return. I watched them as much as I could, for I never had seen such human faces, and I had seen many sorts. Their faces seemed to tell of a long lineage of men all brave and honourable, women gentle and pure. There was not a trace on their faces of any sort of evil in themselves or in anything that had ever really influenced them. They were really saintly faces, the faces of ideal nuns.

"Well, the sirens' faces were like that, only more ineffably perfect. There was no guile or cruelty in them, no delight in the exercise of their power, no consciousness of it, no consciousness of my proximity, or of the spell-bound men, or of the uncountable skeletons of their myriad victims. Their faces expressed but one emotion: utter absorption in the ecstasy of singing, the infinite preoccupation of artists in their art.

"I walked all round them, gazing now with all my eyes, now through my short-focused glass. Their coat of feathers was as if very short and close like seal-skin fur and covered them entirely from the throat down, to the ends of their fingers and the soles of their feet. They did not move except to sit up to sing or lie down to sleep. Sometimes both sang together, sometimes alternately, but if one slept the other sang on and on without ceasing.

"I of course could not hear their music, but the mere sight of them fascinated me so that I forgot my weariness from anxiety and loss of sleep, forgot the vertical sun, forgot food and drink, forgot my ship-mates, forgot everything.

"But as I could not hear this state was transitory. I began to look elsewhere than at the sirens. My gaze turned again upon the men. Again I made futile efforts to reach the sirens, to shoot at them, to aim at them. I could not.

"I returned to my dory and drank a great deal of water. I ate a ship-biscuit or two. I then made the round of the men, and tried on each food, water and spirits. They were oblivious to everything except the longing to listen, to listen, to listen.

"I walked round the windrow of bones. With the skulls and collapsing rib-arches I found leather boots, several leather belts, case-knives, *kreeses*, guns of various patterns, pistols, watches, gold and jew-elled finger rings and coins, many coins, copper, silver and gold. The grass was short, not three inches deep and the earth under it smooth as a rolled lawn.

"The bones were of various ages, but all old, except two skeletons, entire, side by side, just beyond the windrow at the portion opposite where the men sat. There was long fine golden hair on one skull. Women too!

"I went back to the dory, rowed to the camp, shot a hog, roasted it, wrapped the steaming meat in fresh leaves and rowed back to the islet. It was not far from sunset.

"Not a man heeded the savoury meat, still warm. They just sat and gazed and listened.

"I was free of the spell. I could do them no good by staying. I rowed back to camp before sunset and slept, yes I slept all night long.

"The sun woke me. I shot and cooked another hog, took every bit of rope or marline I could find and rowed back to the islet.

"You are to understand that the men had by then been more than forty hours, all of them, without moving or swallowing anything. If I was to save any it must be done quickly.

"I found them as they had been, but with an appalling change in themselves. The day before they had been uncannily unaware of their sufferings, today they were hideously conscious of them.

"Once I had a pet terrier, a neat, trim, intelligent, little beast. He ran under a moving train and had both his hind legs cut off. He dragged himself to me, and the appealing gaze of his eyes expressed at once his inability to comprehend what had happened to him, his bewilderment at pain, the first really excruciating pain he had ever known in all his little life, and his dumb wonder that I did not help him, that it could be possible he could be with me and his trouble continue.

"Once I had the misfortune to see a lovely child, a beautiful little girl, not six years old, frightfully burned. Her look haunted me with the like incomprehension of what had befallen her, the like incredulity at the violence of her suffering, the like amazement at our failure to relieve her.

"Well, out of the staring, blood-shot eyes of those bewitched men I saw the same look of helpless wonderment and mute appeal,

"Strange, but I never thought of knocking them senseless. I had an idea of tying them one by one, carrying or dragging them to the dory and ferrying my captives to camp.

"I began on Frenchy, he was nearest the boat and smallest.

"He fought like a demon. After all that sleeplessness and fasting he was stronger than I. Our tussle wore me out, but moved him not at all.

"I tried them with the warm juicy, savoury pork. They paid no heed to it and pushed me away. I tried them with biscuit, water and liquor. Not one heeded. I tried Obrink particularly. Again he opened his lips. His tongue was black, hard, and swelled till it filled his mouth.

"Then I lost count of time, of what I did, of what happened. I do not know whether it was on that day or the next that the first man died. He was Jack Register, a New York wharf-rat. The next died a few hours later, a Philadelphia seaman he was, named Tom Smith.

"They putrefied with a rapidity surpassing anything I ever saw, even in a horse dropped dead of over-driving.

"The rest sat there by the carrion of their comrades, rocking with weakness, crazed by sleeplessness, racked by tortures inexpressible, the gray of death deepening on their faces, listening, listening, listening.

"As I said, I had lost consciousness of time. I do not know how many days Obrink lived, and he was the last to die. I do not know how long it was after his death before I came to myself.

"I made one last effort to put an end to the enchantresses. The same spell possessed me. I could not aim, much less pull trigger; I could not approach nearer than before.

"When I was myself I made haste to leave the accursed isle. I made ready the second whale-boat with all the best stores she could carry and spare sails. I stepped the mast and steered across the lagoon, for the wind was southerly and there was a wider channel at the north of the atoll.

"As I passed the islet, I could see nothing but the white sand beach that ringed it. For all my horror I could not resist landing once more for one last look.

"Under the afternoon sun I saw the green meadow, the white curve of bones, the rotting corpses, the pink slab, the feathered sirens, their sweet serene faces uplifted, singing on in a rapt trance.

"I took but one look. I fled. The whale-boat passed the outlet of the lagoon. North by east I steered.

"Parts of the Indian Ocean are almost free of storms. The atoll was apparently in one of those parts. I soon passed out of it. Three storms blew me about, I lost my dead-reckoning, I lost count of the days. Between the storms I lashed the tiller amidships, double-reefed the sail and slept as I needed sleep. Through the storms I bailed furiously, the whale-boat riding at a sea-anchor of oars and sails. I had been at sea alone for all of twenty-one days when I was rescued, not three hundred miles from Ceylon, by a tramp steamer out of Colombo bound for Adelaide."

Here he broke off, stood up and for the rest of the watch maintained his sentry-go by the break of the poop.

Next day we towed into the harbour of Rio de Janeiro, then still the capital of an Empire, and mildly enthusiastic for Dom Pedro. I hastened to go ashore. When my boat was ready the deaf mate was forward, superintending the sealing of the hatches.

After some days of discomfort at the Hotel des Etrangers and of worse at Young's Hotel I found a harbourage with five jolly bachelors housekeeping in a delightful villa up on Rua dos Jonquillos on Santa Theresa. The *Nipsic* was in the harbour and I thought I knew a lieutenant on her and went off one day to visit her. After my visit my boatman landed me at the Red Steps. As I trod up the steps a man came down. He was English all over, irreproachably shod, trousered, coated, gloved, hatted and monocled. Behind him two porters carried big, new portmanteaux. I recognized the man whom I had known as John Wilson of Liverpool, second mate of the *Medorus*, the man who had seen the Sirens.

Not only did I recognize him, but he recognized me. He gave me no far off British stare. His eyes lit, even the monocled eye. He held out his hand.

"I am going home," he said, nodding toward a steamer at anchor, "I am glad we met. I enjoyed our talks. Perhaps we may meet again."

He shook hands without any more words. I stood at the top of the steps and watched his boat put off, watched it as it receded. As I watched a bit of paper on a lower step caught my eye. I went down and picked it up. It was an empty envelope, with an English stamp and postmark, addressed:

Geoffrey Cecil, Esq.,
C.o. Swanwick & Co.,
54 Rua de Alfandega,
Rio de Janeiro, Brazil.

I looked after the distant boat, I could barely make him out as he sat in the stern. I never saw him again.

Naturally I asked every Englishman I ever met if he had ever heard of a deaf man named Geoffrey Cecil. For more than ten years I elicited no response. Then at lunch, in the Hotel Victoria at Interlaken, I happened to be seated opposite a stout, elderly Briton. He perceived that I was an American and became affable and agreeable. I never saw him after that lunch and never learned his name. But through our brief meal together we conversed freely.

At a suitable opportunity I put my usual query.

"Geoffrey Cecil?" he said. "Deaf Geoffrey Cecil? Of course I know of him. Knew him too. He was or is Earl of Aldersmere."

"Was or is?" I queried.

It was this way," my interlocutor explained. "The ninth Earl of Aldersmere had three sons. All predeceased him and each left one son. Geoffrey was the heir. He had wanted to go into the navy, but his deafness cut him off from that When he quarrelled with his father he naturally ran away to sea. Track of him was lost. He was supposed dead. That was years before his father's death. When his father nothing had been heard of him for ten years. But when his grandfather died and his cousin Roger supposed himself Earl, some firm of solicitors interposed, claiming that Geoffrey was alive. That was in 1885. It was a full six months before Geoffrey turned up. Roger was no end disappointed. Geoffrey paid no attention to anything but buying or chartering a steam-yacht. She sailed as soon as possible, passed the canal, touched at Aden, and has never been heard of since. That was nine years ago."

"Is Roger Cecil alive?" I asked.

"Very much alive," affirmed my informant.

"You may tell him from me," I declared, "that he is now the Eleventh Earl of Aldersmere."

Iarbas

(A Tale from *The Song of the Sirens and Other Stories*)

When through the fire nothing remained discernible, when peering and gazing they saw only flame within flame, two of her women gently drew Anna away from the pyre. She let herself be conducted across the courtyard and up the easy stone stair to the first gallery. There, hanging over the polished marble railing of the balustrade, her head leaned against one of the columns, Anna watched the burning pyre. It blazed on, even larger and fiercer, for a string of porters and workmen carrying logs or faggots, filed into the court. Each threw his burden upon the pyre and passed out by another door. Others followed in like manner, and, after a time, the same men returned again with fresh burdens.

From her place by the pillar of the gallery Anna refused to stir.

Several of the women carried in a broad, cushioned couch, placed it silently behind their lady and gently induced her to recline upon it. So reclining she leaned her bosom against the balustrade, her arms upon its rail, her head upon her arms. There she fell asleep.

All night, the slaves in single file carried fuel to keep up the blaze. When the first dawn-light appeared in the sky overhead and the pigeons began to coo upon the red-tiled roofs of the palace, Anna awakened and gave a soft-voiced order. The fuel-carriers ceased to file into the court, the last of them went their way and the pyre was left to burn out of itself.

Watching its fury slacken and its blaze abate Anna, partly from innate docility, partly from dazed indifference, passively permitted her maids to bathe her face and hands, to bind up her hair, somewhat to arrange her dress. She even compliantly swallowed some mouthfuls of the bread moistened with hot spiced wine which they urged upon her. She allowed them to unclasp her nerveless fingers from the tear-soaked square of linen they clutched, to place in them another.

Tactfully they withdrew some little distance and left her absorbed in her grief, oblivious of all other things, droopingly half-supported against the balustrade and pillar, watching the pyre sink into a bed of glowing coals. She stared down at it, weeping softly, now and then sobbing, and once and again dabbing at her eyes with the square of linen she held crumpled in her hand. The women slaves, huddled out of sight under the lower arcade, kept up a monotonous shrill wailing, a weird, droning noise which had become less and less insistent as the hours passed. Through it Anna was aware of a different sound.

She heard the clank and tinkle of jangling armour and glanced across the court. Between two pillars of the lower colonnade in front of the main central doorway stood Iarbas. The scarlet plume of his helmet-crest nodded still and waved as his crimson cloak fluttered and undulated behind him with the impetus of his checked haste; the dawn-light and the firelight glittered and gleamed on the brow-piece of his helmet, on the gilded links of his chain corselet, on the burnished scales of his broad kilt-straps, and shone on the great round shield and the broad polished points of the twin spears his armour-bearer carried behind him.

His eyes were bright in his big swarthy face, and roved about the court gazing at the huddled crowd of *servitors* and menials under the side-colonnades, at the dying glow of the sinking pyre, at Anna and her attendants above. He waved his hand backward with a single imperious gesture and strode across the court, Anna heard his tread on the tessellated floor of the gallery and looked around at him, half sitting up, but still limply leaning upon the balustrade, her head against the pillar. She said nothing.

Weeping did not disfigure Anna. Her pale gold hair rippled ever so little over her temples, her pale blue eyes gazed from unreddened lids, her pale pinkish cheeks were not streaky with her hours of tears, her mild oval face was pretty as it had been throughout her past, whether she had been anxious and worried or happy and gay. Iarbas looked her over from the grass-green sandal-straps across the small arched instep showing under the embroidered hem of her sea-green gown to the jade brooch at her shoulder and the apple-green ribbon which confined her hair. He found himself astonished at her comeliness, he had never noted her looks before.

She gazed at him steadily, mute.

"I am a day too late," he said.

She turned from him, buried her face upon her crossed arms, and burst into a passion of sobs.

He stood behind her awkwardly, ill at ease, and silent, until her paroxysm of grief quieted. Exhibition of emotion was no habit of Anna's. She had been a matter-of-fact child, whose hurts made but a passing impression upon her, a quiet girl, the reverse of high-strung; and a housewifely young woman. Embroidery had been her only activity, superintendence of the maids at their spinning and weaving, or overseeing of the cookery and service her chief occupations. She had never been enthusiastic, or fervid, but always very much the reverse.

When King Belus of Tyre died Anna's wailing had been low-voiced, less noisy than that of any of his other daughters. At her mother's burial her grief had been tacit and suppressed. Amid the tumult and alarm following the murder of Sychaeus, Anna had wept for her beloved brother-in-law decorously and briefly. So now the violence of her sobbing soon abated, her soft weeping too ceased before long. She sat up again and again looked at him.

"I am a day too late," he repeated.

"My sister is beyond any reach or any revenge of yours," she said in her even, unemotional tones, her gaze contemptuous. "All that remains of poor Dido is ashes under the coals of her pyre there."

"I had no thought of revenge on her or of violence to her or her wishes," Iarbas disclaimed.

Anna regarded him unwinkingly. Her weeping had entirely stopped, her eyes were dry, as her cheeks. Her many bereavements, her experiences amid assassinations, plots, revolt, exile and colonization had changed her not at all. Her grief for the loss of her last and best loved sister was genuine and keen, but its manifestations were evanescent. Her gaze was almost as placid as her habitual serene look.

"For what are you a day too late?" she asked.

Anna was not argumentative. She never spoke with heat. Her girlish companions had never been able to elicit from her any warmth of utterance except when she enunciated to them her favourite aphorism that a woman should not find fault with her husband, that any woman should be glad to be married and that the sort of man made little difference. Even this pet doctrine she had maintained but tepidly. So also to Iarbas she spoke mildly.

As he stood mute she repeated, tonelessly.

"For what then are you a day too late?"

"To avenge her and myself," Iarbas answered fiercely. "To reach him, to kill him."

"Aeneas?" Anna exclaimed. "You thought you could? Why did you think you could?"

"You must have known, Dido must have known, anybody must have known, that I had spies in Carthage," Iarbas began apologetically. "I have had many and I have been well served. They learnt his habits and informed me. The man was very thoughtless, very heedless or very reckless."

"Aeneas!" Anna interjected, "call it entirely self-reliant."

So be it, if you please," Iarbas consented. Call it what you choose. At any rate, according to the reports I received, he never varied his day's routine.

"About an hour after sunrise Achates drove his chariot into the palace forecourt and waited for him. When he came out he was driven straight to the arsenal. There he inspected the forges, sometimes the storerooms, always the shipyards and docks. When he again mounted his chariot they drove out by the Cothon gate and along the beach past his ships and the three guard-camps, then they wheeled to the left and drove inland to the south side of the Hippodrome. On foot and alone he went the rounds of that, inspecting the derricks and stone-cutting, climbed alone to the theatre, noted the masons there and talked with the architects and overseers. On the north side of that he regained his chariot which Achates had driven round by the quarry road. From there they drove along outside the walls to the Byrsa gate, stopping at each tower where rebuilding or enlarging was in progress.

"Then instead of coming in by the Byrsa gate Achates drove him westward along the cattle track past the foot of Magar hill. They always drove alone and followed the cattle track up the slope and into the wooded depression between the two crests of Magar hill and along through the gully to the north side."

"Yes," Anna ruminatingly interjected. "He told me. He said it reminded him of the glens of Ida."

"In that ravine," Iarbas went on, "they were out of sight and sound of the city. Every day he passed there at the same time, unattended except by Achates. After traversing the hollow they turned east again, skirted Magar hill on the north and re-entered the city by the Magar gate."

"You meant to ambush him in the gorge," Anna said quietly. "How many men did you expect to have with you?"

"A hundred," Iarbas replied.

"Fifty to one," Anna commented. "Surely you brought more than

215

a hundred?"

"I gathered twenty thousand spearmen before I set out," Iarbas told her, "but I intended only a hundred for the ambush."

"When did you set out?" Anna queried settling herself against the balustrade and pillar.

"We left Usinaz a month ago today," Iarbas answered, "but we rode slowly, foresaw no need for haste. We crossed the Bagradas high up and camped this side of Zama. There we stayed several days, six or eight I think, resting the camels and horses, while I compared reports. We were still there four days ago. Three days ago we broke camp at dawn. I meant to catch him early yesterday morning. Runners came to me early with the news of the mustering of the Trojans, of their leaving the city, of the launch of the fleet; but as my forces were camped well back of the dunes and I was on lesser Magar with my guards only, I could not strike in time to forestall their sailing or to prevent it.

"A messenger during the night had brought word that the day before Aeneas had returned on foot through the Hippodrome, sent a runner around for his chariot, spent most of the morning on the beach and re-entered the city by the Cothon gate. But I had paid no attention to the report, thinking that even if he broke his routine that one day he would resume it the next as he had done once or twice before when something held or deflected him from his habitual round. So I missed my chance."

"How did you approach so near?" Anna queried, "without our getting any warning?"

"All the natives are with me heart and soul," Iarbas replied simply. "Many of your citizens are for me, they informed me at once of everything. Word of your poor sister's end was brought me before dusk. I had made my arrangements and did not change them. I assigned one division to Garamas to enter the Magar gate, one to Maurusus for the Cothon gate, and led my own column to the Byrsa gate. They were all opened for us about midnight. There has been no fighting, not a man killed. My men are in possession of all the gates and towers, of the walls, docks and arsenal, of the market, the streets and the citadel. Bitias is under guard in his own house scared and submissive."

"You have done well," Anna declared.

"I have indeed," Iarbas boasted, "Carthage is in my hands. I have been completely successful."

"You prayed to Jupiter to help you before you left Usinaz, I suppose," Anna remarked.

"I sacrificed a hundred white bulls," Iarbas informed her, "all two-year-olds, every one perfect. I was sure of Jupiter's favour."

"He has indeed protected you," Anna said with her nearest approach to a sneer. "You did not meet Aeneas in Magar gorge."

"What do you mean?" Iarbas exclaimed.

"I mean," said Anna, sitting up haughtily, her eyes as near brightness as they were capable of, "that had you met Aeneas in Magar gorge it would have been your last hour. You would have seen a lion's rush, an eagle's swoop, his spear point would have struck you wherever he aimed and that would have been the end of you."

"You appraise me too low," the royal Moor snarled, nettled.

"I appraise you," spoke Anna placidly, "the most redoubtable champion in all Africa, but no match for Aeneas of Troy."

"I should have had my best hundred guards with me," Iarbas reminded her.

"Aeneas," Anna made answer, "without bow or arrows, with javelins only, killed seven antelopes out of one herd the day he landed in Africa. He is no sluggish spearman. He might have killed twenty of your guards, he might have needed to kill only ten. But before him your hundred ruffians would have scattered like a handful of children. You and they would have had no chance against him."

"You talk," Iarbas exclaimed, "as if you admired the Phrygian pirate."

"Never you dare to miscall Aeneas to me," Anna blazed. "You are master of Carthage if you please, but not of me. Go, or promise to speak respectfully to me and of him."

Mighty of bulk Iarbas stood, towering in height, huge of girth, brawny, clad in mail, clothed as well in the elation of his triumph. Anna was sitting half recumbent, small, slight, soft-voiced and almost expressionless, yet before her gaze the eyes of the big warrior sought the floor.

"I promise," he said. "You admire him indeed."

"Naturally," Anna replied, "he is the most admirable man alive, the most admirable man who ever lived."

Can you say that," the tall prince exclaimed, when your poor sister's ashes are not yet cold in her pyre, the day after her wretched death, the day after his heartless desertion of her?"

"No man," spoke Anna steadily, "was ever further from being heartless than Aeneas was and is, no man ever tore himself more unwillingly and reluctantly from the woman he loved."

"There must have been some blundering in the reports that reached me then," Iarbas declared, bewilderedly, "all agreed that from the time he took up his abode in the palace until day before yesterday he lived as her husband and as king of Carthage, that day before yesterday about noon the Trojans began leaving the city by the Cothon gate, that before sunset the fleet was launched and riding at anchor. Two of my messengers told of Dido's begging him to stay, one told of you yourself going out of the Cothon gate to plead with him when the whole fleet was already afloat All the messengers uniformly reported that Dido's suicide was caused by his desertion."

"Before you left Usinaz," Anna began evenly, "you burnt a hecatomb to Jupiter, did you not?"

"I did," Iarbas agreed.

"The omens were favourable mostly, were they not?" Anna inquired.

"Not mostly," Iarbas replied, "all were favourable and very favourable. Not only none of the bullocks stamped, but not one so much as fidgeted or bellowed. As mild and meek a hundred bulls as those never stood about one altar. Every liver was perfect, not one with a shrunken lobe, not one with a white spot, not a streak on any, not a discoloration. So with the hearts and the rest. No man ever had a more unmistakable pledge of his God's approval, no man ever had a more positive authorization from Heaven."

"Suppose some of the omens had been bad?" Anna suggested.

"Anyone is used to that," Iarbas shrugged.

'Suppose they all had been bad," Anna continued.

"I should have sacrificed another hecatomb," Iarbas reflected, "until they came out right."

"Suppose they did not come out right?" Anna pursued, "Suppose they were all bad and continued to be bad. Suppose you had sacrificed a thousand bulls and not one of them but was as bad as possible in every respect?"

"Too improbable to suppose," Iarbas muttered. "That would be impossible."

"Just suppose it," Anna insisted. "Say it had happened so, what would you have done?"

"I should have stayed in Usinaz, certainly," Iarbas ruminated. "Likely I should have disbanded my men too and let them go home. If such a thing could happen and if it had happened to me I should have been too scared to stir out, not merely for an expedition, but even for a hunt or a ride."

"You would have taken it as a plain message from Jupiter imperatively prohibiting you from your purpose?" Anna inquired, "would you not? You would have left Aeneas undisturbed and Dido in his possession no matter how you raged and fumed?"

"I certainly should," Iarbas admitted, "if such an unthinkable accumulation of bad omens had occurred."

"Suppose," Anna resumed, "that before your first sacrifice Mercury himself had appeared to you, spoken to you as plainly as I am speaking to you and told you from Jupiter to give up your purpose and remain quietly at home, would you have obeyed?"

"I should certainly have obeyed," Iarbas declared fervently, "if such a plain warning had come to me from on high."

"You think yourself a scrupulous man," Anna said, "but Aeneas is far more scrupulous than you. Day before yesterday he left the palace on his rounds punctually as usual, as you know; as you know, he returned from the Hippodrome to the beach, spent most of the day there and re-entered the city by the Cothon gate about mid-afternoon. As he came in by the men's forecourt Dido met him. She had heard that the Trojans quartered in the city were leaving by the Cothon gate.

"He bade her a rather bungling, clumsy and tongue-tied farewell. I watched them from the rear gallery and he looked when he came in like a man who had seen a ghost and when he went out like a man going to his death. Dido made me go after him to the beach and plead with him. That was about dusk,

"He stood there with his back to the sea, looking down at me and listening to me with his grave courtesy.

"'I was at the worst of my misfortunes,' he said, 'with only seven ships left and those no longer seaworthy, their crews worn out, all of us in despair, short of food, clothing, supplies and weapons. I was a beggared outcast on an unknown coast. She welcomed me. She did everything for us. She rescued my scattered people and reunited us all. She was the very goddess of generosity and kindness. Apart from all that she is the very handsomest woman I ever saw, after Helen of Tiryns, and gentler and sweeter than any woman ever was. More than that she loves me. And above all, I love her. Yet I must go. My hard fate drives me and tears us apart. I must follow my bitter destiny.'

"Won't your destiny wait until spring?" I asked him. "Does your destiny call any louder than yesterday or the day you landed here?" I did not know what he had said to Dido or she to him and I was angry and hurt all through.

"He looked at me steadily.

"'Anna,' he said, 'my destiny might have called me forever and I should not have listened. Jove has called me and in no uncertain tones.

"'I was sauntering up the cut-off path from the Hippodrome to the theatre. I was happy and humming an air, the air Dido made the morning of our first hunt. I had passed between the two pomegranate trees and up the steps to that shoulder of rock where you can look over the tops of the pomegranates and see the Hippodrome. I stood there awhile looking down at it Then I turned to go up the crooked steps.

"'I heard a whirring in the air like the noise of a flock of doves swooping down to alight. I looked back and up. There was Mercury, as plain as I see you, not five yards from me, almost on a level with me, poised in the air over the pomegranate trees.

"'His attitude was much that of a spear-thrower, all balanced, leaning forward over the left leg, left knee bent, left heel raised, left arm hanging free, right leg straightened and trailing, feet well apart. But his right arm was not raised, it was extended toward me and carried his caduceus. The snakes around the rod squirmed and coiled and recoiled as I looked.

"'The wings on his cap and bracelets and sandals made rainbow colours in the air about his ankles and wrists and temples, like the iridescent shimmer of a dragonfly's wings when it hovers over a pool. I could hear the whiz of their buzzing motion.

"'He alighted not two yards from me on the edge of the cliff.

"'You have seen me more than once at Troy,' he said, 'though not so clearly nor for so long; you know who I am and whose messenger I am. His message is but one word: 'SAIL!' That means sail at once. You have no right to rest or ease or comfort. It was never right for you to linger one needless day anywhere. Still less was it right for you to form ties in any land except the land appointed for you and indicated to you. Least of all is it right for you to assist another race to strengthen a colony. You know all this. Jove reminds you through me. Heed him. *Act! Sail!*

"'Like a bird from a flower he whirled upward, flashed in the sunlight and was gone.

"'Do you wonder I obey? Can I, could I yield to any appeal from you or her or my own heart? Is there any use in saying anything?

"I turned away to my litter and my bearers carried me back to the palace, but I remember nothing of the way home. He was right."

"You sympathize with him!" Iarbas blurted out indignantly. "You take his side."

"Who could but sympathize with him?" Anna maintained. "Really he never knew any mother except his foster nurse Caieta. Since before he was half grown his father was a cripple. From boyhood he never could have his own way about anything. It was duty, duty perpetually. He always spoke beautifully of Creusa, but it was plain to be seen he loved her because he had married her rather than had married her because he loved her. It was plain that he had married her because his father and his cousins, old Sultan Priam and Prince Hector and the rest thought the marriage advisable for state reasons.

"Then they all suffered ten years of unremitting siege. Then he had the horror of Creusa's death to remember and the haunting self-reproach that he had not saved her, as he had saved his father and son from that appalling whirlpool of terrors, the awful night of the sack of Troy. Then in exile he endured years of toils, misfortunes and baffled wanderings.

"And then he had the only taste of happiness in all his life. He was happy for the first time, living with a woman he loved, who loved him, who was fit to be his companion, living as king of a strong prosperous city, as the chief of an adoring, appreciative people. And no sooner had he begun to relish it than he must tear himself away from it, give it all up, leave it behind and go out to more wanderings and toils and sufferings and disappointments and he did not blench. He went.

"He suffered more than Dido, though he talked less. But he never thought of giving up, he accepted his fate as it came to him and did his duty as he found it. Not even his worst enemy could fail to sympathize with him. Even you cannot help sympathizing with him. You know in your heart you cannot but approve of his unhesitating obedience to Jove's behest, you cannot but admire the strength of will equal to such magnificent self-control, you cannot but sympathize with his heartache and regrets."

"Nothing," said Iarbas, "can alter the fact that Dido killed herself because Aeneas left her. Nothing can alter the fact that he is under the curse she laid upon him before she died. The fact of the curse by itself should cut him off from any reminiscent sympathy in your heart, from even the thought of it."

Anna bowed her face into her covering hands and began to weep softly.

The warrior king stood staring down at her helpless and uneasy.

Presently she took her hands from her face, dried her eyes and looked up at him.

"Oh," she wailed, "if prayer or sacrifice or any expiation or incantation might lift that curse I If only it lay within my power to save him from that curse! He goes weighted with it to some dreadful doom and he never deserved it or anything but blessings and good wishes."

"You make me angry," Iarbas growled. "Deserve or no deserve she killed herself because of him. You have no proper clan-spirit or family spirit. You should think only of her suicide."

"I do not blame him for her death," Anna declared. "I blame her. He suffered as much as she at their parting, for he loved her as much as she loved him; more, for she was left with her established city, her sister, her loving people, countless opportunities of usefulness lay before her, countless duties called her. She thought only of her pangs of grief. She selfishly threw away all the noble activities, all the honour and respect her future might have brought her. He rose superior to his anguish, to the black threatening of the future before him, to everything except his duty. He is all admirable. Why blame him because of her weakness? I suffered more than both of them, I have not killed myself. I can bear my misery, why could not she have borne hers?"

"Your misery?" Iarbas cried resonantly.

Anna turned from him, cast her arms upon the broad top of the balustrade, hid her face upon her arms and burst into a storm of violent sobbing.

Iarbas took a step toward her, hand outstretched as if to lay it upon her shoulder. He checked himself, drew up, stiff and straight and tall and stood immobile and mute till her outburst spent itself.

Again she dried her eyes and looked up at him. She was no less beautiful because of her weeping. He could not but notice that, as she could not but notice the harsh query in his suspicious eyes.

"What did Dido suffer?" she argued, "compared with what I suffered, with what I suffer now? She was abandoned, deserted, forlorn, but she knew even in her frenzy that he really loved her and left her reluctantly at stern duty's call. He went away from me forever without any thought of me more than he took of the sands beneath his feet as he stood there and spoke to me for the last time.

"She lost him, but she had possessed him, had seen him utterly swept away in a passion of longing for her, wholly absorbed in adoration for her. Me he had never for one instant regarded, had never thought of as desirable, never considered as anything but placid, mild, easy-going Anna, useful as a confidant, serviceable as a bearer of tokens and gifts and messages, as a smoother-out of misunderstandings.

"She felt his caresses and knew him her own for the time, basked in months of ecstasy; I must keep a serene face and suave tongue and watch their bliss and know that I was absolutely nothing to him and give no sign. I suffered ten thousand deaths a day while their felicity endured. I did not kill them, I did not kill myself, I shall not now. Dido should not have killed herself. She would have outworn her agony in time. So shall I. I believe not in making the worst of anything, but in making the best of everything."

"Now you talk more like yourself," said Iarbas. "I have not known you since I came here this time. I thought you too staid for such vehemence, too gentle for such feelings, too contained to show it if you felt any such."

"That has always been the way since I was a baby," Anna protested. "Father called me his little pillow, because I was so plump and soft, brother Sychaeus called me 'cushion,' even Pygmalion teased me about my tranquillity. Nobody ever gave me any credit for having any feelings."

"I do," said Iarbas.

"You do not show it," Anna asserted.

"Feelings or no feelings as that may be," Iarbas pursued. "You said just now you believe in making the best of things,"

"I do," Anna agreed.

"How do you expect," Iarbas inquired, "to make the best of your present circumstances?"

" I do not expect anything," Anna declared, "and I have no power to make, I can only go on existing, and pray and wait, as a woman must, for what is to come."

"You must have expected something," Iarbas insisted. "You could not help thinking."

"I was too dazed to think," Anna maintained. "If I expected anything it was that Bitias would seize the citadel as soon as he heard of Dido's death and likely enough have me strangled to ensure his control of the city. If he made no attempt at revolution or faction, Pygmalion might appear any day with an irresistible fleet convoying the transports of an overwhelming army. I saw not a ray of hope for the city or for me. Dido had capacity, and popularity and prestige, I have barely the shadow of any of the three."

"And now?" Iarbas queried.

"You are master of the city, you say," she answered. "I am in your hands."

"The logical solution," Iarbas declared, "is for you to marry me and live on as queen of Carthage."

"You hound!" Anna cried. "My sister unburied, and you talk to me of marriage!"

Iarbas stared at her amazed at her outburst.

"You said you were in my hands," he wondered.

"I expected better treatment at your hands," Anna retorted.

"I cannot imagine any better treatment," the bluff soldier king declared. "You say you loved Aeneas and show you loved him. Yet after all I offer you myself. You would be my queen."

"I had rather perish as Dido perished," Anna declared fiercely, "than be your queen."

"You said you believed in making the best of everything." Iarbas reminded her.

"There are some things," Anna told him, "out of which there is no best to make. You care nothing for me. You only want to be king of Carthage."

"I do not need you," Iarbas retorted, "to make myself king of Carthage, Carthage is mine now."

"I am not," said Anna, almost vigorously, her small head erect. "You may control Carthage, you cannot subdue me. You never cared for me, you always loved Dido. The instant she is dead you are for marrying me! I will die before I will be your queen."

"I never cared for you," Iarbas admitted, "until you faced me down and defended that Trojan p—."

He stopped, gulped and began again.

"That Trojan prince, Aeneas."

"There," Anna interjected, "that is better."

"I like your pluck, your grit," Iarbas glowed. "You held your own and showed spirit. You have no idea how beautiful you looked as you vindicated him. I fell in love with you wholly and at once. It is not so much Carthage I crave as you."

Anna looked down at her interlacing fingers.

"Am I to ride away?" Iarbas asked, softly, "and leave you to have your throat cut by Bitias and his party, or to be burned alive by Pygmalion if he comes? I love you and I want you. Apart from loving you I like you too much to leave you to such a fate, as I like you too much to force you to anything. I like you!"

"And I like you," Anna confessed. "I like your self-confidence in imagining yourself a match for Aeneas. You protested nothing when I vilified you, but I understood you never meant to use your hundred guards against him in Magar gorge. You expected them to stand and look on. You fancied yourself capable of overcoming him with no more help from them or your armour-bearer than he would have had from Achates. It was temerity, it was foolhardiness, but it was magnificent."

She gazed up at him.

"I know your decision," he said, "without your uttering any word."

His eyes met hers steadily,

"We must wait till my nine days of mourning are past," Anna demurred, yielding.

"As you please," Iarbas agreed, "but no longer than the tenth day."

"The nine days," Anna reasoned, her matter-of-factness enveloping her, "must count from the day after Dido's funeral, that cannot be until tomorrow."

"I consent," Iarbas replied, "but for no longer postponement than that."

"My women," said Anna, now wholly her matter-of-fact house-wifely self, "should have changed this gay clothing of mine for proper black before now. I must call them. You can occupy the courtyard and rooms Aeneas used."

"Entirely to my mind," Iarbas agreed. "And now I must go the rounds, and see to my posts and pickets. Then I shall arrange for the details of the funeral."

Once again Anna turned from him. She looked down at the sinking coals, dulling and smouldering, their light effaced under the full brilliance of early morning. Again she hid her bowed face on her crossed arms and sobbed pitifully.

The Right Man

(A Tale from *The Song of the Sirens and Other Stories*)

The fifth *ephor*, as least aged, was consulted last. "To sum up the discussion," he said, "we need an unusually capable and very desperate individual for this undertaking. After canvassing every man we can think of we decide that all those sufficiently able are insufficiently desperate and all those sufficiently desperate are insufficiently able. Confessing that we need expert outside advice as to the fitness and recklessness of men of whom we might have thought we confront the dilemma that, including the two kings, no man enough versed in these matters is to be trusted with the secrets of our policy and no trustworthy man seems likely to be able to give any valuable suggestion. Added to which last consideration it is pointed out that any man we openly call in will be besieged with every sort of device to worm from him what he has learned from us. I conclude, to secure an adventurer not yet hit upon, we must consult some man not yet named and consult him secretly."

"Here," said the second *ephor* sourly, "are many long words, worthy of an Athenian. A Spartan should have put that more briefly."

"We need," said the third *ephor* severely, "not flouts at each other nor floods of long-winded epigrammatic antitheses. We need a shining light on the situation."

"If you want to see a shining light," broke in the fourth *ephor*, "look at that ugly mug across the square. I have heard of Clearchos that in a fight his men called his sour phiz a shining light against the enemy. A shining light it is now surely."

"This is an undignified and frivolous interruption," exclaimed the second *ephor*.

"Have we discussed Clearchos?" cut in the first *ephor* softly, with the ghost of a smile.

"An able man enough," said the second *ephor*, "but too glad of the peace and of his return home."

"I should have said that he longs for more fighting," said the third *ephor*. "He was venturesome enough all through the war. If ever a man sought danger, he did. He throve on perils and uniformly came off safe with glory. He seemed to love risk, yet husbanded his men, laid plans with foresight and disposed his attacks with cool judgment. He often flew in the face of death."

"Yes," said the fourth *ephor*, "that was while Kunobates was alive."

"Gorgo's husband?" asked the fifth *ephor*.

"Gorgo's," replied the fourth, "while she was a wife Clearchos never smiled except at imminent annihilation. Now she is eleven months a widow and peace declared, look at him. He is no beauty, but what a grin of satisfaction, what an air of self-confidence, what a stride. He's not for war, he's all for love. No adventures for him."

"Have we discussed Clearchos as an adviser?" queried the first *ephor*.

"Knows all our fighters," said the second *ephor*.

"Totally patriotic," said the third.

"Silent as a tombstone," said the fourth.

"Never dabbles in intrigues or politics," said the fifth. "Has nothing to do with any cabal, faction or party, favours neither of the kings."

"We seem to see a light," chirped the first *ephor*.

Sparta was never a handsome town. Most of its houses were one-storey structures of unburnt brick, white-washed, flat-roofed and, as all openings, save one door, faced the courtyards, presenting blank walls toward the narrow streets. The main square of the town was surrounded by public buildings of limestone painted white.

Of these the largest and finest was the town hall. Its lower floor was occupied by the great dining-room where the officials of the nation messed, and by its kitchen and other service quarters. Round it were the colonnaded porticoes which served as clubrooms to the elders of the outdoor-loving aristocracy. Facing the square it had a second story and in the largest room of this the *ephors*, for the sake of privacy, held their meetings. From the window all five gazed across the market-place at the tall, dark, angular man who strode slowly past group after group, his bronzed, ruddy face lit up by a frigid smile, his look far off, acknowledging each greeting by a stiff nod.

"Send for him," said the second *ephor*.

The fifth *ephor* unbarred the door, stepped out and called:

"Send up my boy."

227

A slave came in, an impudent faced middle-aged Asiatic clad only in a loin cloth and a patch-work cloak most of which dangled behind him.

"Now look me square in the eyes," said the fifth *ephor*, "and be ready to repeat all I say. Go back where you were before and sit down again. Stay there till no one is watching you; then stroll about until you find a slave idling. Instruct him to find Clearchos of Amyclae and to tell him to enter the kitchen and ask for the third cook. Watch the cook and when Clearchos comes in follow him and bring him up the rear staircase without attracting attention. Now repeat all that."

The Lydian went over what had been said, was dismissed, saluted and went out.

For perhaps half an hour the *ephors* dealt with other matters, then Clearchos was ushered in. After the usher left the door was rebarred. Clearchos gravely saluted, without speaking any word, was offered a stool by a gesture of the first *ephor*, and seated himself in silence. He wore a black-felt travelling hat whose hemi-spherical crown fitted close to his head like a cap and whose broad brim shaded his dark face. He kept it on, as it was no part of Greek manners to remove one's hat.

A voluminous red cloak, with a broad wall-of-Troy border done in black, wrapped him from his neck to his ankles. His military boots were of red leather, gilded along the edges of the soles after the fashion of Lydian and other Asiatic bootmakers. Seated he regarded steadfastly this autocratic committee, the five irresponsible senilities who created, guided and drove the entire foreign policy of Lacedaemon. As ostentatious models of austerity they were all barefooted and clad in scanty cloaks of the roughest woollen cloth, woven of coarse undyed wool of black sheep. Their proud, stern, crafty faces suited perfectly with their garb.

The first *ephor* spoke:

"It will be necessary for you to make formal oath of secrecy as to all that passes here," he said. "We desire to consult you on matters of high policy."

Clearchos stood up, lifted both hands palm up and out, after the manner of the Greeks in supplication, and with raised face solemnly invoked upon himself the perpetual wrath of Zeus the Savior and Herakles of Guidance if he betrayed by word, silence, motion or look anything he learned while before the council.

"Will that suffice?" he asked. The *ephors* nodded and he reseated himself, facing the five silent elders. They remained silent for some time, then the eldest *ephor* spoke.

"The late Shah of Persia has left several sons."

"You need not say another word," said Clearchos, "I know just what you want."

"Tell us then," said the second *ephor*.

"Most friendly to Sparta of the present *Shah's* brothers," said Clearchos, "is the *satrap* of Lydia, who has supplied us with money to retrieve our repeated disasters and by whose aid we have finally defeated the Athenians. He poured gold into our often-emptied treasury partly because of his family's hereditary grudge against the Athenians, but also because of his ulterior motives. Not without agreements on our part of furtherance for his schemes has he parted with so much treasure.

"In our last and bitterest need he probably exacted explicit contracts before he aided us. Now that we have succeeded fully, he perhaps demands requital. He aims to oust his brother from the throne and to be *Shah* in his stead. He knows the excellence of our men, drill and tactics. He considers that a compact body of our infantry, well led, would give him the best prospect of victory in his contemplated dash for the tiara. He has perhaps insisted that you fulfil specific treaties to which you are bound by oath."

"Go on," said the first *ephor*.

"If you help him and he fails, Artaxerxes will be bitterly hostile to Sparta and Persia can still do us much harm. If you refuse aid and Cyrus succeeds, his wrath will be a far more serious danger, for he is a prompt and resourceful man and might even yet revive the power of Athens against us with a league greater than ever. You are in a quandary."

"And we ask your advice," said the first *ephor*.

"My business is fighting, not diplomacy," said Clearchos. "I am no originator of schemes. Tell me what you want done and I can accept or refuse. Give me an outline of two or more plans and I can reject all or choose the best."

The *ephors* glanced at each other.

"Tell him," said the fourth *ephor*, "he can be trusted."

The first *ephor* spoke:

"Our plan is to find a man able to attract a large force of volunteers, able to head it intelligently in camp or campaign, able to deal with foreigners, especially Asiatics, able to seem to know nothing, willing to risk his citizenship and life. He must apply openly for permission to raise a force on his own responsibility for operations of his own devising in Thrace: say about Perinthus. We must appear to weigh the matter and to keep him waiting. He must go through the motions of bringing to bear on us all the influence he can command from his family, his connection and his friends.

"We must appear to consent reluctantly, as if overpersuaded. He must raise a force of five thousand men or more, all from the Peloponnesus. He should muster it at Corinth. Then we shall appear to change our minds. We shall summon him to return to Sparta. He must ignore the summons and press his preparations for departure. We shall summon him a second time, threatening him with disgrace, loss of rights and even sentence of banishment or death unless he obeys. This must be done publicly. He must refuse to obey. We shall order the *harmost* at Corinth to request the city to arrest him. He must escape by some trick. Then we shall publicly condemn him to death as recalcitrant. He must carry on his contemplated operations in Thrace until Cyrus needs him."

"And then," said Clearchos as the speaker paused, "if the expedition fails you can disclaim any responsibility and can say to the *Shah* that you had no hand in it, its leader was a disgraced exile, condemned and banished long before the rebellion. If the attempt fails the man will lose his life or, if he escapes, will remain an exile. If the attempt succeeds you might rescind the sentence against him and pardon his disobedience. I see."

"Can you find us the right man?" asked the first *ephor*.

"I need some days to think," said Clearchos, "I do not think promptly. I must make no recommendations that you will reject."

The buildings of a Spartan farm were customarily set round a courtyard upon which they all faced. They were usually of unburnt brick, much like the adobe of Spanish America. The farmhouse was generally a modest cottage, very simple and plain, floored with beaten clay, and roofed with sod or, at more prosperous farms, thatched with straw. Rough, unbarked trunks of young trees, cut with a fork at the top, supporting low shed-like roofs, the prototype of those stone-pillared porticoes which adorned Greek cities, formed a primitive colonnade round the courtyard. In these earth-floored verandas or in front of them most of the household and farm work was done, for the Greeks loved the open air.

The morning of the next day was warm and still, overhead the sky was deep blue and across it marched slowly isolated clouds dazzling white and so clear of outline that they had a convincing look of solidity. Their dun-brown shadows slid serially down the immense slope of Taygetus and swept across the valley of the Eurotas with an alternate impression of ease and effort as their speed increased in diving into each hollow and diminished in trailing up each ridge. An hour or two before noon Clearchos stopped in the gateway and surveyed such a farmyard. In it were a woman, two children and several dogs.

The dogs were no common curs to bark and run and snarl at a stranger. Big Molossians they, short-haired, fawn-coloured, suggesting lionesses in their build and pose, the fine flower of the dog-breeding of classic time. A man might trade a saddle-horse for two brace of them and know that he had made a good bargain, for they were not only strong and fierce but were dependable, canny brutes, quick to fall upon an intruder once they had concluded he was dangerous, murderous to strange Helots, but warily polite to men in gentlemen's garb. Not one of them so much as growled. Two sat up, but the rest merely cocked one ear, and lay as they were, one eye fixed on the stranger, unhurriedly taking his measure.

The children were at play. The girl, a milk-skinned black-haired child of about twelve, bareheaded, barefoot and clad only in a short blue tunic, held a bow and, when Clearchos first saw her, was nocking an arrow. Without moving from her archer's posture, feet wide apart and every muscle braced, she turned her head for one swift glance as the dogs sat up; then she resumed her deliberate aim. The soldier noted that the bow was too heavy for her and that, strain as she would, she could not pull her arrow to the head. She was aiming at an old shield set against the wall of one of the granaries. She hit it fair, a trifle low and to the left. The boy, smaller and younger than his sister, sat on a stool, his tunic was blue also and like her he was hatless and barefoot. His legs were skinny and shrivelled.

He kept glancing at his sister, now and again, but he was, yes he was, (Clearchos looked twice), spinning, really spinning. He was left-handed, held the distaff in his right and twirled the spindle with his left. It reached the ground just as the visitor caught sight of him and he wound up the thread deftly, like one used to it, not at all like a boy playing girl for the moment. He paid no heed to the stranger, who took in all else in the courtyard with a glance or two, and whose eyes thereafter dwelt upon its mistress.

Under one of the rustic porticoes, in a big, solidly-timbered, carved chair, she sat; wearing a soft, pale gray robe. She was spinning, spinning steadily and evenly with a very graceful motion. She was tall, like all Spartan women, with that magnificent poise of the maidens and matrons of Caryae, which has perpetuated its name in our architecture. Fair-skinned, brown-haired and blue-eyed, her bearing interpreted a proud dignity, veiled by gentleness and good will. At sight of the stranger her face set. She gazed at him stonily without interrupting her task. They exchanged no greetings.

"And what brings you here?" she demanded harshly.

"You," answered the man of few words.

"If I brought you here," she said, " I send you away again."

"I shall not go without what I came for," he replied.

"And what may that be?" she queried.

"You," again said the man of few words.

"You will never have me, Clearchos," she said, calmly and seriously. "After all these years you are unchanged. No thought of anything except your purpose and no comprehension of how to attain it. But one instinct, to force compliance. Your brow-beating would turn even a willing woman against you. And I am not willing."

He stood silent and she went on.

"I should have given you a welcome. Be seated."

He sat upon a stool some yards from her, his eyes upon her face. She went on spinning, upon her distaff a large ball of wool, four times as much as a woman would usually take up, but which she held as easily as if the distaff were empty. She did not look at her visitor, but at her task or her children. They kept on with their play, the girl shooting her quiver empty and then going to the shield and plucking out of it the blunt target-arrows, the boy spinning. Clearchos followed her eyes toward the boy. At the moment a cloud shadow covered the yard and made even more pitiful the child's gray, leaden complexion, pimply face and deformed legs. As mother and guest shifted their glance their eyes met

"I had been hoping that you remembered me," he said.

"I am not likely to forget you," she answered.

"I hoped you might remember our childhood, our youth, our love," he groaned.

"I have not forgotten," she said, "not a day, not an hour," she said solemnly.

And does not your heart soften?" he asked. My mother's blood was that of a race of kings," she replied. "We do not transgress our vows. I warned you once, I warned you twice and when finally I swore that everything was at an end between us it was not without days of misery and nights of tears."

"But," he said, "all that is so long ago. I have suffered so long. Can you not relent?"

"My mother," she said, "was Gorgo before me and her mother was Gorgo and hers also and hers. No Gorgo ever relented. Nor I."

"I have been punished enough," he said. "More than enough. And all for a dog and a horse and a slave."

"Clearchos," she said, "you force me to talk. I do not want to talk. You are the only man I ever loved or ever will love. I adored you when I was a toddling child, and you carried me on your back. I loved you all my childish girlhood. Then I worshiped your masterfulness, your sternness, your terrible directness. But when I was a girl grown, almost a woman, it dawned upon me that your savagery was too fierce, too cold, too indomitable. It grew horrible to me. I still trusted you, for I believed you would never be savage to me. But I came to realize that if I stood in your way in one of your rages I should be nothing to you and your rage everything. Then I warned you."

"All vapours," said Clearchos, "evil misconceptions. You keep a grudge too long. And all for a dog a horse and a slave."

"I was angered," she said wearily, "but not so much angered as hurt. I did not care for the dog or the horse or the Helot. I must have held to my vow, but it was not that. I loathed your cruelty or hated your frosty implacability. I loved you, but I came to dread you. And I gave you three warnings."

"All for two beasts and a chattel," he reiterated.

"If you had done it in wrath," she went on, "I might have forgiven it, might not have noticed it, might never have applied it to myself and dreaded you. But you were not excited, you were not wrathful. You were only resolved. You must need teach that dog what you were determined upon. You might have killed the dog at once. I should not have cared. But you must break its spirit and bend it to your will. You told me that no woman could understand dog-breaking. Perhaps I did not, perhaps I do not, though I have seen hundreds of dogs trained, none in that way, but I understand you."

"You did not," said Clearchos, "and you never will. It is a matter of principle with me. There is no use in a disobedient dog, or horse, or slave or army."

"But you were so vindictive to the poor brute," she said, "you felt yourself thwarted unless you wrested its nature to your purposes. You could not kill it and have done. You could not let it be itself. You must torture it toward habits it could not attain."

"Two lives ruined," sneered Clearchos, "all for a dog dead twenty years ago."

"It was not only the dog," she said. "I forgave you that and warned you again. It was the same with the horse. He must be forced to your purpose. You would not trade him or sell him. You could easily have gotten another. But you must needs make him over. And the poor brute tried so and you were so harsh."

"You unhappy, I unhappy," he growled, "all for a horse."

"The second time I forgave you and warned you," she said, "and it was the same with the Helot. You might have led him, or wheedled him or coaxed, you might simply have let him be a while and tried again. But there was no trace in you of trying to learn his nature and make his ways of thought, such as they were, serve you to bring him to what you wanted. No diplomacy for you. It must be coercion, immediate, uncompromising, unrelenting coercion. If you could not succeed by that and at once you felt defeated."

"I have learnt much diplomacy since," put in Clearchos.

"Have you truly?" she asked with an almost startled interest.

"If I have time to think," he replied almost sheepishly. "If an unexpected situation arises I am swept away by my instincts still, and find myself trying to force compliance before I know what I am doing. But give me time and I can temporize and suggest and wheedle with the best of them."

"Well for you, Clearchos," she said, "but of no avail for us. My vow relaxed no more than did your mood. If you had brained the Helot I should not have cared. But he must live and do your will, else you felt thwarted. I saw it would come to the like between you and me, that your inward demon would lash you on to coerce me into alien ways impossible for me. After the second warning I hoped, I prayed that you would not transgress again. But the slave was too much like me for me to be blind any longer. I foresaw years of stubborn tension between you and me, foresaw myself worn out with resistance, foresaw all the more suffering for each of us since we loved each other. It could not be, not for a Gorgo."

"Were you happy with Kunobates?" he asked.

"Happy!" she exclaimed. "All my sons died save that poor child. He was the goodliest of them all and now he is a cripple. There is a Gorgo, there is always a Gorgo. But I have no warrior son."

"I do not mean grief or trouble," said Clearchos, "were you happy with him?"

"No woman," said Gorgo slowly, "is ever happy save with the one man in the world. I was content with Kunobates. He was always kind."

"I had hoped that you might marry again," he said.

"I shall marry Anaxibius," she replied.

"Do you love him?" Clearchos asked fiercely.

"Oh," she exclaimed, "will nothing make you merciful! I love you, I always shall. My vow is between us. This is our last interview. You are tormenting me needlessly. Go. Go."

Clearchos rose, bade her a formal farewell and strode off through the gate.

Two days afterwards he stood before the *ephors*.

"Have you found your man?" asked the first *ephor*.

"I trust so."

"Is he able?"

"That is for you to decide."

"Is he desperate?"

"No man alive more so."

"Name him."

"I am the man."

Dodona

(A Tale from *The Song of the Sirens and Other Stories*)

1

Dexibios was standing under the two lotus trees. On his right hand, forming part of the pedestal to the statue of the Skipping-Satyr with the Wine-Skin, was a comfortable marble seat. Another was on his left similarly part of the pedestal to the statue of the Dancing-Satyr with the Grapes. But Dexibios, buffeted between elation and despair, between anticipation and dejection, was too much in a ferment of hope and fear to be able to keep still or to sit down. He had lain awake most of the night and his fitful sleep had been full of dreams, of dreams maddeningly delightful or black with horror and gloom. He had crept to his post under the lotus trees between the statues of the two jocund satyrs, long before any hint of light. He had tried to cheat himself into believing that the first light he saw was the dawn indeed. He had watched the false dawn fade and die. He had waited for the true dawn, a period that seemed to him the whole length of a long night.

And now at last he saw the dawn begin and brighten and spread her cool, clean light over the garden, till the leaves glistened, the blue and purple blossoms showed sharp and clear, the red and yellow blooms glowed, the white flowers gleamed, each of the throng of statues stood nimbused in a shimmer of radiance, the bronze statues gilded in their aureoles, the marble statues glittering pearly through silver haloes, while myriads of dew-drops sparkled like facetted gems, and the jets of the fountains turned to streams of falling diamonds. The balustrades of the terraces seemed onyx and jasper, the white walls of the villa showed iridescent and opaline, its red-tile roofs, glazed with the night moisture, flamed like coral against the intense sapphire sky.

The doves that fluttered about their ridges and eaves and the peacocks that stirred numbly on the terraces blazed like jewels. The peace,

236

the security, the opulence, the ostentation of his surroundings dazzled Dexibios, stunned him, made him feel small and worthless and impotent. He was abased before the beauty of it all and yet he revelled in it.

Then suddenly, he forgot everything, forgot sleeplessness and anxiety and his own insignificance and the beauty about him.

For Thessa came!

From between the flaring crimson of the two great mallowbushes, laden with deep red flowers, she appeared a small, slender shape, clad only in white and without an ornament. As he sighted her, she descried him. She gestured to her maids and they seated themselves upon a marble bench on the upper terrace, already in the sunshine. Against a tangle of jasmine their blue veils showed plain, and their golden noserings waggled redly in the dawn-rays. Their bench was twice or even three times out of earshot.

And down the marble steps from the first to the second terrace, down the steps to the garden, past the Tritonesses' fountain, Thessa came. Even in the shadows her hair shone more golden than the aureole of any of the sun-gilded statues, her fluttering robe shone more pearly, more silvery than the halo about any one of the statues of marble, her teeth were whiter than the whitest of the dewy flowers, her lips redder than the reddest blooms, her eyes bluer than the bluest blossoms, her smile brighter than the sun itself. For she smiled as she came, she held out her hands to him.

As his arms embraced her hers wound close about his neck, as he kissed her so she kissed him. Almost a princess as she was she was utterly queenly to her lover and her handmaids, all generosity without reserve, all unconsciousness without reflection.

When they had greeted each other Thessa drew him down to sit upon the long marble seat, from which they could look between the statues of the Satyrs over the fountain of the Tortoises across the whole garden to the terrace where the maids were and to the villa's walls and the stiff, erect palms and clumsy leaning date-palms, sharp against the intense azure sky.

"Don't you really love me, Dexibios?" she asked, nestling into the curve of his arm.

"You know I love you, sweetheart," he assured her.

"And don't you know that I love you?" she demanded.

"I most certainly do!" he exclaimed.

"Then why don't you look happy?" she queried. "Oughtn't you to be satisfied, when I come to meet you this way?"

"I suppose I ought," he admitted. "But——"

"But what?" she insisted.

"It seems to me," Dexibios explained, "that if you really loved me the right way we would be married already, instead of meeting by stealth in a garden."

"You silly boy," she laughed at him, "Cyrene wasn't built in a day. Anything worthwhile takes time. We'll be married, I'll manage that But how could we be married already?"

"Hasn't your father promised you," he catechized her, "that you shall choose your own husband for yourself?"

"He has," she answered. Hasn't he pledged himself that he would urge no suitor upon you," Dexibios went on, "that he would say nothing against any suitor to bias your choice, that he would leave the decision entirely to your spontaneous preference?"

"Dear old dad!" she chuckled. "He just has. No other father ever was half so good."

"Hasn't he taken oath to his pledge in Aphrodite's temple before all her priestesses and priests?" he continued.

"You know," Thessa agreed. "You were there."

"Hasn't he had his purpose and his pledge and his oath proclaimed in full market before all the town-hall and the people?" Dexibios pursued. "Hasn't he had it heralded through every city of the Pentapolis, hasn't it been advertised from Paraetoniiun to Sabrata? Doesn't all the world know of it?"

"Everybody knows about it, of course," Thessa asserted.

Won't he keep his word?" Dexibios queried. Of course he will," Thessa triumphed, "that's how I know you and I are sure to be married. I'll never, choose anyone but you. So I never can marry anyone else."

"But if he will keep his word," Dexibios held on, "why do you keep me waiting? Why not tell him I am your choice and be done with it?"

"Because, you silly boy," she said, "that would ruin everything and make it impossible for me ever to be your wife. For Daddy would say that his promise, and his pledge and his oath and his proclamation and his advertising that I was to marry the man of my choice applied only to men fit by birth and station and wealth to aspire to marry the daughter of the richest man in Cyrene, the richest man in the Pentapolis, the richest man in all Libya between Egypt and Carthage. He would say that no one could pretend that his promise and his pledge

238

and his oath and his proclamation and his heralding left me free to choose a pauper orphan hanger-on of his retinue (for you are nothing more than that now, Dexibios dear, and you know it, though I love you better than all the world and though you are going to be my husband and a very great and important and notable man before I get done with you) any more than to a menial or a porter or a slave or a Nubian or a pigmy.

"And all the districts and cities and citizens and town-hallers and priestesses and priests would say he was right. And then he would say my folly said frivolity and undutiful impiety had absolved him from his advertising and his heralding and his proclamation and his oath and his pledge and his promise. And all the priests and priestesses and town-hallers and citizens and cities and districts would say he was right and that what was more he had been wrong even to ever think of such a monstrous innovation as allowing a girl to choose her husband and that nobody but a fool would be so complacent to an ungrateful little pig of a daughter.

"And then I should have to marry some fat, old, red-faced fright with a big belly just like his round money-bags, and with a town house and a country house and a stable of four-horse chariot-teams and a yacht and all that sort of thing and I should be miserable forever after."

"But none of your suitors are old, fat, red-faced men," Dexibios protested irrelevantly.

"Of course not, silly," Thessa retorted, "Daddy's proclamation has gone everywhere, so all the rich fathers have sent their dandified sons and all the rich uncles have sent their handsome nephews, in hopes that I will fall in love with their good looks and choose one of them. But if Daddy were choosing a husband for me all the rich uncles would be after me for themselves, yes, and as many of the rich fathers as happen to be widowers. And Daddy would marry me to the richest man who would make the biggest settlement on me and be content with the smallest dowry, of course, like any other Daddy. And I shouldn't have any say in the matter anymore than any other girl. And you would never, never see me anymore. So there."

"But as it is," Dexibios complained, "you smile at all the handsome nephews and shapely sons, till I am just ready to slaughter the whole convocation of them."

"They are such fun," Thessa gurgled, "but you mustn't want to kill them. They'll want to kill you when I marry you, but they won't.

They'll be polite and congratulate us properly and go off and get married every one of them and forget about us as completely as we'll forget about them."

"I don't see why you are so confident of our getting married," Dexibios gloomed, "at this rate we'll die of old age before we marry."

"No we won't," Thessa exclaimed, "we'll be married soon. I knew I'd find a plan and one came to me, the right one too, the very night after I saw you last. No, it was three nights ago. I had a dream. You know that big picture of Apellides in the south gallery, the Oaks of Dodona? Well, I dreamed that you and I were at Dodona and stood hand in hand on the edge of the temple-platform, and asked Zeus were we to be man and wife. And the Lovers' Oak rustled, every bough of it, and on the Oak of Assent and Refusal the long Bough of Affirmation rustled, all its leaves at once, and the Oak of Prosperity rustled and the Oak of Happiness. Now that dream is a sign. And dear old Daddy will acknowledge it as a sign."

"You'll tell him!" Dexibios exclaimed. "Then why not declare I am your choice without telling him."

"I'll tell him of the dream," Thessa rebuked him. "But I shan't mention you, stupid. I'll tell Daddy I dreamed that I stood at Dodona hand in hand with a man and asked Zeus for countenance and that all the favourable boughs and branches and trees rustled in concert. He'll accede to the indication of the dream and we'll all go to Dodona. I've a splendid plot that will ensure you're being one of the retinue. And I shan't tell you what it is either. And at Dodona we'll question the oaks and when they affirm my choice Daddy can't refuse me."

"Suppose they confirm some other suitor's pretensions?" Dexibios queried.

"You dreadful irreligious boy," Thessa exclaimed. "Didn't I tell you that you held my hand in the dream?"

"Suppose the dream was false or meaningless?" Dexibios interjected.

Thessa clapped her soft little hand over his mouth.

"You awful, sacrilegious, irreverent, blasphemous child!" she cried out. "You'll spoil the blessing of the dream and call down a curse on us! Aren't we sure and certain after such a dream as that? It was as plain as life, plainer. I could hear the gusts of wind and feel the sunshine. We are assured of success. You have nothing to do but keep quiet, be careful not to sulk and let me make my arrangements. Meantime you can meet me here every time you see the signal at sunset and find the safety signal outside the gate. And now it is getting late and you must go."

In fact Dexibios did go, but not at once.

2

Polyteles of Cyrene was certainly the richest man in all Greek Lybia and probably the fondest father in any part of the Greek world. Likewise he was a pious man, with a proper respect for omens of all kinds and for dreams in particular. When his only child and darling daughter told him that it had been revealed to her in a dream that her choice of a husband was to be made at Dodona according to the voices of the speaking oaks, he accepted the dream as a sign from the gods. He proceeded to make sacrifices of the proper number and kind at the proper temples to authenticate the message from heaven.

When every sacrifice came out right the first time he regarded the injunction as unquestionably genuine, as any orthodox being must. Thereupon he made ready for his voyage across the sea to Epirus. The news produced a great ferment among Thessa's numerous suitors and all the harbour side of Apollonia bustled with preparations. The less opulent among the suitors clubbed together and engaged ships in common, some ten to a ship, some eight, some five, some threes and twos. Eight were wealthy enough to have each a ship to himself. Echesepolos of Barca and Locrides of Tauchira, self-sufficient fops, both affluent and ostentatious, must needs have two ships apiece to accommodate themselves, their servants, and their traveling gear and animals; while Mertander of Berenice surpassed them all in pretentiousness as in property and chartered three ships for himself and his following.

Polyteles required but five, one for himself and his daughter and their personal servants and belongings, two for his retinue, and one for his equipages and one for his horses and mules. For, like Mertander, Locrides and Echesepolos, he considered it equally beneath his dignity and inimical to his comfort to haggle for draft cattle at a foreign port and to travel a strange road with beasts equally strange to him and his drivers. Many of the wealthy fathers and uncles were quite willing to lavish money on their heirs for a journey to Cyrene and a residence there and display before Polyteles and gifts to his daughter, but were unwilling to risk their sons or nephews and their cash on the venture of a sea-voyage.

So whereas more than twenty youths from Cyrene itself had aspired to her and more than a hundred had flocked into Cyrene from as far east as the lesser Cathabathmus, from the oases of the south even beyond Agila, Tabudium and Cydamus, from the westering ports past Simnuana and Amaraeas to the north of the Zuchis, full forty of these were cautious or their guardians were timid, so that those suitors of Thessa the daughter of Polyteles who sailed from Apollonia in Cyreniaca for Ambracia in Acarnania were exactly eighty in number and the ships that carried them were twenty-two. So that the fleet that set sail from the harbour of Apollonia was of twenty-eight sail all told, for Polyteles prudently employed Tamos of Naucratis, a skilful pilot, possessed of a stout ship, to sail in the lead and to guide the convoy over the waters.

At dawn on the tenth day before the summer solstice they weighed anchor from the harbour of Apollonia and sailing all day long at full speed under a clear sky before a strong fair south- westerly wind they entered about sunset into the roadstead off Phaestus in Crete. At Phaestus they remained three nights. About midnight of the third night the wind shifted to southeasterly and Tamos, going about the inns and also the camps by the strand outside the harbour, roused the servants of the suitors and lastly the retinue of Polyteles. At sunrise they steered westerly, coasting along the shore of Crete to Cimarus.

From there they crossed past Aegilia to Cythera. As being lovers and bound upon a mission of love they spent the next day in sacrifices and prayers about the temple of the great goddess of Cythera, Aphrodite Anadyomene, whom the Romans later called Venus.

The second morning the wind held and they were at sea before the sun rose. About the slack time of the afternoon they saw the forested ridges of Zacynthus rising in front of them from the sapphire sea. Before the shadows of its peaks were long on the waves they skirted Mount Elatus and came safely into the harbour of Zacynthus town. As the wind again shifted during the night to due southerly they made haste again to put to sea and skimming between the mainland and the flanks of Same, Ithaca and Leucas, they entered the Ambracian gulf and by dusk were moored off Ambracia itself.

At Ambracia they remained three days to rest the horses and mules and to refresh themselves from the sea and in order that the majority of the suitors might have time to chaffer with the dealers and to purchase for themselves riding horses, pack mules, carriage mules, carriages, saddles, and other fittings for their journey. When all were provided they set out upon the morning of the fourth day, departing from Ambracia by the Thesprotian gate and following the road along the left bank of the river Arachthus. Polyteles, always easy-going and fond of ease, travelled slowly and camped early each day, so that they were five days along the road.

Therefore it was the fifth day after the summer solstice they streamed into Dodona, a cavalcade of more than two thousand people, of whom some three hundred were hired Acarnanians, and the rest, more than eighteen hundred in all, reckoning with Polyteles and with the suitors, their serving men and servants and slaves, had come over sea from Apollonia in Cyreniaca. The inhabitants of Dodona declared that no such company had ever come to their shrine upon a private mission, and that even of the ambassadors of kings and the delegates of haughty republics few came with so great a following.

Polyteles lodged with Anaxiboulus of Dodona, a notable man among her citizens, between whom and himself there was an old bond of friendship, since the great uncle of Anaxiboulus had been a guest at Cyrene of Mexides, Polyteles' grandfather on his mother's side. Some of the suitors also found family friends with whom they lodged. Others disposed themselves in the inns and yet others preferred to camp outside of the town.

After all were rested from the fatigues of the journey and the exhaustion of sea-faring, after they had satisfied too their curiosity by visiting all the sights of the neighbourhood, the breeze which had brought them so swiftly from Libya to Epirus continued to blow day and night, increasing almost to a gale, so that every bough of every tree rustled continually and consulting the oracle had to be postponed until the wind should fall. Steadily it continued to blow. Therefore time hung heavy upon the hands of the suitors, whereupon Okypodes of Tubaktis, the best athlete among the suitors and Lerops of Zigrae, who was esteemed the handsomest of them all, proposed that they while away the time with contests of skill and strength, alleging that such would not only be diverting but would win the favour of the god and please the heiress, Dranor of Tarichiae Marcomada suggested that Polyteles and his daughter be invited to be present at the contests.

When Polyteles was approached on the subject he said he must have time to reflect. Thereupon he consulted Thessa. Crafty little Thessa knew just what she meant to accomplish and precisely how she meant to bring it to pass. She saw an opportunity to win a preliminary advantage. She chatted ramblingly and at large. Polyteles had no suspicion that she was influencing him. Quite to the contrary, he imagined she was yielding reluctantly to his more elderly views.

When he spoke to the suitors' committee he spoke positively:

"I won't have my daughter's choice of a husband marred by any fatalities. No all-your-might-everything-fair fighting. Neither of us wants anybody killed or maimed. No, nor anybody dropping dead, either. No two hundred *stade* races, no wrestling. And no boxing, either, we don't want any of you with his front teeth out or an eye gone. Any reasonable contests will please her and please me. But we don't want contests started if they are to turn into a fierce competition, anything to win and all hate to the winner. Let those enter each contest who please and let us all applaud the winner and praise those who did well, all of them, even if they do not win. I myself will provide suitable prizes for all the contests."

There followed competitions in running short dashes, in leaping, in throwing the discus and the spear, in archery, in dancing, in flute-playing. Thessa and her father watched them all and wise little Thessa, who knew just when and how to speak to her father spoke to good purpose. For when they had run several races Polyteles remarked:

"I have a sort of relation here, a distant connection of my wife's. He can run pretty well. I'm not sure that any of you could beat him."

Now Dexibios, though totally without property, was a free-born citizen of Cyrene in good standing. His father and most of his uncles had been killed in the wars with the Ammonite Libyans. His grand-parents and his mother had died of the plague. And the rascality of an elder brother had left him penniless. Except for his poverty he was as good as any of the suitors. It was not possible to object to Dexibios on any grounds. Therefore he raced with the suitors and after many trials over courses of varying lengths he came out a close second to Okypodes himself.

The suitors were ready to defer to Polyteles in anything, of course, and they liked Dexibios, who was always unassuming, and pleasant-spoken and an agreeable comrade. So it came about naturally that Dexibios took part in all the contests. In most he came out second or third and in some even first. He was a perfect flute-player, as good an archer as the best of them and far surpassed them all at throwing the discus. Polyteles was manifestly proud of him and told him so.

"If it hadn't been for you," he said, "all these outsiders would have taken all the prizes. You are the only good man here from Cyrene."

On the fifth day after their arrival, the tenth after the summer sol-stice, the wind fell during the afternoon. At night it ceased altogether. The eleventh day after the solstice dawned dead calm, with faint gusts of breeze now and then, a perfect day for consulting the oracle.

Soon after sunrise they were all assembled on the great stone platform in front of the principal temple.

3

The sacred hill of Dodona with its broad, flattish top and five radiating spurs was much like a clumsy human right-hand laid palm down with the fingers spread out, the thumb pointing northward. The arm of the hand was a spur from Mt. Tomarus, a bare dome of short verdure to the southwest. On the west was the great temple, the lesser temples behind it. The main platform, paved with the porous limestone of the district, was a nearly square quadrilateral so spacious that even ten thousand human beings did not crowd it. From it one could descry a glint of the sea on either side of Mt. Tomarus. Right against the south flank of the mountain, just where sealine and skyline met, the heights of Corcyra would be made out in clear weather.

The ridge which formed the big finger of the hand pointed to Lake Pambotis, and the little finger toward the ranges of Mt. Lacmon, whose vast pine-forests showed as mere streaks and splotches of blackness across the miles between. From the great platform the view all round upon the plain was most beautiful, looking over the infinity of small hedged,, hand-tilled fields, where mattock and spade and hoe had abolished everything like a weed, and where save for some scanty orchards, fully five miles away, not a tree was in sight

That was the most notable factor in the effect of the view from Dodona; not a tree, separately visible as a tree, was in the landscape, except the fourteen huge, sacred oaks.

If one regarded the hill as a hand one might say that an oak grew on each knuckle of it, three on each of the four fingers and two on the broadest and shortest ridge that formed the thumb. Those two were the largest; the nearer called the Tree of Zeus or the Divine Oak was fully a hundred feet high, perfectly symmetrical and with compact branches spreading forty feet in every direction; the outer, called the Tree of Kings or the Royal Oak, was equally shapely and scarcely smaller. On the ridge corresponding to the index finger stood the Tree of Ares or the Warriors' Oak, the Tree of Pallas or the Statemen's Oak and the Tree of Aphrodite or the Lovers' Oak.

On the ridge answering to the big finger of the hand the three oaks stood not at the crest of the ridge but at its extreme edge to the right. They were called the Tree of Hermes or Merchants' Oak, the Tree of Hera or Mothers' Oak and the Tree of Demeter (or of Prosperity) or the Lucky Oak. The outermost and the middlemost of the three on the next ridge, likewise stood far to the right near the marge of the ravine between the ridges. They were called the Tree of Apollo or Artists' Oak and the Tree of the Muses or Poets' Oak. The innermost of those three was known as the Tree of Artemis (or of Happiness) or the Joyful Oak.

On the ridge answering to the little finger of the hand, stood the Tree of Kronos or Accursed Oak and the Tree of Hades or Doom Oak. At its inner end was the Tree of Affirmation or Denial, called also the No and Yes Oak. This last had been broken off short from the ground and stood, as it had stood for countless generations, the splintered top of its trunk pointing to the sky and its only two branches pointing north and south. That which pointed north was called the Bough of Refusal and that which pointed south, all of fifty feet long, was called the Bough of Consent.

The other oaks were all perfect, but except the Tree of Zeus and the Royal Oak, they were trees of ragged outline and open growth, with branches far apart, separate and distinct. Each branch of each oak had its name and to each was attached a particular meaning. The manner of consulting the oracle was to ask one question at a time and observe which bough of which tree rustled next after the question was asked. No branch of the Divine Oak or of the Tree of Kings had any particular name or any special signification attached to it. These trees were held to answer each in its entirety, the definiteness of the answer increasing with the amount of the rustling.

Near the head of the glen between the thumb and the index finger, was a raised platform of pure white marble, about forty feet square. This was called the Suppliants' Stone and from it every one of the fourteen oaks could be seen at one and the same time, no one obstructed by any other. Upon this platform those who consulted the oracle stood with twenty-eight priests, two of whom watched each tree. Under each tree stood two other priests, so that it required the constant services of fifty-six priests to interpret the oracle. For it was a doctrine unassailable and a dogma universally accepted that if there was any disagreement among the priests as to which tree rustled, or any lack of unanimity among the four told off for that tree as to which bough rustled, it must be considered that no answer had been vouchsafed and the question must be asked a second time. Any doubt expressed by the votaries or by the spectators, was also held to vitiate the oracle and nullify the response. Only when all were agreed was it considered that the god had really replied and been manifestly present to his worshipers.

The dignitaries of the temple when informed of the nature of Polyteles' mission were loud in acclamations, holding it a magnificent augury that the five trees he meant to consult, the Divine Oak, the Lovers' Oak, the Lucky Oak, the Joyful Oak and the No and Yes Oak were precisely those that stood nearest to the great platform and most easily seen from the Suppliants' Stone.

Upon that elevated station were packed fully two hundred persons, the priests, the suitors, Polyteles' retainers, Polyteles himself and Thessa. Upon the platform were gathered more than three thousand people, the retinues of the suitors, waiting suppliants with their followings, and curious or idle townsfolk. The proper sacrifices had been offered, the Tree of Zeus and the Bough of Approval had rustled notably and with them the Royal Oak had joined its deepest humming whirr. The priests congratulated Polyteles. By this sign Zeus welcomed him as a king, and honoured him equally with kings.

When the Divine Oak, the Royal Oak and the Bough of Approval on the No and Yes Oak rustled in unison and no leaf on any other tree stirred, the priests interpreted the marked willingness of the god to be consulted and his kindliness toward the votaries. Polyteles then suggested that the suitors stand forth in turn and each ask whether he was to be Thessa's husband. The chief priest, his red streamer fluttering at the end of his gilded wand, signalled to each pair in turn of the priests under each tree. All signified their readiness.

The sky was a strong dark blue, almost the colour of *lapis lazuli*. Not a cloud broke its expanse. No haze showed anywhere upon the hills or plains all round the horizon. Although it was full midsummer and the afternoon would be hot, the noon-heat was not heralded by the morning air, which was fresh and almost crisp. The dazzling sun was already high and poured a flood of brilliance over the world. Everything showed clear and sharp in the abundant light. The sacred oaks stood cleanly-outlined and definite against the sky, till almost every leaf showed separately.

As the sacrifices had been made for Polyteles as suppliant others had to be made for the suitors. For them collectively the chief priest made a prayer and for them all he cast incense upon the glowing charcoal in a bronze brazier standing upon a tall tripod of chased bronze.

Up, up into the clear air rose the thread of incense smoke, straight and unwavering, without a break, and the Bough of Assent rustled softly, while no other tree stirred any leaf.

Thereupon the chief priest affirmed the consent of the god to be consulted by the suitors in succession.

First, Mertander of Berenice stood forth at the corner of the Suppliants' Stone, in full view of all upon it and of the throng upon the platform, bareheaded he stood and with lifted arms and palms turned to the sky.

"Oh Zeus," he prayed, "make answer to me whether I am to be husband to Thessa the daughter of Polyteles of Cyrene."

And he and the crowd and the throng all beheld the Bough of Denial rustle so strongly that its black-green seemed to whiten in the wind, and of the Bough of Affirmation not a leaf stirred nor any leaf of any other tree, unless perchance a faint whisper may have ruffled the surface of the Tree of Kronos and of the Tree of Hades, the dread oaks of Cursing and Doom.

Therefore Mertander recognized that he was not to be the son-in-law of Polyteles and he stood aside.

Following him came Echesepolos of Barca, and Locrides of Tauchira, and they fared even as he.

Then in succession stood up and prayed: Hermesilaos of Assaria, Nephrodoros of Charax, Apostemon of Paliuros, Tamisophos of Megerthis, Mestianax of Tagulis, Brenctor of Zagazaena, Stlengides of Cyrathion and Phlyrax of Leptis; for these eight were those whose wealth had enabled them to have each a ship for himself. But they fared no better than their richer rivals.

Then stood up and prayed Gengron of Simnuana, Rhexenor of Auziqua, Semnotheos of Damae, Praxides of Kerkar, Thax of Amastoros, Aigityps of Tabudion, Opor of Antipyrgos, Lerops of Zigrae, Okypodes of Tubaktis, Dranor of Tarichiae Marcomada and others in succession until all those had prayed who came two or three in a ship. And ever after each prayer the Bough of Negation hummed and murmured and whirred in the gust that rustled its leaves and perhaps the Doom Oak and the Oak of Cursing gave out a ghost of a sound, but upon no other tree did a leaf quiver in the still air and the dazzling sunshine.

Then all the other suitors, even to the eightieth and last, stood up and prayed, and not one fared any better than any other, but in sight and hearing of all the suitors and priests and of all the multitude gathered upon the platform the god manifestly denied that any one of the eighty should be husband of Thessa the daughter of Polyteles of Cyrene.

And when there were but five left to be heard all those few that remained were wrought up with anticipation, for each thought that he was to be the lucky man.

And when but one remained, he was Neptilides of Augila in the desert, who in the competition of beauty had been adjudged third handsomest of all after Lerops of Zigrae, who was adjudged first in looks and Dexibios who was adjudged second. And Neptilides, because the other seventy-nine had been disappointed by the oracle, made sure that he was to win Thessa and her dowry and the inheritance of her father, and he stood forth swelling with elation and self-esteem. But like the rest he was abashed. And, because he had presumptuously made sure of the favour of the god before asking, all the other suitors laughed aloud at his discomfiture and the throng upon the platform hooted in derision.

And then Polyteles stood forth and asked whether the oracle would at all signify what man his daughter should wed. And the Tree of Zeus and the Tree of Kings murmured aloud together in all men's sight and hearing, and the Bough of Affirmation manifestly rustled along all its length.

Then Polyteles queried in what manner the response would be made. And not a leaf of any tree rustled, stirred or quivered.

Then Thessa spoke to her father and he to the priests. And the chief priest lifted up his voice and asked of the god whether the unspoken prayer of Polyteles would be pleasing to the deity. And the answer of the Oaks was as before, favourable and gracious.

Thereupon Thessa, took her stand before the brazier of hot coals, set upon its tall tripod, and sprinkled incense upon the coals and asked aloud whether she would be permitted to address the god. And the Bough of Affirmation was stirred through all its leaves and the Lovers' Oak and the Joyful Oak sang with all their branches at once, and a faint sigh, as it seemed, proceeded even from the great Oaks of Zeus and of Kings. And from the incense which Thessa had offered the smoke rose into the air straight as a peeled wand, forty feet, even fifty feet it rose, and on its blue-gray length against the dark blue sky was not a break or a ripple or an undulation.

Then all the priests sang aloud for joy of the happy augury, and the people shouted mightily.

Then Thessa stood forth and turned her face up to the blue sky and lifted her rosy hands and spread their palms upward and spoke aloud in her thin, clear voice:

"O Zeus, is it your will that I should marry the man of my choice?"

And all the favourable boughs and trees rustled at once.

Then again she asked:

"Is my choice to be binding upon all those who hoped for me and upon my father Polyteles?"

And the answer came as before in all men's sight and hearing.

Then a third time she asked:

"Is it your will that my father and all my former suitors applaud my choice and favour my bridegroom?"

And the ears and eyes of all men recognized the unmistakably emphatic affirmation.

Then Thessa turned and beckoned Dexibios, and he stepped to her side, for he was near, and she took his hand.

"O Zeus," she called, "this is the man whom I love and who loves me, this man whom I hold by the hand. Him have I chosen for my mate. Is it your will that he be my husband?"

Thereupon the Bough of Affirmation buzzed with the gust that whipped all its branches and tore at its leaves, and the Tree of Happiness, and the Tree of Prosperity and the Lovers' Oak sang with all their branches together and the deep booming drone from the Tree of Kings and the Divine Oak sounded strongly.

And all the people cheered. Whereupon thereafter they chanted a hymn of Thanksgiving and that very night Polyteles held the wedding festivities of Dexibios and his daughter Thessa.

The Elephant's Ear

(A Tale from *The Song of the Sirens and Other Stories*)

Hannibal, cum in praealti fluminis transitum elephantos non posset compellere . . . jussit ferocissimum elephantum sub aure vulnerari et eum qui vulnerasset tranato statim flumine procurrere: elephantus exasperatus ad persequendum doloris sui auctorem tranavit amnem et reliquis idem audendi fecit exemplum.

Julius Frontinus, *Strategematicon*, I, VII, 2.

Not another man," said Hannibal, "shall cross that river until those elephants are all safely over. We cannot afford to lose them, and we have none too many men on this side now."

He glowered at his brother with his domineering, preoccupied scowl, his dark face, small as it was between the low browpiece of his severe helmet and his tight curling sable beard, contracted still more in the concentration of his resolve, his black eyes glittering, his eyelids puckered, his brow knitted.

Mago smiled back his big, bland, blond, blue-eyed smile.

"Leave me a third of the cavalry," he said softly, "and I will hold off the Gauls until tomorrow night; yes, and until noon of day after tomorrow—hold them off without half trying. You won't lose an elephant."

"Your one instinct," his brother retorted, "is to get into risky situations for the mere dare-devil delight of seeing how nearly you can go to just missing destruction for nothing and feeling the glow of satisfaction that comes from your dexterity in extricating yourself. We'll get into tight and scary places enough without manufacturing artificial traps for ourselves. Not another man shall cross till the last elephant is over. We are holding back the savages none too handily now. Listen to that!"

The comparative silence about them, disturbed only by the swish of the wind rocked boughs, the murmur of the sulky river, the guttural calls of the *mahouts* and the occasional squeal of an elephant, had been accentuated by the far off fringe of intermittent but fairly continuous shouts, short, barking, yelping calls, long drawn, shrill howlings, and at intervals the faint sound of a sustained burst of ferocious yells or exultant cheers. As Hannibal spoke a longer, louder and less distant outbreak made itself heard.

"I could hold them off easily," Mago repeated. "I could give the *mahouts* all the rest of today and all of tomorrow to work with the beasts."

"I mean to camp three leagues forward tonight," said Hannibal, "and I hope to make six leagues tomorrow. We've no time to waste. And suppose we needed a rest and you could do what you promise, what guarantee have we that the brutes will be any more tractable in a day or in ten? We don't know yet what the trouble is." He turned to the bevy of young nobles who acted as his unofficial staff orderlies.

"Find the head *mahout*," he commanded, "and fetch the interpreter."

Two of the mounted youths galloped off; the rest kept their fretful horses at a respectful distance behind the two generals, who from their knoll overlooked the hopeless confusion of the milling, heaving herd of squealing, recalcitrant elephants, the broad river and the tangled woods on the further side. The woods gave no token that fifty thousand men had vanished into them since dawn, but the other bank of the river, as far as they could see up and down it, was all ropy, greasy mud, puddled to a paste by the convulsive, frantic struggles of the back-slipping feet of the myriads of men, horses, mules and cattle which had scaled it only by the expenditure of their last fraction of strength.

As Hannibal scanned the surface of the river, swirling with sullen eddies, he kept a tight rein on his fidgety little bay. Mago's reins lay on the neck of his tall sorrel, which he sat without visible effort, as comfortable as if he had been on a sofa.

The orderly who had sought the head *mahout* quickly brought him. He wagged his turban, waved his arms and poured out a stream of excited vocables.

"Where's that interpreter?" Hannibal demanded.

Two more orderlies dashed off, and after an interminable wait, which the Asiatic filled with gesticulations and floods of unintelligible gabble, all three returned together. The interpreter was across the river, beyond present reach.

Hannibal cursed the interpreter.

"That's what you get," said Mago with exasperating sweetness, "for your insistence on importing bogus experts from the other side of the dawn. If you had left the vestibules of the sunrise undisturbed and hadn't ransacked the Ganges Valley for alleged adepts at elephant driving we should all be better off. You should have been able to spend on something worthwhile the fortune you lavished on obtaining these dandelion-stem-fingered, spindle-shanked exotic incompetents. And if your elephants were in charge of plain, honest Numidians, even if anything went wrong, which is unlikely, we should be able to understand what it was."

"Talk never accomplished anything," said Hannibal. "Can't anybody else understand this man?"

"I have an idea," said Mago, "that I begin to catch the drift of his repetitions. I have picked up some words of these men's tongue. Shall I try?"

"By all means," said his brother impatiently.

Mago questioned the man, made him repeat his answers slowly over and over, and reported:

"He says the elephants know they cannot climb the further bank and will not enter the river."

"Do you expect me to believe," Hannibal exclaimed, "that an elephant can judge of the practicability of a bank at that distance?"

I don't expect anything," Mago retorted; I'm only telling you what this fellow says as near as I can catch his meaning. Anyhow, you ought to know as much about elephants as I do."

"When we left Carthagena," said Hannibal wearily, "I thought I knew all about elephants. Every day since I've learned something new about them. Now I feel I am just on the verge of beginning to learn about them. I am approaching the point where their probable usefulness in battle in Italy seems no longer to outweigh the difficulties of getting them there. If it were not that they are so very useful at just the right situation, if it were not for the universal and unreasonable dread of them among the Romans, I'd abandon the whole herd here and now. As it is we must get them on."

"Why not take them up or down stream beyond where the bank is mauled?" Mago inquired. "If I understand this man right he says he could have got them over if they had been sent first instead of held till now."

"You know very well," said Hannibal severely, "that we cannot now dislodge the natives from either of the vantage points on the river, nor can we now work round either with the force we have left, and they are being reinforced hourly. No, we must cross here."

He turned to the force of orderlies.

"Scatter!" he ordered. "Find Hannibal at once!"

Hannibal the Scout, the namesake of the great commander, was the most hated and the most feared man in the army, reputed the cruellest man alive and known for the most cool headed, boldest, most reckless, most calculating and most competent man in the whole corps of spies, scouts and skirmishers which he commanded. He had been born in the lowest slums of Carthage on the night when all its rabble were feasting at the expense of Hamilcar Barca, who honoured with lavish magnificence the birth-anniversary of his heir.

After that heir of the great admiral the slum baby had been named by its mother. Before it was three years old its parents died or abandoned it, and the waif grew up into an amazing precocity of vice. Brought by chance to the admiral's notice, the street boy caught his fancy and was taken to Spain. There he developed marvellous capacities of usefulness and had won and held his place as chief scout. He had a knowledge of men such as only slum dwellers acquire, and a store of woodcraft wonderful even for one forest bred and more than miraculous for a former wharf-rat.

Promptly he came, leaning on the neck of his lathered calico pony, his escorts of ragged outcasts half surrounding him, half following. On his right rode his trusted helper, a Spanish tribesman incredibly tall, incredibly lean, long necked, lantern jawed, mounted on a flea-bitten white pony. The remainder were unsavoury rogues; Spanish, Mauretanian and Numidian irregular horsemen and Mauretanian runners—scantily clad, gaunt figures, all cheek bones, collar bones, ribs and staring, skinny joints, but running easily and long-breathed among, alongside of or behind the scampering ponies. Their leader was a dark man—darker than his dark namesake the swarthy commander. He ranged his pony by Hannibal's horse, listened to his chief's laconic explanation, questioned the head mahout (he knew something of every language spoken in the motley host), confirmed Mago's interpretations and asked what was wanted.

"Get them across, and at once," Hannibal commanded.

The scout was perhaps the only subordinate who did not stand in awe of the redoubtable leader.

"That is always the way," he snarled; "any difficult and dangerous task is put on me, and no thanks after I do it."

"Keep your temper," his general told him. "Can you do it?"

"I can," the scout replied.

"Then do it and no more talk," said the general.

"I cannot guarantee to get them all over safely," the scout warned him. "This is worse than any river they ever swam. I may lose one or ten."

"Do your best," said Hannibal. "I give you a free hand."

"One more point," said his namesake. "I must have your leave to kill one after I get them over."

"Kill one!" the general exclaimed indignantly. "Nonsense! What for?"

"I won't say what for," the scout replied. "I know how to get the herd over if you will let me, but I refuse to do it unless I may kill one of those I get across. If you refuse I wash my hands of the job. Get 'em across yourself. You may for all of me, but I help not a particle."

The chief measured with his keen eyes the sulky scout.

He read men instantly.

"Have your own way," he said.

"Pledge it in plain words," the scout insisted. "I'll have no blame through any uncertainties as to orders."

"Get the elephants over and kill one afterward if necessary."

"It will be the least valuable of the lot," the scout told him. He spoke to the *mahout*, who ran beside his pony as he trotted off. Arrived at the herd, Hannibal the Scout asked:

'Which is your most intractable beast?"

"Barranith," the *mahout* replied.

"Point him out," the scout commanded. The *mahout* did so.

"Get chains, mallets and stakes and peg him down tight by the river bank, facing across the river," the scout ordered.

Barranith was by no means the largest bull elephant of the herd. A dozen exceeded him in height and weight. But it took the six biggest, hustling him on all sides, to hold him while the dodging, skipping, squeaking *mahouts* pegged him down tight.

"The instant you displease him he is worse than a wild elephant," the head *mahout* told Hannibal the Scout as they watched the operation.

When Barranith was secured sufficiently, to the *mahout's* satisfaction, the scout commanded:

"Now double chain him."

When Barranith, still grumbling, but no longer resisting, had been fastened as they would have fastened a mad elephant, the scout ordered the other elephants taken some fifty yards back from the river and gave orders to feed them slowly.

He questioned Barranith's own *mahout*.

"What does he like best to eat?"

"Millet cakes and honey," said the Asiatic.

"Got any millet cakes?" the scout queried.

"Yes," said the man.

'Give me three," he commanded.

Then he galloped back to Hannibal and Mago on their knoll. It was about noon and Hannibal was fuming with impatience.

'What now?" he inquired.

"I need some honey," said the scout, "and some pepper. Is there any left of either in the army?"

"My cook has pepper," Mago put in.

"Is he on this side of the river?" his brother demanded.

"I believe so," Mago ruminated doubtfully.

"Send an orderly after him," said Hannibal, "and get that pepper, or go yourself if you like."

Mago sent an orderly.

"And the honey?" the scout persisted.

Mago again came to the rescue.

"My surgeon has a kidskin of strained honey to dress wounds with; but he won't give it for anything else."

"Is he on this side of the river?" Hannibal queried again.

"Yes," said Mago positively.

"Well, get that honey," his brother ordered.

"How much do you need?" he asked the scout.

"Enough to fill the hollow of my hand," he replied.

Orderlies set out in search of the surgeon. Presently one brought the pepper. From the surgeon came a refusal.

"Go get the honey yourself, Mago," said Hannibal, in his most imperious tones.

Mago, his kindly eyes a-twinkle at the humour of the situation, signalled two of the orderlies with a gentle nod and an easy wave of the hand to each. The three galloped off, and when they returned one of the youths carried a small kidskin bulging under his arm.

After he had been provided with sufficient pepper and honey Hannibal the Scout left the two generals and their escort on their knoll and cantered down to where Barranith was fastened. He dismounted some distance from the animal, beckoned to the *mahout* and conferred with him. He took the three fat, moist cakes, smeared honey on two, made with his finger a hole in the third, put in the pepper and plugged the hole with a bit of the cake. Then he told the *mahout* to stand behind his charge. He went in front of the anchored beast. Putting one of the cakes on the point of his spear he held it toward Barranith. The elephant smelled it, took it and engulfed it in his crimson bag of a mouth with visible satisfaction. The scout approached until he was just out of reach of the trunk and held out another cake.

Barranith's trunk reached for it. But the scout backed off a pace, held the cake up and made as if to throw it. Promptly Barranith curled his trunk high up in the air over his forehead and opened his slack, slobbering cavern of a mouth. The scout threw the cake straight and true, and Barranith's approval was visible all over his huge bulk. Then the scout backed off another pace and held up the third cake. Again Barranith spread wide his mouth, again the scout threw accurately. Then, as the pepper took effect, the great dun beast made good his claim to the title of "the trumpeter," tooted, squalled and blared his rage, strained at his shackles and strove to reach his insulter.

"Will he get loose?" the scout called.

The *mahout*, peering from the bush where he had hidden himself, squeaked out a quavering reply.

"Not yet, lord. He is safely held yet."

The scout slowly drew near again to his victim. The elephant, shaking with fury, tugged at his fastenings and bawled his hatred. The scout eyed him, shifting the grip of his spear.

At that moment Mago, watching from his horse on the knoll by his brother, saw a boy running toward the scout. Recognizing him for the absent interpreter's son, one of the bare half dozen boys with the expedition, he realized the situation and put spurs to his horse. Both the skulking *mahout* and the intent scout were unaware equally of the racing boy and of the hurrying general.

The scout watched his chance, avoided the swaying trunk and drove his spear point through the long, tattered flap of the elephant's forward-held left ear. The brute shrieked with pain, impotent rage and outraged pride. As the spear head tore sideways from the bleeding ear the boy yelled out, "You are hurting my elephant!" dashed past the animal, leaped at the scout and wound his arms and legs about him.

The unforeseen onset pushed him still further from his victim. Hannibal was so staggered by the unexpected attack that he lurched back, and, strong man as he was, could not instantly free his arms from the boy's wiry grip. He cuffed at the lad's head, and then his hand went to his dagger. He would have slit the boy's throat or stabbed him as automatically and unhesitatingly as he would have crushed a loathsome insect. Before he could draw his dirk Mago was on them. Wrenching his horse round almost in its own length, he reined it back on its haunches and seized the boy's left arm.

"Let him go!" he commanded.

His practised lift, reinforced "at just the right instant by his horse's onward movement, tore the boy from the scout and laid him helpless across the horse in front of him.

"Be still, you little fool!" he admonished him. "Do you want to be killed for an elephant?" Wheeling round, he cantered back to the knoll with his prisoner.

"Always your everlasting sentimentalism," growled Hannibal. "Why did you have to interfere?"

"I couldn't see a child killed for his folly," Mago retorted. "Give him a chance."

"We've no room for folly and sentiment on this expedition," said Hannibal sourly. "If he ever catches my eye again with any such behaviour I'll have him put out of the way instantly. I'll tolerate no such weakmindedness."

"Give him a chance," Mago repeated.

"Tie him up, anyhow," his brother ordered.

While two of the orderlies tied the boy hand and foot the scout resumed his tormenting of Barranith, Trunk and spear, never touching, fenced in the air, the elephant shrilling his indignation. Then a second time the javelin tore through the thin flesh of the flapping ear.

"Be warned, lord," the *mahout* called from his bush. "His strength is as his rage. Anger him yet again and he will tear free."

"Is he angry enough?" the scout inquired.

"Too angry already, lord," the *mahout* replied. "Much too angry already."

"Keep back there," the scout called sharply. "Don't let him see you."

The *mahout* retreated through the bushes; the scout made a detour about the frenzied elephant and joined the *mahout*.

They walked to where Hannibal's horse was held by one of his underlings.

"Did he see you?" the scout inquired.

"Perhaps," the *mahout* answered doubtfully, "certainly he heard me."

"Does he blame you?" Hannibal went on.

"If he does," said the *mahout* resignedly, "he will assuredly kill me. If he does not kill me you will know that he does not blame me. I think he blames only you."

"Will he remember me?" the scout demanded.

"As long as he lives he will remember you. If you go near him again you are a dead man."

"Will he chase me?" Hannibal pursued.

"That will he," the *mahout* ejaculated; "to the ends of the world will he pursue."

"How far off am I safe?" the scout continued.

"Only when out of his sight," the *mahout* affirmed, "and an elephant can see further than men would believe."

"Would he recognize me across the river?" Hannibal concluded.

"Yea," asserted the *mahout*, "and twice as far. He will know; he will not forget."

The head *mahout* had joined them while they talked. To him the scout turned. He had assumed his intensest air of command.

"Now attend to me!" he ordered. "When I am out of sight quiet this elephant. As soon as you think it safe remove his fetters, except one shackle. Bring up the others and have them lined up three or four to right and left of him, and the rest in the rear of the foremost row. Arrange them so that their formation is deeper than it is wide, and those in the rear can see as little as possible of what is going on ahead of them. Choose for the front row the tallest elephants, and among them those at once promptest to obey and most easily excited. Have the *mahouts* mounted and ready with their goads. When all is prepared signal to my men on the further bank. When Barranith enters the river urge on the elephants; they will follow."

"Truly, lord," said the head *mahout*, "your words are wise. You surpass us at our own trade."

The scout swung himself into his saddle, drove his heels into his pony and galloped off up stream, his tatterdemalion escort following in their usual haphazard fashion.

Barranith's *mahout* gingerly approached him. The elephant was rocking from side to side, rumbling and whining piteously, the big tears streaming from his eyes. He did not grow angry at sight of his driver, but he did not quiet down, either.

From the knoll Hannibal, Mago and their escort surveyed the scene. Behind them the boy had struggled into a sitting posture. He peered between the legs of the horses.

"Let me go," he begged. "Let me go comfort my elephant."

"May I cut him loose?" Mago asked Hannibal. "It can do no harm now."

"I've a mind to have him speared for a nuisance," Hannibal growled.

"Oh, give him a chance," Mago reiterated for the third time. His face wore its kindly, compelling smile. Hannibal grunted an assent. Mago signed to one of the orderlies. He drew his dagger, cut the cords and in an instant the boy was scudding down the hill. He dashed in front of the elephant and began to coo to him, fondle him and pat him. Barranith stopped his woeful noises, ceased his rocking and responded to the boy's caresses. The *mahout* left the boy and elephant together and fetched water from the river. He and the boy washed Barranith's ear.

The brute was then sufficiently quieted for the *mahout* to remove all the chains except one to each hind leg. Barranith was still shedding occasional tears and moaning over the indignity he had suffered, yet he felt himself in the hands of friends and his bad tempered little eyes roved over the prospect without catching sight of anything that irritated him. The elephants were being ranged in rows beside Barranith and behind him.

Next him on his right was the tallest elephant, and aloft upon it the head *mahout* alternately viewed the proceedings of his subordinates and scanned the further bank of the river. Most of the bushes near the bank had been broken and tramped flat in the passage of men and animals. Just opposite two dumps were left at the lip of the steep bank, and beyond them was a gentle slope clear of trees for a dozen yards. The scout's escort of mounted Numidians and half-naked Mauretanian runners emerged from the woods on the left.

The runners were spearmen and swordsmen; the spearmen carried with miraculous ease their amazing twenty-four foot lances, with heads shaped like smilax leaves, three feet long and sharp as razors all round; the swordsmen carried their equally amazing Tingitanian two-handed swords, four feet long, straight, two-edged and with great cross guards at the hilt. Four approached the two clumps of bushes; two, one swordsman and one spearman, hid in each clump. Then the lean man on the white pony stood up in his stirrups and waved his hand. His shout reached the head *mahout*. He looked behind him, swept a glance over the serried elephants, called a question, gave two guttural orders and then in his turn stood up, gestured and shouted.

Two ponies dashed out of the woods, one ridden by a Numidian nondescript, the other, a roan, carrying a figure cloaked to the eyes. They reached the top of the bank between the clumps of scrub, and then the swathed figure swung off the roan pony, shed one cloak after another till he had handed five to his companion, who promptly spurred away, carrying the cloaks and leading the roan pony.

Hannibal the Scout stood unhelmeted and unbooted, bareheaded and barefooted, clad only in his waist cloth, at the top of the bank.

Scarcely had he shed the last cloak when Barranith trumpeted. Hannibal the Scout danced on the edge of the river bank, waved his arms and yelled. Again Barranith trumpeted and all the herd took it up. In the silence following this outburst Mago and Hannibal heard the snap, snap of Barranith's leg chains. Again he trumpeted, again the herd reinforced his defiant outburst. Mago and Hannibal, watching intently, caught a momentary glimpse of Barranith's broad rump silhouetted against the yellow surgings of the river as he tilted down the bank. The herd heaved behind him, he trumpeted a third time and surged forward, the *mahouts* plying their hooked goads.

Down the bank they slid and into the river, till its yellow water was spotted with erect *mahouts*, each with a trunk held aloft and part of a gray head visible before him and part of an unsubmerged gray back behind him. Hannibal the Scout danced and gesticulated on the bank. Barranith, without any *mahout* astride his back, swam two lengths before the other elephants. As he reached the bank and began to struggle up it Hannibal the Scout looked over the edge, gave a last teasing yell and then turned and fled for his life. As he turned, as Barranith toiled up the yielding bank, the four Africans, two above and two below, began to sneak out of their clumps of bush.

When he had his head above the bank, had caught sight of the scout running toward the forest and was making his last spasmodic effort to reach the level above, as they felt sure of his ignoring them, they crawled toward him, clinging to the slippery face of the bluff. Below and behind him they neared him just as he gained sure foothold. Before he could make the first stride of his pursuit Mago and Hannibal, watching from across the river, saw the two big Mauretanian swords flash to right and left of him, saw him sink down like a hamstrung horse, saw the long spears thrust home. The four men scampered away to right and left as the herd behind began to breast the bank, their *mahouts* yelling and pounding them with the spiky goads.

"*Baal* be thanked!" said Hannibal, "they will make it."

"*Baal* nothing," Mago snorted, "Hannibal be thanked! You could have prayed to *Baal* till next summer and they still be on this side. Your scout did it."

"Like enough he is praying to *Baal* yet," Hannibal rejoined, "and he will not lose one in the river. None is being swept down."

Mago scanned the turbid surface.

"Look there!" he exclaimed, pointing below the herd, now more than half across. Two heads bobbed in the current. They watched them till they gained the banks. Barranith's *mahout* was one and the boy the other.

"If that little idiot makes any more fuss I'll have him thrown back into the river," said Hannibal savagely.

"Give him a chance," said Mago for the fourth time.

"Where a boy can swim there can I," said Hannibal without replying.

"Don't you venture it," his brother protested. "If we lose you we are all dead men together. Cross in a boat."

"Example counts," snapped Hannibal, "I swim. As for you, off with you. Now is your chance for one of your favourite rear guard actions. Send me all the divisions except your own as promptly as you can. Don't lose more men than you need lose. Take Gisgo and Hasdrubal. I keep the rest."

The two young nobles he designated followed Mago away from the river, the rest followed Hannibal toward it.

As the last elephant scaled the further bank Hannibal spurred his horse into the yellow current, his escort beside and behind him. When they topped the further bank nothing living was in sight save a gray faced Hindoo and a sobbing lad sitting huddled by Barranith's carcass. Hannibal gave but one glance at them and spurred his horse past them into the forest

The Fasces

(A Tale from *The Song of the Sirens and Other Stories*)

Cneius Pompeius minantibus direpturos pecuniam militibus, quam in triumpho ferretur . . . adfirmxavit . . . se potius et moriturum, quam licentiae militum succtunberet, castigatisque oratione gravi laureatos fasces objecit, ut ab illorum inciperent direptione: eaque invidia redegit eos ad modestiam.

Julius Frontinus, *Strategematicon*, IV,V, I.

1

Faint and blurred, but unescapable, the vast hum from the roaring early-morning activity of Rome reached their ears above and through all nearer sounds. About them the bustle and hurry of the camp, its clatter and rattle, its buzz and drone, enveloped them with insistent noise. Yet the two women faced each other with a mute hostility so tensely silent that the spiritual hush inside the tent seemed an immense stillness pervading all the world. Except their own and each other's breathing they heard nothing.

Through the entrance of the tent, past the edges of its drawn-up flaps, they could see, on either side, an elbow of an immobile sentinel. But the two sentries might have been of bronze for all the two women noted them or thought of them. They felt alone and they were alone, for across the whole width of the big, gorgeous tent they were out of earshot of the guards.

They gazed at each other for some moments.

Pompeia spoke first:

"There is no need," she said, "to tell you how astonished I am to see you here. To say how much I disapprove would be waste of breath."

"Your assumption that I care nothing for your approbation," Mucia replied haughtily, "is as baseless as it is undeserved. I have always striven to win your approval. Your behaviour and your utterances today are But one more instance of your determination to find fault with everything I do, to pick flaws in anything.

"Your surprise at my being here is natural, but your censure I do not deserve. I have broken no family law, and surely there is nothing very reprehensible in transgressing a clan-custom which never had any sense in it. Why should I be bound in these progressive times by a narrow-minded adherence to a mere whim of tradition just because all other women of my clan have observed it?"

Your clan?" Pompeia exclaimed fiercely. It is no longer your clan. When my brother married you he made you, worse luck, a member of our clan. You are not bound by the customs of any other clan or by the statutes of any other family, and if you were, nobody except your own blood kin would know or care. Nobody pays any attention to such things. No more do I. You know well that is not why I am incensed."

"If not, then why, in Castor's name?" Mucia queried amazedly.

"It should be unnecessary," said Pompeia coldly, "and it is probably useless, to point out to you the indelicacy of driving out here in a closed carriage with a man who is not your husband. You must have started long before daybreak."

"It seems to escape you," Mucia retorted indignantly, "that you have yourself done precisely the same thing."

"Not precisely nor nearly," Pompeia argued hotly. "I am a widow. I came with my cousin, who grew up with me and whom no one has ever suspected of being an admirer or gallant of mine. Your escort was a man wholly unrelated to you in any way, whose attentions to you have been the talk of Rome for a year."

"Clodius," Mucia disclaimed, "is my husband's friend."

"Clodius," Pompeia rejoined, "is nobody's friend. He is his own worst enemy; his country's worst enemy; your worst enemy, if you but knew it; and beyond peradventure, your husband's worst enemy."

"You are blinded," Mucia sneered, "by your own sour, vinegary spirit. Your bile and spleen miscolour all the world for you. Clodius has his faults, but he is far from being as bad as you make him out. He could appear such only to one blinded by mere gall."

"I may be blinded by anything you choose," said Pompeia fiercely, "by the worst quality your hatred can think up to accuse me of, but at the worst you can make me out, I would be far better than the bad wife of a good husband blinded by an unholy love for another man."

Mucia looked unaffectedly shocked.

264

"Can even your malice and venom imagine," she cried, "that I could be in love with Clodius?"

"Everybody thinks so," Pompeia told her, triumphantly, "all Rome is sure of it."

"I don't believe a word of it," Mucia exclaimed. "Because you hate me you want to think the worst of me, and because you credit anything, however improbable, you persuade yourself that all Rome believes what your malignity conjectures. The idea! Pompey is the handsomest, the kindest, the most fascinating, the most agreeable, the most popular, the most successful, the greatest man the world has ever seen. The idea of me, who am lucky enough to be his wife, so much as thinking of any other man, absurd! and you know it is absurd!"

The aversion all vanished from Pompeia's handsome, domineering countenance. She gazed at her beautiful sister-in-law with a sort of impersonal fascinated interest.

"Really Mucia," she asked, in a tone entirely inoffensive, wholly disarming, "do you truly care nothing for Clodius? Do you believe in your heart you care nothing for him and everything for Pompey?"

"Truthfully," said Mucia simply, "I do."

"And do you really believe that Clodius is Pompey's friend, showing you attentions for your husband's sake only?"

"I genuinely do," Mucia affirmed sincerely.

"I feel, somehow," Pompeia admitted, with an expression of wonderment, "that you are telling the truth."

"You could scarcely," Mucia proudly said, "fed anything else."

Pompeia's dark face suddenly flushed and her eyes blazed.

"You dolt," she exploded, "almost anyone would believe the exact reverse. And I believe you against my will and against my wish. I have never liked you, as you well know, and as I have never concealed. I began by seeing you frivolous and light-headed, I went on to think you flighty and capricious. Later I made sure you were vain and reckless. At last I judged you cynically shameless. I hated you all the while. But I wronged you, I deceived myself. You never deserved hatred; you are not worth hating, you are not a bad woman, you are worse. You are a fool. I hate you no longer, I despise you!"

The fury of the outburst dazed Mucia and her face showed it.

"O, I've no patience with you," Pompeia went on, "to be so shallow, so easy a dupe. Clodius has never been actuated by any motive but self-seeking. Out of that grew envy of Pompey. Pompey has never said or done anything that could give Clodius a chance to injure him, has never made any mistake in war or politics, Clodius has watched in vain for an opportunity, for a pretext against him. Once Pompey was off for the East and you left behind he naturally cast his eyes on you, and schemed to hurt or injure or discredit Pompey through you. When he found himself kept away from you by Caesar, he plotted to smirch you with innuendoes about Caesar's relations to you. You were silly enough to act so as to lay yourself open to his slanders and to come near disgrace from pure unthinking folly.

"Then, when Caesar avoided you in disgust, Clodius laid siege to you and you fell into his trap at once and more and more. Everybody but you sees through him. Everybody knows he cares nothing for you. Everybody sees what he is trying to do, what he has been doing. Day by day he has alienated you from your husband and ingratiated himself with you, till you echo his thoughts and words as an adoring bride does her bridegroom's utterances. Everybody in Rome can see it but you. And you lend yourself to his plans, let him lead you on to humiliate the family and help him compass Pompey's ruin, and never see what is going on. Oh, you incalculable fool!"

Pompeia stopped for mere lack of breath.

Mucia, pale and wrathful, spoke slowly and contemptuously.

"It is astonishing," she said, "how you very good women, who radiate virtue from every pore and make righteousness a profession and rectitude an art, can descry nothing but wickedness or folly wherever you look, can view nothing but evil anywhere. Your habit of censorious criticism becomes a bias of spiteful malignity and prevents your seeing clearly or thinking rationally. There is not an approach to truth in anything you say."

"Is there not?" Pompeia began again. "Do I not see clear? Do I not see that you are merely a simpleton? All Rome else believes that you are in the plot, that you have abetted Clodius to devise this threatened mutiny, that you have come out to your husband's camp today, as all Rome predicted days and days ago that you would come, to behold the outburst of the mutineers and gloat with your lover over your husband's discomfiture."

"Pompeia," Mucia said solemnly and with conviction, "you are surely insane. I know of no plot. What is this talk of mutiny? The daughter of Pompeius Strabo should not speak lightly of mutinies. Are your wits diseased? Is this a delusion of your own? Have you imagined mutiny impending? Or is there really anything behind what you say? If you are in your senses, let me hear you talk sensibly."

266

"I am talking sensibly," Pompeia protested. "From the day the army began to disembark at Brundisium, Clodius has had his agents among the men. They inflamed the soldiers' cupidity with exaggerated accounts of the value of the booty brought home, set them calculating the probable amount each one would receive and then, when they were busy with anticipations of how they would spend their prospective wealth, the rumour was spread about that Pompey would turn the entire spoil into the treasury and the men get nothing but their bare pay. They feel defrauded already. When Pompey announces how much is to go to the treasury and how little to the men, as he will today, they will feel robbed and are likely to break all restraints. That is Clodius' calculation."

"This is a tissue of absurdities," Mucia exclaimed.

"I knew you would not believe me," Pompeia breathed wearily. "I knew it would be useless to talk with you."

"I do not credit a syllable of what you say of Clodius," Mucia answered, "all the more since I know the falsity of your aspersions upon me. But you forget how much I love my husband. I have little faith in your wild talk of mutiny planned. But I am ready to oppose the most phantasmal shadow of any danger to Pompey as vehemently as if it were a tangible reality, a dreadful certainty."

"It is a certainty," Pompeia averred.

"I will not ask you," Mucia went on, "how you came to believe all this or where you heard it. But thinking you knew it you must have told Pompey. If warned he can easily provide against any danger."

"That is just what he will not do," Pompeia declared. "I might as well have been Cassandra of Troy pleading with Hector."

"What did he say?" Mucia asked.

"'Sister,' he said, Pompeia replied, 'our father's grave is a witness that any army, if misunderstood and mismanaged, may mutiny, however causelessly and unexpectedly, and that when they have once transgressed discipline the men may go to any length. But I never fail to understand and to manage my men.' That is what he said, then what could I say?"

"Obviously nothing," Mucia agreed, "and more than likely he is quite right and would foresee any such danger as you imagine long before you or anyone else could hear of it."

At that moment they became aware of the sound of many feet approaching, not the foot steps of casual passers-by, not the tramp of soldiers in rank, but the noise of men walking together. The two women ceased to look at each other and faced the entrance of the pavilion.

2

The two sentinels wheeled stiffly to face each other, presented arms and stood at the salute. Between them a tall, well-knit man strode springily into the tent.

Mucia gave a little cry, ran to him and threw her arms about his neck. He started in surprise and then caught her to him. She fairly hung upon him, laying her face to his, kissing him again and again, and between tears and laughter repeating:

"Five years, Cneius, five years!"

He said nothing. When her transports slackened, he gently disengaged himself from her caresses. Holding her hands in his, he kissed her gravely, as an indulgent uncle might salute his niece, without warmth and as a sort of matter of routine.

"This is indeed a surprise," he said, "and the greatest pleasure of my homecoming. I feel greatly honoured."

"And you do not disapprove?" she queried, half timidly.

His self-contained calmness, his total lack of any loverly ardour, his obvious preoccupation with other thoughts, piqued and displeased her.

"Certainly I approve of your coming," he told her, "but I am still astonished. Why did you come?"

"Chiefly because I wanted to see you," Mucia answered, adding with a sudden brilliant inspiration of solicitous mendacity, "and particularly to warn you that there are rumours of dexterous and well-laid plans to foment a mutiny which is expected to break out this very day."

Pompey laughed gently and softly, but he laughed. He still held Mucia's hands, holding her away from him and looking down at her.

Pompeia, withdrawn the width of the tent, gazing from under her raven-black hair, her brown eyes wide in her proud swarthy face, not only admired her brother, but confessed to herself that they were a well-matched, well-looking pair. He was very handsome; bareheaded, after the Roman fashion; his hair glossy brown, soft and wavy, his face healthily tanned, and ruddy; his eyes a very dark bluish-gray, transparent and bright; around big, black pupils.

He was wearing the embossed body-armour of pure gold which the city of Antioch had had made for him, which he had declined, as he refused all gifts everywhere, but which he had so admired, that he bought it from the goldsmiths at its full value. His crimson cloak, fastened by a big emerald brooch on his left shoulder, hung behind him. His bare arms were round and muscular. From under his military kilt of broad leather straps, plated with scales of chased gold, his knees showed brown and sinewy. He wore the half boots of a Roman nobleman, made of crimson chamois leather, with tiny gold crescents dangling by short chains from their tops.

Before him Mucia gazed up at him adoring and rebuffed, her yellow curls rippling down past her flushed, sea-shell cheeks, her pale blue eyes ready to fill with tears, a lovely figure of a young matron still girlish, palpitating with anxiety, but already dashed by her husband's coolness.

"Why do you laugh?" she pouted.

"People tell me I am the greatest general the world ever knew," he said.

"Your wife knows well that they do," she chimed in, "and proud of it she is."

"You dear little girl!" he exclaimed. "Can you not feel why I laughed? I have lived in camps since I was fourteen. I grew up on incipient mutinies. I deserve as well as I can what men say of me. And you come of a family whose men have been priests and advocates and farmers, but which has never given a general or admiral to the republic, which has so avoided camps, that you are the first woman of your blood to set foot inside one. This is your first hour in a camp and you instruct me how to manage an army! You bring me warnings! Do you wonder that I laughed?"

"You might pay attention to your wife," she pouted.

"Not her warnings, certainly," he said, with an air of finality. "Attention to her I might pay if she had notified me of her coming."

"I wanted to surprise you," she protested.

"You have," he acknowledged, "and so much so that I must forego the pleasure of showing you over my camp. That would be a rare treat, to show my best-beloved, a woman so appreciative and enthusiastic, what she would see for the first time, I have shown many ladies many camps, but never any to a lady who had never seen one before. I should enjoy it of all things could I watch your pleasure. But all my time is taken up. I could hardly snatch these brief moments with you. I must turn you over to one of my aids."

He led her out of the tent and presented her to his staff. Gabinius, splendid in gilt armour. Labienus, thin-lipped, adequate, envious-eyed, conspicuous in his plain leather corselet; Cato, sour-faced and monosyllabic; Afranius, mild and mellow as a full moon; Petreius, emaciated with fever, but resolutely erect; and a dozen more.

"And you remember Mark Antony," he said presenting a curly-headed, blue-eyed dandy, a trifle too plump. "He shall have the pleasant duty of showing you the camp. You will find him an agreeable guide. And now I must go. Business presses."

In a moment he and all his staff save Antony were gone.

3

Mucia found herself looking up into the very eyes Cleopatra of Egypt was to love so well twenty years later. All women admired Antony and liked him. Mucia liked him.

"You did not remember me really?" he began. "Am I not right?"

"No," she admitted, "I did not."

"No wonder," he agreed, "I went away scarcely more than a boy: I feel every inch a man now as I come home."

"You look it too," Mucia assured him, "and what is more you are."

She understood all the arts of coquetry and not least those by which women no longer young flatter youths. Antony responded to her words and tone. An atmosphere of intimacy enveloped them at once. From within the tent Pompeia glowered unnoticed, unheeded, forgotten.

"Do you really want to go over the camp?" Antony queried. "All camps are alike."

"But I have never seen a camp," Mucia exclaimed.

"Never seen a camp!" Antony echoed. "Do you mean that?"

I truthfully do," Mucia confirmed.

"How on earth can that be possible," Antony wondered.

"I come of the Scaevolas, you know," Mucia reminded him.

"Oh yes," he drawled, ruminating. "Seems to me I remember that their women must never enter a camp. But I thought of course you'd left all that behind when you married."

"Not till today," she exclaimed.

"Showing you about will be a treat indeed," he laughed delightedly.

Mucia, in her interest, walked rapidly, scorning the suggestion of a litter and bearers for her comfort. Antony had never convoyed a lady who made the round of the camp so fast. When their tour was fairly complete she burst out.

"I don't care about so many square feet for so many horses nor anything like that. A camp is fascinating and you are a good showman, but you have shown me everything except what I want to see. I want to see the treasure, the ingots, the coins, the goblets, the vases, the bowls, the statuettes, the tables, the sofas, the rugs, the tapestries, the hangings, the awnings, the embroideries; all they will carry in the triumph. And especially the jewels; the jewels most of all."

"That is the only thing you could ask to see," Antony replied, chapfallen, "which I cannot show you. The treasure is under strict guard and the orders are unequivocal, to let no one see it."

"Not even the commander's wife?" Mucia pleaded.

"Pompey makes no exceptions and tolerates no transgressions," Antony declared. "No one dare break his rules."

"But even if no one else dare break one," Mucia insinuated, "you might know a way to get round this one quietly."

"Circumventing Pompey," Antony told her, "is likely to be as disastrous as disobeying him. Kind-hearted as he is, bland and deliberate as his habits are, he can be terrifyingly sudden and inflexibly stern on occasions."

"He wouldn't be savage on the eve of a triumph," Mucia wheedled.

"Technically," Antony agreed, "we disbanded at Brundisium and are here informally waiting to march in the celebration. Actually his authority is as autocratic as while we were still under oath and his discipline as exacting. He would not hesitate, I believe, to touch an offender with his baton if he thought the offense grave enough, and the offender would undoubtedly be stoned instantly."

"His hold on the men is good then?" Mucia queried.

"Perfect," Antony affirmed.

Mucia, inwardly self-congratulatory at this refutation of Pompeia's alarms, became altogether irresistible in her fascinations. Antony yielded after a little more talk.

"I'll take the risk," he agreed at last. "But I cannot arrange it at once, nor while you are with me. If you are willing to stay quiet a while in a tent by yourself, I'll find out if it is possible, arrange it if I can and in any case come back quickly to let you know."

"Where must I stay?" Mucia queried. "I am quite willing."

"Here," Antony indicated. "See the sentinels before those six tents, they are reserved for conferences of visiting politicians. If one is empty I'll leave you there safe under guard. No one can know you are there or can disturb you."

He spoke to a saluting sentry, they stepped past him and in a moment Mucia found herself alone in the glimmer of a closed leather tent.

She had barely settled and composed herself for her waiting when she heard talking, evidently in the tent adjoining hers. To begin with she was merely aware of the murmur of two men's voices. Then she made out that they were talking Greek. Then she recognized Clodius' voice. Very much to her own astonishment she felt herself thrill at the sound of it. She had been entirely sincere in talking with Pompeia. She herself was as far as possible from realizing how completely Clodius had ingratiated himself with her. He had been tactful, deft and unhurried, had never gone too far in word, tone, action or demeanour.

She had accepted his attentions without concern because she was wholly absorbed in thinking of her husband. Convinced that she herself idolized Pompey she had thought of him as idolizing her, had pictured him from moment to moment as not only her husband, but as her ardent lover kept away from her by unwelcome duties. She had been wrapt up in her dreams of her ideal. Now that ideal had been displaced by the actuality of a cool, preoccupied and externally indifferent husband, who put her aside mechanically and continued absorbed in his duties, her recollections of the attentions of Clodius came over her, a pleasant throng of memories, of compliments, flatteries and kindnesses.

At first she could only recognize the voice, but could not hear the words, then he spoke louder.

"Crassus," he said. "Can you see a flaw in the arrangements?"

"Not a flaw," Crassus drawled, his fat, suety tones trailing glutinously into each other, "when we sit here and talk it over, it seems that everything has been considered, everything provided for and nothing forgotten."

"We are certain to succeed," Clodius exulted.

"I am not certain by any means," Crassus replied. "You forget the man we are dealing with. Pompey has been in ten thousand tight places. He has always come through safe. Time and time again his enemies have thought they had him. More than once, since I have been pitted against him, I have thought I had him. Just when it seems everything is adverse to him and no loophole of escape possible, he escapes or he turns the whole circle of menaces to his own advantage. He has a way of grasping the entirety of a situation in the twinkling of an eye, of comprehending all the factors better than anyone else could and of doing just exactly the right thing, just exactly the one thing no other man alive, no other man that ever lived, could have been capable of conceiving and executing, and it is always the right thing to a hair and he always carries it out without an error. He's the factor which is likely to put all our calculations to naught."

"Whom the gods mean to destroy," Clodius quoted, "they first make mad. The man is insane with self-esteem, with self-confidence. His foolhardy recklessness is going to deliver him into our power tied hand and foot. His success against the fleets of the pirates and the hordes of a dozen *sultans* has so puffed him up that he thinks no harm can befall him, that he only has to will anything to have it go as he wishes. He is no longer his old wary self. I have not told you, but I know from reliable sources that he has been advised of our tampering and warned of our plans, has been warned by at least six different individuals. He laughed at them. He refuses to heed. He is deaf and blind. His folly will make us sure to succeed."

"It does look that way, I allow," Crassus admitted grudgingly. "But he may fool us yet. However it turns out you certainly have taken endless pains. You puzzle me, I can't see what you are in this for. I can see what I am to get, what the others are to get, but I can't see what you hope to get."

"I," said Clodius intensely, "hope to get Mucia."

Mucia hearing the passion in his voice, felt an answering tingle in her blood. She realized that the man loved her. All their hours together, all their words together suddenly appeared to her in a new light.

"Mucia," Clodius repeated, his voice dwelling on the name. "Mucia is what I hope to get."

Crassus snorted.

"Why man," he exclaimed. "You've had five years to get her in, with Pompey half a world away, and you've spent most of your time on her for three. If you haven't got her already, you'll never get her now. And if you could I don't see how a mutiny of his troops will help you."

"Of course you don't see," Clodius retorted. "Neither should I, if I had not been forced to see, and even now I cannot credit my senses. Mucia likes me, likes me so much that I should be sure that any other woman liking me as much loved me completely. Perhaps she does, if I could only make her realize her feelings. But she does not realize them. She delights to be with me, she enjoys my solicitude for her, she accepts all my attentions, but she accepts them as if I were her brother or her father. Off and on I believe she loves me, not for an instant have

I believed that she feels that she does. She is walled, towered, bastioned and moated about with her love for Pompey.

"Not for Pompey as he is, but for what he seems to her. She worships that outward semblance of faultless, impeccable capacity and uprightness which he presents to her as to all the world. Once I show her the fellow as he really is, and she will see what a sham he has always been. He has succeeded all his life because he has succeeded, not from any real strength of character, not from any ability to command success. His life has been a series of dazzling windfalls of luck. He has never wrung success from adversity or risen superior to disaster. He never will. One failure will be the end of him, and his one failure is not two hours off.

"At this moment he is the hero who has swept the seas clear of all our enemies, abased our most dangerous foemen, avenged the massacre of our slaughtered countrymen, gathered the vastest treasure any Roman general ever captured and brought home the biggest army that ever claimed a triumph. By sunset he will be only the bungler who permitted the most dangerous mutiny a Roman army ever burst into. Whether they kill him or he survives he will be remembered only as a colossal failure. Either way Mucia will know him for the imitation he is. Either way I get her, for she will realize what it is to be loved by a real man."

"You are not a man," Crassus retorted. "You're a reptile."

"Mind your words, Crassus," Clodius warned him. "You don't want to quarrel with me. Our interests are identical."

"As far as Pompey goes, they are," Crassus admitted. "When I think of his cold scorn I rage."

"You hate him politically," Clodius added, "as much as I hate him personally. Today is the end of Pompey. His sanctimonious assumption of perfection comes to an end today and we shall have—"

His voice suddenly ceased.

Crassus gave an inarticulate grunt and then both were quiet

4

Mucia, listening intently, heard no footsteps nor any human movement, nor yet any stir of a tent-flap. Through the silence following the sudden hushing of the two voices she felt the presence of a third person in the next tent, rather than heard him enter it. She divined a mute interchange of keen glances.

Then Clodius spoke again.

"What brings you here, Caius," he said, in no tone of inquiry.

"Don't you dare to call me Caius," the newcomer rapped out, sharply. "Call me Caesar when you speak to me. You've no manner of pretension to any degree of intimacy that would justify your Caiusing me."

"All right Caesar," Clodius asserted easily. "No harm done."

"Harm enough," Caesar growled, "to be smirched with the stench of your effrontery, you nasty little tadpole. Keep your foul familiarities for those too low to resent them. Don't you dare to try them on me."

"All right Caesar," Clodius repeated. "No offense intended. You haven't told us why you came, though."

"Nor shall I unless I choose," Caesar replied. "Nor until I choose."

Thereupon Crassus interposed.

"If you won't treat Clodius decently for his own sake," he said, "treat him civilly because he's my friend. Do you hear?"

"I hear," Caesar answered, "and it's little I heed. You can hang all the hay in Italy on your horn, but you can't frighten me. You're like many another sham that's marked dangerous, you scare only the scary. I know you for what you are. You try to make believe you're the bull of the herd and you're nothing but a bogus bullfrog blown up with wind, you great scurfy toad!"

"Come, come Caesar," said Crassus. "You must be in a pretty humour with somebody, but that's no reason for insulting me. Remember that I've paid your debts, financed your election, and that you have me to thank for getting Spain as your province for next year. Be civil."

"I'll be civil or not as I choose," Caesar rejoined. "I'm in a bad humour with just precisely yourself. As for my election and my province, your cash would never have gotten either for me without my control of votes, and if you paid my debts it was in exchange for votes I swung as you wished, and you thought it a right good investment, too."

"Come, come Caesar," Crassus repeated, "out with what you have to say. I know you quite as well as you know me. You're not a man to waste breath on epithets. Tell us your business here. You never came merely to insult us two."

"Insult you two," Caesar sneered. "Impossible! You're beneath insult. It's a condescension to go through the motions of insulting you. You great pair of fools! I came in specifically to tell you that you can be heard outside. I heard you. I fancy the sentry may have heard you. You could be heard in either adjoining tent. You don't know that they are empty. If you must talk, talk lower."

"No need of that," Crassus replied, "we do know that the nearby tents are empty and the sentries don't understand Greek. If you came here to tell us we talk too loud you may go away again."

"I'll go away when I please," Caesar said sternly, "and you'll listen to me as long as I choose to talk. You babble of Pompey's self-conceit and over confidence. You two are a hundred times worse. You yoke of asses! You plume yourselves on the scheme you have fostered and are about to hatch out. You are boobies. I'm here to make you see your folly, to persuade you to give up your purposes."

"You are always doing unexpected things, Caesar, and in unexpected ways," Crassus spoke in his tallowy voice. "But this passes belief. Do you really expect to persuade us by misnaming and browbeating us?"

"I am bursting with arguments," Caesar replied.

"You may argue till the Greek *Kalends*," Crassus affirmed, "but you'll never persuade me to halt now. No conceivable argument could make me forego this chance of pulling down that smug, opinionated, insufferable paragon of a Pompey."

"I tell you," Caesar asserted, "you are a fool. Instead of working against him you ought to make him work with you. Think of the team you and he and I would make. I control the voters, you have more money than any ten men alive and he has the entire army and navy ready to do anything he asks."

(Mucia could almost feel the gesture by which Crassus kept Clodius mute.)

"Instead of plotting to abolish or weaken his hold on the military, you ought to use it. If you ruin him some other man will come up with whom you can make no arrangement. Through me you can make one with Pompey."

"I have tried over and over to make a dicker with him." Crassus growled. "I've got for my pains nothing but scorn and that cool, exasperating contempt of his. I hate him and I mean to get even with him at any cost. You can't change me."

"Nor me either," Clodius put in.

"Even if each of you," Caesar pursued, "is too blinded by hatred to see your own advantage as it is, you might be alive to considerations of prudence. Starting a mutiny is as easy as starting an avalanche, one rumour is like one rolling stone or sliding snow-wreath. Once under way an avalanche is no more unmanageable than a mutiny. A mutiny can no more be directed than a tempest or an earthquake."

"What's the use of your talking about mutinies to me," Crassus rumbled. "You know about slum-votes and election-trickery, you know nothing about soldiery."

Just wait till I get to Spain," Caesar bragged. I'll show you what I know about soldiery. When I come back you'll confess I know how to manage soldiers as well as any man alive."

"That's neither here nor there," Crassus objected. "That's all in your mind. It may prove true, but most likely it is mere dreaming. You don't know any more about mutinies than I do. Clodius knows all about mutinies, he's engineered three already. They turned out as he forejudged."

"A mutiny in Syria or on the banks of the Euphrates," Caesar argued, "was a very different proposition from a mutiny at the gates of Rome. Before Artaxata you risked one entire army, yourself included, in the face of the enemy. Your plans succeeded, you substituted a timid sluggard for a dashing martinet and a cowardly retreat for a glorious advance. If you had failed you had your chance with the rest of getting home. There was no danger of the mutineers killing more than a fraction of their officers, they were irritated only against Lucullus and his loyal subordinates. You only had to spread a panic against further advance and a demand for a retreat. Once turned homeward all discontent vanished.

"Here, to spite Pompey, you have turned the men against discipline itself, irritated them with all their officers, weakened the hold of their oath upon them, stopped the foundations of patriotism and embittered them against the nobility, against any wealthy family, against Rome itself. What you are risking is neither more nor less than the entire republic, the city and all in it, the whole present and future of Rome. Surely that is too much risk for mere private revenge."

"Revenge!" Clodius exclaimed. "Talk of revenge to Crassus. Hate drives him. What drives me is love. You can't move me by talking of risks, or of Rome. Not all Rome, not all the Empire, not all the world would be too much to risk to gain Mucia."

"Mucia!" Caesar sneered. "Love! You pose or you misuse words or both. You aren't capable of love and such as you are you do not so much as imagine you love Mucia. Why you are cruising on the offing of half the pretty women in Rome, and you'd tack inshore toward any port not well guarded. You'd be philandering round my wife if you dared and you'd dare if I were not careful and watchful. You love Mucia! You, ready to risk anything, let alone everything for her sake! Nonsense."

"No nonsense," cried Clodius with spirit, "but the plain truth."

Mucia, listening, heard no trace of insincerity in his tone. For her, for the moment, it seemed the plain truth indeed, and a pleasant thing to hear.

"Man, man," said Caesar, "granting that you are in love, have you spark of patriotism left? You've little enough. For your own mean spite and personal profit you ruined between Tigranocerta and Artaxata the most splendid campaign Romans ever fought. You thought little of patriotism then in your rage against Lucullus, and he your brother-in-law! But here and now cannot anything reach your better feelings? Did Rome escape Hannibal and all the power of Carthage, did Sulla save her from the Samnites twenty years agone, did she barely escape Catiline and his ruffians to be burnt in a mere mutiny and that not spontaneous but stirred up for the sake of a woman? Think of all the blood and tears that have gone to make Rome what she is. Must all be in vain because you are made reckless by a woman's indifference to you?"

"I mean to have Mucia," Clodius replied stubbornly. "To get her I must destroy that sham idol of a husband whom she worships. To do that I'll risk Rome, yes and ten Romes, or the world entire!"

"You two are a pair of lunatics," Caesar sighed.

"I should say," Crassus cut in, "that you, Caesar, are merely an alarmist. You seem to assume that the mutiny is bound to get wholly beyond our control. There is no likelihood of that. Clodius has all his plans well laid."

"What are they?" Caesar queried.

"Do you think it likely," Clodius retorted, that we would tell you?"

Something in Clodius' tone struck Mucia unpleasantly as he spoke.

"I did not think so till you spoke those words," Caesar rounded on him, "I am certain by your intonation that you have no plan at all."

For a moment silence followed.

"You ninny!" Caesar began again. "You haven't any plan! Crassus, what sort of man are you to be led off by such a shallow fool? If you two cannot be moved by considerations of prudence or of patriotism, you might be alive to the thought of your own safety. Can't you realize that if the soldiers get out of hand you will be among the first men killed?"

"We knew we were risking our lives when we went into this scheme," Crassus affirmed.

"You risked your lives, of course," said Caesar. "But you never foresaw how or how much. I can see it on your faces. I've one more question to ask before I go. Can you stop this thing yet?"

No answer came to Mucia's ears. Again she heard Caesar's voice.

"You cannot! I can see that on your faces, too. You are a pair of fools indeed. You're a laughing stock for gods and men.

"You congratulate yourselves on your astuteness, you preen yourselves over your policy, you fancy you are paying off old scores, gratifying old grudges and getting even for old slights. You bat-blind idiots, you're worse off than the man in the fable, who dug a pit to snare his enemy, found himself trapped in it and starved to death there; you're worse off than the slave in the old joke who sat on a limb of a tree and sawed it off between himself and the tree trunk. You're in the position of the carpenter in the comedy who lay down drunk to sleep in his own shavings and drowsed off giggling while he set fire to them to spite the saddler next door.

"You've got up a beautiful plan to discredit Pompey and what does the plan amount to? To ruin him you have arranged to put the city at the mercy of the one thing worse than a plundering army of foreign savages, and that's a frenzied mob of indignant soldiers. You've got up a scheme for the massacre of all the notable families of Rome, men, women and children alike. Incidentally you two are certain to be butchered in the first outbreak, along with every other man of importance who happens to be in camp when the row starts. Yes and all the women visitors too. The soldiers will butcher every lady and gentleman in sight. You two and I will be among the first killed. Yes and Mucia besides."

"A nice mess you've led me into, Clodius," Crassus gloomed.

"You don't mean to say you believe all this?" Clodius exclaimed.

"I do," Crassus snarled, "and so do you, Caesar is right. You've led me by the nose into a trap. This can turn out but in two ways. One way we shall owe our lives to Pompey and shall have increased his prestige enormously, the other way we lose our lives. I see it clear now."

"And you've had enough of Clodius, I conjecture?" Caesar put in.

"More than enough," Crassus assured him. "If I come out of this alive I'll stand in with you on any dicker you arrange. Just now the point is, do you see any way of saving our lives? I can see Clodius is helpless."

"I see none," Caesar stated calmly. "Nor my own for that matter. As for myself I could find a horse and gallop for the horizon, say toward Capua. I might get into the city in time to have my dear ones out of the Porta Salaria before the soldiery burst in on this side. But that would do no good; once the news goes all Italy will rise; the Samnites and the Gauls and the rest will slaughter us Romans everywhere.

"No, I'll stay and see this thing out. It will be worth seeing. I could laugh with my last breath at the folly of you two, you weave a snare for Pompey and the result is that at this instant you two are dead men if Pompey does not save you. Pompey alone stands between us and death."

"Caesar," said Clodius, and Mucia could hear the shake in his voice—"you do not believe your own words. You never could be so cheerful in the face of death."

"You could not, you insect," Caesar sneered. "I am a man. When I really look on the face of death I shall not blench. I've seen death close a hundred times, as light-heartedly as today. Think of the excitement of it. Men get worked up over dice. But what a game this is, Rome the stake and our lives to boot and it all turns on Pompey. This beats chariot-racing for any wager."

Mucia heard a movement behind her and turned around.

'What are you listening to?" Antony asked.

"I was trying to hear what is being said in the next tent," Mucia coolly responded. "There are three men in there, talking excitedly in Greek. But they talk so low that I could not make out a word. At first I thought I knew the voices, but I could not even recognize them. However, listening has passed the time for me. Am I to see the treasure?"

5

Her heart palpitating with conflicting emotions, her mind whirling with antagonistic ideas, Mucia went to her sightseeing woodenly and numbly. Yet her instincts of coquetry and finesse made her counterfeit a delighted interest which completely deceived Antony.

Inwardly she was torn between loving admiration for Pompey, pique at his coolness, even resentment against him, leaning toward that furious rage for revengefulness which woke so easily in a Roman woman. She was divided between distrust of Clodius and the newly realized fascination he had long exercised upon her. Fearing for her own life alternately woke to frenzied panic and calmed under the spell of exultant confidence in her incomparable husband. Solicitude for his lofty reputation and for him struggled against indignation at his curt ignoring of her attempt of a warning. The black certainty of impending doom surged up and drowned her spirit in despair and then again she told herself she had heard merely the inventions of three politicians talking for effect.

With these and a thousand other contending sensations and thoughts seething within her she kept up her judiciously interested smile, shot her dazzling glances at the proper moments and gurgled expressions of pleasure which she herself could not hear and knew were successful only by watching Antony's face. She felt ready to faint more than once, yet congratulated herself that her companion perceived nothing wrong.

When he showed her the wagon-loads of jewels, she suddenly forgot all about Caesar and Crassus, Clodius and Pompey, mutinies and intrigues, forgot herself and spoke naturally.

Antony was amazed. She swept away his attempt at reply in a second outburst, which he only half understood.

"You certainly seemed to enjoy the bulk of the treasure," he groped; "why are the jewels such a disappointment?"

"Naturally," Mucia replied, "these coffers of loose pearls and turquoises, of heaped sapphires and rubies, of unset opals and diamonds mean nothing to me. The romance, the glamour was all taken away from these stones when they were torn from their settings. No stories cling to them, no perfume of the past lingers about them. I am ready to burst into tears at the sacrilege. Mithridates had gathered the spoil of a hundred conquests into Amisus, his sixty *sultanas* had wonderful diadems, necklaces, bracelets and amulets.

"Every piece had its history. Archelaus had taken in Sparta all those rings and belts which the tyrant Nabis lavished on his women; and with them the ornaments of his chief wife Pheretime of Barca, the very trappings the first Pheretime wore when the Persians helped her punish the rebels and she tortured them and their wives. From Antioch Tigranes carried off the seven strand necklace the mother of Darius wore when Alexander captured her at Issus. He got the best of that share of Alexander's treasure which Seleucus kept.

"I expected to see all those glorious things and more, and you show me meaningless stones bereft of their souls.

"It was such a silly thing to do! The greater bulk of the wrought jewellery would have made only a trifling difference in transporting it and guarding it. And the authentic, original curios could have auctioned for ten times as much as you will ever sell these bleak pebbles for. Merely that is a pity. But the loss of their associations wrings my heart.

"I am so disappointed. I expected to thrill so at the sight and touch of them. They symbolized the power and majesty of the tyrants and kings and sultans who bestowed them, the glory of their conquests and kingdoms, the beauty of the women who wore them, the dangers and toil and triumph of the campaigns in which they were won. They would have preserved all that forever. Now it is all lost, gone from them irretrievably."

"Oh, the pity of it!"

"Don't talk to me. I am cheated with heaps of gems where I anticipated seeing the embodiment of the arrogance Rome has abased, of the courage and skill that accomplished so much for Rome, of the power and prestige and glory Rome has won."

Antony looked at her, bright-eyed, ten times handsomer than she had thought him.

"The embodiment!" he exclaimed. "You were never in a camp till today? Have you ever seen and touched fasces or standards or an eagle?"

"Fasces I have seen, of course, but never touched," she beamed, catching fire from his enthusiasm. "But I was a child when Pompey returned from Sicily and Africa and triumphed. I never saw an eagle or any standard."

"I should have thought," Antony wondered, "that you would have had Pompey take you to the treasury and show you his fasces and standards and eagles while they were deposited there."

"One never does the sightseeing that is easiest," Mucia replied. "If I had thought of it I should have put it off, and in fact I never thought of it at all."

"Then," Antony exulted, "I can show you what you want to see, the embodiment of the soul of Rome."

The tent to which he led her was guarded by a detail of brawny self-important giants. Inside it they found a dozen centurions, grizzled veterans every one, scarred, seamed and weather-beaten. Their fierce old eyes glared kindly admiration at her from under their bushy brows, their mouths widened into smiles of a truculent good-nature which made her quake at the thought of fifty thousand such men suddenly frenzied with ferocious indignation. These old warriors were all awkward complaisance tremulously pleased at her presence, but their faces had that odd animality which results from sound teeth shortened by long grinding of gritty bread, an approach of nose and chin very different in its effect from the outcome of toothlessness, but productive of a sort of senile brutality which the grins only accentuated. They had been handling long narrow cases of red leather.

"We are just in time," Antony remarked, they are taking out the standards for the parade. The soldiers are going to turn out to hear the general's speech."

Mucia shuddered. Everything hinged on that speech. Then the awestruck reverence with which the veterans opened the cases riveted her attention upon what they contained. From their swathings of fine crimson cloth and delicate white wool padding appeared the standards; each a ten-foot pole of carved wood gilded with gold-leaf all over; shod with a bronze spike below a chased silver rosette, bare for some feet above that; then to the top set close with thick corrugated silver disks, like cups trodden flat by an elephant; topped off by a cross-bar from whose ends hung streamers of crimson silk tipped with tinkling tassels of silver ivy-leaves. The names and numbers of the legions chiselled on the cross-bars, the dates and names of localities embossed on the saucer-shaped disks woke Mucia to palpitating delight in their crowding associations. She overwhelmed Antony with questions which he answered indulgently.

Yes, this was the first standard of the first legion. No, those disks did not recall Pompey's victories, the legion had won them under Lucullus. From the top down the disks commemorated the relief of Cyzicus, the capture of Heracleia, the storming of Sinope, the passage of the Halys, the taking of Amisus, the blockade and entry of Tigranocerta and the storm of Nisibis. Yes, the second standard commemorated Pompey's victories. No, there were no disks for any of the successes against the pirates, he had considered them too easy. They commemorated the night victory on the Lycos; the forcing of the Phasis, the storm of Artaxata, the taking of the castles in the Caucasus, and the entry into Jerusalem. So they went over them all, she bubbling delight, he pleased, enjoying her enjoyment, adding to it with brief sketches of battles or anecdotes of sieges and marches, but mostly watching her and talking tolerantly.

This was the eagle of the legion. No, eagles were not always of silver, in fact, they had always been of bronze until Aemilius Paullus had silver eagles made from the Macedonian booty; Scipio plated his silver eagles with gold after he defeated Antiochus of Syria; Pompey was the first commander to have his eagles of solid gold; actually this was the first eagle of cast gold ever made.

"And now," said Antony. "You shall see the fasces."

"The fasces!" Mucia exclaimed. "Has Pompey two sets of fasces?"

"No," Antony answered, "only this one set."

"But how can they be here?" Mucia queried staring at the fasces the centurions were lifting out of their cases, "Are they not being carried before him?"

"Did you see any *lictors* when you saw him?" Antony suggested.

"I shouldn't have seen or noticed *lictors*," Mucia retorted, "if there had been ten dozen instead of two. I was not looking for *lictors*. I saw only Pompey."

"There were no *lictors* preceding him," Antony said simply.

"But why?" she marvelled. "How can that be?"

"You see," Antony exclaimed. "Technically we disbanded at Brundisium. Nominally we have not been an army since we came ashore, nor Pompey a general."

"You mean," Mucia panted, "that the men are no longer under oath?"

"Certainly," Antony answered easily. "Not since the day after they disembarked."

"But what holds them together?" Mucia asked wide-eyed and breathing fast, her heart thumping.

"Pompey," was Antony's sufficient reply. "They are gentle as lambs. He is paying the expense of rations and everything else out of the booty account, and the technical irregularity will be overlooked, for it forestalls all chance of the quarrels, fights, stabbings, brawls, affrays, riots, pillaging, robberies and burnings that would certainly occur here and there as the men got to drinking, if they straggled up to Rome afoot, in loose bands without officers. The saving is obvious and great. As it is they have been as orderly as on campaign, not a squabble or row anywhere. But they are held only by custom, convenience of tenting and messing, their ingrained habits of obedience, the after effects of their oath-bound years and their reverence for Pompey."

Mucia ruminated in silence, choking. Here was an opportunity indeed for plotting an outbreak. Nothing to hold the men but Pompey's personal magnetism, no legal power behind him, no authority lodged in him, no bond between him and the men, no consecration of duty, no curse upon malcontents.

"And that is why the fasces are not carried before him," she quavered, "why no *lictors* precede him?"

"Just so," Antony agreed, "he could hardly parade the sacred legal symbols of powers he has solemnly surrendered. But the fasces will be displayed, carried behind him on the platform with the standards and eagles when he makes his speech today. The men would miss the tokens of command to which they are accustomed, and the violation of the law will be winked at and ignored."

Mucia bent over the fasces, forcing herself to seem interested in these emblems so full of weighty import, the grim bundles of gilded wands bound together with crossed red-leather thongs, each including a broad-bladed keen-edged axe, silver-mounted and its handle silver-ringed. She bent over them and forced herself to her expected outward semblance and to ask questions. Antony expounded as before.

Yes, these were the very fasces Pompey had assumed in Sicily with Sulla's permission, when he was only twenty-two. The laurel-wreaths were pure gold, the same he had added with Sulla's consent when he returned from Africa and triumphed and his men saluted him as commander. After he returned from Spain the fasces had been in the treasury from the end of his year of office until he set out against the pirates. Yes, the rods were birch, you could see that through the gold leaf if you looked carefully. Corinnos of Rhodes had forged and inlaid and chased the axes and carved their handles.

Yes, the tassels of the straps were silk, these were the first silk tassels ever put on fasces, before Pompey they had been of wool only. Could these very rods be used for flogging? Indeed they could and had; many a thief or skulker had been cut to ribbons with them; afterwards the blood was washed off and the rods regilded. And could these very axes behead a man? Actually one or another had been used more than once.

"We were just in time, as I told you," Antony concluded, "here are the bearers come for them."

The two dozen bare-headed, bare-necked *lictors*, jaunty in their short crimson cloaks, filed in silently, eyeing the lady curiously, nudging each other and whispering that she was the general's wife. As they softly fell in to go the standard bearers edged their way in, received their precious charges from the old centurions, and tramped off behind the *lictors*.

When they were gone Mucia, bright-eyed and quick-breathing, faced Antony. "Do you know," she said, "it was not the fasces and standards themselves, not even the eagles, that impressed me most, it was the way the men handled them. No young mother ever hung over her first baby boy more solicitously than those hard-faced old warriors over these cases. No priest ever touched any amulet or Palladium more reverently than they dealt with those standards and fasces and eagles; their battered, gnarled hands grasped and lifted them as delicately as a lady's fingers would her fancy work. The tears came into my eyes to see it."

"You have the right kind of heart," Antony told her delightedly. "You have true sympathy. That is just what I wanted you to see. All the toil and sweat and determination of their marchings and trenchings and waitings, all the grim resolution that carried them through starvation and sickness, all the hopeless valour of their chums and cronies who died on forlorn hopes and fruitless assaults; all the heartbreaking doubts of night surprises, the furious uncertainties of the crisis of battle, the tumultuous exultation of the moment of victory; all the ecstatic enthusiasm of recognition of their commander's worth in strategy and tactics; all their adoration of his still composure, of his unexpected revelations of insight beyond their comprehension; all that and more, all their successes and hopes they see in their standards,

"All their army's reputation and prestige and glory is manifest and visible to them in their eagles. And all the majesty and might of Rome, all the accumulated power and authority of her conquests, all the magic of her sway is for them inherent in the fasces. For them the standards are the visible soul of the army, the eagle the living presence of Rome's glory, the fasces the personality of her puissance. They might ignore the holiness of consecrated ground, they might violate a tomb or a temple, they might lay violent hands on the statue of a divinity; before the fasces they are deferential, before the standards they are obsequious, to the eagle they bow in awe.

"A soldier has often little enough respect for a court or a judge, but the fasces are for him the concrete embodiment of right and justice, he would give his life rather than see them dishonoured. He might be never so drunk and never so weary, but every fibre of him would wake to energy to protect the standards; he might be so lost and degraded as to kill his own father and mother, but he would hesitate to do wrong to an eagle. I see you comprehend all this. Few women do. It will make you enjoy the assembly all the more. You will realize what is behind Pompey's speech."

Did she not realize? She shook inwardly as she realized it, shook outwardly, almost tottered before she mastered herself into external decorum as she suffered Antony to escort her to the platform.

6

From the platform of a Roman camp, orders of the day were read, news cried, notifications given, also addresses made to the soldiers by officers or the commander. This platform was in most cases a substantial structure of earth faced and topped with sod, in temporary camps; or in permanent camps with stone, of which it was sometimes entirely constructed, as was the platform toward which Antony conducted Mucia. The rank and file of men were assembling before it; the centurions, nearly six hundred of them, on either side of it facing the soldiers; upon it stood Pompey, his chief officers on his right, on his left the visiting notabilities, behind him his *lictors* and the standard bearers.

Farther back on the platform, upon its three raised tiers, were massed the officers, the staff and others above the rank of *centurion*. On Pompey's left, among the visitors, were a dozen or more ladies, Pompeia with them. Mucia noted her, and nearby Crassus, Clodius and Caesar. For Antony did not conduct her up to join the rest until he had led her entirely around the platform, so that she might get the men's view of it from in front. Pompey, sweeping his outlook with keen eyes, stood at the edge of the platform, midway of its front.

The crimson horsehair crest of his helmet rippled in the breeze, his blue eyes sparkled, his gallant bearing, his golden armour, his crimson cloak and big green shoulder-brooch set him off splendidly. Still more was he set off by the tiers of serried officers behind the standard bearers and *lictors*. Against the deep azure of the morning sky spread the golden wings of the ten eagles, gleaming in the sun. The masses of gorgeous colouring of the uniforms made a background which would have swallowed up and extinguished almost any other general, but against it Pompey stood out conspicuous, his ineffaceable distinction making his armour seem more golden, his cloak more crimson than any of those behind him, as his face seemed nobler and his eyes brighter.

Mucia admired him unreservedly and her sense of pique at his coolness lessened. She comprehended why Sulla had accorded him his title of "the Great Man;" if at that moment his shoulders bore the whole weight of Rome's destinies he looked fully equal to the load, looked the visible incarnation of the majesty of Rome. Beside him Clodius seemed a poor creature.

Yet Mucia ruefully reflected that appearances were very little likely to avail in the approaching crisis. Clodius looked the shrewder, if the meaner man.

Before Antony went his way to take his place among the younger members of the staff he left Mucia next Pompeia. Looking about she found Caesar on her left between her and Clodius. Clodius did not meet her eye. Crassus behind him looked pasty and mottled.

Caesar had hitched his belt askew into that rakish position, the habit of which had made him so conspicuous as a lad. He seemed to Mucia masking a cynical bravado under an inscrutable air of rollicking jauntiness. Pompeia gloomed darkly, tense and over-wrought.

The *centurions* had flowed round in a crescent and stood facing the platform leaving a few yards of ground bare before it. Behind them was a jam of the rank and file, armed and helmeted as for review, but collected like any crowd without formation. They were ominously silent. Their one cheer was lifeless. Pompey began his speech as lifelessly. As she listened to his cold, formal periods Mucia wondered was he really the sham Clodius made him out. The men, she could see, listened without enthusiasm as he frigidly enumerated those names of victories which, if glowingly delivered, should have roused his auditors to a frenzy of ardour. Clearly he spoke and audible to the last man at the rear of the listening thousands, but his utterance, precise, almost mincing in its exactness, carried no warmth.

The senate had graciously acceded to their request for a triumph. They were to be accorded full measure of recognition for their valour and their success.

There were to be two separate processions on succeeding days. The first day would commemorate the annihilation of the pirates. The army would act as escort only. The second day would celebrate all the land victories. The spoil . . . (at the mention of the spoil Mucia felt the strained attention of the men, their readiness to take offense), the spoil would be displayed on sixteen hundred wagons. It would be deposited entire in the treasury. Each man would be paid his allotted stipend at once and in addition in place of any division of booty would receive the amount of two years' wages, paid in silver.

At that word the storm burst. The roar of the angry men drowned Pompey's voice and swelled into a tide of sound that seemed capable of drowning all the noises in the world. It lasted on, roar following roar in pulsations, blent into one unbroken cataract of noise. All the men were gesticulating and here and there a naked sword flashed aloft above the mob. The tossing sea of waving arms and contorted faces made a terrible spectacle.

Mucia realized instantly the fatuity of Clodius and Caesar's unerring prescience. She knew her last hour had come, unless Pompey was strong to save. She knew that upon him hung, not only her life but the lives of all those about her, that upon him depended the salvation of Rome and of all the Roman world. She realized how imbecile had been any pretensions of Clodius towards keeping in hand and guiding the tempest he had aroused. She had a staggering prophetic vision of what the platform she stood on might look like at sunset, her draggled corpse among others heaped pell-mell. Equally clear did she behold the impending horrors of Rome pillaged, burning, then obliterated forever.

In all this instantaneous realization of threatening doom she did not lose her composure. The Romans were an amazingly excitable race, quick to yield to any passion, and by no means controlled in the outward expression of their feelings. Their women screamed easily, their men, even in public, commonly burst into tears, even multitudes of them together, upon provocation that would move no Teutonic or Saxon crowd to any exhibition of emotion whatever. Contradictorily they were extremely capable of self control in respect to anything infringing their idea of dignity. The nobility especially valued a dignified exterior above all the other possessions of their souls.

Mucia came of a family believed to be descended from an ancestor capable of thrusting his right hand into a fire and holding it there unflinchingly till it charred. She lived up to her family traditions in general. Now she did not shriek or faint. She was of that blood which bred those contained matrons whose poise and serenity we may still view mirrored forever on the faces of such portrait statues as have come down to us. She had not their height or majesty of form, she had the Roman soul of the tallest of them. Inwardly overwhelmed with dread, she coolly took in the situation. She had had her eyes on Pompey's face and she saw him for one heart-beat thunderstruck with astonishment, saw that he had anticipated no such situation, saw him wholly unprepared to deal with it.

The sea of faces before her heaved like a whirlpool. The next breath it might become an irresistible torrent of utter destruction. There would be one chance against it and only one.

The women about her she saw as unperturbed as herself, true to their ideals of demeanour. Yet their impassive countenances were deathly white every one.

On the faces of the more comprehending men she read dazed terror; Crassus was blotched and speckled with hues of fright, Clodius was gray with the fear of death; Caesar clothed in cynical patrician effrontery gazed unmoved at the riot, cast a glance of amused contempt at Clodius and fixed expectant eyes on Pompey.

Mucia's followed his. She had borne up in spirit against her inward shudders at the men's outburst, now she nearly fainted under the hot wave of reassurance that surged through her.

Pompey's face was the face of the practised fencer who knows his own skill, knows just what he means to do and confidently waits his certain opportunity.

The roar for gold, gold, gold filled the air. The first syllable of "*aurum*" pulsated in a "*wow*," "*wow*," "*wow*" like the snarl of a horde of ravening wild beasts. Ravening wild beasts the men would be next instant unless Pompey saved the situation. Calmly and resolutely he faced them until they hushed from mere breathlessness.

Then his voice rang out, clear, magnetic, full of resonance and fire. "You want gold?"

Again the roar, the harsh, hoarse, rasping roar of fifty thousand angry fighters, again he waited for it to die down.

"You want gold?" he repeated.

The roar redoubled and through its continuance Pompey's face was not that of a man baffled and defeated, not that of one in a quandary, it was the face of a capable man seeing his opportunity and rising to grasp it. It was not the face of one who doubts or fears. It wore the expression of the man who comprehends his countrymen to the recesses of their souls, knows all the modulations of their heart-strings, understands a situation in all its complexities and means to do the one thing sure to touch the right chord.

Silence fell again, not so much now that the men were breathless as that those in front felt the compulsion of Pompey's magnetic gaze, those not so far off yielded to the spell of his masterful attitude, and the thrill of their submission communicated itself to the entire throng.

Transfigured and sublime, his presence thralling the whole vast concourse, he stepped back half a pace. With each hand he seized the fasces from the nearest *lictor* to right and left of him. To the earth before the platform he hurled them. Through the stunned silence his voice bugled:

"If you want gold, begin on that: . . or that!"

The stillness became as if no breathing thing but himself existed. Stepping back again he seized the two standards of the fourth legion.

"Or on that!" he called as he hurled the first, "or on that!" as he hurled the second.

Across the dazed hush his clarion voice carried far.

"Think what you are doing. The gold I shall turn into the treasury is no more yours to covet than the bullion on the fasces, the metal of your standards, or the gold of the eagles."

He seized and hurled the great gold eagle of the seventh legion.

"If you must and will have gold," he called, "begin on that!"

The tension snapped. A tenfold roar effaced the brief silence. It was a roar of weeping men, abashed, abased, brought back to their senses, those behind trampling those before as they surged forward. From the dust they lifted their desecrated standards, their eagle, the dread fasces. Tenderly they brushed them. On their knees they begged for pardon, with streaming eyes and babbling tongues choked by sobs they proffered unalterable fealty.

When the tumult slackened Pompey held up one hand. Every man in whatever attitude he might be was frozen mute. Pompey gave a low-voiced order. The two *lictors* and the three standard-bearers went down into the crowd, retrieved their precious charges and returned to their places, no other man moving the while.

Mucia looked about her. Crassus she saw, but not Clodius. In fact she never saw him again that near, never at all again to speak to. Caesar's eyes met hers with an expression of relished amusement

She looked again at Pompey, at the deity who had saved her, had saved Rome.

He surveyed the throng before him,

"Further details of the arrangements will be communicated to you by your *centurions*," he said. "After the spoil is in the treasury you will be paid your stipends and the amount of *one* year's wages apiece paid in silver."

He paused.

Not a sound did any man make.

"Magnificent," Caesar whispered to Mucia. "Almost too risky, but perfectly successful."

"You will now fall into ranks," Pompey continued to the men. "You will march past. From the march past the whole army will double-quick the six miles to Antium. There you will be allowed one draft of water each. You will then double-quick back to camp."

He paused, and stood imperiously dominating the ensuing silence, completely master.

In Roman civil life, in all state affairs, still more in all military matters women were not supposed to exist. If present they effaced themselves, tolerated maybe, but ignored. But now Mucia rushed to Pompey and threw her arms about his neck.

He caught her to him, not perfunctorily, but greedily. Before all his staff and army he kissed her lips.

Then did the men burst into vast, ringing cheers.

"No danger now," Pompey whispered to Mucia as he released her. "After that cheer they are mine, heart and soul."

The Swimmers

(A Tale from *The Song of the Sirens and Other Stories*)

*Liburni, cum vadosa loca obsedissent, capitibus tantum eminentibus
fidem fecerunt hosti alti maris ac triremem, quae eos persequebatur,
implicatam vado ceperunt.*

Julius Frontinus, *Strategematicon*, II,V, 43.

The inner waiting-room of the imperial palace was just then at its
fullest, Togaed senators bulged in creaking armchairs; couriers, gaudy
in embroidered habiliments, lounged everywhere. Military-men, fresh
from the frontier and uncomfortable in parade-uniforms, fidgeted
impatiently. Some of Rome's richest land-owners, ship-owners, or
money lenders, fuming hot in their oppressive state-*togas*, collogued
in low voices. Women were many too, and the rustle of skirts and the
flutter of fans pervaded the apartment. There was much moving about,
changing of seats and rambling from group to group. The buzz of talk
was continuous, but mostly under breath. For an atmosphere of uneas-
iness pervaded the place. Elated faces, eager for an interview, were few.

A rumour had been circulated that the emperor was out of sorts.
An adept might have inferred as much from the demeanour of the
two tall *pretorians* who guarded the inner door or from the air of the
silked and jewelled pages who came and went softly. The difference
was subtle, and would have wholly escaped a stranger, but it was real.
To the best of his ability neither guard nor any one of the pages gave
any sign. There were men present who would have given their weight
in gold for a hint as to the form of the emperor's ill humour: whether
it was flaring rage, sullen vindictiveness, or, worst of all, his dreaded
ironical blandness. To none was any hint given. They conjectured in
vain. But imperial irritation cast a gloom over the assembly. A subdued
and anxious gathering they were for the most part.

If the emperor's wrath might be supposed to threaten any one in

293

particular, his displeasure plainly impended over one alcove, midway of the windows on the side opposite the sun. Its shaded recess was tenanted by a man and two women. They had sat together, almost without stirring, since the first comers were admitted. No one had spoken to them, no one had accosted them, no one had greeted them, even in passing. Those who approached their nook, sheered off at sight of them. The alcoves on either side of theirs were filled with indifferent courtiers, insolently sure of their own standing, without cares, whiling away their time with mere chatter. No other groups settled near them and those least distant drew away as much as possible. They were ignored with sedulous caution.

The man wore the uniform of a commodore, but was without sword, scabbard or sword-belt. His blue cloak hung stringily behind him, he sat lifelessly, his broad shoulders stooped over his big sunken chest. His cropped hair had a suggestion of waviness even in its shortness. He should have been handsome had he not seemed so dispirited. His complexion was of a peculiar hue, as it were, of youthful flesh, long tanned by wind and sun, grown pallid for lack of light and air.

His attitude could hardly have been more listless, more hopeless. His pale blue eyes had in them no sparkle, no light at all. They stared out of the window over the city roofs glittering in the sun or at walls or floor, unseeing, gazing anywhere except at the young woman who sat by him, holding one of his hands in both of hers. She was a sort of human doll, very graceful, and very pretty, even while in tears, manifestly a pampered beauty who had lived all her life on admiration.

The elaborate arrangement of her lusterless gold hair had been a good deal disturbed. She had reddened her eyes with weeping, and they filled with tears again and again, she dabbing at them ineffectually with a pitiful wad of a drenched handkerchief. At intervals she gave way to sobbing, leaning against her mother, who half held her, half supported her.

The three had spoken seldom and then in whispers.

"You ought to have let us try, Bassus," the girl moaned. "You ought to have let us try," she reiterated.

"You did right, Corinna," he told her. "It was braver of you. And remember, it was wisest Anything you might have done would only have sealed my doom. If I have any chance it is only because we have kept silent and made no move."

"But it is so dreadful!" she said, "to get you back after all that nightmare of grief and uncertainty and horror, to watch you recover and then to have to keep silent and remain inactive and see you go to death unhelped! To regain you only to lose you again! Oh, it is too dreadful!"

His face was the face of a man who beheld death close, indeed. But collapsed as he was he made a brave effort.

"Try to think of the brighter side of things," he urged.

"There isn't any brighter side to any of it," she declared.

"Yes there is," he insisted, "at the worst of it he can only order me to death, and I ought to have died long ago. No man has any right to survive such a fiasco. I should have died with my men!"

"Judging from your wounds," Corinna's mother put in, "you tried hard enough!"

"I did indeed!" he ejaculated, "and that is some comfort. And if I die now there are other comforts. For me death will be better than degradation, than living on in contempt, out of service and despised."

"We could be married at once," Corinna sobbed, "and live all our lives at Sirmio. What could be lovelier than that? What would disgrace and shame matter there together?"

"I could not be happy, sweetheart," he said gently, "even there, even with you, if I were dishonoured."

"If you had let me do as I wanted," she insisted, "you might have been vindicated."

"There can be no exoneration," Bassus maintained, sadly, "no extenuation even, for a commander who loses a whole squadron of warships to an inferior enemy and is himself the sole survivor. And if there were anything to be said in my favour it would have no weight. I must be made an example of. There is no use trying to deceive our minds. I go to death. My only chance is one of his whims. It is a small chance. Let us hope till the end. But even if death is a certainty for me, let us not forget what we have to rejoice over."

"Rejoice?" the girl whispered bitterly. "Joy? For us?"

"Rejoice that you have made me glad," he said. "A man has but one life. I have had much joy in mine. My misfortune has brought me more joy than I should have thought possible. I knew I loved you, I was wild with elation at the thought of returning successful and marrying you. But what was that to the joy of knowing that you loved me well enough to cling to me, a failure, an outcast, a prisoner! Your first letter was a joy too great to be described. I thrilled with ecstasy at the thought of your loving me well enough to burden your estates to ransom me!"

"And it was all for nothing," the girl wailed. "If you have to die anyhow."

"Not all for nothing," he argued, "there are deaths and deaths. It is bad enough to have to die young. But to die clean and fed and clothed as a Roman should be is far less terrible than to die as I should have died, racked with fever, starved to a skeleton, slashed with festering wounds, shackled in a vile hovel in the mountains, a sty, dark, noisome, filthy and verminous. You saved me from all that."

"But what use was it" she repeated, "if I must lose you after all."

"Even if I must die now," he said, "I had all the bliss of coming back to life and love under your care. I can go bravely remembering all those delicious hours of solicitude and affection; and you must always remember how much it meant to me, how utterly I revelled in it all."

The inner portal opened and between the immobile guards there staggered out a spectre of a general, gray-cheeked, too brow-beaten to hide his condition from the throng. The room fell silent as he tottered through it to the outer portal. After he was gone conversation was even more subdued than before.

Presently a page approached the three in the alcove.

"Bassus?" he queried, curtly.

Bassus stood up.

Regardless of the throng Corinna clung to him, kissing him repeatedly, and sobbing.

"Be brave, dear," he said, gently disengaging her arms from his neck. "A scene can only worsen my slender chances. Be brave. Goodbye."

He kissed her gravely once; kissed her mother, pressed a hand of each, and followed the page.

In the small private-audience room Bassus found an emperor not irate nor glum, nor sarcastic, but plainly and unaffectedly ill in body, haggard and worn with worry, weary in mind and weighed down in spirit with care and disappointments. He was leaning back in a deep armchair upholstered in green leather, against which his face showed also an almost greenish tinge. His neck was scrawny and stringy to the edge of the dark crimson, elaborately embroidered robe which wrapped him about to his ankles. His feet were on a hassock and the gold thread eagles worked on his light blue shoes showed conspicuously. There was a low backless chair beside him.

He looked at Bassus with no symptom of his dreaded dissimulation, but openly wrathful in expression, his eyes glaring, one just visible across the bridge of his hooked nose.

He spoke harshly.

"Are you well enough to talk to me? Mind, I won't be bothered with any more unrepaired wrecks. If you need nursing go back and get well."

"I am entirely myself again," Bassus asserted.

'Sit down,' the emperor commanded, motioning to the low chair beside him. "No, don't hesitate, sit down!"

Bassus, bowing deeply in silence, obeyed.

The emperor glowered at him.

"I am cursed with bunglers everywhere," he said.

"I am one of them!" Bassus admitted. "I know it. I was surprised at your sending for me.

"I suppose," the emperor ruminated peevishly, "I should have sent you word to make away with yourself. I didn't want to see you or to talk with you. But I need some of the information you might give me for the benefit of the next man who is to try where you failed and then—" He broke off and fidgeted fretfully.

"I'm ashamed of it," he went on, "but I am consumed with curiosity to know by what recondite imbecility you arranged for such a complete disaster."

Bassus sat silent

"So I sent for you," the emperor concluded.

Thank you, Sir," Bassus said respectfully.

'Now you are here," the emperor demanded, "what have you to say for yourself?"

"Nothing," Bassus replied simply.

"This is your last chance!" the emperor admonished him.

"Why say anything?" Bassus gloomed. "You know all the facts, you have made up your mind!"

"Assumption of disfavour," the emperor told him, "is sometimes as foolish as assumption of favour. And you err. I have not all the facts and my mind is not made up. Speak out."

"If I knew what you think you do not know," Bassus began.

"I do not know," the emperor cut in, "whether Vespillo behaved as a cowardly subordinate to you or as a prudent husband of his own ship."

"No fault can be found with Vespillo," Bassus told him straightforwardly. "Frankly I believe he hated me and was glad to see me in trouble, but he did exactly what he should have done. If he had attempted to come to our rescue he would have lost his own ship to a certainty. Nothing he could have done could have helped us a particle."

The emperor's yellow gray face became almost animated, almost flushed.

"Pollux!" he exclaimed. "There comes the puzzle of it again! How could you lose five men-of-war at once and to a horde of naked pirates? You were supposed to have an overwhelming force at your command, and you get gobbled up like a sausage by a mastiff. Explain! Tell me your story, man, come closer."

Bassus hitched his chair sideways and leaned over.

"I knew they had gathered a big flotilla at Toluca," he began, "a bigger flotilla than they had ever before got together. I knew they were planning some more outrageous venture, farther than they had ever raided and for a greater prize most likely, I judged them elated and rash and thought it the right time for a surprise. There were no better *triremes* afloat than my six and they were in perfect condition to the last spike, to the last rope. My rowers were all sturdy men and they were well fed and fresh. I trusted all my commanders absolutely, except Vespillo, and I knew he would do his plain duty, though he might trick me on any ambiguous order.

"The weather suited us. There was no high wind, but favourable breezes all the while, with much fog and rain, so that we had every chance of approaching unseen. We actually sighted not one vessel all the way up to Mexa, There we anchored in the seaward harbour. The scouts and our other friendlies uniformly reported no signs of wariness at Toluca, but much roistering and recklessness. Meanwhile it poured rain in torrents, yet our measures kept all the men healthy and everything ready.

"The second night after our anchoring it stopped raining and fell dead calm. We could hear the roaring of the uncountable brooks tearing down the sides of the mountains back of Mexa all over the island. About midnight it cleared, with a fine booming wind. I had the hawsers buoyed out ready on the instant. Before dawn a fisherboat of one of our friendlies brought word that the flotilla was coming out. We slipped our cables and were off, round the south end of Mexa and straight before the wind for Berega, which was exactly between us and the mouth of Toluca harbour.

"We drew up to Berega before it was really light I knew my gentry relied wholly upon sails and that it was rush or nothing, for of course they could out-distance us before the wind on the open sea, and if they once scattered we could catch only a few in the maze of inlets. So we stored sails, lowered yards and unstepped masts and generally stripped. It was done promptly and we were under way again. As we rounded the north headland of Berega the sun came up over Apson directly ahead.

"It was as fine a picture as a man ever looked at. "The sky all blue without a cloud, except some crimson streamers from the sunrise, Apson black against the redness, its shadow shortening on the sea in front of us, the sea emerald green up at the margin of the yellowish water that fanned out from Toluca harbour, where all the rivers converged their swollen torrents of freshet-mud. Well out on the yellow fan was the flotilla, scudding side on to the wind, as their fashion is; not an oar among them all. And to the left the slopes of Gifetta, rosy in the sun, overlooking everything."

"You have the localities better than I," the emperor put in. "I know them only as nameless islands and mountains. Go on."

"The flotilla was in a sort of crescent formation, bulged toward us, about two miles from tip to tip and each tip about two miles from the nearest shore. They were all heeling over in our direction, every sail bellying out, every *felucca* running evenly with every other, a magnificent spectacle.

"The instant they sighted us the most amazing alteration in their movement took place. They seemed seized with a mad panic. The *feluccas* yawed crazily about, rammed each other, ran together by threes and fours, and hung, held by a jumble of shattered masts, intertangled yards and snarled cordage. Those that ran free zigzagged about, now aback, their lateen sails slatting in the wind, now ducking and scooting this way and that.

"The masthead lookout called that all the crews had jumped overboard at once and were swimming back toward the harbour.

"I judged that we could catch up with them and run them down long before they reached it, and my chief pilot agreed. I had detailed Vespillo to act as a reserve and he had aboard spare crews and extra marines and all that sort. I signalled him to fall behind, to seize and man all the *feluccas* worth capturing and to ram or burn the rest at his discretion. Then I signalled the others for battle-front full speed. We gathered way abreast, two of them on each side of me. Through the *feluccas* we drove, veering aside so as not to be delayed by ramming any. Between the flotilla and the harbour all the water was yellowed by the outrush of the freshets.

"Across it we could see the swimmers, ten thousand black heads bobbing in the current, not scattered much but swimming in a fairly compact crescent. It looked like an annihilation for the enemy, for they were all of a mile from any beach still, and the current was against them. There was no noise, our crews were quiet and I could hear the time-beaters' gongs on the other *triremes* ringing sharp and quick in perfect unison with ours. The oars dipped and flashed, we were at top speed, all of twenty miles an hour, and the bobbing heads seemed just where we had first sighted them.

"'The current is too much for them,' Euphranor chuckled to me as we stood on the upper platform, 'they are practically stationary.'

"I gave the order, the lookout signalled, and all together the five ships swept round in a wide curve so as to take the strung-out swarm of swimmers diagonally and drown as many as possible at the first onset. We came among them at terrific speed. I was standing with my feet wide apart and my arms stretched out leaning with both hands braced against the platform bulwark rail. So I was not thrown down like most of the rest, and saw the whole thing. For as we drove into the mass of heads we ran hard and fast aground, all five ships at once. Half the oars snapped, of course, so we were utterly helpless.

"Nearly every standing man was hurled flat or flung overboard or from his platform to the deck or into the waist. We were in the utmost confusion. Anyhow, as against undisciplined irregulars, we had no boarding netting out, being all for the attack and defence un-thought of.

"And as we struck the whole ten thousand savages stood up and yelled."

"Stood up!" the emperor interjected. "Stood up?"

"Yes, Sir," Bassus went on. "Stood up, not a man of them over knee deep and many not ankle deep!"

"On what?" the emperor queried, mystified.

"On the bar," Bassus explained. "Mud-flat or sand-bank or what-ever it was. You see, the water was all so muddied no one could see the difference between deep and shoal water by colour as in dry weather. The current was far slower than we thought, and not a ripple showed the shallows. Those rascals had been belly flat on the mud, going through the motions of swimming, to trap us."

The emperor threw back his head and laughed.

"Pollux!" he exclaimed. Then he laughed again, a genuine hearty laugh that lasted long. He wiped his eyes and surveyed Bassus, his expression altered from grim sternness to a tolerant smile.

"The weather helped them," he chuckled. "Everything helped them. They fooled your pilots, they fooled you, they would have fooled me if I had been there, they were wily."

"And brave too," Bassus assured him. "They took their chances which were to be run down. Some were certain to perish as we drove into them, many did. Tanno's ship was on our port quarter as we made our curve, and I could see the heads smash like melons under her cutwater. Yet not a man made any attempt to escape by standing up. They played their game of pretending to swim until we were all aground."

"Yes," said the emperor, "the scoundrels were brave. But just think of the glee the scamps must have been in, of the hilarity they shook with, their backs barely awash, realizing what was coming."

He laughed again, heartily.

"They had you trapped of course," he said, and what happened then?"

The commodore's face darkened.

"They yelled again and came at us. They swarmed up the oars, up the sides of the ships, over the bulwarks, like rats, like ants. I had a moment's glimpse of the other ships, each like a bear at bay buried under a pack of dogs. After that one glance I had no eyes except for my own ship, and soon I could see nothing beyond my own sword's length, as long as I could see anything."

"The Ripustians respected you, I gathered," the emperor remarked.

"They never hinted it to me," Bassus replied with a wry face.

"I inferred," likewise the emperor pursued, "that they did not treat you any too well."

"Shackles riveted on my ankles," Bassus told him. "Cross bar, between them; chains a plenty. I was about as comfortable as an animal in a cage, no cleaner, and not much better fed."

"You've no love for the Ripustians, that's plain," the emperor drawled, still smiling.

"Not a bit," said Bassus fervently.

"You'd like to get even with them, I presume?" the emperor asked.

"Just wouldn't I," Bassus ejaculated.

"I've a notion to let you try again," the emperor said.

"Sir!" Bassus exclaimed.

"No," said the emperor. "Don't stand up. Stay where you are. I fancy no man is likely to display more zeal against the Ripustians than you would. And after your experiences I doubt if any man living could be more prudent and wary than you will be. Likewise you are too angry to be timid. You can't raise Euphranor to life again, but you will find one of his family or some other pilot as good. No one will choose pilots or crews or ships better than you and I've a notion I can manage to impress it upon my army and navy that your case will not establish a precedent and that losing a squadron will not assure promotion to anyone else. No, no thanks, let me talk. I was a good deal interested in you by Corinna's behaviour. After seeing her, still more after listening to her chatter, anyone would have expected her to shrug her shoulders, forget you, and marry anyone convenient within a year.

"When she besieged her guardians until they mortgaged her estates and ransomed you the gossips were all agog. I heard of it And then I felt uneasy. I expected her to unleash on me not only all your relations, but her own uncountable, pertinacious clan. Nobody has so much as hinted at intervention in your behalf. They have let me alone, all of them. They have had the marvellous good sense to pay me the compliment of supposing I can make up my mind rationally for myself. That makes me like Corinna and like you too. I'm going to give you another chance. She deserves you and you deserve her. Did you come here alone?"

"No, Sir," said Bassus simply. "Corinna and her mother came with me."

The emperor clapped his hands twice.

A page came, was given his orders, and in a moment ushered in Corinna and her mother.

"No," said the emperor sharply. "No kneeling! No hand-kissing! Sit down, all three of you. I meant to be severe with Bassus, to make an example of him. But he made me laugh! The first real laugh I have had in months. I had a soft spot in my heart for him anyhow. The man who transformed the most fickle and capricious *coquette* in Rome into a paragon of constancy deserves consideration. He is a marvel. So I'm going to give Bassus a chance to do better against the Ripustians. This time he shall have ten ships, if he wants that many, and he can pick his choice of ships, men and stores at Ravenna or at Misenum also, if he likes.

"But there are two conditions. First, you two must be married today. Not any later day, but today. In the second place you must report him well enough for duty before he so much as smells at an arsenal. I'll give you two months if a month won't suffice, I think one month might do."

"And now, one question, Corinna," the emperor said, fixing her with his big, dark eyes; "was it your idea to let me alone without bothering me with pleas and petitions, or was it Bassus that suggested it?"

"It was Bassus," Corinna answered. "In his first letter to me, before anything else, he wrote: 'Don't intercede with the emperor!' And he repeated it in that letter and in every other."

"Good," said the emperor, "that is one more reason for reinstating him. He has sense. And so have you. You have been docile in a difficult matter. You will be an obedient wife. Go now and get married. No, no thanks! No thanks! Go and get married. And come back a month from now and show me how fat he is.

"And now go, I've less pleasant and more pressing business to transact"

The Skewbald Panther

(A Tale from *The Song of the Sirens and Other Stories*)

His face was the face of a man glad all through. He was standing, his knees against the coping of the inner wall. He looked down into the deserted arena, across it, at the great sweeping curve of tier above tier of blank, tenantless, stone benches and up at the sagging, saucered, spider-web of radiating or cross-knotted guy-ropes. Far away on the opposite side of the amphitheatre several workmen were busy with those same guy-ropes, had flung some temporary tackle over one of them and were hoisting up a boy to make repairs or adjustments; otherwise the Colosseum was empty save for himself. He had the air of a man enjoying its emptiness.

The sun had risen but a few moments before and its slant rays struck on the gayly painted awning-poles and on their gilded ropes. The interior of the building was coolish with the dawn-chill of masonry grown cold under autumn stars, and he kept his new, white, crimson-edged *toga* wrapped about him, both his arms under it to the wrists. Yet he snuffed joyously at the early air and breathed long breaths of its coolness, turning from side to side his uncovered curly head, rolling his gaze relishingly about.

As he stood there another head, a big close-cropped, bullet-shaped head, raised itself slowly above the top rail of the entrance stairway behind him, a florid, round moon-shaped fleshy face came above the rail and its small, brown good-natured eyes peered at him. Then there came into view a neck, which would have been long if it had not been incredibly thick, nearly as thick as the big head. The owner of the head moved cautiously, like an overgrown boy playing blindman's bluff. He was a man huge in every dimension, wrapped in a very thin, very white toga with a very broad crimson border.

As he trod softly round the end of the railing he showed foot-gear of pale green buckskin, much like Wellington boots, but shorter, with a gold crescent on a little gold chain dangling from the top of each. He was followed by an enormous fawn-coloured dog; heavily built, square-jawed, short-haired, which moved as silently as he. Padding noiselessly up behind the absorbed gazer he slapped him boisterously on the shoulder. The smaller man turned round.

"Lucius!" he exclaimed, "what good luck brought you?"

"Precisely to find out," said Lucius, "what whim led you in here. I saw you entering, stopped my litter, got out and followed you. What on earth made you come in here, Quintus? There's no show today."

"Show or no show," said Quintus, "this is the Romanest thing in Rome and I am just famished for Rome. I've been hungry for Rome for five years."

When did you get back?" Lucius asked.

"Day before yesterday," answered Quintus. "Just in time for a good bath and a good dinner. I paid all my official visits yesterday. Today I'm my own man until lunch-time at the palace and I mean to stroll about and just bathe in the sensation of being in Rome again."

"Well," said Lucius, "while you are bathing, as you call it, you might just as well bathe sitting as standing. Let's sit down."

He settled himself ponderously into one of the ample, heavy-timbered, leather-bottomed, front row armchairs. Quintus took the next. The dog curled up at Lucius' feet.

"Were you at the emperor's reception yesterday?" Lucius asked,

"I was, my boy," said Quintus, "and very kind he was too. 'You're the right sort, Proculus,' said he, 'you do things. You've earned a rest Hope you'll enjoy it and go back and do more things. No time to talk now. I've sixteen yoke of horses to look over and I want to get this tedious ceremonial done. Come to lunch with me tomorrow and tell me your adventures.' Rather gracious for Commodus, don't you think?"

"Most unusually gracious," said Lucius. "Wish I could extract something like that from him for me. Wish I had been there to hear it. I didn't see you."

"I was early," said Proculus, "too early for you. I'll bet you were one of the last half dozen."

"I was the very last," said Lucius with a twist of his face. "And I caught it, Commodus burst out at me.

"'Last again, as usual. You are a nuisance, Balbinus; you're one of those unimportant important men that aren't worth noticing and must be noticed. You haven't anything to do but eat and sleep and you do too much of both. I've quantities of things to do far better worth doing than eating or sleeping or ruling and you keep me here in this everlasting tedium longer than there is any necessity for, when I must be here too long anyhow. See you're early tomorrow, or I'll think of something to make you remember. You're too fat!' said he. I never had such a scolding. That's why I'm up so early today. I was on my way to the palace, trying to be first. But I have plenty of time yet to be early enough. There is no hurry."

"You are fat," said Proculus, running his eyes over his friend.

"Not a bit of it," the other denied vigorously. "I'm big. Last time I was at Cossa I climbed into the pan of the bale-shed stilyard at the wool-house. I weighed two hundred and sixty. But I haven't a pound of fat on me. I'm all muscle, stronger than ever. Feel me anywhere. And I keep in the best condition. Swimming Tiber three times is nothing for me. I never make it less than five and generally six, and when I'm in Rome I haven't missed a day, except holy days, for years. I look suety, but I'm all hard flesh over big bones and sinews, stronger than ever."

"I believe you are," Proculus admitted after an investigation.

"My wits may be fat, as Commodus says," went on Balbinus. "I can't get over your thinking of coming in here today. I might be away from Rome for ten years, and frantic to get back, but I should never think of coming in here when there was nothing going on."

"You think so now," said Proculus, "but if you had had two years of frontier fighting, let alone five as I have had, you'd have thought over a hundred times everything you could see at Rome, you'd want to see them all at once, and you'd get around and see them all as quick as possible."

"You've been on the Rhine, it seems to me," Balbinus ventured.

"Rhine!" Proculus exclaimed. "Not a bit of it I've been in Dacia."

"But there have been no wars in Dacia," Balbinus demurred.

"No wars!" Proculus ejaculated. "Perhaps not. Do you remember how Opsitius Tanno used to get drunk?"

"Used to," said Balbinus. "He does yet only not near so often. He'll take a notion, you can't tell when, and from beginning with the rest of us like everybody else he'll make each bowl more wine to less water until he's pouring it down pure and unmixed and the strongest in his cellar. He'll keep on till his blood is just raw wine. And then when his fit's over no more till next time."

"Just so," said Proculus. "And you remember what he said to Faltonius Bambilio?"

"Can't say I do," Balbinus ruminated. "What was it?"

"Why after Tanno was well over one of his drinking-spells some of the boys were joking him and Bambilio had to join in, 'You ought to be like me, Tanno,' says he, 'I'm never drunk.' 'No,' says Tanno, 'never drunk and never sober either.'"

"What's that got to do with Dacia?" Balbinus demanded.

"Everything," Proculus replied. "Dacia and the Rhine frontier are just like Tanno and Bambilio. When you've got a war on the Rhine you've got war sure enough. It takes every town, fortress, camp, cata-pult, spear and arrow you have and every man and boy you can muster to hold the frontier and stave off an invasion. You have to deal with this or that keen ambitious chief, full of dreams of conquest, glory of wealth and power and ease, backed by a compact coherent nation of devoted warriors, hard fighters all, with good swords, good spears, good shields, good hearts envenomed with envy and hate, and then when they are beaten, you have peace, safe, dependable peace, until the next time. Dacia is different.

"No definite nations there, no chiefs worth reckoning with, no point of special danger, no period of rest. Just indefinite swarms of insignificant tribes of dirty, runty savages on rough-haired ponies, and only half-armed with bad lances, worse bows, wretched arrows, mis-erable shields and long raw-hide nooses. They have no dreams, no plans, no intentions. They are always on the verge of starvation, never half-clad nor half-housed. It is just raid, raid, raid, summer and winter wherever they think they see a chance for food or clothing, weapons, cattle, horses or slaves. They keep us going. It is exhausting work. If you had been through what I have been through you'd be wild for a sight of the Colosseum, even with nothing going on. Not but that I'm impatient to see a show too."

"You'll be here tomorrow, of course," said Balbinus.

"If I don't drop dead first," said Proculus fervently. "And I don't know what gate to go to. Commodus has changed the arrangements and regulations so I don't know where I am entitled to sit. I was hop-ing he would ask me to a place on the dais with him. But after all the officers on leave I saw at the reception yesterday morning I don't believe there's a chance of that, so many outrank me."

"There may be a chance anyhow," Balbinus told him. "Commodus is a whimmy creature. But most likely he won't. If he don't, come with me. One of Commodus' changes has been granting each Senator the right to bring in a guest to a front seat. I sit just over there, where you see that panel of gouged rollers."

"I'll be delighted to come with you," said Proculus. "I can't be too far forward for my taste. I want to see everything."

"You shall," said Balbinus, "and now let's go."

"Certainly," said Proculus, but he did not move. "Where did you get that dog? I think he is the biggest, strongest-looking, fiercest looking and quietest dog I ever saw."

Balbinus settled himself again in his chair.

"That dog," he said, "used to belong to Fonteia."

"Did she give him to you?" Proculus enquired.

"Not a bit she didn't," Balbinus disclaimed. "She never gave me anything but the cold shoulder. One of her uncles sent her that dog all the way from Tolosa. They had him chained up for a door-dog. He used to growl at everybody. He growled at me every day, going in and coming out. One day he was loose and sprang at me. You know when you are surprised you think mighty quick. It came over me all in a flash that Fonteia was so determined to get rid of me that she had ordered the dog let loose just so he could get at me; for a hint you know."

"Pretty positive hint," interjected Proculus.

"Well she had nothing to do with it, I found out afterwards," Balbinus went on. "But that was the way the idea rushed over me as the dog sprang. Anyhow, it made me so furious that, instead of smashing him on the nose, I just caught him by the throat with both hands and stood right there without moving either foot and choked him till he was limp as a towel. I had a half mind to give him a wrench and break his neck, but I was afraid Fonteia would be angry. So I just flung him into his kennel and went on into the atrium. They were all out in the garden under the big lotus tree. Vedia Philotera was there and Entedia and dear old Nemestronia and some more and of course there were three men to every one of them.

"I couldn't get near Fonteia. They were all listening to an interminable recitation by one of those pestiferous poets Fonteia always has hanging round. It was all about Tiberius the Divine and his campaigns in Pannonia. Some of it was lively, exploits of Velleius Paterculus, hard fighting up gorges and on mountain spurs, but most of it bored me. Presently I felt something under my chair. Do you know, it was that dog; licking my feet too. The moment he had come to himself he had crawled after me. Presently Entedia smelt him, though how she can smell anything but the perfumery she uses is more than I could ever make out. She objected. Nemestronia backed her up, though why anybody that keeps a pet leopard should object to a clean dog is beyond my guessing. When the recitation came to a pause they spoke to Fonteia. She called a slave to take him away.

"He wouldn't stir, showed his teeth. She sent for the door-keeper. The dog snapped at him. Then she sent after her slave lashers. They came and all five of them were too few to move that dog. Then Fonteia got up and tried herself. He snarled at her. Then I said if she would tell me where she wanted him to go I would take him there. And I took him to his kennel and chained him up. He stayed there till I went home and then he broke his chain at one tug, and followed me home: precious scared my bearers were too. He has never left me since. If I want to go anywhere without him I have to chain him up myself. He won't let anybody else chain him. To hold him takes two chains, fastened to rings at opposite ends of his kennel wall. A single chain too strong for him to break is so heavy it drags down his collar even when he is lying still and chafes his neck sore."

"You don't mean to say he goes into the palace, with you?" Proculus demanded.

"Oh," said Balbinus, "he'll stay by my litter if I tell him to. He knows that whenever I leave my litter I am sure to come back to it. He's obedient enough. I like that dog. I never liked a dog before. But he'd let me twist his ears off, if I felt like it. He's my dog."

"Thought you said Fonteia didn't give him to you," Proculus remarked.

"Neither did she," said Balbinus. "Next day she asked was I a dog-stealer. I said no, I hadn't stolen her dog, she could get him if she sent after him. She said that wouldn't do, I must bring back the dog and leave him or pay for him. I asked how much she wanted. She said twenty thousand *sesterces*. I said that was too much for any dog. She said to bring him back then. Finally I paid her the money. What does she do, but buy a turquoise brooch with it."

"Queer how those red-headed women do run after blue," said Proculus.

"Red-headed!" exclaimed Balbinus. "Nonsense, Fonteia's hair isn't red. It's the finest imaginable gold-copper. There isn't a handsomer head of hair in Italy."

"Certainly," Proculus hastened to admit. "But what about that brooch?"

"She bought it of Orontides," Balbinus went on. "Said she had been wanting it for a year. Showed it to me the next day. I told her I would have given her a dozen of them if she had hinted that she wanted one. She said that was different. I said I couldn't see the difference. She said I was stupid as usual. Anyhow, I have never seen her since without that brooch. She wears it no matter what colour she is dressed in, red or yellow, green or violet, brown or gray."

"Don't you understand why?" asked Proculus.

"Not a bit," confessed Balbinus.

"Then you are stupid as she says," said Proculus.

"I suppose so," Balbinus admitted. "I'm generally stupid. I don't understand about Dacia. I know about the Rhine frontier, there's Gaul to sack on this side and all those ravening kinglets with their unhesitating hordes on the other. You've something to defend and something to fight But by your own showing no Dacian would ever try to cross the Danube. Why not leave that as the boundary and let the Dacians cat each other up? What is there in Dacia worth fighting for?"

"Dacia, mostly," Proculus replied, the aggressive light of the enthusiast for a new country shining in his eyes. "Dacia is bound to be the very jewel of the Empire. It is no teeming land of easy plenty like Egypt, no trimmed and clipped garden of glorious abundance like Syria or Asia, never can be such a country as Italy or Spain or even Gaul; but it is enormous, and full of possibilities. It has immense plains, flat as the sea, the finest horse-breeding territory in the Empire. It has vast stretches of rolling country, nothing better in the world for grain. It has uncountable chains of mountains covered with the finest timber, full of mines of iron and lead, silver and gold. Oh, it's all worth fighting for, every foot of it."

"What's the use of all that without colonists," Balbinus demanded.

"Without colonists!" Proculus exclaimed. "It's filling up fast, much of it has filled up. The bridge is jammed from sunrise to sunset, and as I came southward I passed colony after colony. The roads are thronged all along."

"Got roads there, too?" Balbinus queried.

"As fine roads as any in the empire," Proculus asserted. "With good spile bridges at every river and some stone bridges. More than a thousand miles of perfect roads, ditched and curbed, paved and full twelve feet wide. They fork beyond the bridge. One to the westward runs to Porolissum, the middle one strikes Sarmatagete and runs on to Apula, the third swings eastwardly through Maluensis to Zusidava. They are well used all spring, summer and autumn."

"But how on earth," said Balbinus, "can you get colonists to go there in the face of all that raiding?"

"You don't understand," said Proculus. "We keep pushing the frontier back all the time. Where I was fighting in an absolutely wild country the first year I was there, is perfectly peaceable now, not only not a massacre, nor inroad, but no disturbances of any kind, not so much as a murder. The farms are thick set all over the country and the people live on them the year round, entirely fearless."

"What do they raise?" asked Balbinus.

"It varies with the part of the country," said Proculus. "Cattle and horses and sheep on the plains, wheat and barley and rye on the farmlands."

"No olives?" asked Balbinus. "No wine? No fruit r

"They'll never raise olives there," Proculus conceded. "But they'll raise vines yet. They are trying everywhere. And they make a sort of wine out of barley. It's not bad when you are used to it. And for fruit they have cherries and apples finer than anything in Italy and in season you'll find as great a variety of garden fruits and fresh vegetables in the town markets as in any town market in Italy."

"Towns!" Balbinus exclaimed. "What sort of towns?"

"Hasty towns most of them," Proculus answered. "Not much better than a winter camp. The colonies run about five thousand persons and they are not rich to begin with. Stone work is slow and dear, while timber is cheap. They build timber houses and fortify the towns with a deep, broad ditch, a high earthwork and heavy log stockade with log towers. But the later colonies are bigger, some of twenty thousand, and they are better equipped. It is wonderful how rich they get in two or three years. Nearer the bridge many of the towns already have well built stone or brick temples, basilicas, baths, amphitheatres, circuses and other public buildings and fine stone city walls."

"How do they get rich?" Balbinus asked.

"You ought to see the roads," replied Proculus enthusiastically. "Droves of cattle and horses, great flocks of sheep, thousands of wagon-loads of sides of pork, hams and such, endless mule-trains, panniers full of crude iron and lead, yes, and silver and gold, too. The Danube carries fleets of grain and timber ships all summer; they go round by Byzantium."

"The people are well off by your account," said Balbinus.

"They are," Proculus boasted. "It is a cold country, but they will soon be as well-housed as people in Gaul or Britain and they have even a superabundance of clothing and food. Furs are good and cheap, wool and flax plenty. Everybody is well-fed, all the slaves are fat, no one poor anywhere."

"You make it out a fine country, if we can hold it," said Balbinus.

"Hold it!" Proculus cried. "Well hold it forever. We'll push on beyond the Carpathians up to the Dniester."

"Where can the Empire ever get men for such a conquest?" Balbinus wondered.

"From Dacia, of course," said Proculus. "Dacia makes men. It not only will soon furnish enough men to hold its own frontier without a single legion from outside, but will push on west- ward, swing round the Yazyges and swallow them whole, and press on Germany from the rear till we crush it between Dacia and Gaul and colonize it up to the Baltic."

"These are all wild dreams," Balbinus protested. "Come down to facts. How do you hold Dacia now? If what you say is true it is already nearly as well worth looting as Gaul and will soon be richer. How do you hold off all those desperate nomads of the north? You can't set up a cordon of legionaries shoulder to shoulder, over a thousand miles of frontier. You can't ditch, stockade and tower any such endless line of defence. You can't even have posts close together. How do you hold off the raiders?"

"The legions do it handily," said Proculus, "Hold them off and push them back too."

"You can't make me believe that," Balbinus objected, "A legion can't catch nomads any more than a sow can catch larks or a mud turtle can catch butterflies. The raiders must slip in between your posts and tear up the country. As it gets richer and more peaceful they will have more temptation. The first war elsewhere that calls off some of your outpost garrisons, you'll have a series of inroads and the whole province will go up in smoke."

"Dacia will take care of herself in a few years," Proculus argued. "And until then our outposts let no raiders through between them. The savages have learned better. We've plenty of local friendly cavalry, same kind of fellows as the raiders, confident in the backing of the legions, and aching to pay off old scores on their tribal enemies. And we modify the legions to meet the local conditions. Besides their regular equipment every man has a bow and quiver. Out of a legion we get four thousand men fit for volley archery, two thousand of them make good archers and one half of those get to be experts while on horseback.

"Then a legion can fight afoot with their regular shields and formation or we can use any advisable proportion of the men as archers and shift from one arrangement to the other as we please. Changing their heavy shields for bucklers, we can use as many as a third of a legion as mounted archers. And we can make any combination of mounted and foot fighters we need. We can fight a legion as a whole, or break it into *cohorts* or *maniples* and scatter them about We teach them, besides their own natural methods, the nomad tricks and outdo the raiders at their own game."

"But how do you think of such innovations?" Balbinus wondered. "I have often considered about that. Somebody must have thought of everything first, I know. But I simply can't imagine it. I can do anything when someone explains it to me. But I should never think of making any variations. How do you do it?"

"Don't know," said Proculus. "Seems simple enough to me. Don't you think it's time we were going?"

"We might go," said Balbinus, rising. "But I've time to spare yet."

Proculus rose and surveyed the building with a lingering, loving gaze. The sunlight now bathed the interior opposite him, although some of the lower tiers of seats were still in shadow, as was the arena, which was, however, lit up by the glaring reflections from the higher expanse of sunlit marble.

"What's that up yonder?" he inquired, point ing to the far end of the arena.

"Oh," said Balbinus, "they're turning one of the animals loose. That's another of Commodus' notions. He says the beasts get dull and stupid in cages and he has the pick of them let out in the arena, one at a time for air and exercise."

"But what kind of a beast is it?" Proculus queried.

"Panther," said Balbinus.

"Nonsense," Proculus objected. "That can't be a panther. A panther is spotted yellow and brown, or is solid black. That creature is black and white like an Epirote bull or a Carthaginian watch-dog. There never was a panther like that"

"Never was, maybe," said Balbinus. "Maybe never will be again, but there is now. Why you must have seen that brute before you left. She's been here for four or five years."

"Five years!" Proculus exclaimed. "Why no animal lasts five years in the Colosseum: few ever fight twice."

"That panther," said Balbinus, "will last ten years. She has a charmed life. She'll die of old age, like as not. She has fought at least two hundred times. And never varies when she is let out. Watch her." And he sat down.

Proculus, reseating himself, watched as he was bid.

"Watch her," Balbinus repeated. "She always makes for that same panel of rollers over there—the set that is so gouged and clawed—and tries to climb up. She never tries any other panel, and she always tries there at least three times."

The panther loped easily across the sands, crouched, sprang vertically and caught the third of the wooden rollers set along the face of the wall to protect spectators from any possibility of any animal scaling the enclosure of the arena. Her claws sank into the wood, but the lurching turn of the two-foot roller threw her back upon the sand.

"That was not much of a leap," said Balbinus. "I've seen her touch the sixth roller. Those claw-marks are nearly all hers. You can see from here some on the sixth roller. See, the sun has just reached it. She has never touched the seventh roller. There she goes again."

As he spoke the panther shot into the air. She got a hold on the fifth roller and clawed wildly with her hind legs at those below, but as they yielded to her weight and revolved on their bearings she slipped down again.

"She's only playing," said Balbinus. "When she is really in earnest she does better than that. My seat is right above that panel, almost exactly in the middle of it, and sometimes I think she's going to get her claws over the coping. If I am looking over when she springs it seems she is coming right in my face."

The panther sprang a third time and fell back at once.

"She won't try again," said Balbinus. "Sometimes she tries six or seven times."

She walked nosingly around the edge of the arena, flicking the end of her tail. She lay down, rolled over, sprang up lightly and continued her nosing progress.

Proculus eyed her as she went.

"Did you ever see a black dog that had been scalded?" he asked, "with white hairs grown out on the scars?"

"I have," said Balbinus, "but the white hair would only be in little streaks. She is more than half white."

"Her belly is black," said Proculus, "and her tail is black."

"If she had been scalded over as much of her skin as shows white hairs, she would have been killed," Balbinus argued. "I believe those are natural colours on her. The edges of the white are too irregular for scald marks. Look at her face now while it is towards us. That black patch over her left eye and ear looks perfectly natural."

"Perhaps it is natural," said Proculus. "But I never heard of such a beast."

You must have heard of her," said Balbinus. That is the very panther that killed Fonteius Bucco."

"Killed Fonteius Bucco!" Proculus exclaimed.

"Oh well," said Balbinus. "He had no right to the name of course, but he had passed under it."

"But which Fonteius Bucco," queried Proculus, "and how did she come to kill him?"

"Do you mean to say you never heard of the murder and the trial and all that frightful scandal," demanded Balbinus.

"Lucius," said Proculus. "I have heard nothing for five years except the wind howling over the plains, the moaning of the forests at night, the roaring of great rivers at their fords, the yells of Scythian robbers, the blare of bugles, the whine of well-sweeps and such like noises of campaign or camp. I have seen nothing but camps, or stockaded forts, or miserable, raw, timber towns, or the wild mountains and the weary plains of Dacia. I have had no time to read, no time to talk. It's been day-and-night riding and fighting, or desperately hasty ditching or breathlessly driven sword, spear, shield, helmet, shoe, harness, tent, or tool-making.

"Little news has reached me and no gossips Please assume that I know nothing. Tell me everything you know and by all means tell me about Bucco and the panther."

"You remember Decimus Fonteius Bucco?" Balbinus asked.

"Fonteia's uncle?" Proculus asked in turn.

"No," said Balbinus. "Not old Decimus, young Decimus."

"Fonteia's brother?" Proculus queried.

"As you and I knew him," Balbinus agreed.

"A vile whelp," said Proculus. "The worst specimen of a noble family ever I saw. I detested him. How such an unsavoury pup could be Fonteia's brother and Causidiena's son I never could make out."

"He really wasn't," said Balbinus. "But I'll get to that later. Causidiena died before you left I believe."

"I was at the funeral," said Proculus, "and very sorry I was. She would have turned into a lovely old lady like Nemestronia."

"Well," said Balbinus. "Even before she died, what with old Fonteius Bucco's blindness and the invalidism of Marcus, young Decimus was more and more unmanageable. Marcus Bucco never could control any of his children, not even Fonteia. Naturally being the best man of the family Caius Bucco had charge of all the estate, and when his father and Marcus died about the same time, a little after you left, it hardly increased his power over the property. Old Decimus stood out of the way and never claimed any of his privileges as elder brother. Young Decimus kept getting into trouble, and though Caius was kind to him, he quarrelled with his uncles continually.

"Then Caius was found murdered, most atrocious butchery too. Everybody thought it was one of his slaves; he was a very reckless man about slaves, bought all sorts with no guarantee of good character and gave them a loose rein. But when the investigation was no more than started suspicion turned on young Decimus. Proofs accumulated and it was soon clear he had murdered his uncle. He was convicted. Then one of Marcus' slaves confessed that Decimus was her son, she had substituted him for Causidiena's baby, and never been suspected. The legitimate heir had died on her hands before he was a year old. Of course that mitigated Fonteia's shame, but still she had grown up with him as his sister, and felt the disgrace of the trial terribly.

"After he was proved a slave the lawyers had a fine wrangle over the sentence. One lot said he must be sentenced as a slave. The other lot held out that as he had had the status of a free man when the crime was committed and was constructively related as a son to his victim he must be punished as for parricide by a citizen. Then Commodus cut in. He said he didn't mean to interfere with the dispensing of justice but he suggested that, instead of wasting time deciding whether to crucify him as a slave or drown him, sewed up in a sack with snakes, dogs and monkeys, as a parricide, why not compromise on throwing him to the beasts in the Colosseum?

"That would be more of a lesson to others, as being visible to a greater crowd, and it would be more spectacular. Thrown to the beasts he was. It was four years ago, four years ago tomorrow. Fonteia was there. She had been sorely tried at first between her genuine dislike for him, her abomination of him as a murderer and her love for her uncle on the one side and her mother's training in family duties and loyalty on the other. Once he was proved a slave and no kin of hers she behaved as if he had never existed. But the spectacle here shook her nerves for all her self-control.

"I sat on this side then, just where the Vestals sit now, about three panels nearer the dais. She sat with the Vestals, where I sit now above that panel the panther tried to climb. Several batches of criminals had been disposed of when they cleared the arena, sanded it afresh and turned him into it alone. He had nothing on but a waist-cloth, and carried a short dub, to let him feel as if he had a chance and to make it interesting. They let out six panthers from six different inlets. Two began snarling at each other at once and paid no attention to anything else. The one nearest the fellow went straight for him, and, do you know, that cowardly scoundrel showed just one flare of courage in his desperation.

"He ran at the beast, hit it on the nose and drove it away. He scared off the next, too. The fifth was afraid of the crowd and the shouts and all that and tried to get back through the grating down the inlet. While Bucco had been setting the crowd wild with delight by scaring off the two panthers in succession, that she-demon down there had never moved. When he paused and glared round she began to crawl toward him. The moment he saw her coming he yelled, threw away his club and ran. She never hurried, just crawled steadily. He scudded to that panel of rollers below the Vestals.

"There was Causidiena, the eldest Vestal, and Fonteia, who had known him as nephew and brother, and Gargilia, the youngest Vestal whose cousin he had courted. It was harrowing to see him run and hear him yell. And the panther never hurried, just kept on crawling. Fonteia sat as if nothing was going on, but the Vestals leaned forward; Causidiena was very bitter over her brother-in-law's murder. Then . . . have you ever seen one of the log-walking contests?"

"I haven't seen one amphitheatre show where you have seen a hundred," said Proculus.

"I mean," said Balbinus, "when the arena is flooded and they throw in a dozen or two logs and then offer a prize for anyone who can stand up on one. And first they let a batch of street urchins try, and they wade out to them and scramble on to them and try to stand up and always get thrown off when the logs turn."

"I've seen that," said Proculus.

"And then, you know," Balbinus went on. "Slaves and rabble try and not one of them can stay on a log. Then an acrobat minces out on a slack-rope, and takes a long jump for a log and lands neatly on it and stays there. And he dances and skips and makes the log turn under him and pirouettes and turns flip-flops and walks on it on his hands and stays on."

"Yes," said Proculus, "I've seen that too."

"You know what a peculiar trick of balancing he has so the log never lurches and throws him off?"

"Yes," said Proculus.

"Did you ever see anybody climb arena-rollers with a similar trick of balancing?"

"No, I never did," said Proculus, "and I don't believe it could be done."

"Neither would I have believed it," said Balbinus, "until I saw it. That frantic murderer jumped for the lowermost roller, and somehow got his right arm and right leg over it, hugging belly-flat to it. He hung on when it turned. Then he clung to it with both legs and one arm and got his right arm over the second roller. Then he got both arms round the second roller and steadied himself. Then up went his right leg and he was sticking to the second as he had stuck to the first. The whole audience was dead still, everybody that could see him watching breathlessly and the rest silent because the others were.

"The panther never hurried, just crawled steadily, her eyes never leaving him. By the time she was below him he was on the fifth roller and she crouched flatter and flatter while he worked up to the sixth roller. When he put up a hand for the seventh she sprang. Her paws clawed into him, one on his ribs and the other on his left thigh, and she gripped a mouthful of his right flank just above the hip, her teeth must have met in his liver. He gave one frightful screech as they fell together. She landed on her feet and instantly gave him a cuff with her forepaw alongside the head. It tore the side of his face off and must have broken his neck.

"Then she set her teeth into his throat and lay down flat, holding on. The audience had given one barking shout as they fell and then hushed again. When she lay motionless they yelled over and over. And through it all Fonteia sat bolt upright, fanning herself quietly and keeping her countenance, though she was dead pale. And she has never missed a spectacle since; too proud to give anyone an opportunity to say she stays away because of her memories. She always comes with the Vestals, too. But they were so affected by the panther's regularly repeated efforts to climb those rollers that Causidiena petitioned Commodus for a different place.

"He was just making his revision of the seating regulations, and he changed them to this side. Quite by accident my new seats happened to be where theirs had been. I don't wonder they were upset, it makes my flesh crawl every time that brute tries to climb up, not that I am afraid she is coming over, but because she reminds me of Bucco and all that. Fonteia hates the sight of the beast, a hundred times more than I do, I know. I used to hope each show would finish the creature. But she has killed any number of criminals. She has fought goats, antelopes, elks, bulls, buffaloes and all sorts of horned animals. She has set to with dogs, panthers, tigers, lions and come off alive. She has escaped numbers of gladiators, bested some, killed one or two, and been let off by the favour of the audience over and over.

"When I gave up hoping that she would be killed, I tried to bribe the keepers to poison her. But they wouldn't hear of it. I bid them up to two hundred thousand *sesterces*, but they said Commodus had taken a special fancy to the beast and they dare not take any bribe to poison her. I would have paid four hundred thousand to get the creature out of the way. I know how Fonteia feels, though she holds her head high at the shows and never mentions the panther at any time. She can't help being reminded of all that hideous humiliation and she not only can't help remembering the horror of Bucco's death, but she must recall her baby days with him before he developed his ugly traits. It must tear her heart to see that panther. I am sure nothing would please her as much as getting finally rid of the beast."

"By your own account," said Proculus, "you are no nearer winning Fonteia than you were five years ago."

"No nearer and not any more hopeful," said Balbinus. "But just as determined."

"Doesn't the turquoise brooch make you any more hopeful?" asked Proculus.

"I don't see what that has to do with it," said Balbinus.

"That's just it," said Proculus. "You don't see."

"One thing I do see," said Balbinus. "She doesn't seem to care for anyone else. She has any number of suitors, but never treats anyone any better than she treats me; or any worse, for that matter."

"I believe you are more hopeful after all," said Proculus.

"Not a bit," said Balbinus. "Whenever I talk marriage to her she says Helvacius was a man who did something and she'll stay a widow for life before she'll marry a do-nothing. She says if I'd only do something she'd think about it."

"Why don't you do something?" Proculus inquired

"Can't get a chance to do any of the things I can think of," said Balbinus. "And can't think of any more."

"What did you think of?" his friend asked.

"I went to Commodus," said Balbinus, "and asked for a province. You know the way Commodus looks at you, like a stupid countryman who has not understood what you said?"

"Yes, I know," said Proculus, and he laughed grimly.

"Well," said Balbinus, "he stared at me in his red-faced goggle-eyed fashion and burst out:

"'Make you a *prefect*! You manage a province! You never managed anything in your life.'

I manage my estate,' I said. 'Don't put on airs with me,' he growled. 'You talk as if you were your rich cousin. You aren't *the* Caelius Balbinus. Your estate is no wonder. There are a hundred men in Rome richer than you.'

"'I'm not putting on airs,' I told him. 'I know where I stand and what my estate is. Such as it is I manage it.'

"'You do not,' he snapped like a dog. 'It manages itself. You've bailiffs and overseers and inspectors and bookkeepers and managers. Your father trained them, yes and your grandfather, in the ways his grandfather's grandfather before him didn't so much as start, but only had to keep in motion. The estate runs itself as well as if you had been born deaf, dumb and blind; runs itself no worse and no better. You manage nothing.'

"'Men less capable than I have provinces,' I said.

"Then he did puff and glare.

"'You think,' he bellowed, 'because I don't wear a long beard and keep a glum face like my father that I'm a fool. You think because I enjoy a good time and don't consort with dreary old shaggy-faced, shaggy-cloaked philosophers, that I care nothing for the Empire. You think because I love horse-racing and archery and beast-fighting and gladiators and all sorts of really entertaining things, I am no judge of men. I know men. I love best a man who can do things with his hands, a good swordsman or fighter. I love best a man who can distinguish himself in the amphitheatre. That's the best kind of man. But I love any sort of capable man. You senators think I hate you all. I don't hate senators, I hate loafers. You are about as active as a row of hay-ricks in the sun.

"'Get out and do something, any one of you, and I'll be the first one to give you credit for it. If it's worthwhile I'll love you for it. I know men. You take me for a fool, but you are wrong, all of you. I'm no fool and I care more for the Empire than any man m it. I know whom to appoint and whom to reject. You run a province! You couldn't attend to a rabbit-hutch. You great, bloated, lard-bag, you! you sit like a toad on a mud-bank gaping for flies to blunder into his mouth. You never did anything in your life. Get out and do something.'

"'What am I to do?' I asked. 'I want a province and you refuse and then tell me to do something. What am I to do?'

"'Men who do things,' he said, 'don't need to be told what to do, they see things for themselves. If you only once did something I might think of you.'

"'But what,' I insisted.

"'What?' he roared in rage. 'Anything! I'd like to see you spit once as if you really meant it; I could forgive you if you'd up and kick me under the chin, if you thought of it for yourself. Go home,' he said. 'Get out of my sight!' And I went. I don't care about the province, and I don't care whether I please him or not, but I do want to do something to please Fonteia. Only I suppose nothing I could do would please her."

"I believe," said Proculus, "that she is much better pleased with you than you suspect and I believe Commodus likes you too."

"They have a queer way of showing it," Balbinus gloomed.

"You could please them both at once," said Proculus.

"I wish you would tell me how," said Balbinus. "Hang him I say. Yet I shouldn't mind catching his eye. For her, I'd do anything, as you know."

"Do you really mean to say," demanded Proculus, "that you don't see for yourself what to do?"

"Not a bit I don't," said Balbinus.

"Not with such an opportunity staring you in the face?" Proculus demanded. "When the gods have loaded the dice for you and all you need is to make the throw?"

"If you see anything to do," said Balbinus, "you tell me and I'll do it quick."

Proculus looked around. Several gangs of workmen were busy, but none near them. He stood up, walked to the rail of the stairway and peered down it. Then he came back to his seat.

"Now listen to me," he said, "and don't interrupt me till I am done."

Balbinus listened, mouth and eyes open. When Proculus was done he objected.

"It won't work."

"Are you afraid?" asked his friend.

"Not a bit," said he. "It would be easy. But if they refused two hundred thousand *sesterces* before how can I bribe them now?"

"Don't you see how different this is?" asked Proculus. "They have no dead panther to account for, only a natural failure to notice some rollers out of order, and you won't be dealing with the same set of men, anyhow, not trying to bribe men who have once shied. These will only have to invent a story to explain a perfectly usual occurrence. Did you never know of rollers jamming?"

"Often," said Balbinus.

"There you are," said Proculus, "and now let's go. It's getting hot here and you'll be none too early at the palace by now."

"Your advice is good," said Balbinus. "I'll take it."

Therefore the moon that night looking down into the Colosseum saw a group of figures in the arena by the enclosing-wall. One was a very big man with two attendants. The others were regular keepers of the amphitheatre. They talked a long time and there were many explanations and much assurance that there could be no mistake. A bag of coins changed hands.

Next morning, so early for holders of senatorial seats that they found the chairs all about their own still vacant, Balbinus and Proculus settled themselves into their places.

"One drawback about festival days," said Balbinus, "I always have to chain up my dog, I miss him and he misses me. He hates to be chained up."

"I sympathize with him," said Proculus, half shutting his eyes against the dazzle of the sunlit sand, and snuffing joyously at the perfumed air. "I'd hate to be chained up today. But don't you think he'd interfere with our purpose?"

"We had best not think of our purpose," said Balbinus, "until the time comes to carry it out. I have never been nervous in my life and I don't expect to be now, but I want to run no risks. Let's forget our little secret until the moment for action arrives. There's plenty else to think of."

"The greatest plenty," Proculus agreed. "And more for me than for you. What makes the sand sparkle so?"

"Notion of Commodus," snorted Balbinus. "His father saved so much money he's afraid he can't spend it fast enough. So he has gold-dust sprinkled over it. Fine bit of fool ostentation."

"Wish he'd save the cost and spend it on Dacia," said Proculus earnestly.

"Can't you forget Dacia for one day?" Balbinus asked banteringly. "Isn't this enough to make you think there never was a Dacia?"

"Indeed it is," Proculus replied.

"Well, forget it then," his friend advised. "And enjoy yourself."

"I can't help that," said Proculus. "It's almost as novel to me as if I had never seen it before."

"Then you ought to be able to answer a question I have heard debated," said Balbinus. "Does the Colosseum look bigger when full or when empty?"

Proculus ruminated, gazing about him. The arena had in it only a few sweepers, the Imperial platform was untenanted save by the sentinels, most of the movable armchairs in the foremost rows were not yet occupied; but the second wider belt of stone seats devoted to the wealthy nobility of lower than senatorial dignity was already well filled; the third yet wider division of stone benches was crowded with gentry; the fourth steepest circle was overflowing with the populace; while behind them, on the uppermost level, was a packed jam of standing rabble.

"I don't know," he answered. "Yesterday it seemed enormous, today there is something choky about the crowd. Yet the unvaried variety of all that flickering waving of fans and turning of faces and moving hands and arms, gives one a sensation of immensity too."

"What strikes you most?" asked Balbinus.

"The flowers," said Proculus.

"Don't you have flowers in Dacia?" Balbinus inquired.

"Dacia won't be forgotten," laughed Proculus. "Yes, we have flowers there, even some roses. But when we have games the spectators just sit on the grass slopes or stand along the edge of the arena like our ancestors of old. You don't see the wreaths as you do here, and there they are mostly made of strange wild flowers, not a bit home-like to see. These are uniformly roses, and such roses! there must be wagon loads of them. When the seats are all full, allowing a dozen roses to a wreath, there will be twelve hundred thousand roses in this building."

"More," said Balbinus. "But hang the wreaths. I'm afraid mine will tilt over my eyes at the critical moment."

"Shall I pull it off your head as you rise?" asked Proculus.

"I'd thought of that," said Balbinus. "Better not. It might disconcert me. I'll risk the slipping."

"We agreed to keep off that subject," said Proculus.

"We did," Balbinus admitted. "But it will come back. Yet it's not worrying me any. I'm as cool as possible."

"You look it," said Proculus, "and that's more than most of the audience look. I think it will be a hot day."

"It's cool enough here," said Balbinus, "but the upper tiers look hot already."

"I should think they would be," said Proculus. "Piled against each other as they are. I never sat before where I could see the top rows opposite me. You senators get a fine effect here, able to see up under the awning, clear to the arcade and the awning-poles. You can't imagine what a difference it makes."

"I can," said Balbinus. "For I never could see that much before. The sag of the awning, at its inner edge on the farther side, always cut off my view of everything above the top tier of seats."

"I thought it was all because of our location," said Proculus. "What makes the difference?"

"It's the awning," said Balbinus. "It's the lightest they ever put up and it sags correspondingly less."

"What's it made of?" asked Proculus.

"Silk," said Balbinus. "Pure silk. Commodus started the fashion of full complete silk clothing for men and all the dandies are imitating him. Linen and wool for me though, yet. But Commodus, not content with dressing in women's textures must needs commit the extravagance of an entire silk awning."

"It's beautiful," said Proculus. "But I should say it is too thin to do much good."

"It's hard to get a satisfactory awning," said Balbinus, "they have tried all sorts in my time. One thick enough to stop the sunrays altogether is so heavy it sags till the inner edge cuts off the view of the upper tiers over the farther side of the arena, and besides it makes the place look gloomy. So does any awning all one colour. Brown and gray are coolest, but very dingy. Blue and green make the people look ghastly and the women ugly, white and yellow make a glare no one can endure and red makes the place look hot. This awning is about the best I ever saw. It's light and not too thin, the pattern is gay and the red and yellow, blue and green make a pleasant variety of bright colours on the audience."

"Too much red," said Proculus.

"That's Commodus again," said Balbinus. "He likes red."

"Speaking of red," said Proculus, "what have you on under your *toga?*"

"Tunic, of course?" said Balbinus.

"But what colour?" Proculus queried.

"Crimson," said Balbinus.

"But why?" Proculus persisted.

"I might get scratched," said the strong man, "and I don't want to show it if possible."

At this moment several senators with their wives and guests came to fill the chairs to right and left of them. Greetings, introductions of Proculus to the newcomers and various chat occupied some little time. By and by Proculus came to a lull in his talk with his left-hand neighbour and found Balbinus momentarily disengaged and questioned him.

"Is Fonteia with the Vestals? I can't make her out?"

Balbinus peered across the arena. The Vestals had just entered and were settling themselves in their chairs.

"That's Fonteia in lavender. She's between Causidiena on her right with gray hair, and Manila; Gargilia is the one with the black hair on the left end."

"Fonteia is too young and too slender for lavender," said Proculus.

"That's what I tell her," said Balbinus. "I say lavender is for fat old women. But she will wear it."

Just then the imperial cortege began to fill the dais and the audience burst into the quick *staccato* three-bar song of greeting to the emperor, thundering it over and over until he was seated and held up his hand for silence.

At once the shows began. Proculus, watching with unsated eyes the succession of beast-fights, acrobatic feats, and killings of criminals by various beasts, was, even in his interested state, aware of the lack of enthusiasm in the audience. He was too far from the dais to make out the emperor's expression. Commodus was hardly more than a great hulking, overgrown lad, with all a boy's impatience and petulance. Not much could be expected of him in the way of dignity. He sulked often and at the smallest pretext. Yet Proculus perceived, or thought he perceived, a more than usually obvious posture of bored irritation, of disappointment with the progress of a very tame, usual and uninteresting series of shows.

He saw, or imagined he saw, an emperor wearied with what he

had seen over and over and eager for some diversion, something new, something unusual. Fonteia's face he could not read where she sat. It was all one could do to identify a known figure in a known seat at that distance. Yet he reflected that she could not but see Balbinus, the biggest-bodied man in the senate, in the front row. As he looked on with a return of half-forgotten reminiscence, he realized that no one could see everything when so many things went on at once, that no one group in the arena, still less any one figure, caught the eyes of all the throng.

Yet when the splotched panther appeared from one of the beast-inlets, it seemed to Proculus that all eyes followed her, as, ignoring everything in the arena, living and dead, she galloped in a straight line across the sand. His eyes he certainly kept on her till the coping cut off his view. Then he saw Balbinus slip the *toga* from his shoulders. Both of them sat well back and strove to appear unaware of what their strained senses expected.

That the panther had sprung and had not fallen back they were apprised by a universal yell from all parts of the amphitheatre from which she was visible, by an alarmed shrinking back of the senators and their guests near them, by little screams from two ladies who had been looking over the coping and who shrank back abruptly. Proculus pressed himself against the back of his chair and over its left arm, to give Balbinus room. He heard in front of him a scratchy clawing, heard it even above the redoubling waves of excited yells that rang from all around the arena; heard it all the more when those yells subsided suddenly into a tense hush of expectation, when the seventh roller failed to turn.

A paw clutched the coping, a splay paw with four translucent horny claws that slipped on the polished stone and caught on the interlaced leaves of the carven vine on it, a puffy paw with dingy black hair between the claws. Then beside it and by no means close to it another paw, white-haired and paler-clawed, hooked its talons into the carvings.

A head came up, a head with a black ear and a white ear with irregular marblings of white and black, with two round-pupiled yellow-gray eyes, one looking out of a black patch and one out of a white. It had a moist, black muzzle, and as it rose the lips curled, the mouth opened and Proculus found himself trying to push back his chair as he recoiled from a jagged snarl. He was looking past incredibly white, unbelievably sharp teeth into an unforeseeable immensity of scarlet mouth and throat

There was more all too audible scratching and the head elevated itself on a black and white neck, Proculus did not see Balbinus move, but he did see a big, beefy, pink hand round that neck, the thumb on the gullet.

The spectators, who had first yelled in mere blind excitement and then stilled in mere unconscious strained attention, saw the panther's head above the coping, saw the senators tumbling over each other to right and left, saw the two occupied chairs in front of her, saw the distracted arena-guards, some ineffectually rushing for the nearest exits, vainly trying to reach the podium before the animal cleared the copings, some vacillating on the sand below, eager to shoot the beast and fearing to loose spear or arrow for fear of wounding one of the senators.

Then they saw a big, crimson-tunicked figure erect, its long arms stiff and straight out before it, the panther's throat vised inside its big hands, the beast's fore legs beating the air in front of her, her hind legs lashing wildly against the top roller and the bit of wall below the coping. They followed breathlessly the gyrations and throes of the lithe body until it hung limp and motionless, straight down from the unaltering grip of those big hands. Then they stood up and howled, and stamped, yelling wave after wave of cheers till they were hoarse,

Balbinus stood motionless, the panther dangling against the coping, his tense arms streaked with the streams that gushed from a dozen gashes.

When the cheering died of itself he straightened his arms again till the carcass hung clear of the wall, gave it a flirt to the right and flung the flaccid, broken-necked carrion into the arena.

The wave of cheers that followed after he sat down made all that had gone before seem whisperings.

When the first lull came between the gusts of cheers, Commodus, standing up on the seat of his throne, his voice broken by excitement to a cracked *falsetto*, sent down the whole length of the arena, audible to everyone, a shrill yell of:

"*Macte virtute esto Balbine.*"

The cheering rose again like a storm-wind. It was very pleasant to Balbinus. He sat bolt upright in his chair, his *toga* wrapped round him to the throat, his arms under it. He was staring across the Colosseum at a lavender-clad figure in the front row facing him.

327

Disvola

(A Tale from *The Song of the Sirens and Other Stories*)

As he penetrated more deeply into the wood, continually scrambling up hill, hampered by his armour and hindered by low boughs and undergrowth, it appeared to him that, slowly as he seemed to advance, he was drawing away from his pursuers. Instead of shouts and widespread cracklings in the underbrush he heard only occasional snappings of branches and the footsteps of but one man. He stopped, listened attentively, made up his mind and turned like a wolf at bay. The fight was brief. In a moment he tugged his dagger out of his pursuer's ribs, drove it three times through his throat to make sure, and plunged it repeatedly into the cleansing earth. Sheathing it he stood up and hearkened. He heard only the woodland noises. Rapidly he divested himself of his armour. Settling his sword-belt anew he continued his flight, bareheaded and still panting, until he gained the lonely recesses of the mountain forests.

There he sat down to consider his situation.

He was of a buoyant disposition and the mere fact that he, unhorsed and encumbered by his mail, had hacked his way through a press of eager foes, had eluded and outdistanced a hue and cry of victorious and triumphant enemies, appeared so notable an exploit that the thought of it seemed to give him confidence and to cheer him up.

He needed cheering.

At sunrise he had known himself the most formidable, the most dreaded, the most renowned condottiere in Italy; before sunset he found himself a solitary fugitive. He had ridden out at dawn the leader of eight hundred reckless and obedient spearmen; in the dusk he crouched alone, destitute of food, water, friends, shelter or refuge.

He tried to review his chances of life and rehabilitation.

At first he could think of no chances of either.

In any city where he was a stranger he would either be killed at sight as a dangerous alien, or clapped into a dungeon as a suspicious outlander and later handed over, as a peace-offering, to some one of his implacable enemies.

Implacable enemies he had by thousands.

Scores of the cities where he was known had always been his implacable enemies. He had been among their foemen from his childhood. Some he had sacked, some he had helped to sack, others remembered citizens who had died by his sword in fair fight, had been slain by his men-at-arms, had been butchered by his orders.

Most of the cities where he would be recognized were still more envenomed against him as a perfidious ally who had betrayed them to their ruin or deserted them in their bitter need.

He could not think of any walled-town in all Italy where he could find safety, protection or even mercy.

Merciless to all men, he knew that to him all men would be merciless.

As a lonely wanderer, without money or armour, but girt with a sword and *poignard*, any village would greet him with volleys of stones and curses; any country-side would band to hunt him like a stray wolf; any farmstead would loose its dogs on him; any labourer, goat-herd or wayfarer would raise the hue and cry against him.

For a while he raged at his luck.

This day was to have set him, secure and above the caprices of fortune, upon the pinnacle of prestige and fame. It had all been arranged. In the crisis of the battle, just in the nick of time, he and his men were to have changed sides, annihilating their frigid associates and winning both the everlasting gratitude of their admiring adversaries and undying glory for himself as a lightning strategist and wily diplomat.

But everything had gone wrong. His employers had suspected his perfidy, had come to an understanding with their antagonists, the battle had been a sham, a parade, an elaborate snare laid to trap him and his company into shame and massacre. At the crisis of the day both leagues had laid aside their age-long enmities and feuds and had joyously united in the pleasant pastime of butchering his men. Many of them had been slaughtered. But some, taught by long service with a leader who had changed sides whenever it suited his advantage, had won honour in a new service by joining in the carnage and helping to exterminate their less facile comrades. Most of his mercenaries were dead, not one of the survivors would ever again own Melozzo

Carpineti for his master.

He could hardly believe that he was Melozzo Carpineti.

He resolved that no man should take him alive, that he would never be a prisoner to be taunted, insulted, tortured, shamed.

He thought of falling on his rapier-point, he fingered his throat and half drew his *poignard*.

Then he remembered Fabrizia.

He had not thought of Fabrizia for years, for ten years at least; at least fourteen years had passed since he had seen her.

He recalled their parting, she leaning out of the window, he clinging to the face of the castle-wall, his elbows on the window-sill, his toes on his familiar scant footholds in the inequalities of the stonework. He recalled her last kiss, her parting words.

"Melozzo," she had said, "I shall never cease to love you. No power on earth, no wheedling, no threats, will ever make me marry any other man, or enter a convent. I shall be yours until I die or until you return to claim me. Every night, while I live, my lamp shall burn at this window as tonight, so that you can see it across the valley. Every day I shall wish for you, every night I shall expect you. I shall never change or forget."

Melozzo Carpineti stood up, made sure of his direction and began to work his way southward. His first care was to find a rivulet, to make sure he was the only man in that solitude, and to drink his fill; then, all night he made his way along the mountain-side keeping well down from the crests of the ridges, but following their general direction. The night was clear and he guided himself by the stars. Towards dawn he found a well-hidden nook and curled himself up to sleep.

He wakened near sunset, famished, but not yet weakened by fasting. He was well pleased. Another night of thridding the hillsides ought to put him well beyond peril from any organized pursuit He had escaped his relentless enemies and infuriated allies.

The next morning he had luck. From his hiding place he overlooked a hut and saw its occupants go off about their daily tasks, goat-herding and such like. Venturing near he found the hut indeed untenanted and stayed his hunger on cheese and rock-hard bread. Likewise he took with him a supply of both.

Steadily then, without hurry, sleeping by day and slinking by night, he made for Vola. Good fortune attended him. The weather was dry and warm; he throve on the food he was able to steal; twice only did he have to fight for his life, and then he left no adversary alive to betray him; he slept soundly; he was a ragged scarecrow, but strong and lithe as a panther.

During the twenty days of his journey, he had plenty of time to think. His thoughts at first surprised him, then absorbed him so that they seemed merely natural. He did not plan or fear for his future; he did not brood over his past; he forgot his treacheries and crimes, his feats and triumphs, his disappointments and failures, his hatreds and ambitions. He thought only of Fabrizia. It seemed to him that, somehow, deep inside of himself somewhere, he had always loved Fabrizia.

Certainly there could be no doubt that he loved her now, loved her consumingly, loved her more every day. His flight ceased to appear to him an escape from doom and a quest for security. He forgot both the imminence of danger and the prospect of safety. His advance seemed a pilgrimage towards Fabrizia. She appeared the only prize in the world really worth striving for. The goals towards which he had striven so eagerly for so many years all of a sudden seemed to him the veriest trifles, matters of no importance.

His one aim in life was Fabrizia. To find her, to possess her, to make her happy, to atone to her for the long years of his neglect. He was indifferent to peril or dominion. He desired only Fabrizia. He longed for her hungrily, frantically.

Before dawn of the twentieth day of his skulkings he descried, far ahead to his left, the unmistakable, familiar, well remembered outline of the great castle of Vola. That was only a glimpse. It required a long night of his utmost effort to bring him near enough to behold at the next dawn the bold grim shape of Vola, dominating the landscape from its magnificent location on the end of a sheer mountain-spur. Then he was on the wrong side of it and had to work round it in a long circuit before he found himself in line with Fabrizia's window. There he slept.

In fact, he overslept.

He woke in the pitch dark, under a moonless, starless, cloud-obscured firmament. Everything about him was inky black, except, far across the valley, a pin-point of radiance.

Fabrizia's light!

The instant he recognized it every conceivable and inconceivable misgiving began to torment him. Like a swarm of impish gadflies they buzzed inside his brain, like virulent gnats they tortured him. Never once did he doubt Fabrizia. If she were in fact alive he was certain that she was expecting him, love in her heart, eager to do all she could to welcome, to succour, to protect, to relieve him. But all the other Disvole had hated him consumedly and they were the most unrelenting, the most pertinacious, the most rancorous family in all Italy. For tenacity of purpose, for subtle craftiness in revenge they surpassed any stock on earth. He feared them, frankly he feared them. He shuddered, shuddered undisguisedly as he thought of them.

Grim old Zenone Disvola, Fabrizia's father, was dead, he was sure. He had heard of his death too circumstantially to be in any doubt as to that. Also, he would now be of an incredible age: he had been a very old man fourteen years before. Melozzo knew he would not have to reckon with old Zenone's icy malignity. Also he seemed to have heard of the deaths of Vincenzo and Romualdo, Fabrizia's two brothers. He could not make up his mind whether he had heard that they were dead, or had heard some ephemeral rumour, soon contradicted.

He ruminated, inclined first to the notion that they were out of the way, then to the opinion that he had no grounds for supposing them dead. There was little comfort for him in either supposition. If they were alive, if either were alive, he had to expect hatred only a shade less malign, less ingenious than their father's, and if they were gone, there remained Bauro, Bauro the Bastard, brawny, sinister and ferocious. He shivered at the thought of Bauro.

Bauro or Romualdo or Vincenzo, it was all one to him. He stood up, his purpose indomitable. He would go straight to Fabrizia's light. If she was alive and waiting for him, he would reward her as far as lay in his power for her loving fidelity. If she was in duress and the light a lure, at least she might have the poor satisfaction of knowing that he had remembered, that he had returned, had tried to reach her. If she was dead, and the light indeed a decoy, he would at any rate find out the truth. His life was little to pay for that, now. If she was not in the world the world meant nothing to him. As well one death as another. In his days of brooding in the forests Fabrizia had revealed herself as all the world to him. If she was not in it the world mattered nothing. Nothing mattered but Fabrizia.

In this exalted mood he started down into the valley. Within an hour his feet were on the old familiar path, the path his feet had trod so many nights in his golden youth to reach the stolen kisses of his unattainable darling. Tonight he found the path unaltered. He crossed the Latte at the old ford, and not a stone seemed a finger breadth out of place. He breasted the ascent.

At the cleft rock, where he used to hide love-letters for Epifania

Varese to find and carry to her mistress, where Epifania used to leave missives for him to find with tokens warning him that he must not venture further that night, or other tokens, assuring him that the coast was clear, at that cleft rock he halted.

He felt in the cleft. It was empty, of course. He unbuckled his belt and bestowed it in the hiding place. One might enter Vola sword in hand, clad in mail, at the head of six hundred men-at-arms. One might enter Vola weaponless; either was rational, though venturesome. But to enter Vola, unarmoured, yet with a sword and *poignard*, was to seem ridiculous. Melozzo had committed crimes and blunders, but he had never made himself ridiculous. Bareheaded and weaponless he climbed the steep rock path, the path that he alone had ever trod, a path that a goat could hardly have followed. His feet knew every inch of it.

Above him the brute bulk of Vola, haughty and menacing, loomed huge against the darkness.

When he stood on the narrow ledge below the castle wall, he leaned against the stone until his breathing quieted. Staring up he saw the battlements, a solider blackness against the sable firmament of cloud. Also he made out above him to the right the faint outline of that great iron bar, projecting from the coping, from which the lords of Vola were in the habit of hanging whomsoever it seemed good to them to hang.

He smiled to himself in the dark.

When he felt rested he began the last stage of his ascent. His fingers found at once the familiar handholds and his toes the inch-wide footholds in the masonry. He clutched the sill at last, drew himself up and looked into the room.

It was unaltered in fourteen years, the vaulted ceiling painted in arabesques, the rich tapestries hiding the walls, the stone floor bare, the whole empty save for two chests against the arras and the big table midway of the floor, and two armchairs. On the table stood two lamps; one at its nearer edge, a lamp with a tall standard, the lamp that sent its rays across the valley; the other stood at the further comer to the right, a lamp with a short foot, its flame near the table-top. By the shorter lamp sat a woman embroidering.

It was not Fabrizia!

At first he did not recognize her. Then, just as he knew her, fourteen years older and stouter, for Epifania Varese, she turned and saw him.

"*Ecco!*" she said. "*Il Signor Melozzo! Entra, Messer Melozzo.*"

She stood up.

Melozzo put a leg over the sill, pulled himself up and vaulted to the floor.

"My lady will be overjoyed to see you, Messer Melozzo," spoke Epifania.

The tattered, grimy spectre of Melozzo Carpineti before her eyes had appeared to crouch and shrink away. At her words he flushed a hot brown-red under his month-old scrub of beard and seemed to swell and grow as she watched him. His chest expanded. Fabrizia was alive and free!

Epifania clapped her hands. Presently two pages, rubbing sleepy eyes, entered the room. Epifania gave them succinct orders. At once, deferentially, they conducted Melozzo into an adjoining apartment of three rooms. In one they bathed him, shaved him and combed his long hair. In the largest they set him, clad only in a bathrobe, before a table spread sumptuously with viands: cold pigeon pie, cold roast wildfowl, cold ham, bread and olives, a variety of sweetmeats, and two great flagons of wine, one white, one red. There by the light of six lamps he ate his fill. Then in the third room his attendants composed him in a big, soft bed.

He slept soundly.

When he woke it was broad day and the two *servitors* were watching him. Obsequiously they inquired whether it would please Messer Melozzo to rise. Deftly they habited him in luxurious garments, fit for a great lord, but without belt, dagger or sword. Respectfully they led him in the large room where he had supped the night before. There was no crumb of food there, this time. There they left him, closing the door behind them.

A moment later the door opened again. Melozzo looked up. In the doorway stood Bauro Disvola, swart, vast and truculent, hand on hilt.

Melozzo stood up.

They eyed each other.

Bauro spoke, suave as a troubadour.

"Greeting, Messer Melozzo."

"Greeting, Messer Bauro," Melozzo replied.

"May I come in?" Bauro asked, urbanely.

"Enter, Messer Bauro," said Melozzo.

Bauro closed the door, swept the room with a swift glance and said:

"Let us be seated, Messer Melozzo."

They took chairs. Bauro pulled his close up.

"Messer Melozzo," he said, "my father and brothers detested you more than any other living being. They foresaw the eventuality of your return here. They laid their plans accordingly. They gave explicit directions. You know the family history. The Disvole have always been vengeful, but they have never been satisfied with any brutal and obvious revenge; they have had a pretty taste in retaliation and their vengeances have been delicate, fantastic, recondite,

"I must now tell you, Messer Melozzo, what I have never told any man, what I shall never tell any man but you.

"After our father's death Vincenzo neglected me, ill-treated me, insulted me. I had no reason to expect any better treatment from Romualdo. Vola, you should know, is not a fief held from the emperor, from the Pope, from any overlord. Under God the lord of Vola owns no master. Vola belongs to its possessor, absolutely, without qualification. Its owners may sell Vola, may give it to anyone whim suggests, may bequeath it as caprice prompts, being accountable to no higher authority. When its holder dies Vola passes to the next heir, who for it does homage to no *suzerain*.

"With Vincenzo and Romualdo out of the way Vola must pass to me or to Fabrizia. I was exceedingly popular with the garrison and vassals. Fabrizia was as docile to me as to Romualdo or Vincenzo. Considering all that I sounded a medico. He declared himself my man, promised a sure and swift poison, and gave me what he prepared, with instructions. Vincenzo died at once and painlessly, without any suspicion. But the poison worked on Romualdo differently; curse him, he was tougher or protected by magic. It worked, but it worked slowly. He knew himself a dying man, but he did not die at once. He suffered and he suspected. The medico was tortured, he confessed. I was pounced upon and haled to the upper room where the high door opens out over the cliff beneath the iron bar. The door was wide and across its sill I saw the Latte a ribbon of blue-green water a thousand feet below at the bottom of the valley. The rope was ready, rove through the pulley at the end of the bar, the executioner held the noose in his hands. Romualdo was there, writhing in his litter, groaning and gasping, his face contorted with agony.

"'Bauro,' he said, 'you are meat for the crows. You should have swung beside your apothecary leech. You shall, if I give the word. You are a murderer. You killed Vincenzo, you have killed me. I am a dying man. I shall not live to accomplish what I most desire. But I should like to die knowing that what I most desire will be brought to pass after I am dead. If you will swear to carry out my instructions you shall not hang today. You shall have a respite until such time as you hand Vola over to your successor. You shall have a chance, a small chance, one chance in a million, but still a chance, of living after you hand over Vola to your successor. Meantime, be it days or years, you will be Bauro Disvola, living and lord of Vola. Will you swear to carry out my instructions?'

"I looked round the room, I looked out of the open door in the wall, down at the valley of the Latte, up at the blue sky.

"'I will swear,' I said, 'and I will carry out your instructions.'

"Then, grunting and wheezing, he gave me his instructions, his tortured head on one side, his wry face leering at me.

"I was dumbfounded at his instructions as you will be astounded when they are carried out I swore to carry them out.

" 'Yea,' said Romualdo. 'You swear and you shall swear a very different oath, a very different oath.'

"Then they carried him in his litter all the way to the shrine of the Madonna of Lattemaggio, they haled me all that road. Before the statue of the Madonna they set me, he in his litter behind me. There he made me repeat his instructions, word by word, my hand on the knee of the Madonna, on the worn shiny spot on her knee, where the blue robe has been rubbed smooth by the hands that have been laid on it by men taking solemn oaths, making solemn vows. So standing, my hand on the blue robe at the Madonna's knee, I rehearsed his instructions and I swore.

"Romualdo grinned, a twisted grin.

"'Let him loose,' he said. 'Give him his sword and *poignard*.'

"They girt my belt on me. 'Men,' said Romualdo to the guard, 'the moment I am dead you are to take orders from Messer Bauro as you take them from me, as you took them from Vincenzo, from Ser Zenone. The moment I am dead Messer Bauro is lord of Vola.'

"Back to the castle we fared. In the courtyard Romualdo repeated to all the garrison what he had said to the guard in the church at Lattemaggio. Before sunset he died. For six years I have been lord of Vola.

"Now the time has come for me to carry out his instructions, instructions very little to my taste, wholly contrary to my taste. But you comprehend, I swore with my hand on the knee of the Madonna of Lattemaggio."

Bauro was mottled as he spoke the last words.

Melozzo nodded, sympathetically. He had broken oaths without number, but he knew that, had he sworn an oath by the Madonna of Lattemaggio, his hand on her knee, that oath he would keep to the last particular.

Bauro stood up.

You are hungry, Messer Melozzo," he said, I also am hungry. Let us proceed with the first part of my instructions, which are likely to please you well. You are to be shriven, houseled and married. Then we are to have breakfast."

"Married!" Melozzo's mind leapt at that word. It would be like the sly indirection of the Disvole to plan to marry him to some horrible creature and afterwards to parade Fabrizia before him. He resolved that no threats, no tortures would force him to marry anyone but her. To meet the utmost test he steeled his fortitude.

He had no need of it.

In the courtyard he beheld Fabrizia, arrayed as a bride, accompanied by four bridesmaids; Fabrizia looking not a day older to him than she had looked fourteen years before; Fabrizia, looking so girlish and so lovely that he could not believe her thirty years old, that he could not credit what he saw.

Across the courtyard she smiled at him and he smiled at her. Separately they entered the chapel, separately they were confessed and absolved. Melozzo felt the load of his crimes fall from his shoulders, felt himself a new man, made clean for Fabrizia. Together they knelt or stood through the long ordeal of a nuptial mass; side by side on their knees, they received the host. Side by side, her hand on his arm, they left the church.

Except that he was without sword, *poignard* and belt there was nothing to remind him that he was anything else than a chosen bridegroom, a beloved brother-in-law, a welcome guest. The breakfast was lavish and savoury; Bauro, at the head of the board, beamed at the guests, the great hall was bright with flowers and gay with banners.

After the breakfast they were conducted to Fabrizia's apartments and there left alone, Epifania and one of the pages within call. Undisturbed they passed the day together as they pleased. Alone together they dined and supped.

They told each other all their lives during those long fourteen years, he recounting numerous exploits and adventures; she telling of the slow monotonous life at Vola.

Again and again she clasped him crying:

"Oh, my love, I am so frightfully afraid Romualdo has planned some hideous pang for us, some unforeseeable ingenuity of deviltry!"

But when he strove to conjecture what might impend over them, she stopped his mouth with kisses.

"At least," she said, "we have this day, this hour, this moment. Let us not waste an instant of what we have, let us make the most of every minute."

Next morning they slept late, when they were dressed they were summoned to breakfast in the great hall.

Again everything was as friendly and pleasant as possible. When the breakfast was over two pages brought in a huge tray filled and heaped with magnificent jewellery. By Melozzo they halted.

"Messer Melozzo," spoke Bauro from the head of the table, "it is known to you that it is customary for a bridegroom, if he is well-content with his bride, to make her a present on the morning after their bridal night."

Melozzo, eyeing Bauro, eyeing the jewels, said nothing.

"Messer Melozzo," Bauro continued, "are you well satisfied with your wife? Is she all you anticipated? Did you find her as you expected to find her?"

"Yea," Melozzo exploded, "I found her faultless, body and soul; I found her all any bridegroom could wish for, more than any bridegroom could hope for."

"Such being the case," Bauro went on, "it is fitting that you present her with a morning-gift. Choose then from the treasures on the tray. You may take what pleases you, but only so much as you yourself can here and now place upon your bride, only so much as she herself can wear becomingly at one time."

Suspicious, darkly pondering, puzzled, wholly perplexed, Melozzo examined the gems and gold, conning them, lifting them, rummaging among them.

So overhauling them he considered Fabrizia. She wore not one single jewel. The neck of her gown was cut low and round and the brilliant light blue of the silk emphasized the whiteness of her neck. Her small ears were exquisitely shaped and placed.

After he had delved all over the tray Melozzo spoke to Bauro.

"Messer Bauro, I should like to adorn my bride with a necklace and ear-rings. I find none."

"There are no ear-rings among those ornaments," Bauro answered. "There is no necklace among them. Be content with what you find,

Messer Melozzo. There is a duke's ransom on that tray."

Melozzo chose a high filigree comb set with rubies and emeralds, a sort of diadem that matched it, bracelets the gold of which was almost hidden among the sapphires they carried, and a belt on which turquoises and sapphires cut flat and set deep, alternated, close together, with little gold showing between and around them.

When he had loaded Fabrizia with all she could wear at once he said:

"I have chosen, Messer Bauro."

Bauro dismissed the pages.

When they were gone he said:

"Ask your wife to stand up, that we may judge of the effect."

When Fabrizia had turned round he asked:

"Are you proud of her, Messer Melozzo?"

"The archangels in heaven," Melozzo replied, vehemently, "are not so proud of the Madonna."

"Are you tired of her yet, Messer Melozzo?" Bauro went on. "Do you find matrimony tedious? Have you been married too long?"

Melozzo swore aloud, a solemn oath.

"By all that and more," he said, "no man would ever weary of Fabrizia. A thousand years would be too short a time in which to enjoy Fabrizia."

"Let us go outside into the courtyard," spoke Bauro.

Hand in hand Melozzo and Fabrizia walked, Bauro beside them. At the door he said:

"Look behind you, Messer Melozzo."

Melozzo looked. Half way down the hall, between them and the tables, a double line of men in mail, standing shoulder to shoulder, extended from wall to wall. The rear rank advanced with arms locked, a human chain; the front rank carried their daggers bare.

"What is this, Messer Bauro?" Melozzo queried, his eyes on Bauro's, his voice steady.

"Merely a reminder, Messer Melozzo," Bauro answered, "that we go forward into the courtyard, that there is to be no retreating."

Melozzo turned his back on the armed men and paced sedately towards the door, his hand in Fabrizia's.

Outside he beheld the courtyard lined with a similar double row of men-at-arms, rear rank elbows interlaced, front rank with naked *poignards*.

Also, he saw midway of the pavement, the block, and beside it the headsman leaning on his axe.

Melozzo, all an Italian and therefore half a mystic, was capable of quaking endlessly at peril barely guessed and wholly indefinable. Before the face of unescapable doom he became valiant, almost elated. He drew himself up to his full height, stiffened his shoulders, threw out his chest, held his head high, and trod straight towards the block. A pace further he felt his shoulders seized by two heavy hands and knew that two big ruffians had approached him from behind.

He pressed Fabrizia's fingers, loosed his hold on them, dropped his arms to his sides.

"*Addio*, Fabrizia," he breathed, his eyes on her face. She was regarding him strangely. Somehow not her blue-clad shape, not her jewelled hair, not her inscrutable face made most impression on his vision. He seemed to see only her slender white throat.

Then, to his disdainful, insulted amazement, two more burly varlets caught him by each wrist, two hulking bullies flung themselves flat on the pavement and seized each of his ankles, and the giant of the garrison caught him round the waist from behind, locking his hands before him.

"What?" he thought, indignantly, "eleven rascals all at once to hold one prisoner? Do they expect me to struggle like a child?"

Clamped to the pavement he looked at Fabrizia. She was a pace or two before him, gazing back at him over her shoulder, gazing wistfully. Her bare white neck shone.

"*Addio*, Melozzo," she said.

She took another pace.

A man at arms on either side seized her by the elbows.

She took another pace.

Then, all at once, Melozzo realized that he was held stationary to watch her being led to the block.

It took every thew of his eleven guards to hold him fast Like a wild beast he strained and strove.

In vain!

His fury of effort had blinded him. In his relaxed helplessness his sight cleared.

He saw Fabrizia kneel.

He shut his eyes, he could not look.

He kept his eyes closed until the gripping hands loosened and he stood free.

Then he gazed, he saw the huddle of silk that had been her body,

the spout of blood across the stones, the head, the head, red neck up!
He looked away, looked about him.

Beside him stood Bauro, no longer florid and ruddy, but lead-gray all over his huge face.

Then he was aware of a page offering him a sword-belt. The belt was new, but he recognized his own dagger and sword which he had hidden in the cleft-rock.

"Gird yourself, Messer Melozzo," spoke Bauro.

Mechanically he fastened the belt about him. The feel of the sword at his thigh half restored him to sentience. He heard Bauro speak aloud:

"Hearken all men. Here before you stands Messer Melozzo Carpineti, lord of Vola. He has been lord of Vola since the death of Ser Romualdo. For six years I have been his deputy holding his castle for him, awaiting his return that I might deliver to him his own. From this moment you are to take orders from him as you took orders from Ser Romualdo, from Ser Vincenzo, from Ser Zenone, Salute the lord of Vola!"

The salute crashed out from every throat.

Bauro mute bowed low before Melozzo.

"Messer Melozzo," he said, "you are now lord of Vola. These men will obey your orders, your orders alone, any orders of yours."

"Any order of mine?" Melozzo queried.

Bauro, his face ashen gray, echoed:

"Any order of yours."

"Messer Bauro," said Melozzo, "you Disvole have a pretty taste in vengeance."

"A pretty taste," Bauro echoed, even grayer.

"You Disvole," Melozzo continued, "will give much for vengeance."

"We will give much," Bauro echoed.

"Even sometimes your lives?"

Again Bauro echoed.

"Even sometimes our lives."

The Flambeau Bracket

(A Tale from *The Song of the Sirens and Other Stories*)

Gentlemen, calm yourselves, there is no occasion for an uproar. Be seated again, be seated, all of you, I beg. Honour me with your attention for a moment. Signor Orsacchino has called me a murderer. He need not repeat the epithet. We have all heard it. Some of you gentlemen—I did not recognize the voices—so far forgot yourselves as to suggest that I should cross swords with Signor Orsacchino here and now, or that I should call him out and fight him at once. Gentlemen, I brook no suggestions as to what I should or should not do upon any point of honour. I permit no man to school me as to when or to what extent I should consider myself offended. Still less would I fail to resent any question of the propriety of my ignoring what other men dare not ignore.

Signor Orsacchino has shown his courage by applying to me, before so many of you, a term of such serious import. He can incur no dishonour by hearing out in silence what I wish to say before we proceed to a final settlement. As victor in some score of duels I pray your indulgence if for once in my life I depart from my habits, and instead of fighting at once and keeping silence, talk first and fight afterwards, or not at all. You, as my friends, will do me the honour to listen to me. Signor Orsacchino, as my enemy, will do himself the honour to hearken. A young man, and one who has never yet taken part in a serious combat, he has exhibited his conscientious conviction of the justice of his views, and proved his valour and daring by bearding a master of fence who, in fifteen years, has never failed to kill his man.

As a skilled swordsman I should feel myself a murderer indeed were I to take upon my soul his blood in haste. The *Signor* is young; the wine has passed rather freely; we are heated. I say earnestly—let no man interrupt me—that if Signor Orsacchino tomorrow in cool daylight chooses to reiterate his words, I shall take them as a deadly insult and shall challenge, meet, and slay him without compunction. If, on the other hand, after I have told my story, he does not repeat his accusations, I shall regard them, all of them, as not merely withdrawn, but as things never said at all.

Signor Orsacchino has called me a murderer because I killed in a *duello* his kinsman. General della Rubbalda. That was more than fifteen years ago, and it was my first formal dud. So far from being a seasoned fighter who butchered a feeble and heartbroken old man, I was then a boy, very raw, and to a great extent unpracticed, pitted against a cool, dexterous, and envenomed adversary. In the many encounters through which I have since passed I recall not one which taxed me more severely or in which I ran a greater risk. In fact, the general would assuredly have killed me had he not chosen to fight with a sword, a perfect mate of my own, which I knew and recognized—a sword the sight of which converted me from an excited lad into a being strung far beyond the reach of any personal or paltry emotions; a thing all muscle, nerve and will, perfectly co-ordinated; an infallible supernaturally accurate incarnation of unhurried, predestinate vengeance.

We met in the meadow outside of the river gate. Our seconds are all alive, men of unimpeachable integrity, nobles of the loftiest traditions, of the most honourable lineage. There were other witnesses of the fight which was scrupulously fair, and which I won by mere force of right and justice. I believe that, when I have had my say, all of you and Signor Orsacchino not least, will admit that I had just cause, more than just cause, for any vengeance upon the general—that to treat him as a man of honour and meet him sword to sword was a condescension upon my part. So far from having forced him to meet me, hid challenge to me was simultaneous with mine to him. Signor Orsacchino has insinuated what, if he were ever to put into words—no, *Signor*, hear me out, you may then say what you please—I should resent far more bitterly than the epithet of murderer.

You will all recall the sudden and lamented death of Signora della Rubbalda, more than two years after that of her husband. You will all remember that she, the most beautiful woman of our city, who was mourned by unsuccessful suitors beyond any count, left behind her a reputation for saintliness, such as few women have ever attained to. I had, indeed, seen the *Signora* before my combat with her husband, but I say solemnly that until the Carnival ball I had never spoken to her, that until the morning after, just before the duel, I had not known whom I so admired. I admit that he challenged me upon her account, but his jealousy was as insensate as the spleen that drove him, whose household had escaped loss, to press an imaginary grievance upon me, whose house was most desolate of all, upon a morning of general sorrow and desolation.

If the story of my grievance—all too weak a word—against him, has never before been told by me, it is not because I have any reason to be ashamed of it, but rather chiefly that I was not willing to smirch the name of della Rubbalda with a tale of villainy so cynical, and, after the custom of our family, I reserve everything involving penitence or repentance for my confessor. You shall judge whether I am right in confessing to you all. I shall detain you but a few moments longer.

Without penitence I cannot speak of my brother Ettore, at the thought of him I am convicted of ingratitude, that most universal, most unforgivable of the sins of youth. I failed to appreciate my brother Ettore. He was to me not merely a beloved comrade, he not only more than filled for me the place of the father I had lost, but also of the mother I had never known. His tenderness was as exquisite as his precepts were wise, his concern universal, his care constant. I loved him, loved him with the ardent adoration of an unproved boy for a young, handsome, accomplished cavalier who is and does all that the boy longs to be and do.

Yet, although he stinted me in nothing, fulfilled for me all my reasonable desires, granted most of my wishes, humoured my whims and bore with my moods, some malignant fibre of my heart drove me into perpetual opposition to him. His solicitude irked me; for, with a boy's folly I mistook stubbornness for resolution, recklessness for valour, and self-assertion for independence. I misconstrued supervision as espionage. Resenting it I began by evading perfectly natural questions as to my whereabouts and doings. From that I grew into a contemptible habit of petty and unnecessary concealment as to my outgoings, incomings, and occupations. He bore this patiently, not showing any change of his affectionate and kindly bearing.

Presently my perversity drove me to run counter to his wishes in first one thing and then another. Because he had advised me to cultivate certain of my associates I drew off from them; because he had warned me against others I made cronies of them, although I liked them little or not at all. I felt myself manlier for this sort of folly. I consorted with persons of dubious character or manifestly beneath me, resorted to quarters of the town I should have avoided. When I should have been diverting and improving myself in the best company possible for a young cavalier of our part of the world, I was roistering—by no means enjoying it—with fellows I heartily despised. I lost much money gaming, yet Ettore refilled my purse without chiding me in words, his manner conveying the just disapprobation I would not heed.

I came home many times so late or so early that I found our porter difficult to wake, and more than once was nearly compelled to find shelter elsewhere. Sometimes I returned so disordered that I shrank from ascending the grand staircase and slunk around the courtyard under the galleries to the *servitors'* stair. I became habituated to low taverns across the river, where I naturally became involved in wine-room quarrels and street brawls. I flattered myself that I comported myself well in these senseless melees. I dealt some shrewd wounds and came off unscathed. I felt all the man, the man of pleasure.

Then one night I was entrapped, I never realized how, in a street fight with several rufflers. One of my comrades fell and the rest fled, and I was left alone, my back to a barred door, facing several blades which I barely kept off, when a tall man appeared behind my assailants, fell upon them without warning and promptly beat them off. After the sound of their fleeing feet had died away in the alleys I found myself face to face with Ettore, wearing a cap without a feather, and a plain brown cloak. He asked only:

"You are not wounded?"

"Not a scratch," I replied.

"We will walk together, if you do not object," he said. "Which way are you going?"

"Home," I answered.

As we traversed the crooked streets, crossed the bridge and made our way home, he kept silence at first and then led me into some light gossipy talk, making no remark upon my silly foolhardiness, nor saying anything relative to his sudden appearance or my rescue.

I should have been touched by his solicitude, but with a boy's folly, instead of being overwhelmed with gratitude to him for having saved my life, I was merely indignant at his having followed me and watched over me, and furious at the thought that he had felt that I, who aspired to be redoubtable, might be—as I was too headstrong to confess I had been—in need of assistance.

After this adventure my perversity was aggravated. I took the most sedulous precautions for my own hurt, doing all I could to preclude the possibility of Ettore's ever again being able to protect me from any possible consequences of the dangers into which I needlessly thrust myself.

Throughout the carnival time I fairly lived away from home, mostly, and this, with Ettore's full knowledge, at the Palazzo Forticello with wild Gianbattista and his wilder brother Lorenzo. I took perverse care that Ettore should not be able to recognize me, changing my dress often and wearing a variety of masks. Throughout the carnival I had been hoping to encounter a lady whom I had first seen the previous autumn, whom I had caught sight of but twice during winter, whom I had watched for in vain at the Cathedral, and in the search for whom I had fruitlessly haunted every church in the city.

It had so happened that on each of the three times I had seen her I was alone. My descriptions had been unrecognizable to those of my friends whom I asked to enlighten me. When I had described her to Ettore he had maddened me by saying that he knew well who the lady was, but declined to tell me, advising me to think no more of her, as her husband was devoted to her and a spleenful, dangerous man.

I spurned his advice, but my fevered efforts won me no success. I had no due to her, and even during the delirium of the carnival time I had sighted no one whom I could take for her. This failure diminished my enjoyment of the week of revelry, but I had at least the satisfaction that I had not seen Ettore. No sense of his presence, of his hovering influence, dimmed the glow of my delight in feeling myself my own master and perfectly able to take care of myself, in getting into scrapes, as I did, and getting out of them as I might, untrammelled.

On the night of the great ball I was dressed as a troubadour and was very proud of my becoming costume. No sooner had Lorenzo and I entered the theatre then I saw the lady of my dreams. She wore a very narrow mask, no more than an excuse for a mask, and was dressed in fanciful garb, the significance of which I did not try to guess, but with the effect of which I was enraptured. She was with a very young man, and after a word with Lorenzo, using the freedom of the festal time, we accosted them. Lorenzo engaged the attention of her escort, while I gained possession of the lady, I may say that we spent the evening together, dancing countless dances, partaking of refreshments, strolling about, or seated on one or another of the benches in the corridors or loggias.

So engrossed was I that it was only occasionally that I remembered to look about for Ettore. I never saw him, nor any figure at all suggesting his. But each time I looked among the crowd, the parti-coloured brightness of which was accentuated by a liberal sprinkling of cavaliers in black *dominoes*, all alike slender, youthful, and tall, I saw somewhere one figure that, as it were, stood out among the rest—a tallish spare man of erect carriage, stiff bearing, and moving in a way not at all suggestive of youth, most absurdly and unbecomingly habited as a buffoon, not after the manner of our theatre, but in the French fashion, all in white, with a tight-fitting cap and a full false face whitened with flour, a loose, white blouse, with huge, white buttons big as biscuits, loose, wide, white trousers, and white slippers with white rosettes.

This costume, odd enough on a young and plump figure, had an uncanny effect preposterously hung about the leanness of an elderly and frigid form. It was so unpleasantly weird that more than once my gaze dwelt on it for an instant before it returned to peering through my dear comrade's mask at the half-revealed wonders of her dazzling eyes. Our conversation was very innocent, witty we thought, delightful we felt. It was near the unmasking time when, as we gave ourselves to the intoxication of one of the last dances, I heard Ettore's voice whisper in my ear.

"Take care. Do not go home alone. You have been three hours with the wife of the most jealous man alive."

I turned my head, and as well as I could in whirling through the whirling crowd, I looked about for Ettore. I did not catch sight of him, nor of any costume such as he might be likely to wear. I saw only the everlasting parti-coloured whirl, the iterated black *dominoes*, the inevitable misfit zany.

At the end of the dance the youth, whom Lorenzo had removed for me, claimed my partner so peremptorily that I could not but resign her—and she, addressing him as cousin, went off with him. They had scarcely more than disappeared when, as I stood leaning against a pilaster gazing across the press of dancers who thronged the floor at the dazzling parties which crowded every box of the seven tiers, a woman's shriek filled the hall. The next instant came the cry of "Fire," and almost before the boxes opposite me emptied the blaze ran across the ceiling. I took no part in the mad panic which ensued. I stood petrified, as did a few others, and recovered my senses only when the billows of smoke rolled to the floor.

Then, from under dropping masses of blazing decorations, through doors empty save for the trampled shapes of dead or insensible victims of the rush, I made my way from the auditorium. How I so made my way out, and by which door I do not know, the spectacle of the trampled women so sickened me that I marvel I ever escaped at all. For, at the sight of a corpse not of my own making, I have always turned, I confess, utterly a coward. To gaze at a man dead by my sword does not disturb me. I see in it only the evidence that heaven's justice has made use of my hand to give a scoundrel his deserts.

But a glimpse of a dead body, that of one not slain by me, makes my head swim, my eyes dazzle, my sinews loosen, my knees knock together. Before such a corpse I am—I may apply to myself what no other man would venture to hint—no better than a craven. Therefore, I shall never know how I came out of that furnace. I was delirious with horror—a mere animal driven by the primitive instinct of the dread of fire.

The corridors and passageways were almost as full of smoke as the theatre itself, and, it seemed to me, more aflame. I dare not venture to say how many stairways I seemed to find ablaze. The rush of the fire drove me in frantic flight hither and thither through several narrow doors and—for down every stair I saw climbing flames—up more than one stair. I realized that I was quite out of the theatre and on an upper floor of one or the other of the long-disused, deserted *palazzos* which flanked it. I could not guess which, and whichever it might be, it was certainly as much on fire as the theatre. I recall rushing through room after room all filled with smoke, often turning back, finding no outlet and no way down.

Several times I scrambled over heaps of what seemed to be old stage scenery. Once I stumbled and fell, jammed in a forest of broken laths and scantlings. I do not know how I reached the window at which I finally found myself, nor where I was joined by that sinister figure, in the white clown's dress, which I had remarked so often during the dancing. I was first aware of him beside me when I pushed vainly against the shut lattices of the window, and it was his strength, not mine, before which they gave way—not opening on their hinges, but carrying with them their crazy rotten frames, wrenched loose from the stone work of the window and falling altogether with a splintering smash upon the pavement below.

The noise of their crash struck our ears, while our eyesight was yet stunned by the impact of the hot brilliance with which, as the dislodged woodwork left the window aperture clear, we were flooded, diving upward, as it were, from the smoky obscurity of the interior into an intense ruby glare. We both scrambled upon the sill. There was no balcony outside. We were looking into a courtyard so filled with crimson radiance that not only were the walls opposite us bathed in an intense light, but the dark corners were penetrated by a weird carmine-tinted glow even in the deepest shadows.

There was not a human being in sight—the court was deserted. It was of considerable size, paved with big square blocks of black-and-white stone. I could make out on the side opposite us the opening of a wagon archway, yawning like a black throat. No arcades flanked the courtyard, and every window I could see was shuttered fast. There were six stories of windows, and we were at one of the fifth story. The roof cornice beetled above us, the roofs above the court were silhouetted against the inflamed sky, and overhead poured the vast inverted cataract of sparks which streamed up from the holocaust we had not yet escaped.

We spoke no word. He stood upon the left side of the window, I upon the right. My lute I had, of course, thrown away, my mask I had on no longer. I had lost both sword and *poignard*, my whole belt was gone. I had nothing in my hands, which were torn and bleeding. The buffoon had a naked dagger in his right hand, a piece of rope in his left. He leaned over and scrutinized the outlook, as I did. We were a frightful distance above the pavement, and even had we been lower, dropping to the pavement would have been certain destruction, for precisely beneath us was a long narrow area, about a yard wide, and how deep I could not guess, constructed to let light into some cellar.

The coping along its edge, where the pavement ceased, showed as a line of dull light in the appalling illumination. There were no balconies to the windows below us, or to any of those immediately on the right or left of them. About halfway down the face of the wall, from just below the left of the window in which we were to the corner of the courtyard on that side, ran a broad stone cornice, wide enough for a lean man once standing upon it to walk along it .without holding to anything. About halfway to the corner of the court a metal rain-spout ran down, making a conspicuous elbow over the jutting stone shelf. Once set on his feet upon this cornice, either of us was sure of escape. The end of it was not precisely below the left side of our window, but a little to the left

All this I took in in a moment, so, apparently, did the other man. There were many flambeau brackets projecting from the walls of the courtyard. There was one beside each lower corner of our window. The buffoon took his dagger in his teeth, kneeled down, reached over and fastened one end of his rope to the flambeau socket. He did not hurry, but made sure of his knots. Then he dropped the rope and, holding to the bracket with his left hand, shook the rope into undulations with his right, peering down to descry its end. Its end was all of ten feet above the level of the cornice, too far for a man holding the extreme end of it to set his feet on the cornice top.

To jump for that cornice, or to drop upon it from even a yard above, it would have meant the certainty of going down to be dashed to pieces on the cruel flagstones below. The buffoon pulled up the rope and stood up, his dagger still between his teeth, projecting from under the false face which it thrust away from his own, and through the eyeholes of which I seemed to led his eyes fixed upon me. We could hear, above the roar of the fire, the confused hubbub of shouts from the crowds which thronged the square and the streets round about I had called for help when first I reached the sill, but my bawling, lost in the steady deep, rumbling note of the fire and in the confusion of voices beyond, won no response.

Now I yelled again, screamed, shrieked, but no one heard. The buffoon echoed my outcries, but not as if assisting them, not as if hoping against hope for rescue, not as if, like myself, merely giving way to terror and despair, but rather with derisive mockery in his rallying halloos. I felt totally helpless. If I were to escape at all it would be through him, yet I felt him as an inimical presence and feared him almost more than the fire behind us. He stood with the rope bunched inside his fingers, it seemed to me nervously knotting and unknotting it, then he let most of it go slack, a coil of a loop or two swinging back and forth in his left hand, his face toward me and his eyes I felt steadily on me. The tiny threads of lazy smoke that had been faltering out of the window under the lintel increased from a thin trickle to a continuous stream.

Through the door of the room behind us was visible a faint blush of blurred brownish light. As I looked at it I saw the door darken suddenly. A man rushed through it, incredibly alive out of the throttling reek, crossed the room in a bound, and leaped upon the sill between us. He was all in black—black cap, black mask, blade *domino*, black hose, and his sword in a black scabbard. So swift was his rush, so impetuously did he leap, that I wondered whether he had meant to set foot on the windowsill or had expected to land on a balcony outside. As it was, he planted his feet fairly on the sill, but just missed pitching forward into space. He toppled, bent double, and saved himself only by touching the outer sill with the outstretched fingers of his tense arm.

At this instant, as the masked, black *domino* rocked unsteadily, head and shoulders into the outer air, the zany flung the noose—for it was by no means a snarl of rope, but a cunningly knotted slip-noose, which he had held inside his closed left hand—over the newcomer's head, and, with one lightning movement, half dragged, half hurled him from the sill. In the air the victim spread out arms, legs, and cloak, like a huge bat. His hands windmilled wildly, searching for the rope, and failed to touch it. For a horrid instant, as the rope checked its headlong dive, the inverted body gave a jolted bob upward before it turned, then it lurched over, the hands making one last clutch for the rope, and again missing.

The cord drew up straight as a rapier blade and held. The body was violently and convulsively agitated once or twice, and its sword, tossed out of the upturned scabbard, struck the corner of the cornice with a sharp clang, bounded up, flashing in the red glare, and shot down a long line of light to the pavement. Its owner's corpse writhed sinuously and then merely gyrated limply at the end of the rope. Its feet were not much more than a man's height above the cornice. My abomination of the sight unnerved me so that my impulse to hurl myself upon the murderer was swallowed up in a physical sickness in which I nearly fell from the sill. As I clung to the stone jamb the malignant white shape, dagger in hand, addressed me:

"Sir, I know who you are. I was about to piece my rope with your carcass. Since this intruding stranger has spared me the necessity, and since the rope is now long enough to be useful, I offer you the courtesy of the first opportunity to descend."

Speechless with horror and loathing I tottered, a helpless jelly, against the jamb. He stood, his long dagger in his right hand, eyeing me through his whitened mask.

"Ah," he went on. "You hesitate. You can pass me easily, descend by the bracket, the rope, the cornice, and the rain-spout. You will not? Then you will pardon me if I leave you. You will find it warm here before long. Nevertheless, if this place is more to your liking than the street, I do not dispute your right of choice. A goodnight to you. I am tempted indeed to put this dagger into you before I go. But I reflect that, though you do not look it, you might have the strength and sleight to avoid my thrust, and perhaps even throw me down. I shall not risk it. If you overcome your panic and are not burned here or killed by falling, if, in short, you get down alive and get home, you shall hear from me in the morning."

He leaned over, tore off and threw away his false face and revealed to me a countenance I did not then recognise. Next, his dagger in his teeth, he dived for the bracket, caught it with both hands, swung himself off into space, gripped the rope, first with one hand, then with both, went down it, stood on the dead man's shoulders, let himself down the rope till he clasped the corpse, wriggled down it, embracing it close, dislodging the cloak which sailed down the air like some huge bird and settled upon the pavement far out into the court near the sword

The escaping villain finally gripped one ankle of the corpse with each hand, swung himself and all above him gently sideways until his feet found the cornice, steadied himself by the feet of the corpse, let go and stood up, edged gingerly along the cornice to the rain-spout, and slid down it smoothly. Once on the pavement he leaped into the air, clapping his hands and crowing, scampered briskly across the court, stopped to pick up his victim's cloak and sword, turned to glance up at me, waved me a derisive farewell, and, after a hideous caper of joy, vanished into the black throat of the wagon archway, running like a fiend.

My eyes came back to the dangling body, revolving slowly now. Its mask hung beside the neck and the back of the head was toward me. I felt myself doomed. I knew I could never summon up resolution to escape by that road. In fact, I am sure that from losing my hold, as I actually later descended, and being dashed to pieces on the pitiless stones, nothing saved me but the set fixed purpose of vengeance, which made me not a man, but an automaton.

I looked behind me. The glare of the fire was bright through the smoke, dense volumes of which poured out of the window above my head, and the heat of which I could feel.

At that instant came a terrific dragging crash, a brief darkness, and an agonized wail of groaning shouts. The roof of the theatre had fallen in. The smoke sucked back through the window above me, and momentarily I felt cool air on my face. The next instant the volume and intensity of the light redoubled as the overarching stream of sparks became a firmament of fire. The court grew bright to the deepest, darkest corner, eddies of air swept past me, the corpse swung round, its mask blew away wholly. Hideously bowed the head was, the chin driven into the bosom. But I knew the face of my brother Ettore.

Azrael

(*Matrimony*, 1932)

My nursemaid used a cruel plan,
To curb her charges' play,
By tales about the Bogyman,
Who carried you away.

I used to wake when I dreamed
And, in the inky night,
I sat up in my bed and screamed
With childish fear and fright.

I dreamed about a lovely land
And there a girl and I
Were faring forwards hand in hand
Beneath a sunlit sky.

Then as we went, the sky grew dark,
The shadows thickened round,
I seemed to palpitate and hark
For some approaching sound.

On the unstable verge of sleep
I swayed, appalled and numb;
I knew the Bogyman, to leap
On one of us had come.

My Love, your finger wears my ring,
My heart is in your keeps;
Our lives are at their perfect spring,
Our harvest yet to reap.

Let us be happy for a span
Together, while we may;
For, all too soon, the Bogyman
Will carry one away.

Floki's Blade

1

Thorkell Vilgerdson was not only reputed the handsomest youth in all Norway, but was famous as a redoubtable champion, who had unfailingly killed his man in every combat, and who was so skilful with weapons that he had never been seriously wounded in any of the countless affrays in which he had taken part. Therefore, although every one of the thirty-nine other men on the *Sea-Raven* hated him venomously, not one challenged him, or provoked him, or affronted him in any way, but all were most scrupulously civil.

They all hated him. The three chieftains, Halfdan Ingolfson, Kollgrim Erlendson, and Lodbrok Isleifson, who owned the ship and had planned the adventure, hated him because, to their incredulous amazement, they found themselves indubitably afraid of him. Their six thralls, Vifill, Ulf, Hundi, Kepp, Sokholf and Erp, hated him, even more than they hated their own masters, for his air of ineffable superiority. The twenty-six other Vikings hated him because they felt themselves his inferiors and were unwilling to acknowledge it, even in their thoughts. Most of all his four perfidious sham friends, Hrodmar Finngerdson, Sigurd Atlison, Gellir Kollskeggson and Bodvar Egilson, who had hatched the plot to hire him to his doom and put him out of the way, and had enticed him to join the expedition, hated him for his beauty, his grace, his jaunty demeanour and his vivacious wit. Attack him they dared not, and, sulking inwardly, they bided their time, outwardly suave; and smiling, but with furtive winks at each other.

Their opportunity came after a storm which drove them, they knew not where or whither, for. in those times, stars were the mariners' only guides. Throughout three nights and three days they saw neither star nor sun; in fact, could see barely two ships' lengths through the driving scud and sluicing rain; and all that time they dared not set so much as a rag of sail, but, taking turns, every man of them, thralls, warriors and chieftains alike, with but brief snatches of uneasy sleep, laboured mightily at the oars, to keep the ship head to gale, or bailed furiously to keep her afloat. So terrific was the tempest that Kollgrim, their acknowledged leader, was unwilling to relinquish the helm and clung to it until exhaustion compelled him to rest. Even when he signalled for a relief neither Halfdan nor Lodbrok showed any alacrity for undertaking his momentous task. As they hesitated, although only for an instant, Thorkell seized the tiller just as Kollgrim's grasp loosened. So well did he steer, so completely did he justify his reputation as a seaman, that thereafter it was rather Kollgrim who acted as relief to him than he to Kollgrim: every man of them all, Kollgrim included, felt safer with Thorkell at the helm.

An hour or two before sunset of the long northern day the storm blew itself out, the sky cleared, and the wind slackened and shifted to a fair breeze. They stepped their mast, hoisted their yard, set a full sail, and, Halfdan at the tiller, and Lodbrok on lookout at the prow, the rest feasted. Champing and munching unhurriedly they despatched a vast quantity of food, washed down with copious drafts of mead. When no one could swallow another mouthful, Sigurd took the helm and Bodvar the lookout's place, and, while Halfdan and Lodbrok ate, the rest disposed themselves to sleep, most of them to larboard, on the spare oars and coils of rope, under the rowing-benches.

During the brief northern night Sigurd and Bodvar set the *Sea-Raven* on a true course by a whole sky full of brilliant constellations, but, before dawn, they saw the stars hidden all round the horizon and gradually higher up, until only a few showed blurredly directly overhead; so that, when the sleepers waked, they found themselves enveloped in dense fog, and, soon after dawn, the wind slackened until they had to man the oars to keep headway on the ship. The weary thralls and Kollgrim roused last. After Kollgrim waked Thorkell was the only sleeper and he slept heavily, exhausted by his over-exertion at the tiller.

Eyeing him as he lay on a coil of rope, Hrodmar and Gellir beckoned Sigurd and Bodvar. They resigned their posts to willing reliefs and picked their way amidships over and among the resting men and toiling rowers. Kollgrim. Lodbrok and Halfdan joined them and the seven conferred. All conned Thorkell and all agreed that he was fast asleep and far from rousing. Then the three chieftains beckoned their six thralls and instructed them. Erp and Ulf took convenient lengths of ratline and knotted in each a clean-running noose. Vifill paired with Hundi and Sokholf with Kepp, each pair choosing a length of light rope, thicker than a big man's thumb. Cautiously the six crawled towards Thorkell, every man aboard, except a few sleepers and such oarsmen as were abaft of Thorkell's position, watching their approach with malicious relish. Hundi and Vifill slipped their rope under Thorkell's knees; Kepp and Sokholf took a turn with theirs round his ankles, Ulf and Erp each noosed a wrist: when all six were ready they looked towards Kollgrim, and, at his nod, the two nooses tightened and the ropes were knotted fast round Thorkell's knees and ankles. Even that did not waken him and, as Erp and Ulf pulled their cords and dragged his arms wide, his four pretended friends sprang on him, turned him on his face, and, after a violent struggle, for, even with knees and ankles lashed, Thorkell fought like a wildcat, they pinioned his arms behind him and turned him once more face upward, trussed and helpless.

Then they gloated over him, told him what they really thought of him, and insulted him to their hearts' content. Halfdan, who was an acclaimed *skald*, composed and chanted over him an impromptu *drapa* of triumph. Even the thralls expressed their envious malignity. Gellir proposed to run him through and Bodvar to throw him overboard. But Kollgrim demurred. The thirty-four freemen had taken oath to a pledge of mutual fellowship, as was customary in all Viking voyages, and he pointed out that they were bound, all of them, by their oath and must keep its letter, if not its spirit.

Lodbrok thereupon suggested that they set him adrift, bound as he was, in their smallest boat, which had been half stove during the storm and was presumably leaky; putting into it with him a small hide flask of water and one smoked fish. Then they could accuse him of wilful desertion.

By then it was nearer noon than sunrise, but no sight of the sun had they had, nor could any man, in that fog, conjecture the sun's place in the sky. Their outlook was all grey mist and smooth groundswell, for there was not a catspaw of breeze.

From the boat they took its sail, mast and oars; but they did not search it carefully. In it they laid a leather flask of water and two little smoked fish. In it they laid Thorkell, trussed as he was, but, as they launched the boat, Kollgrim cut the ropes at his knees and ankles.

As boat and ship drifted apart his enemies mocked him, their grinning faces peering between and over the shields which lined the low rail.

'Hoist your sail!' Bodvar jeered at him, 'and make for Norway or Iceland, as you prefer. You are about as far from the one as from the other. You have no worse or better chance, either way.'

'Hope you relish your provender!' Gellir called,

'You'll need both oars soon,' Hrodmar shrilled, 'and I don't see either.'

'Don't you wish you had a bailer!' Sigurd shouted.

Soon he saw only fog.

He eyed the dirty water sloshing about in the dory's bilge. The boat was not leaking rapidly, but it was leaking. No water had lapped over the gunwales and the big groundswells were long and smooth. Of air there was not a breath. For the time being be had only the leaks to fear. And, in the bow, jammed under the tiny fore-thwart in the triangular cubbyhole, he saw a small wooden scoop-bailer. It meant more to him than the two little fish and the leather water-bottle under the after thwart.

He conned the edges of the gunwales and thwarts. He saw two sharp splinters. The larger and sharper was where he could not use it; but, painfully and with great exertion, he wriggled, hunched and wrenched himself until he brought the cords which bound his wrists against the other splinter. With efforts distressing at once, and not long afterwards agonising, he sawed the rope against the splinter. Panting, a jelly of exhaustion, shivering and sweating, he all but fainted; but he found fresh energy every time he glanced at the bilge-water.

At last, just as hope and strength together were failing him, the cord parted. A few jerks and twists of his arms and hands and they were free. He shook himself, beat his arms against his chest and sprang upon the bailer. To his great satisfaction it was not long before no deftness could scoop it up half full; the boat was not leaking too fast for him.

As the dense fog and breathless calm continued to brood over the waters and the slow groundswell even abated, his cockleshell kept afloat not only all that day and night, but throughout the two following days and nights. But the third night after he had been set adrift found him near exhaustion. More than half his time was occupied in bailing and his muscles ached. He was afraid to sleep for fear of foundering before he woke. Once, in spite of himself, he fell deeply asleep and roused to find the gunwales almost awash, so that the most desperate fury of bailing barely sufficed to save him. In the flurry of effort his remaining fish went overboard in a scoopful of water, unheeded. His flask he had emptied by dusk of the second day, control himself all he could.

As the slow dawn whitened the fog after the short arctic night he thought he was delirious, for he seemed to hear the roar of surf on rocks and not far off.

Then, suddenly, all at once, the fog thinned, sun rays lanced the last wisps of it, the air cleared, he saw the sun plain, saw the sky cloudless, saw the horizon all round and beheld, close to him and opposite the just-risen sun, a rocky coast.

Instantly he realised that his enemies had been vastly in error as to the position of the *Sea-Raven* and had set him adrift only a few leagues east of Iceland. In spite of his buzzing head, his parched mouth, his shivering and trembling limbs, his general faintness, he felt new vigour infused all through him. With his pitiful beechen scoop he alternately bailed and paddled. The current, he felt, was drawing him towards the cliffs. He saw a headland close. With his bailer he strove to guide the skiff towards it. The currents were kind and towards that headland he drifted, he saw no beach, but many flat-topped rocks just awash, some hardly wet by the lazy surges. Between them and him he saw no broken water. If his boat dashed into or scraped against a rock, he might leap to it without a ducking.

Actually he had the luck to achieve just that and saw his boat stove and smashed after he had firm footing on almost dry basalt.

He stood in his doublet, hose and brogues, with only his inner girdle, without belt, mantle, sword, dagger, or even belt-knife. Everything on him was damp from the fog and the splashing of his long bailing; but, though his teeth chattered in the chilly morning air, doubly chilly to him after the milder temperature out at sea, he was not the half-frozen waif he would have been if he had had to swim ashore.

To his left, to southwards, the cliffs seemed beaten by the surf. Before him, to westwards, he thought he espied a bit of beach not far ahead. To his right, northwards, he seemed to descry a headland afar across a fiord. He walked westwards, swaying, tottering, stumbling, even staggering, but keeping his feet. Gulls and other sea-fowl wheeled and screamed above and about him. Not a hundred paces from his landing-place he came upon a little rill trickling down a nook in the cliff. He knelt and scooped up a handful of icy water. Then he lay beside the rivulet and counted a slow hundred between each handful of the water and the next. Before his thirst was entirely quenched he stood up.

Then he scanned the rocks for birds' nests. He saw many; but, of the scores of eggs he broke, but one was eatable. This he sipped and slowly swallowed its contents. He felt new life all over him.

Not stumbling now, he stepped heedfully forward. He felt strangely large and light and whatever he gazed at looked dim and vague. But he felt really able to walk. He rounded a jutting elbow of the cliff.

Before him, irradiated by the slant sunrays, he saw three handsome young noblewomen, walking arm in arm. All were bareheaded, each with a forehead-ribbon round her flowing hair. The middlemost was tall, full-contoured, with very black locks. She was enveloped in a crimson mantle. The girl on her right was of medium height, slender, with glossy brown tresses and wore a mantle of dark blue. The third was small and very lovely, her hair golden, her cheeks pink, her eyes blue, all set off by a mantle of bright grass-green.

Thorkell thought them *Norns* come to escort him to Valhalla. A cloud, grey and then inky black, swept between him and his outlook. He felt himself topple.

2

When Thorkell came to himself he was in bed in the pitch dark. He felt about him and found that he was in a sort of bunk, a wall on his right hand and, on his left, a polished board, he ran his hand along its upper edge. He was rather deep down in his berth and under him was an infinity of yielding feather-bed. He was well covered with warm quilts. He tried to stretch, but the space was too short for him. He composed himself and slept again.

When he woke the second time it was daylight and he saw by his bunk a tall, spare, elderly noblewoman, severe-looking, hatchet-faced, with a lean and stringy neck and grey hair. She was clad in garments of undyed wool of the usual rusty brown.

'Son,' she warned him, 'you must not try to speak. Drink this slowly.'

And, as he weakly tried to raise himself in the wall-bed, she supported him with her right arm, at the same time holding to his lips with her left hand a silver goblet, Thorkell lasted a delicious posset, compounded of milk, mead, honey, barley-meal, and of other ingredients unknown to him. He swallowed most of it, fell back among his down pillows and slept again at once.

His third waking was again in full daylight. He felt more like himself. He saw that his bed occupied most of one side of a fair-sized

room, wainscoted in dark wood and with a low ceiling, similarly pan-
elled. Opposite his bunk stood a high, narrow table. In the wall by
the footof his bunk was a low doorway, its door shut. In the opposite wall was a window, whose contracted casements had small panes
of fish-gut membrane, stretched across wooden lattices. The panes
were bright with the glare of brilliant sunshine full on them and
much light filtered through, so that the room was well-lighted. By
his bed, facing the window, in one of the two chairs, sat a tall, mag-
nificently dignified, elderly man, grey-haired, ruddy of complexion,
broad-shouldered, wrapped in a reddish-brown mantle of line wool.
He wore a gold neck-chain from which hung a large, flat, oval gold
amulet-case.

'Son,' he said, 'you must not yet attempt to speak. Hearken and
remember. You are housed at Hofstadir, on Revdarfiord, by Faskrudness, on the east coast of Iceland. I, Thorstein Vilgerdson, am master
of Hofstadir. We know nothing of you except that my daughter and
my two nieces found you early in the morning, day before yesterday,
on the strand by Faskrudness. My wife has been caring for you and
she now tells me that you will soon be able to be up and about. Only
after you are well and strong will I permit you to tell your story.
Meanwhile you are our guest. Do as I bid you. Be silent, compose your
mind, repose yourself, and help my wife to restore you to strength and
vigour. When you are yourself we shall talk again. Now sleep.'

Thorkell was compliantly mute and his host rose and left him.

Two mornings later Thorkell woke to find Thorstein again seated
by his bed. And he saw, on the table opposite his bed, a tray with a
goblet and a bunch of bread on it.

'Son,' the old man queried, 'are you entirely awake?'

After Thorkell's affirmation Thorstein said:

'My wife judges that you are now sufficiently recovered to tell your
story. But you had best first fortify yourself with some food.'

And he himself rose and fetched the tray from the table. Thorkell
acquiesced and swallowed a few mouthfuls. Then he settled himself
back on his pillows, his host resumed his armchair, and Thorkell began
his story by naming himself.

'A Vilgerdson!' the old man exclaimed, 'and from Rogaland! We
must be cousins, however distant. In my long life I have never known
or heard of any Norwegian Vilgerdsons; as far as my knowledge goes
our family has long been wholly Icelandic. We are descended from
Floki Vilgerdson, of Rogaland, the first voyager who ever wintered in

Iceland. A hundred and thirty-six years ago he sailed past the headlands of Faxafloi and wintered in the Breldifiord. But he and his associates were so carried away by the abundance of fish and the ease of catching them that they neglected to cure enough hay and their livestock all perished. Therefore, he sailed home next spring. But, twenty and more years later, when past middle age, after most of the west and north of Iceland had already been settled, Floki returned and chose a home here in the east on this very spot. I am his great-great-great-grandson and heir to him and all his.'

'I,' said Thorkell, 'am great-great-great-great-grandson to Snorri Vilgerdson, younger brother to Floki the Viking and settler. For both were sons of Vilgerd Vilgerdson of Rogaland.

'Then,' said his host, 'you are a fourth cousin to my children and they are your fourth cousins. You are one of us. And now tell me your story.'

When Thorkell had said his say and had answered all his host's questions the old man said:

'My wife opines that it will now benefit you to be out of bed and in the open air. My younger sons, Thorgils and Thorbrand will help you to dress and will assist you to walk about, for, although you may resent the suggestion, you are not yet strong enough for it to be well for you to attempt walking unassisted.'

And he called his sons, handsome youths, who clasped hands with Thorkell, called him 'cousin' after their father's explanation, and, when the old man bad gone out, assisted him to rise. He found he needed assistance. They helped him to don a shirt of the finest linen, knitted hose of soft wool, noblemen's shoes, a doublet of the best woollen cloth, and a fine crimson mantle of wool delightful to feel and handle. They girded him with an outer belt, but there was no sign of swordbelt, sword, poniard or knife. Each of them wore a belt-knife with a stag-horn heft, and a dagger and sword, with steel guards and hilts of walrus ivory, pommelled with gold.

One on each side of him they supported him as he strove to stand and they guided him through the doorway into a spacious, plank-floored, high-raftered hall, lighted by many small windows placed high up in the tall gable-ends; low, narrow doors were all down both long sides, with an ample fireplace in a big chimney-piece midway of one side: at one end was the main doorway, at the other a door almost as large. His helpers conducted him out through the main doorway and to a bench in the sunlight where they seated him.

Thorbrand sat by him, Thorgils walked away.

Thorkell found the cool, soft breeze invigorating and yet mild, for it was near midsummer and as genial as it ever is in Iceland. The slant sunray swarmed him. He basked and gazed about him. He saw close by a strongly built storehouse of stone and great ash beams, high-gabled, though its roof was not as steep and tall as that of the mansion. Further away he made out a big sheepfold, with sheds, a large cattle-byre, an ample stable and two very large barns. In whatever direction he looked the extensive level space in which the buildings were grouped was bounded by a stone wall, breast-high, and not of boulders, but of roughly squared blocks.

Some two hundred yards or more distant, topping a low hill, was a temple; for, with its great size, its high and steep roof, its scalloped shingles, its horse-head and fish-tail ornaments at the ridge-pole ends and eave-ends, its carven gable-ends, ii could be nothing else.

Some of the thralls were busy about the buildings and several maid-servants passed in and out. Thorkell saw no men-at-arms, nor any of the family except the two brothers. Thorbrand sat smiling, but mute. Thorkell kept mute and basked. After a time Thorgils came back and Thorbrand strolled away. When Thorbrand returned he said:

'Mother thinks that you were best back in your bed."

Thorkell acquiesced and suffered himself to be escorted indoors. In bed he ate some food brought by a tow-headed serving-maid. Soon he slept.

He woke near dusk of the long northern day and again ate what the same maid brought him and was again soon asleep.

Next morning Thorstein was again sitting by him when he woke. As before; he enquired how he felt and himself served him with food and drink. When he had reset the tray on the table and reseated himself he said.

'Young man, I and my family have talked over you and your story. I and my daughter and my nieces believe you. But all five of my sons, my two daughters-in-law, my accountant, my *seneschal*, my *skald* and everyone, of my men-at-arms are convinced that you are not a castaway from any ship, though likely enough a Norwegian and no Icelander. They are unanimously of the opinion that you are a spy craftily insinuated into our community by our enemies. They point out that your clothing was dry when you were carried in here, that neither it nor your hair showed any signs of your having been swimming; that such a marvel as your having leapt ashore from a ship's-boat drifting without sail, oars or rudder is too improbable for them to believe it other than a clumsy invention. They all insist that I would imperil myself and all my household if I were to accept your story and keep you here as a guest. My word is law here, but I feel that it would be unwise for me to disregard so unanimous, so insistent and so clamorous a dissent from my views.

'Now, young man, if you have in fact been sent here by the Miofifirthers or the Seydisfirthers you had best admit it at once and make a clean breast of the whole matter. You shall not be harmed in any way. I will have you fed and cared for until you are fit for a short journey, and then I will equip you with flint and steel, a belt-knife, a dagger, a sword and sword-belt, a horseman's cloak, a good horse, well bitted, saddled and girthed, and a supply of food; and I will send a thrall to guide you round the head of Revdarfiord and to speed you on your way. But if you are what you assert you are and claim our protection and hospitality as the dues of a castaway, you must convince, all my household of the truth of your tale.'

'I am Thorkell Vilgerdson of Rogaland in Norway,' he replied. 'I know nothing of any Miofifirthers or Seydisfirthers or of any foes of yours. I never set foot on Iceland until I leapt ashore from my drifting boat soon after sunrise of the morning on which I encountered your daughter and nieces. I have never, in Iceland, set eyes on any Icelanders except members of your household. What I have told you is true in every particular. But how may I convince you of its truth?'

'As you must know from my name and my sons' names,' Thorstein answered, we are steadfast adherents of the old faith. Those who suspect you, and my wife, the most embittered of those against you, in particular, would be at once convinced if you take formal oath to the truth of your statements, an oath sworn upon your own blood and the sacred ring of our holy temple, calling Thor and Odin to witness. If you are willing to take oath, as I suggest, no one here will any longer doubt you.'

'I am entirely willing,' Thorkell declared. 'I am more than willing, I am eager. The suspicions of your household are natural, it you have crafty enemies near at hand and live under threat of being raided. I will swear as you suggest.'

"I infer,' said Thorstein, 'that you also, then, like all here at Hofstadir, are a firm believer in the gods of our fathers.'

'I am indeed,' Thorkell affirmed.

'Have you met Christians?' his host queried.

'Too many,' said Thorkell, 'too many by far.'

'Have you talked with any about their beliefs?' the old man inquired.

'With many,' Thorkell said.

'And what do you think of them?' Thorstein pressed him.

'It seems to me,' said Thorkell, 'that they claim to have a system of sorcery and magic far more efficacious and far cheaper than ours. That is about all I can gather from their talk. Their religion costs far less than ours because they hold that no blood-sacrifices are necessary, stating that one man, hundreds of years ago, achieved one sacrifice by which all men may benefit forever, no other being required after that one. How this could be or can be I cannot conceive. But such appears to be their view. Then they seem to think that priests can be largely dispensed with: certainly they have far fewer than we and their priests are cheaper to maintain than ours, as they require less in the way of ornaments, raiment, food and servants. Then, though no one of them has conveyed to me what they mean, they all allege that their invocations win surer and more effective responses than those which we receive from our deities. That is all I can make out about their novelties.'

'Your impressions,' Thorstein said, 'tally with mine. Christians are utterly incomprehensible to me. In particular, they all rant about peace on earth and good-will to men. Yet, since they became Christians, the Miofifirthers and the Seydisfirthers are just as implacably hostile to us here as before. My father repeatedly made overtures to them proposing conferences to negotiate for a reconciliation, for mutual concessions, for laying our differences and the damage done to each side before the Althing for reference to the courts and for a decision and settlement, for a termination of the feud and the establishment of harmony and amity. I have made similar proffers. But they have been inexorably hostile. In fact, since they became Christians, they seem, if possible, even more ferocious, rancorous and bloodthirsty than before.'

'That,' said Thorkell, 'is just about the attitude towards us heathen of all the Christians I have ever met or heard of. Their idea of peace is unqualified submission or total extermination for us, and complete triumph and unquestioned domination for themselves. Not one will listen to proposals of compromise, accommodation or mutual forbearance.

They seem to me opinionated, bigoted, fanatical, overbearing and arrogant. We must fight or perish, there appears to be no other way.'

'You speak sensibly, my son, it seems to me,' the old man said. 'You have convinced me that you are sincere. Your oath in the temple will convince ail my household and all my retainers.'

Then he rose and went out.

3

Again Thorgils and Thorbrand entered the bedroom and helped Thorkell to dress. This time he needed little assistance. And this time they girt him with a sword-belt, and equipped him with a handy belt-knife, a line dagger and a sword in a decorated scabbard. Out they escorted him, Thorkell now walking easily and unaided. In the open he found awaiting him Thorstein, his three elder sons. Thorfinn, Thorgeir and Thord; a handsome and very blond young giant who was presented to him as 'Finnvard Sigurdson, of Faskrudsfiord, my future son-in-law,'

Thorstein's house-*skald*. Olmod Borkson; and his *seneschal*, Ari Gormson. There were a score of men-at-arms lounging about.

After the presentations they set off towards the temple, Thorstein linking arms with Thorkell and leading the way.

'I myself,' he said, 'am *Gothi* of this temple, which my grandfather, Thorleif Vilgerdson, built with timber fetched from Norway.'

The temple, Thorkell judged, was a fall hundred feet long. Temple fashion the end under the gable which they approached was doorless. The side-wall had two ample doorways, each near an end. They passed in by that nearest them towards the right end of the side-wall, and turned to their left. In behind them straggled the men-at-arms, who had trooped after them. Thorkell could feel the reverential awe with which the great, hulking, burly, truculent spearmen entered the holy place.

Midway of the opposite long-wall they passed the High Seat, between the tall pillars, each with its three consecrated bolts of gilded bronze. They were visible even in the dim light afforded by the small latticed windows, gut-paned, high up in the gable ends. Towards the end of the temple they entered the oval, defined by a ring of thin slabs of stone set on edge. Inside the oval, near the end of it towards the further gable of the building, was an altar of the customary form, a great thick slab of dressed stone, full three ells square, supported by four stone posts, squared, carved with runes, and set deep in the beaten earth floor. The slab of the altar was also carved with runes. On it the great holy ring, of solid silver, weighing fall thirty pounds.

Thorstein lifted the great ring and slid it up his right arm to the shoulder. There Thorfinn tied it with a crimson wool ribbon, slipped under his father's left arm-pit and crossed on his left shoulder; so that, the ring would not slide down the arm. Then, standing on Thorstein's right, Thorkell unsheathed his dagger and with its point lightly slashed the back of his left hand, tilting it till the dagger-blade ran with blood. Then, placing his left hand on the temple-ring and holding the dagger point down over the centre of the altar, he swore:

> As my blood drips upon this altar from the point of this dirk, so may my blood and the heart's blood of all my kin, of any wife I may wed, of any children I may have, of all those dear to me, be spilt upon the earth, if my oath is not truthful. I swear by my own blood, by the holy ring which I grasp, by this altar, by the pillars of the High Seat, by their sacred bolts, before Thor and Odin, that I am Thorkell Vilgerdson of Rogaland in Norway, and that I am newly castaway on the coast of Iceland and have never, in Iceland, seen or spoken with any Icelander excepting dwellers here at Hofstadir.
>
> If my oath is false may my heart's blood and the blood of all those dear to me be spilt upon the earth as my blood now drips from the point of my dirk. Before Odin and Thor, I have sworn.

Thereafter Thorfinn removed the *Gothi's* ring from his father's arm and he and Thorstein laid it in its place midway of the altar-slab.

Outside the temple Thorgils dressed the slash on the back of Thorkell's left hand. Then Thorstein first and after him his sons in the order of their ages, clasped hands with Thorkell, each uttering the formula:

> You are our clear and trusted cousin.

Finnvard followed. Then Ari, Olmod and the men-at-arms saluted Thorkell, crying:

> We are brothers in arms.

From the temple Thorstein led Thorkell into the storehouse and into that part of it which was used as an armoury.

'Look over these weapons,' he said, 'and select a sword, poniard and belt-knife to your mind. Try first those you now have; if they suit you, keep them, but be sure that the balance of the sword is precisely what you prefer and that you are armed as you desire."

Outside, in the mild sunshine of a day unusually mellow for Iceland, they sat on the benches flanking the doorway and chatted until after midday. Then Thorstein cautioned Thorkell that a man who had been exposed and exhausted as he had had best lie down an hour or so before his first heavy meal after his privations.

When Thorgils wakened and summoned him he found in the great hall a numerous assemblage. He was presented by Thorstein to Thorkatla his wife, to his daughter Thorgerd and his two nieces Thorarna and Thordis, whom he had encountered on the beach. Thorarna was the tall, full-contoured, black-tressed beauty, and Thordis the exquisite blonde whom he had thought the most beautiful of the three. Thorfinn's wife Arnora and Thord's wife Valdis were personable young women.

Thorstein occupied the High Seat, facing the fireplace. To the left and right of him sat his family, on benches ranged along that side of the hall, but far enough from the wall to leave space for anyone to walk behind them and to pass in or out of any door. On the opposite side of the hall, flanking the chimney-piece, was a similar row of benches, occupied by the men-at-arms, more than forty together. Towards the ends of the hall sat such dependents and thralls as were not busy serving the feast. The servitors carried in more than eighty light, collapsible tables, each in three parts, a square top and two trestles. One was placed before each diner. The fare was varied and abundant, but notably characteristic of Iceland.

There were unlimited supplies of fresh whey in jars, pitchers and bowls; bowls of curd: platters heaped with slices of cheese, both new and aged; there was even an overabundance of smoked and fresh fish, cooked in every known manner; plenty of tender fat mutton, beef and veal, and, each borne in by two brawny thralls, two great platters, one piled with convenient cuts of stewed horseflesh, the other with similar collops of horse-flesh roasted. There was a moderate supply of manchets of excellent rye, barley and wheaten bread, handed along in smallish flat osier baskets or on similar trays. Maids continually passed and re-passed proffering basins of warm water and towels; for, in those days, forks were unknown, and, besides plates and spoons of beechwood from Norway and bell knives, fingers were the only table implements, and frequent washing of the hands was necessary for comfort.

Thorgils and Thorbrand, between whom Thorkell sat, plied him with offerings of every viand brought in and saw that his goblet was kept full of well-aged, fragrant mead. Even more than the large household and lavish fare Thorkell was impressed by the chimney-piece, which faced him on his left, and by its fireplace, not aglow with smouldering peat, but ablaze with a generous heap of crackling drift-wood, he commented on this to Thorbrand.

'I have never seen any other chimney or fireplace except ours,' was his reply. 'It is said that two halls in the river-valleys about Faxafloi have chimney fireplaces, and that there is another in a mansion on Breidifiord. But none of us have seen any. My great grandfather had this built of native stone, for there is much fire-resisting rock on our island.'

'This,' Thorkell said, 'is the only chimney fireplace I have myself ever seen. My home, like every other hall I have ever entered till now, has only a fireplace midway of its floor, so that the smoke blackens the rafters before it finds the hole in the roof.'

After the feast Thorstein called for silence.

'We have with us,' he said, 'what is almost as good as a visiting *skald*, a guest who has had marvellous adventures. All of us will now listen to Thorkell Vilgerdson of Rogaland in Norway, if he will be so good as to accede to my request that he tell us of his dangers and of his escape.'

Thorkell blushed, but was encouraged by the smiling, eager faces turned towards him. He took courage, stood up, and told his tale, halt-ingly at first, later more fluently.

After he had finished and sat down Olmod twanged his harp and recited a *drapa* describing and praising the exploits of Floki Vilgerd-son the Viking and settler. When he ceased the company dispersed to bed.

During the ensuing days Thorkell became well acquainted with Hofstadir, its *denizens* and its neighbourhood. As soon as he felt his full strength and vigour return he spent his mornings with Thor-gir, Thorbrand, Thorgils and Finnvard at fencing, target practice with spears or arrows, wrestling, and other such manly exercises. At all of these he excelled, yet his genial demeanour was so winsome that his easy victories gave no offence to his companions.

They also went swimming together, and fishing, both in the many nearby streams, and off shore in a very handy small boat, heavily built, blunt bowed, yet a good sailor. Thorkell was amazed at the numbers of fish and at the rapidity with which they could be caught, A hook thrown into the water was taken almost at once.

They rode about the neighbourhood on fine mounts, for, in those early days, Icelandic horses were still fully equal to Norwegian horses, as the breed was kept up by constant importations of tall, strong, speedy and spirited stallions.

After not many days Thorkell learned the country further afield, for he was invited to accompany Thorstein on a tour of inspection of his district; for he was not only *Gothi*, that is, priest, of the temple at Hofstadir. but also *Gothi*, that is, magistrate, of a district called a *gothorth*, all Iceland being divided into *gothorths*. Thorstein made his tour attended by his five sons; by several cousins, among whom were Thorlak Vilgerdson of Thelmark and Thorvald Vilgerdson of Husavik; by many thingmen, dependents and yeomen; and *by* a strong guard of well-horsed spearmen.

Thorkell was much edified by Thorstein's promptness at settling controversies and redressing grievances. The old man displayed an uncanny intuition and seemed to know all his vassals' thoughts, motives, wants, desires and needs without being told.

After the tour was over, at a moment when Thorstein was at ease, Thorkell ventured to express his admiration.

His host smiled.

"A chieftain,' he said, 'must possess the faculty of seeing into his vassals' hearts and of knowing their thoughts without question asked and answer given; even without any uttered word. A man who cannot divine the unspoken thoughts of his dependents will not long retain the prestige vital for a *Gothi*, or for any sort of chieftainship. Necessarily, I know much without being told, with hardly even a glance. Mostly for instance, I can foresee months in advance, sometimes even years in advance, what girl each youth will woo for his wife, what maiden each lad desires, even what lad finds favour in each maiden's eyes. Such must any chieftain divine.'

At Hofstadir Thorkell was soon at home among the buildings. Not less than by the chimney, inset fireplace and lavish wood fire was he impressed by the fortifications of the homestead. It was protected all round with a dry moat, the earth from which, thrown up on the inner side, formed a considerable rampart, topped on all four sides of the enclosure by a solid wall of large, roughly squared blocks of stone. At the corners were jutting, bulging circular bastions well stockaded with birch logs, set deep in the earth, butt up and touching each other, everyone fully three spans broad at the upturned butt, for, in those early days, the primeval woods of Iceland furnished logs much larger than any now obtainable on the island.

The stockades, like the walls, were breast-high. Thorkell had never seen a bastion before, nor heard of one, and was much impressed by the novelty, originality and manifest adequacy of the device. The idea of a bastion, that it affords defenders of a fortification an opportunity of shooting sideways at an assailant crossing the fosse or scaling the parapet, appears so obvious to us that we can scarcely realise that there ever was a time when it was unknown. Yet, hundreds, even thousands of years after it was common and a matter of course in the Mediterranean countries, it had not yet penetrated the ruder northern lands. In fact, in all parts of the world, men were not quick to conceive the idea, and, as with other devices, very slow to adopt it. from foemen.

Almost as much was Thorkell impressed by the bath-house, a small structure, one might say a hut, built of sod and stone, with a low door and only one very tiny window. Inside there was room for only one person and a pail of water beside a very small stone stove. This was heated almost red-hot and then the bather, with a dipper, poured on it water which at once filled the hut with steam, both cleansing and refreshing.

On either side of the chimney-piece in the great hall was a sort of trophy of spears, shields and swords arranged in a pattern like a six-pointed star; six short pikes crossed and lashed to pegs, six small round shields set between the radiating spears, and twelve swords, two by each shield. Above the fireplace was another, of six long swords, their points together, their hilts apart, with shields between,

Thorkell, inquiring about these, was told that they had been placed there by Thorstein's grandfather, Thorleif Vilgerdson, who had built the hall and temple. The spears and swords forming the two flanking trophies were fine and valued weapons of former Vilgerdsons: the trophy over the fireplace was formed of the very sword worn all his life by Floki Vilgerdson the Viking and settler, and of five cunningly exact replicas of it, made at Thorleif Vilgerdson's command by Hoskuld Vestarson, a famous smith.

'I do not myself know,' said Thorstein, 'which is Floki's blade. My father told me that he did not know. No one knows. No man has used any one of those six swords since before I was born. It is told that Floki's blade is enchanted, that no one except a Vilgerdson could wield it, that to anyone not a Vilgerdson it would be heavier than a thick bar of iron; but that, in time of peril to Floki's heirs or kin, it is magical to infuse into its wielder super-human valour, swiftness, dexterity and strength, it is also told of Floki's blade that it blows friend from foe and will not smite a friend, no matter how frenziedly its wielder believes him a foe, nor yet will it fail to smite a treacherous foe, no matter how implicitly its wielder trusts the traitor. We have come to regard these swords as almost as holy as the bolts in the pillars by the High Seat in our temple, as almost as sacred as the temple ring itself. Their presence in our hall we regard as a protection and safeguard to us all, as a sort of talisman for Hofstadir. We all and all my men-at-arms and thingmen and retainers reverence and treasure them.'

Thorkell could see that they were very handsome swords.

He learned that Thorstein never had fewer than sixty men-at-arms on duty, but not all of them were ever at Hofstadir itself. Some were on watch along the cliffs, on the lookout for an attack from seaward. There were always two or more patrol-boats on the offing conning the sea northwards. The lookouts on the cliffs also watched the fiord for signs of an attempt to attack in boats from its northern shore. And some men-at-arms were always scattered about at the farmsteads of Thurstein's thingmen and other dependents, especially towards the head of Revdarfiord, round which must come any attack in force by land.

Thorkatla he found kind-hearted, but taciturn, sharp-tongued when she did speak, and of a very stern, harsh and austere disposition. Thorgerd, staid, astute and shrewd, was yet, by nature, trustful, unsuspicious, confiding, artless and unaffected. She gave Thorkell an experience entirely novel to him. For she displayed for him a warm sisterly interest, as to which she was entirely frank and open, while indubitably ardently in love with her handsome Finnvard.

Thorarna and Thordis he greatly admired and liked, he could not make out at first which he liked better. That both were manifestly deeply in love with him he took as a matter of course. He had long become habituated to having attractive maidens fall in love with him on short acquaintance and show it.

The immemorial usages of Scandinavian life made it absolutely unthinkable, in the Iceland of those days, that a young man and a young woman should ever be alone together, even for a moment. But, on the other hand, life in Iceland was so free, open, frank, spontaneous, unconventional and inartificial that not only were lads and lasses constantly encountering each other about the dwellings, but that not merely was chatting a matter of course and unremarked, but that such young folk as Thorkell, Thorarna and Thordis might and did walk about together out of doors, and sit together side by side conversing for hours in the hall, in full sight of those about them, unnoticed and left to themselves.

In this way Thorkell became rapidly well acquainted with both his host's nieces and heard from each her story; stories very much alike and of a kind far too common in Iceland at that period, and for centuries later. The envenomed and unremitting enmity between the Revdarfirthers and their neighbours the Miofifirthers and Seydis-firthers had resulted in recurrent reprisals.

Thorarna was the only survivor of an overwhelmingly successful assault upon her father's homestead. Her father, Thorstein's brother Thorleik, had been killed in the fighting, and, when the buildings were set on fire by the victorious assailants, all the family had perished in the flames except Thorarna, who, a child of three, had been saved by her faithful nurse.

Thordis, the only daughter of Thorstein's brother Thorgest, was the survivor of a similar massacre.

Much of the evening leisure at Hofstadir was taken up with tales of such atrocities as these and of like assaults on homesteads, some by one side, some by the other; some craftily planned, artfully delivered and overwhelmingly successful; others resulting in drawn battles and leaving the homestead in mourning for some of its defenders, but unpillaged and unburnt; yet others unplanned, impulsive, foolhardy, undermanned or bungled in delivery and resulting in the utter dis-comfiture of the assailants. Thorkell sat in silence and listened to many long tales of this kind from Olmod the house-*skald*, from Thor-stein himself and from his elder sons.

From them also he listened to even longer tales of complaints against one or the other side before the Althing at Thingvellir, nearly every year at the two-weeks summer meeting of this national assem-bly. They told in great detail of the impassioned accusations of the plaintiffs, of the indignant rejoinders of the defendants, of the cita-tions of the respondents before the high court of justice, of the evi-dence of the witnesses for each side, of the arguments of the lawmen, of the disagreements of the judges, of their occasional agreement, of their verdicts and judgments and of the indemnities they assessed upon the convicted aggressors.

In almost every case Thorkell heard of the ignoring or flouting of the court's decision and of yet further reprisals, duels, forays and out-rages. What astonished him most was that, in all these tales of duels, murders, treacheries, ambushes, pillagings, outrages, butcheries, mas-sacres and arson and of their consequences, the narrators talked as if the Althing were an efficient legislature with power to see to it that its enactments be observed as the law of the island; as if the courts had the authority they assumed to have and could enforce their judgments, verdicts, decrees and penalties; as if, in truth, law and Justice did exist in Iceland: whereas, in fact, it appeared from every tale he listened to, from every detail of every narrative, that their vaunted Althing was merely a turbulent yearly social gathering, accomplishing nothing except the waste of time in futile wrangling, making a vain show of counterfeiting a sham legislature, which empty pretence all Icelanders kept up with a curious mingling of unconscious self-deception and shame-faced effrontery; that the courts, while generally spoken of with respect, were in fact derided by all malefactors, and unable to give effect to their decrees, judgments and verdicts, to enforce their penalties or to exact the indemnities they granted, so that they were, on the whole, a costly, time-wasting, exhausting and pitiable farce.

It was plain to Thorkell that the Icelanders, if his host and his household were fair samples, had somehow duped themselves into fancying that they had courts which dispensed justice and a government which maintained law and order; whereas it was manifest that they lived in a condition of utter anarchy, where there was no protection for life or property except the fighting prowess of the men of a homestead as concerned themselves, their folk and their possessions; or of the men-at-arms of a chieftain for him and his.

It was plain that beautiful Thordis, magnificent Thorarna, lovely Thorgerd, fair Arnora, dainty Valdis and stern Thorkatla were living in daily peril of a horrible death and were safe only in so far as their men could protect them. Yet they, like their men, boasted of the noble freedom of life in Iceland, pitied the servile condition of Norwegians under their tyrannical king, vaunted their island institutions, and lauded the system of local *gothorths*, yearly elections, yearly assemblies at Thingvellir of their unwieldy and ineffective Althing, and the complex, lengthy, laborious and fruitless procedure of their fatuous courts. Local pride seemed a passion which blinded them to the most glaring imperfections of anything Icelandic.

4

But it mattered very little what was the subject or the nature of the conversation, Thorkell found himself more than contented with any length of time which he might spend with either Thorarna or

Thordis. Yet, after not many days, he was aware of a difference in his feelings for the two and of theirs for him. Thordis never avoided him, but never put herself in his way. If everything was favourable and they happened to be thrown together accidentally, she frankly enjoyed being with him, but never did anything to prolong a chat or bring one about. Thorarna, on the contrary, was most ingenious in postponing the termination of a colloquy, and was most fertile in clever, adroit, and unobtrusive devices which resulted in their being together,

Before many days life at Hofstadir, for Thorkell, consisted chiefly of endeavouring to be with Thordis. Once, when he was basking in her smiles, her face suddenly clouded and she said:

'There! Thorarna has gone! Please, please try to spend more of your time with her and less with me. From childhood she and I have been happy together, and nothing has ever blurred our love for each other and our unreserved mutual confidence until she began to grow jealous of me. Since she fell in love with you we have become alienated; she is chilly to me, distant, reticent, even unfriendly. I grieve that we are estranged. I love her and I want her to love me. I do not want her to hate me. Please do all you can to placate her. She keeps her countenance and is always outwardly serene, sedate and stately. But she rages inwardly and is so infuriated when you talk to me that I dread her. Please avoid me and propitiate her all you can. Please promise me that you will do as I ask.'

Thorkell promised, and, for some days, barely greeted Thordis and had no converse with her whatever, whereas he spent long hours with Thorarna, and, to his amazement, found that he enjoyed her society keenly; yet, even more to his amazement, felt that, when he was not with Thorarna, he longed for Thordis so acutely that he could hardly restrain himself from seeking her out and telling her how much he loved her.

The long spell of clear, mild weather merged into weather decidedly warm, weather which would have been warm even for Scotland or England. Thorstein, with a large retinue of spearmen, rode out to visit and inspect the outlying fringe of farms tenanted by his dependents or thingmen. It was a very fair day and they had expected an easy jaunt and an early return to Hofstadir. So it turned out for Thorstein and most of his company. But, early in the day, they heard a report, hardly more than a rumour, of distress at a farmstead isolated among uplands at the extreme southwestern point of Thorstein's *gothorth*, very much out of their way. Thorbrand offered to ride there and investigate and Thorkell volunteered to go with him. He demurred to his father's suggestion that he take some of the men-at-arms, declaring that he and Thorkell could make better time alone. Off they set.

Their errand was easily accomplished and the rumour found untrue and everyone safe and well at Mossfell. But, on their return, they encountered conditions peculiar to Iceland. There it frequently happens during a prolonged spell of warm weather that great quantities of snow are melted high up on the plateaus or in hollows among the upper foot-hills, and, very occasionally, that the waters are dammed back by ice accumulated in some valley, ravine, gorge or glen, and, if the hot weather lasts on, are suddenly released by the crumbling of the ice-dam. Such a sudden and terrific freshet roared across their homeward way and presented a torrent of deep water not only unfordable, but impossible to swim. They were, perforce, compelled to await the ebbing of the transitory flood and so did not reach Hofstadir until the gradual twilight, insensible gloaming and lingering dusk had melted into semi-darkness.

Thorbrand, sedulously careful of their weary mounts, bade Thorkell go at once into the hall. Between the stable and the mansion, out of sight of either behind the storehouse, he encountered Thordis.

She burst into tears; crying:

'Oh! My Love! My Love! Ref and Karli rode in after sunset on lathered horses reporting that you and Thorbrand had been ambushed and killed. Oh! My Love! My Love!'

Thorkell caught her in his arms and they clung together, she sobbing, her head on his breast, he with one arm about her, his other hand stroking her hair, whispering:

'My Darling! My Darling!'

Suddenly her arms relaxed, she pulled away from him, pushed him from her, and cried, in a strangled whisper.

'Let me go! Thorarna might see us! Be careful! Thorarna must not see us together! Let me go! Avoid me! Keep away from me, hardly speak to me! She must not see us together! Let me go!'

And she sprang away and vanished like a frightened hare.

The weather, for two days afterwards, was not merely warm, but hot, weather which would have been hot anywhere; an occurrence very unusual for Iceland, but not unknown, especially on the east coast. On account of the heat the fire in the hall was allowed to go out entirely, and, at the evening meal, two of the benches of the men-at-arms were set across the fireplace, close against the stone work of the chimney-piece.

During these two days Thorkell spent as much time with Thorarna as he could arrange, and found her fascinating, but moody, high-strung and capricious. He sedulously avoided Thordis. Only for one moment did they have an opportunity to exchange a few words. Then Thordis, on the verge of tears and gasping, said:

'Oh! I am so afraid of Thorarna. I don't know what I dread, but I am in the most fearful dread of her. She is very suspicions of you. I think she conjectures that you and I love each other. You are too distant with her for her peace of mind. Thorarna, like all her mother's family, is petulant, choleric, touchy, irascible, hot-tempered, acrimonious, vindictive, impulsive, precipitate and hot-headed. Oh, I am so afraid of her!'

Thorkell tried to calm her, but could not.

Early the third morning, just after dawn had brightened into day, the lookouts gave the alarm.

And too late!

For, when the garrison of Hofstadir had barely armed and were not yet all at their posts, there fell upon them three simultaneous and perfectly coordinated assaults; from the west along the strand, from the south down the slope, and from the north, from across the *fiord* by a party which had made an unopposed landing on the shore.

Thorkell was among the defenders of the western side of the enclosure, and, despite the hard fight he and his companions put up, their assailants succeeded in crossing the trench and scaling the wall. But thereupon they were beaten back by a desperate rally of the *denizens*, in which Thorkell played more than his part, for he, single-handed, successively slew five formidable antagonists. As their foemen wavered he sprang at a sixth, parried his thrust and got home a deadly stroke on his helmet.

The sword snapped!

As his adversary was half stunned and wholly dazed by the force of the blow Thorkell whirled about and made a dash for the hall. There he leapt upon one of the benches set across the fireplace, seized the hilt of one of the six identical swords, wrenched it from its fastenings, and, waving it, dashed out.

As he cleared the doorway he heard elated shouts and an exultant cheer. Glancing to his right he saw men in chain-mail hauberks vaulting the eastern wall of the enclosure. He recognised, in the lead, Lodbrok and Halfdan, the chiefs, Gellir, Sigurd and Bodvar, his treacherous friends, and others from the crew of the *Sea-Raven*. He instantly divined that they had blundered into Miofifiord or Seydisfiord, had fraternised with the Seydisfirthers and Miofifirthers and had readily agreed, for their share in the prospective loot, to take part in capturing and sacking the richest homestead in eastern Iceland.

On fire with his chance of revenge he flew at Lodbrok, and, as he charged, it seemed to him that never had he run so swiftly, never had he felt so strong, so capable, so eager for a fray, so sure of success.

He beat back Lodbrok's guard and swung a full arm sweep of his blade at his head. The sword went up like a feather and came down like a battle-axe. As if through cheese it clove helm, skull, jaw and chin down into the breast-bone. Lodbrok fell like a pole-axed ox, and, as Thorkell saw him go down, almost in two halves, he realised that he was wielding Floki's blade.

He whirled on Gellir and the sweep of the sword cut clean through not only both forearms between wrist and elbow, but also through the stout ash shall of the pike he wielded. Behind Gellir was Halfdan, no mean adversary, truculent, wary and skilled. He held his bright, round, arabesque shield close against his left shoulder and lunged cunningly and viciously. Barely parrying his thrust Thorkell swung his great sword, and, lo! it shore clean through shield, gorget, hauberk, shoulder and arm, so that his left forequarter fell clear of Halfdan and he was dead before he crumpled on the earth.

Similarly, Thorkell slew Bodvar, Sigurd and Hrodmar. Two the sharp sword beheaded at a single sweep, one it cleft under the sword-arm, through his ribs, into his liver; of the fourth its point pierced his heart through shield and hauberk.

Instinct made Thorkell spin round and he faced Kollgrim Erdlendson, leader of the Vikings and most redoubtable of them all. Their swords clashed and Kollgrim's failed, snapped before the hilt, so that Thorkell's blade shore off his right shoulder, slicing through the rings of his chain-mail hauberk as if it had been of hemp, and he died as his fellow chieftain Halfdan Ingolfson had died.

Although their chiefs were all dead the Vikings, descrying but one defender before them, were swarming over the wall. Among them Thorkell dashed and at each stroke of Floki's blade a foeman died. Yet Thorkell must have been overwhelmed by mere numbers if some of the Vilgerdsons and their men-at-arms, now victorious to north and south, had not flocked to his aid, amazed to see that Hofstadir had been saved by his unaided valour and spurred on by admiration of him.

Thorkell at their head they drove the survivors of the *Sea-Raven's* crew in headlong flight across the wall and trench, and Thorkell beheld in the distance the thralls Erp, Ulf, Hundi, Kepp, Sokholf and Vifill, standing ready with spare shields, spears, bows and quivers, cast away their burdens and him in flight before the foremost of the fleeing Vikings reached them.

The fight was over. The assailants were everywhere beaten and routed. Thorstein forbade pursuit on foot, and only some twenty of the men-at-arms found horses ready, mounted and sped out of the main gateway of the enclosure to complete the rout of the assailants, who left more than forty corpses behind them.

Of the victors twelve spearmen had fallen and with them seven of Thorstein's dependent yeomen, four of his thingmen, and two cousins, Thorberg Vilgerdson of Snowfell and Thorod Vilgerdson of Gelsbank. Thorkell, Thorstein himself and Thorfinn were the only unwounded warriors among the defenders. All the rest of the family, all the cousins, thingmen, yeomen, and men-at-arms had suffered one or more wounds; but, of the family, only Thord was wounded seriously. His wounds were at once bound up and the blood staunched.

Then, with one accord, every warrior of them all acclaimed Thorkell as their saviour. They cheered him and saluted him as 'hero.' Thorfinn and Thorgeir seized him by the elbows, and, following their father and followed by the cheering throng, marched him into the great hall and up to the High Seat. There Thorstein stood aside and motioned Thorkell to mount the dais and occupy the High Seat. Before his dazed astonishment could protest, Thorfinn had gently forced him into it. There he sat, Floki's blade, still red, point down between his knees, his hands crossed on the pommel of the upright hilt.

Thorstein shouted:

'Mead for the hero! Not a man of us shall touch horn or bowl to lip until the hero has had his fill of my best mead. Mead for the hero!"

At the call Thorarna appeared from the kitchen through the rear doorway carrying with both hands a great bowl high before her. Down the hall she came, her face lit with a triumphant smile, magnificent and stately. Before the High Seat she knelt and offered the bowl to Thorkell. The fighters cheered again.

As Thorarna held up the bowl, Thorkell, to his horror, felt his right hand grasp the sword-hilt with a grip he could not loosen, felt the sword raise itself and his arm till the blade swung high above Thorarna, felt the magic of the sword drag down his arm in a deadly sweep, felt and saw the blow descend, felt and saw the blade shear through Thoron's left shoulder, shoulder-blade, collar-bone and ribs, cleaving her to the very heart.

She crumpled in a horrid welter of spilt mead, gushing blood, disordered raiment and huddled flesh.

The onlookers stood, frozen mute.

Into the hall rushed Thordis and Thorgerd, screaming;

'Do not drink! The mead is poisoned! Do not drink! The mead is poisoned!'

At sight of the High Seat, Thorkell on it and what lay before him, Thordis collapsed in a faint. Thorgerd was at once absorbed in tending her cousin.

Thorstein shouted for his thralls.

'Ref! Karli! Mar! Odd! Remove that carrion! Cleanse the dais!'

And, when his orders had been obeyed and the dais and hall were again seemly, he called once more:

'Mead for the hero!'

Thordis, now restored, though tottering, her golden-haired, pink-cheeked, blue-eyed loveliness amazing even in her confusion, herself carried to Thorkell a horn.

He took it, quaffed it as he sat and handed it back to her. Then Thorstein shouted:

'Mead for all of us, and more mead for the hero!'

Maid servants flocked in with bowls, horns and goblets and behind them thralls with pails of mead to replenish those drained. All drank, Thorkell too, a second horn offered him by Thordis. From her knees he raised her and made her stand beside the High Seat.

Then Thorstein shouted:

'Hail the hero!'

Whereupon all the warriors cheered Thorkell until they were hoarse.

Into the ensuing silence Thorstein spoke clearly and gravely:

'Tomorrow we shall revel in honour of our deliverance, victory and safety. And the banquet shall be the wedding feast of my niece. Thordis and of her bridegroom, my cousin, Thorkell Vilgerdson of Rogaland in Norway, our hero!'

The Buzzards

(*Bellman*, July 25,1908)

Her ears were keen. As she sat on the porch, her workbasket be-side her on a chair, her lap littered with sewing, her needle flying fast, she could hear through the intervening sitting-room and passage the clink of a glass in the dining-room. Her all-embracing smile vanished. A third time she heard it. Her face clouded, her brows puckered, she brushed back from her face with an impatient gesture a stray wisp of her straight, light hair.

A tramping of heavy-booted feet sounded inside the house. Her brother appeared in the doorway. His face was knotted and scowling. He had a week-old scrub of stubby, blonde beard which added to the truculence of his air. His blue eyes were bloodshot. His greasy-grey, battered felt hat was on the back of his head, a briar-wood pipe in his mouth, his rough tweed coat open. His brown flannel shirt showed a white pearl button where his necktie should have been, his corduroy trousers were objecting to being tucked into his muddy, tan, boots. He held a gun in the crotch of his left elbow. His sister, watching his face, took no particular note of the gun.

"Curse the pipe," he said.

He stood the gun against the jamb of the door, took the pipe out of his mouth.

"Thunder," he said. "I forgot to fill it."

He fumbled in every pocket, swore, began all over again and found his tobacco pouch. He filled the pipe, lit it and took the gun again.

"Jim," she said. "Did you really need three drinks?"

"There you go," he snarled. "Nagging again. You know it all. Drink is my failing of course and I must be nagged about it. It is good for me. You have your failings, too. Suppose I nagged you about Pierre Beaumont."

380

"It would be rather a relief, I think," she said. "You are nastier sulking than scolding."

"You women," he sneered. "Don't care whether you are right or not as long as you seem right, and you have the last word."

He stamped off and disappeared behind the barn.

She slipped her hand into the front of her shirt waist and took out a note. She kissed it twice, opened it and read it over.

Darling,
You shall not give me up for Jim's sake. I know you love me and I won't let you.
You know I love you and you will yield yet. I shall be at the old place at the usual hour on Thursday.
　　　　Eternally,
　　　　　　Pierre.

She kissed the note again before she tucked it back into her bosom.

As she sewed she let her mind dwell on Pierre Beaumont, chiefly contrasting him with her brother. He was, if anything, bigger and stronger, but Jim's strength was all surface violence, whereas Pierre's was all quiet reserve, and the eyes! How much difference there was between Jim's fierce, hard, blue eyes and Pierre's brown eyes, almost womanly in their softness.

Sewing on, she let her gaze rove lovingly over her wide outlook: the farm buildings, the stubble field behind, the field of clover beyond that, the bit of farm lane leading to the hill-fields farthest from the house, the peach orchard, the field of corn, the waving woods beyond it, on the hillside the bit of pasture visible between the woods. High over the woods and pasture lot, several buzzards were sailing in slow circles. Beyond them was the varied green of the mountain side, with the blue-black cloud-shadows marching along it. Over all, the dark blue sky with a few clean, white clouds in it.

She saw a figure appear in the bit of lane.

"What on earth is Jim going to the back of the field for?" she exclaimed aloud. "And afoot, too."

He vanished at the point beyond which the lane was no longer visible. She continued to stare at that part of the landscape. Then again her gaze went to the wheeling buzzards.

A chubby, moon-faced *mulatto* girl came round the corner of the house.

"Miss Nancy," she said. "Abner says kin you stitch up his coat fuh him. He done toe de ahm hole."

She held up a faded blue jacket, one sleeve half ripped away.

"Give it to me, Mary," her mistress said, "and come get it before he finishes his dinner."

Mary scampered away.

Nancy selected and threaded a needle. Then she adjusted the coat on her knee. Something crackled inside it and she searched the pocket. She drew out an envelope, sealed, stamped and directed in her own handwriting.

Her face blanched as she read the address:

Mr Pierre Beaumont,
Rockledge,
Virginia.

She tore it open, it was the last note.

Monday night.

Pierre, Dear Pierre,
You mustn't call me darling anymore, and you mustn't try to see me. Above all don't try to come to the old place. Jim has been suspicious lately and he is so surly and gruff he must be in a very bad temper. If he meets you, there is no telling what he might do, no telling. Don't come Thursday. I shall expect you to obey me in this, and I shall not meet you.

Nance.

She read the letter with dilating eyes. Hastily, she thrust it in her bosom. She pushed the coat from her knee and let it fall upon the porch floor. She stood up. Her eyes scanned the view. Nothing living in sight except the half dozen turkey buzzards, their unmoving wings spread wide, soaring in lazy arcs against the far, clear sky.

Suddenly she ran into the house to the gun rack. The rifle was gone. The rifle! Why had she not noticed it! Now she recalled distinctly that she had seen the rifle in the crook of her brother's arm. Her eyes had seen it but her mind had not realised it.

She dashed out of the house again, hatless as she was, and made straight for the stable. It was empty. Her bridles and saddle hung on their peg, but Miss April's stall was vacant. Why should her riding horse not be in the stable? She could think of no explanation and her bewilderment and surprise added to her alarm.

She slipped out of the farther door of the stable and began again to run, not up the lane, but across the apple orchard, following the track she knew as "Jake's Path", made by their occasional negro man-of-all-work on his way to and from his cabin.

She was a strong girl and she ran well and steadily, not in any panic of fluttering over-exertion, sure to collapse soon into helplessness, but with a restrained evenness, intelligently determined to last over the interval she had in mind, to reach the point she aimed at in the shortest possible time. Her path was all uphill and the distance was by no means short. In the orchard, where the grass was eaten down to the earth and there was nothing in her way but a few clumps of jimson weed, ironweed and milkweed, easily avoided, she went quickly.

The fence she vaulted cleanly as a man, her skirts not hampering her a particle; the field beyond hindered her a little, though the sharp ends of the stubble stabbed her ankles as she ran.

Through the clover field, the path ran along the edge by the boundary fence. The clover delayed her, but she did not gather up her skirts. She ran, elbows back, hands at her waist, head up, glancing indeed now and again at her path ahead of her, but mostly looking toward the sky above the woods where the buzzards sailed idly in their wide circles.

Through the peach orchard the tall weeds held her back. By the time she entered it she was all a flame of heat. As she tore through the waist-deep ragweed she began to pant, and two spots of crimson deepened in her cheeks. The fourth fence she did not vault but half climbed it, half fell over it. The earth between the rows of corn was soft, for the weather had been dry since the last time it was cultivated. Her breath began to wheeze in her throat and the throbbing of her heart jarred her painfully. The cornfield was divided down its middle by a broad strip planted in tomatoes. In this freshly hoed ground she stumbled and her stride lost its swing. She half staggered in her run.

When she was about halfway between the corn behind her and the corn in front, a rifle shot rang out from the direction of the pasture lot. She checked with a rending sob which shook her from head to foot. She reeled, put out one hand toward nothing, steadied herself, threw back her head and gazed up at the sky. There were three buzzards in sight over the woods. They were wheeling in circles shorter and shorter, flying faster and faster, lower and lower.

She gave a second sob and started once more to run. Into the corn she plunged and through it she dashed. Breasting the slope, she went as fast as if she were fresh-rested and going downhill. The long, sharp-edged leaves of the corn slashed at her face and flailed across her bosom. She burst from the corn and half leaned, half fell against the fence, her arms across it. Close to her, but a few yards above her head, swept the black, hideous, shape of a buzzard. She gave the ghost of a smothered scream. Her eyes scanned the knolly field before her. Nothing alive was insight save the scuddard buzzard flying low and flappingly. A narrowing edge of woods half-divided the pasture. Round the sharp end of this, the bird swooped and disappeared into that recess of the field. The path led through the jutting triangle of woodland. She darted across the close-cropped grass towards Jake's stile.

Opposite the gate, she paused and gazed down the lane. Just topping the first hill she saw her brother. He was running. His back was the back of Cain fleeing into the wilderness.

Another buzzard whizzed over her head, flapped upward and vanished over the near screen of trees.

At the stile, she checked again. She simply could not go on. She cried aloud.

"His eyes! His brown eyes. They will begin on his eyes."

She screamed twice, strangling choked screams, barely a sound at all.

She clutched at the fence, leaning against the panel next to the stile. Then again she spoke aloud.

"Perhaps he fell on his face."

She scanned the sky. There were five buzzards in sight, all flapping steadily and pressing toward the recess of the pasture.

She heard a noise, as if there was a foot on the stile.

She turned. On the stile she saw Pierre Beaumont, his face bright and smiling.

She screamed a clear, high scream and collapsed into the weeds by the fence.

★★★★★★

When Pierre succeeded in bringing her to consciousness, she clung to him, sobbing crying and laughing all at once.

"What on earth is wrong?"

"Oh!" she gasped, I thought you were dead. I thought Jim had killed you."

"But why?" he wondered.

"He shot something. He had his rifle. Oh, why did he have his rifle? Why did he run away?"

"He wanted to spare you," Pierre said. "That was why he did not tell you. Miss April had to be shot. She broke her leg yesterday morning. He had been nerving himself up to shoot her all day yesterday. When it came to the shooting, he broke down and I had to shoot her for him."

"You!" she cried. "He knew you were here?"

"He was in Rockledge yesterday," Pierre exclaimed, "insisting on Schoff's trying to set Miss April's leg. I did my best to persuade Schoff to try. So we made it all up."

"And he didn't tell me," she wondered.

"I suppose," Pierre said, "that he could not without mentioning Miss April."

"Oh," she said. "An hour ago I should have thought losing her dreadful, but now I can think of nothing except that I have you."

"Yes," he said, "you have me."

The Death Rattle

(*The Bohemian* September 1909)

1

Crosby married young. In fact, he married the day after his twenty-first birthday. Some parents would discountenance such early mating. But Ned Crosby's father had married very young himself and had been very happy. Ned had grown up in a household where a large family lived comfortably on a small income. Ned's mother was up early and to bed late and forever dragged this way and that between attending to her house and table and caring for her children. She did a great part of her cooking herself, most of her sewing and all her mending. She had no more hesitated to sweep off her front steps and pavement in the morning, if there was no one else to do it, than her husband felt it beneath his dignity on a hot afternoon, to adjust his hose for himself, sit on these same front steps and water that same pavement and a generous portion of the street beyond.

And as he throve on his breadwinning, so she throve on her family cares and housekeeping. They were a generous but at the same time an economical pair. They no more thought of going to the country for the summer or any part of it than of starting for the North Pole. They were city folk and lived comfortably in the city, except for an occasional excursion. They never thought of missing pleasures other people regarded as necessities, and they continued healthy and raised a healthy family of affectionate children.

They were loverly up to their silver wedding and after it and the atmosphere of conjugal felicity which filled his boyhood home naturally coloured Crosby's outlook upon life. To fall in love, marry, get along somehow, stay in love, and be happy where one happened to live or what one happened to have seemed to him not merely normal human life, but the real summit of human blessedness.

His married life did not disappoint him. His bride was a pretty girl, a sensible girl and a good girl. But besides she was a cheerful, merry girl, with a multitude of graceful, unexpected ways and sayings entirely her own. An above all, from Crosby's point of view, she moved softly and gently and had a very agreeable voice. For the Crosby's, with all their straightforward simplicity and industrious self-helpfulness, had a great deal of really fastidious delicacy of their own kind. Crosby inherited it, absorbed it, and retained it. He disliked levity of soul, was nauseated by cheap attempts at false humour, revolted from irreverence, flippancy or making fun of serious subjects, and detested coarseness of thought or speech and boisterousness of behaviour.

In particular he loathed loud laughter and assertive talk, and harsh shrill voices. For sounds, more than sights, struck upon Crosby's consciousness, caught his attention and remained vividly in his memory. He revelled in his bride's daintiness of movement and unconstrained musical utterance. He delighted in the quiet rhythm of her even breathing. When he happened to be awake at night he would lie and listen to it with the same sort of enjoyment with which he would have listened to a symphony.

The two were very happy and very conscious of it. They lived very simply, very economically, for Crosby's salary was small. They had a few of what people call pleasures, but all through his long day over his books, all through her long day at home, they had the pleasure of anticipating being together. That seemed to be the only pleasure they longed for, or craved.

After they had been married a year or more, they began to debate the question whether they would not be happier if they had a baby. But they came to no conclusion. They rather supposed they would. But often as they discussed it they never seemed to take precisely the same view twice in succession. One time both thought they would, next time one would take one side and one the other; next time likewise, except that they had changed sides. Again, both would agree that they would not. Always they were sure if they would be any happier with a baby to love they would have to be very, very happy indeed, for they were so extremely happy as they were.

His wife's illness came as a thunderbolt to Crosby and each worsening stage of it was as much a dazing surprise as the preceding. It was one appalling succession of horrors to him.

And, as all his life, it was not the sights which were dreadful enough and all too dreadful, but the sounds which made the most poignant impression upon his flayed, quivering memory, it was not so much her pathetic attitudes of pain, as the sound of her tossing and moaning and of her harshening breathing and gasping that harrowed him with recollections he could not put away. No pictures of her torments and of her death were before him to be curtained away in any drudgery of waking industry or in any oblivion of dreams. He was haunted by audible recurrences of sounds. He never saw in his mind's eye the intense sunlight and the shadows of the maple leaves on the black-clad figures and fresh green grass and raw ochre heap of moist, lumpy earth by the yawning rectangle into which her coffin vanished, but he heard a hundred times a day the echo of every shovelful of clods from the first to the last and most of all the hollow thud of the first.

2

No healthy, normal young man of barely twenty-four is likely to cling overlong to mere brooding on his grief for any loss, however frightful. Life opens out wide with possibilities at twenty-four and it is not good live alone.

Crosby began to realise something of this not long after the anniversary of his bereavement. He took hold of himself and strove to look at his life and his future squarely and without self-deception. He concluded that he could never find a mate as perfect as Minnie had been, that he would do nothing to search for another mate, but that it would be folly and wickedness to shut himself up in himself. He made a brave effort to circulate with his friends of his age as he had before he met Minnie. But it was sorry labour.

Then he met Claire Figeac. Her father, who had been agent for a Paris firm of glove manufacturers, had died some two years before they met. Her mother was a thrifty Frenchwoman of the usual town type, saving pennies and hoping to marry her daughter to a thrifty young man. She was not unhappy in America, and had either no wish to return to France or no relatives to return to. She made the best of her transplanted condition, but remained entirely French.

Claire was a novel and fascinating blend of most of the best she had acquired from her French heredity and her American environment, with a dash of spicy frivolity wholly Gallic and to her seldom or never misbecoming. She made the best of everything. She had a figure scarcely good, yet her way of making or selecting her clothes and of wearing them made her seem strikingly graceful even when contrasted with girls far better endowed by nature. Her face had not one perfect feature, but they were all passable and, by some magic inherent in herself, she made the total effect so charming that she was universally called very handsome.

She fascinated Crosby and he pleased her mother and ended by endearing himself to her. She really fell in love with him deeper every day. She palpitated at every imperceptible alteration in his manner, bearing, look, words, tone of silence that told of a warmer feeling and a closer intimacy between them. She knew him already too solicitous for a friend, she watched rapturously his approach to loverliness and his intensification in loverliness. She knew, at last, that it could not be long before he declared himself. Tacitly there was a perfect understanding between them, they were in love, they knew it and they were glad of it.

Their courtship had been simple. He was, since his wife's death, living with his parents and saving every cent he could put away. She and her mother lived in four small rooms on a third floor. But her tiny parlour had, in its arrangements, touches of Claire's individuality that made it heavenly to Crosby. He adored her for the way she put a stick of wood on the grate, or stirred up the failing fire. His evenings with her in the winter were full of romance for him.

With the warm weather their romance did not lose its glamour. The spring gave them opportunities for outings which seemed to him presages of a long life of happiness together.

Then came the hot weather. Indoors was unendurable. They sat on the white marble front steps of the house where she lived she on a cushion on the sill of the outer doorway, her feet on the top steps; he on that top step at the other side. So they sat for the first time the first suffocating evening.

He had made up his mind to tell her he loved her and to ask her to marry him that very evening. And she knew it. But it was evident to both of them that the chance would not come until late. After an hour of happy chatter and happy silence, he proposed a stroll.

Naturally for them it led to a drugstore on the corner, and to its soda-water fountain.

Claire wanted raspberry flavour without cream. She took it through the two paraffin paper straws the soda-fountain boy put into her glass. She stirred the ice with them and said its drinking made her cool. She smiled at the boy and told him he had put too much syrup in her soda and would he please put a little more water in it. He filled it up for her and fizzed it and she sipped at it and prolonged her enjoyment of it.

When the liquid was low, she clinked the ice around and around and drew up the last of the soda-water slowly. As the liquid ebbed through the ice lumps at the end of the straw, the air came up them with the last of it in a crackling gurgle. Claire laughed merrily in Crosby's face and remarked:

"That's the death rattle."

Crosby had a self-control unusual for a young commercial American. She did not notice his sudden pallor, and his expression change slowly.

She did realise the altered quality of silence in which they walked back. But she was utterly stunned with astonishment when at those same white marble steps, he stopped and abruptly said:

"Goodnight, I must be going now."

Still more was she amazed when he strode off without shaking hands or any other farewell

★★★★★★

Next day Crosby told his employers he would accept their proposal that he go to Chicago as their assistant bookkeeper there.

After some days of bewilderment, Claire collapsed with wretchedness and wrote him a long, wild letter. But her pride made her tear it up. Through many weeks she wrote many more, wrote them sobbing and abject. But she tore them all up.

He never wrote to her.

She never saw him again.

www.ingramcontent.com/pod-product-compliance
Lightning Source LLC
Chambersburg PA
CBHW020932020726
47495CB00002B/466